AMONG THE BEAUTIFUL BEASTS

AMONG THE BEAUTIFUL BEASTS

A NOVEL

LORI McMULLEN

SHE WRITES PRESS

Published 2021
Printed in the United States of America
Print ISBN: 978-1-64742-106-9
E-ISBN: 978-1-64742-107-6
Library of Congress Control Number: 2020922470

For information, address:
She Writes Press
1569 Solano Ave #546
Berkeley, CA 94707

Interior design by Tabitha Lahr

She Writes Press is a division of SparkPoint Studio, LLC.

For Lee, for everything.
And for Taryn, Emily, and Tessa, for making
it all worthwhile.

"Is it any wonder that south Florida, this new Florida, is young and hopeful and confident? The tired ways of the old countries and of the north have no meaning for us, who are conscious of the banner of a great new belief."

—MARJORY STONEMAN DOUGLAS
from "The Galley," *The Miami Herald*, 1920

CONTENTS

WEST OF MIAMI, 1920

I can't see the mosquitoes, but I hear them coming. They swarm through the darkness in a cloud of buzzing night-song, eager to feast. This is their warning, their war chant, yet somehow I am still startled when they descend. In a cloud of a thousand or more, they force their sharp suckers through the veil of my clothes, then my skin, and they pull. Pull and pull with Bacchanalian fervor, delicate bodies straining until my blood drains away, a millionth of a drop at a time.

This is love, I think. This is the only kind of love I've ever known.

Around me, beyond the roar of mosquitoes, the swamp gurgles and slurps, a nocturnal commotion that is stranger than any I've ever heard. If I stare long enough into the dark, alligator eyes start to appear. Luminescent pairs of pinkness, sprinkled across water so black it might as well be the abyss. They are so patient, those eyes. So preternaturally calm.

I am thirty years old and at the edge of the civilized world with an impossible choice: remain trapped where I am, or step into the wild, wild unknown—an unknown that teems with birdcalls and howls, where freedom is rabid and dogged and as relentless as the water that flows and flows forever south to the bay.

My head throbs. My fingertips buzz, and, as the mosquitos gorge on what's left of myself, I realize that I have no idea what to do.

PROVIDENCE, 1896

We used to walk, my mother and I, over the sleeping streets of Providence, Rhode Island. Her hand was nearly as small as mine and softer than the gardenia petals on the bush near our house. I held onto her hand more and more tightly as night came on.

The air on those evenings smelled of pine and soot, of salt off the sea and drying horse dung. Windows, like stars, lit up with haphazard timing. There was, all around us, a sense of brief otherworldliness, as if the crisscrossing streets of the city had lifted and settled again on a faraway planet.

"Look," I'd say to Mama, and we'd catch glimpses of our neighbors' lives being lived before the curtains were drawn.

We knew most of the people inside those houses, but there was a thrill to watching them unaware. Sometimes, Mama would gossip. Nothing too scandalous, but still things that I, at five years old, shouldn't have known.

"Does Mr. Carson really have another wife in Colorado, Mama?" I asked when she told me about the people in the brick house on the corner.

"That's what I heard, love," Mama answered.

"I wonder how he keeps their birthdays straight."

"I'm sure he manages somehow," she said, squeezing my hand.

With these secrets tucked in between us, we'd roam the neighborhood—laughing at stories that might have been true, and delighting in the closeness of each other.

3

Mama didn't stop to talk to anyone during our night-time walks. Even if she saw someone she knew, she nodded and smiled but never slowed down. This made me feel very special. Surely, whoever was on the receiving end of Mama's quick greeting looked at me and knew I must be important.

"That one," Mama would sometimes say out of nowhere. She'd stop walking and kneel, pressing her pink cheek to mine.

"Which one, Mama?"

I'd follow the line of her finger through freckled night sky. She'd point over the trees at the brightest white star.

"That one, Marjory. That's me. I'm your north star."

"Yes, Mama," I'd say, believing.

We'd walk past my school, past Grandmother Stoneman's vine-covered house, past my bedtime. No matter when we arrived home, though, Papa would be there, candles lit and Lewis Carroll in hand.

"Good walk?" he'd ask, lifting me as I nodded, suddenly taken over with sleep. Then Papa would carry me upstairs and read to me until I drifted away in his arms.

In those years, music filled our house like constant birdsong. It was there, always, even when it wasn't, because the memory of it swirled in our heads and through the small rooms: Mama singing; Mama strumming; Mama tapping the keys of the ancient Steinway. And yet, because Mama was Mama, some music managed to be even better, managed to rise from the rest like sweet cream and offer itself as the best kind of gift.

Mama was generous with these gifts and often gave concerts after dinner in the reception room of our old duplex.

"Set up the chairs, Frankie, would you?" she'd ask as soon as Papa came home. "I've got an audience tonight. You'll set the chairs up won't you, Frankie?"

Papa would, of course. Those were the days when he'd do anything for Mama.

"You got it, baby," he'd say, then lift her like a small bird and place her atop the piano. "Rows or along the walls?"

"Along the walls," was always her answer, then she'd swing one slender leg under her skirt like a metronome, keeping time as Papa arranged the seats.

When the blue-black of night filtered into the room and my words were sluggish with yawns, Mama would dip to one knee and sweep the hair from my face.

"You had enough supper?"

I'd nod.

"You had enough hugs?"

I'd shrug, and she'd give me one more.

"Now, you go upstairs, little love, and lay on your bed and listen for it, O.K.?"

"Yes, Mama."

"Promise?"

"I promise."

From my mattress in the corner of my upstairs bedroom, I'd hear the house swell with familiar voices. Neighbors, mostly, but also Mama's friends from the library and sometimes Papa's brother, Uncle Ned, when he was in town. Mama's accompanist, a nice neighbor lady, would run her fingers over the piano keys to settle the audience, and that's when I knew to strain my ears hardest.

"My girl is upstairs," Mama would announce to the crowd. I imagined her looking to the ceiling as she added, "Goodnight, sweetheart."

Then the silky strains of her violin rushed up the stairs and into the sleep-ready room, and I'd fall away as the sounds of Brahms' lullaby played just for me.

Mama was everything but, still, Papa was lots. He was stories at bedtime and lamplight on fall afternoons. He was, with his list of failed businesses and sheepish return from out west, ambition diverted, the American dream shaken awake. His voice boomed louder and louder when he made plans for our future, which made him sound less and less sure that each new business adventure would work. More than all of that, though, Papa was strength. He was my strength before I needed my own.

When we were together, we wrapped ourselves in blankets of words, words printed in leather-backed books laced with gold thread, words that Papa braided into magical stories I wasn't quite sure of. After I got glasses to stop my left eye from watching my nose, the words on those pages made sense to me, too, and I began reading to Papa as often as he read to me.

We took turns with Longfellow's *Hiawatha*—Papa read a page, I read a page—and because my reading was not yet fluid and smooth, the truth of the story revealed itself almost in hiccups.

"Wait," I said to Papa when we finished chapter eight. I looked at him through the bubble of my new glasses.

He peered down the slope of his aquiline nose, witnessing my slow, shocked comprehension.

Tears welled on my lids. "Did Hiawatha really ask the birch tree to give up its bark?"

Papa nodded.

"For his canoe?"

Papa nodded again.

I chewed at the skin near my thumbnail—the idea that someone could ask for the biggest part of another living thing and expect it to be handed over made me queasy, like when cousin Forrest demanded some of my Easter candy, but worse. I threw myself into a heap on my father's lap and grieved for that sorry birch tree.

My shoulders shook and tears slicked my nose and it didn't take long for the glasses to slide off my face. Papa caught them, folded the arms, and set them on the table beside him. Then he wiped my cheeks with his big thumbs, the way he did when I had jam on my face. Maybe, somehow, he already knew how much like the birch tree I was to become.

I was a pudgy child, with limp brown hair and those glasses that gave me the half-stunned look of a raccoon caught in the trash. I bit my nails. I tugged at the collars of my second-hand dresses until the buttons popped off and Grandmother Stoneman complained to Mama that I was indecent.

"She's six," Mama would say. "She can't be indecent."

Grandmother Stoneman would *tsk-tsk*, purse her small lips, and say, "Well, it reflects badly," before leaving the room. On whom it reflected badly, Mama would later say, we weren't sure.

And yet, I felt possessed of a beauty I couldn't explain. To be so young and so loved—this was the magic of Mama. This was what happened when she looked at me, brown eyes swelling with joy, and told me she was so happy I was her baby. *Surely*, I'd think, watching the smooth skin on her neck ripple as she spoke, *a woman as lovely as Mama couldn't have made me without a bit of her grace passing on.*

It was easiest to think this way in the bathtub. Mama would gently take off my glasses, set them on top of my waiting towel. Then she'd wet my hair, smooth it back from my face, let the water darken the strands to near-black like hers. She scrubbed me gently but thoroughly, washing away whatever judgment from Grandmother Stoneman I had endured.

"Bubbles?"

I always said yes.

Once, when the Barney twins next door were in the bath at the same time as me, we discovered we could hear each other through the duplex's shared wall.

"Hello! Hello! Hello!" we shouted, thrilled with this development. "Hi-ya! Howdy!"

But we could say variations of hello for only so long. Soon our bathing rooms fell quiet as we considered what to say next. Lingering drops plinked into the tub. Mama used bubbles to turn my knees into snowcapped mountains. I gave her a bubble beard, which she wore proudly until the suds fell away. Then a voice, one of the twins, pushed through the wall.

"Is your mother there!"

"Yes!"

"Will she sing!"

I looked at Mama, who smiled and shyly tucked a piece of hair behind her ear. She nodded.

"Yes!"

"Hooray!"

And then Mama's voice filled our room and filled the room of the Barney twins too, and I imagined them lying in their bathwater, smiling like I was, happy like I was, and warm and coddled and safe. No one's mama, anywhere, I thought, was as perfect as mine.

Until, suddenly, she wasn't.

It was summer the first time she broke. Late June, the air sunbaked and still. Mama and I sat on the back porch. She plucked at the banjo while I played at her feet, eating raspberries from a bowl and making shapes with sticks I'd gathered that morning. It was the kind of afternoon I'd wrap up and put in my treasure box if I could. At some point during our plucking and playing, Cousin Forrest came around the side of the house, heavy feet stomping up the porch stairs. He stood panting at us for a while, his eyes wide-set like a bulldog's. I rounded my back and blocked my stick shapes with my body. Cousin Forrest was the kind of boy who'd step on my work just because.

"Grandmother Stoneman says supper's at five," Forrest finally said.

Mama kept plucking the banjo as she spoke, turning her words into a kind of a song. "We're not going to Grandmother's for supper tonight, baby. Frank's out looking for work, and he'll want to come home."

Forrest huffed, big eyes bulging.

"But Grandmother said."

"I said too," she replied, still strumming. "We're not going to Grandmother's for supper tonight."

Forrest lifted his fat foot and brought it down hard on the porch.

Two of my sticks cracked apart.

"She said for you to come."

Mama set the banjo down, leaned it against the seat of her chair. She smiled at him. "Forrest, you just broke Marjory's treasure."

"A stick is a stupid treasure," he huffed. "And Grandmother wants you at dinner."

"Forrest, your grandmother's a witch. Were you aware? She has a foul heart and foul breath and mean eyes that are utterly incapable of seeing any goodness at all. I'm tired of her eyes, Forrest. They've judged me for so long. You understand that I'm tired? And, so, as I said, we are not going to her house for supper tonight."

I gasped. Although I knew that Papa's mother was unaffectionate and gruff, and that she never thought Mama got the floors clean enough, I hadn't, in my whole six years, heard her spoken of so bluntly before.

Apparently, neither had Forrest.

Forrest attacked. He threw his thick body at Mama, knocking her out of her chair and sending the banjo into the brick wall of the house. He drew his right elbow back, clenched his fat fingers into a fist, and though he had the determination of the dog he resembled, he was weak in both mind and body. Mama, little Mama, was able to keep him from throwing the punch by holding tight to his wrist.

But something snapped as she lay there, fending off blows from her nephew. Mama turned her head, black hair falling like shadows over her cheek, and she began to laugh.

"What's funny, Mama?"

Mama laughed harder. The sound was eerie, hollow and endless, interrupted only by her breath sometimes tripping over itself. I knew I would never unhear it.

Moments like that have no room for reason, and I truly believed I could make the sound stop by fixing the banjo. If Mama could just start picking the strings again. If she could just make her music instead of that howl. I crawled around Mama and Forrest, who was trying to wriggle his wrist free of her grasp.

The banjo lay near the back door. Its neck was broken, held together only by the perfectly tuned strings. I bent the neck forward and back at the crack. It would never, ever be played again.

Mama finally let Forrest go. Her laughter dribbled to silence.

"Mama?"

I crawled to her, afraid, for some reason, to stand.

"Mama?"

I was right in front of her now, looking straight into her beautiful brown eyes. Still, she did not seem to see me.

"Mama?"

The word was a soft as a whisper and as desperate as a plea.

Mama stared past me, so sharply focused on something beyond, that I turned to see what was there.

Forrest staggered away.

"Crazy whore," he sputtered. "Stupid, crazy woman."

My eyebrows jumped over my glasses. I thought only grownups could curse.

"Mama," I said, breathless. "Did you hear what he said?" She hadn't heard. Not that she was ignoring him. She listened to something else instead, something far off—something I could not understand. But I did not want to let her disappear without me, so I climbed into the space between her folded legs. I lifted her limp arms—one, then the other—and draped them over my shoulders like overall straps. Then we sat like that for a very long time.

Hours later, when my feet were tingly from sitting so long, when the treetops covered the sun, when Forrest and Grandmother were likely sitting down to supper, Mama finally eased me off her lap.

"Let's walk," she said, and though it sounded like there were cobwebs in her throat, she looked almost right.

I twisted one leg over the other, squeezed them together, damming the pee.

"I have to use the two-holer, Mama."

She smiled.

"Me, too."

When we'd gotten that business taken care of, Mama and I walked farther than we ever had before. We walked until the streets were dark and the banana moon began to rise. My legs ached. I was hungry and tired. I wanted so much just to read with Papa about that silly Cheshire Cat and get tucked into bed, but Mama seemed fine while she walked, as if the motion held something at bay. I would not be the one to end that all-rightness. So I scrambled beside her, clutching her hand, weighted by exhaustion and the first heavy press of a burden I could not yet define. We walked and walked until my heels leaked blood.

Home. Finally. Papa paced the front porch with a lantern. I did not read with him or even change into my nightclothes. I simply fell on my bed—a small cot in the corner of my parents' room. Blanketed by the belief that our walk had cured Mama, I sank into the nothingness of sleep.

But I did not stay there long. In the dark, hourless sea of midnight, I became unmoored. Not awake or asleep, I struggled to understand what was happening. Mama leaned over me. She was crying, and hot tears plinked onto my face. Between sobs, Papa called to her.

"Lillian. Come to bed. Lillian. Please. You'll frighten her."

"You're going to take her, Frank, aren't you? You're going to take her. You're going to kidnap my baby. Aren't you Frank? That's why you want me to sleep. So you can take her. Right, Frank? Frank? Frank!" she howled at Papa. She seemed unable to stop.

Under the storm of their voices, I squeezed my eyes shut and pushed my face to the pillow.

"Please, Mama," I whispered. "Please go to sleep."

For a few weeks, it seemed like maybe I'd imagined it all. Maybe Mama was fine, and I was the one who'd misplaced reality that awful day, like the time I'd thought I'd lost my glasses but then found them on top of the piano. I welcomed this possibility more than I welcomed the other because if I were the one who'd gone crazy, at least Mama would be there to fix me.

When Papa was home, I looked to him for clues. He seemed to be treating me gently, as if I were a torn page in one of our books.

"More butter on that biscuit, Marjory? Pass it here. I can spread it for you."

He spread carefully, swirling the knife until the entire surface glowed with warm butter.

"Thank you, Papa."

"Here, pass the other half, sweetheart. I'll do that one, too." With Mama, though, he acted the same as he always did—smiling at her over the top of the newspaper, patting her knee when they sat next to each other.

"I'm talking to someone tomorrow, Lillian," he said to Mama one evening. He always shared good news with her right away. "About a new opportunity. Really good one this time. You'll see, Lillian. This could be it."

With Papa treating me extra gently and treating Mama the same as always, I convinced myself that I'd been the one going mad a few weeks before. Of course it was me with the problem, not Mama, but the delusion didn't last long.

One morning that August, when I was again playing with sticks on the front porch, Mama appeared in the doorway, a tattered valise in each hand. She wore her pink Sunday dress, even though it was Saturday. Her hat sat too far back on her head and one strap of her brown brassiere fell below her cap sleeve. I peered around her legs, looking, hoping, for an instrument case. Violin, banjo, anything. But there was none.

"Come, Marjory," she said, not looking at me. Sweat streaked over the swells of her cheeks.

"Where, Mama?" I asked.

"Taunton, Marjory. We're going to Taunton." Taunton was up in Massachusetts. "Now, come along." She glanced at me. Her red lips quivered. "Please," Mama added, almost begging, then looked away again. She took a deep breath and pressed her mouth into a line.

"But, Mama."

I didn't know what to say next. Did words even exist for something like this?

Mama walked down the stairs, paused at the bottom. I wondered how long she would wait.

Papa stood in the doorway, as sad as I'd ever seen him. When our eyes met, he would not look away. His stare was telling me something I could not understand.

"Papa?"

He didn't answer.

Slowly, I stood. I brushed the dirt from my knees, adjusted my glasses, and stepped closer to him.

"Will you come for us?" I whispered.

Papa nodded. A rolling tear got stuck in his whiskers.

"Promise?"

Papa nodded again. This seemed, right then, the best I could hope for.

"Mama," I called loudly. "Just wait a minute. Please."

I ran past my father, into the house. Upstairs, in the study, on the third shelf from the bottom, I found our old copy of *Alice in Wonderland*, the one with Papa's thumbprint accidentally stained on the last page. I grabbed it, held it close to my chest and hurried downstairs.

"Don't forget," I whispered as I rushed past him. Papa would come. I knew he would. But Mama needed me now.

We arrived at the house on Harrison Street in the early evening, with the warmth of our Providence porch still in our hair. The train ride had calmed me a little, but the walk from the station had recharged my jitters.

"Well, Marjory, there it is," Mama said, looking up at her childhood home.

The big house hid behind four apple trees, waiting as if it had known all along that Mama would return. Shutters, like eyelids, were flung open wide, and I felt the house watching to see if we'd step closer.

"It's staring at us," I told Mama.

She nodded as if this made perfect sense. "It does that."

The front steps were swept and painted but screeched like a cat under our feet.

"Do they know we're coming?" I asked.

"They won't be surprised."

Mama hadn't answered my question, and I wanted to point this out, to ask my question again and again until she answered me right. And I wanted to ask her my other questions, too, like how would the Barney twins know where I'd gone and did this house have a bed ready for me because I was suddenly so very tired.

Mama opened the front door without knocking. She'd left the valises on the porch, so I dragged them in with us and dropped them on the shiny wood floor. The thud echoed in the house's stillness, though somehow, I could tell the stillness was not emptiness. People were here. I just didn't know where.

Mama seemed to know exactly where they would be. I followed her past the stairs and down the hall, trying not to breathe because the sound might disturb the silence. When Mama turned, I turned, and suddenly, there they were. My Taunton family, seated around their dining table.

"Oh, hello," Grandmother said, without interrupting the *poke-and-pull, poke-and-pull* rhythm of her knife and fork.

I squinted and pushed my glasses up my nose, but I still couldn't tell what kind of food was on their plates or whether they were enjoying it or whether they were going to part with it long enough to come greet us.

Grandfather sat at the short end of the table, tipped forward for a bird's eye view of his place setting. Grandmother sat on one long side, framed by the window behind her, and Aunt Fanny sat across from her, facing away from the doorway where I stood with Mama. Aunt Fanny did not turn around, so I stared at her back. I liked the blue-flowered fabric on the shoulders of her dress.

"We thought we might stay a while," Mama announced.

Poke-and-pull, poke-and-pull.

No one responded to Mama. Maybe they also liked the sound of Grandmother's eating utensils.

Finally, Grandfather looked up. Wooly eyebrows stretched over his forehead.

"We've got a toilet indoors now, Lillian," he said. "First house on the street to get one." Grandfather punctuated this statement with a forkful of food.

Mama's messy lips trembled. The old people chewed. And the house, this big, watchful house—it shifted and champed, joists smacking, beams straining, noises that, piled together, sounded like the house was getting ready to swallow me whole.

"Can I use it?" I blurted. "The special toilet?"

Aunt Fanny's chair scraped back, and she stood, unfurling in ripples of flowery blue.

"I'll show her," she said.

Grandfather nodded at his plate, whispered something that sounded like, "It *is* special, that toilet."

Aunt Fanny approached. At first, all I noticed was her puckered expression, all parts of her face pulled toward a soured middle, as if her supper plate had been full of lemons.

"This way," Aunt Fanny said, and as she stepped past me, I saw it—ferocity under the scrunched up features, like she might roar if given the chance.

Aunt Fanny tap-tapped to the back of the house, and I fast-walked to keep up.

"Pull that chain when you're done," Aunt Fanny instructed. "Give it a really good yank, okay, or else it will get stuck and have to be cleaned, and I have enough to get done tonight."

The toilet was something. It really was. Almost a miracle, if you believed in such things. I might've even liked it if I hadn't had to abandon my house and my father and my whole life to use it.

When we got back to the dining room, Mama sat in Aunt Fanny's seat, and all the used dishes had been pushed to the far end of the table.

"We told you, Lillian," Grandmother was saying, shaking her head. Though she didn't have a French accent, exactly, I heard a lilt to her words. *We told-uh you, Lilliannn.*

"He was going to take her, Mother. He was going to take her."

Mama's voice seemed to come from the dark corners of the room, a voice that was everywhere and nowhere at the same time. Outside, the sky got ready for night, dropping a blanket of purple clouds over Taunton.

"Mama?" I said.

She stared at the clouds.

"Mama? I'm tired."

It was happening again, that thing where she couldn't hear me. I stepped closer, put one hand on her shoulder, but still, she didn't turn.

"Aunt Fanny?" I asked.

Aunt Fanny paused, her hands filled with dirty plates.

"Is there someplace for me to sleep?"

"Of course there is, Marjory. Take that bowl, please. Come with me."

I started to follow Aunt Fanny, then stopped with the bowl in the doorway.

"I love you, Mama," I said, so she could be sure.

When Mama didn't respond, Grandmother filled in the blank.

"Go on now, Marjory," Grandmother said, breath whistling through the gap in her teeth. "Go on to sleep."

I was to share the double bed with Mama in the front chamber upstairs. The pillow was softer than my pillow back home, and I liked the shadow that the black walnut armoire made on the wall—wide and tiered, almost a castle. Even though it wasn't used anymore, a beautiful porcelain pitcher and bowl sat on a side commode by the window.

"Good night, Marjory," Aunt Fanny said when I was settled. I knew Mama wouldn't hug me tonight, but I thought Aunt Fanny might hug me or kiss me or wish me sweet dreams. She didn't. But she did hesitate at the door, and I told myself that she'd thought about doing at least one of those things.

I pulled the covers higher. This Taunton house might have a toilet, I thought, but it didn't have very much love.

Was it one night that first week or another soon after? The nights melted together in a mess of no-story-first slumbers, descents into Papa-less sleeps that I endured because I had to and survived with the comfort of Mama's soft snoring. I tried to sleep through the whole night because the gradual remembering that happened each time I woke was painful enough in the mornings. I did not need to go through it twice.

But sometimes I woke in the night despite my best efforts. The high headboard and footboard pressed from each end like a vise, holding me in place, and I tried to be still and go back to sleep before the remembering stirred. A few times it worked. When it didn't, I reached for Papa's *Alice in Wonderland* book, which I kept under my pillow, and hugged it with both arms in the deep dark.

That night, though. That night Mama's laughing yanked me from sleep, jerked me to awareness with such sudden force that I didn't notice at first Grandfather sitting beside me, holding me in his arms.

"THE-OAK-FELL-IN-THE-PURPLE," Mama yelled from her side of the bed, then she burst into laughter so deep I thought she would drown in it.

I hugged Grandfather tighter, shoved my head into the space between his chest and arm. Though the moon glowed through the high window, he was fully dressed, as if it were midday instead of the depths of the night. His suit jacket covered my face. His heart ticked in my ear.

"BUT-THE-PURPLE-TOOK-THE-TRAIN-TO-MINNEAPOLIS-AND-THEN-THERE-WAS-NO-MILK-FOR-THE-KITTEN! HA-HA-HA-HA-HA-HA-HA-HA-HA-HA-HA!"

"Grandfather?" I whispered, and he pulled me closer.

The laughter went on and on, like waves during a storm, a relentless onslaught with only half-breaths of reprieve.

During one of these moments, the bedroom door opened. Aunt Fanny and Grandmother crept into the moonlight, clutching each other and moving as one.

"Lillian," Grandmother said from quite far away. "You must stop this now—"

Grandmother might have said more, but Mama sprang to the foot of the bed and screamed with a blackness that didn't sound human. The laughter was gone. Now she just screamed, her voice pushing Grandmother and Aunt Fanny back, back through the door, into the hall, where they huddled together and trembled so hard I felt the floor shaking.

Grandfather held me until Mama wore herself out. She collapsed in a heap at the end of the bed. When we were sure she was sleeping, I slid off the side and let Grandfather lead me through the dark to the extra bedroom in the attic. He left me when Aunt Fanny came. This time, she kneeled near my head and stroked my hairline with her soft fingers.

"Dear child," she whispered until sleep arrived.

Mama slept for two days. I peeked every hour through the crack in the door, unsure whether I wanted to find her awake. On the third day, a nurse came. She wore a white uniform and was thick in places I didn't know a person could be thick, like her elbows. She marched up the stairs while the rest of us waited in the parlor below, watching the ceiling as if we could see through it.

"It must be going all right," Aunt Fanny said.

Her words unleashed fury above. A shriek and a thud— the nurse pushed to the floor? And then the unmistakable crash of the porcelain water pitcher. Mama screaming. More crashes. The nurse rushing downstairs with blood soaking the kerchief she pressed to her arm.

"She needs to go to Butler's," the nurse said in a voice she forced steady. "Would you like me to make the arrangements, or shall you do it yourselves?"

My grandparents and Aunt Fanny looked at each other, talking with their eyes the way grownups seemed to be able to do. No one looked over at me. Maybe they couldn't. If they had looked at me, though, if they'd asked me my opinion on the matter, I would have told them that, yes, Mama should go to Butler's.

And I should go with her.

So, quick as a lick, I had no parents. Well, I had them. But they weren't with me, which, frankly, is like having no parents at all.

"How long will Mama be there?" I asked Aunt Fanny as she salted a chicken.

"As long as it takes, Marjory."

Whatever that meant.

"Can I go live with Papa until she gets back?"

Aunt Fanny set the chicken down as if it were very heavy. She wrung her slimy hands in the air.

"No, Marjory. For the last time, you cannot go live with your father. He is not a reliable provider."

Books. Hugs. A ride in his arms when I was tired. As far as I was concerned, Papa provided for me very well.

"Fine," I said to Aunt Fanny, knowing how sassy I sounded. "But he's coming for me one of these days. He promised."

Aunt Fanny hoisted the chicken again.

"That man has promised a good many things, Marjory," she said.

I sat with my chin in my palm and watched Aunt Fanny finish up with the chicken. The warm afternoon light was good for daydreaming, and I pictured myself riding a bicycle (never mind that I had neither a bicycle nor the foggiest idea how to ride one) to Butler's Sanitarium. Mama was small. She could perch on the handlebars. Once I had rescued her, I'd pedal us to our old duplex in Providence, where Papa would toss me high in the air, and the three of us could restart and pretend none of this had ever happened.

The sunlight shifted. My daydream grew cold. I chewed on my thumb and decided there was only one thing I could actually do in this situation: I could read.

The writing room was above the front parlor. It was small and dusty and did not have a writing desk, but it did have a very big bookcase. The bookcase was so full that some volumes were jammed in sideways, on top of upright ones, making it hard to pull any one book off the shelf without pulling twelve others down with it. I decided to start at the bottom.

Oliver Twist. A whole set of Encyclopedia Britannica. The fourteenth edition of *Gray's Anatomy.* A history of the Chicago fire. The complete Shakespeare in print so tiny I could read it only when I slid my glasses to the end of my nose like an old biddy. *A Tale of Two Cities.* The history of the Johnstown flood. Poetry by Byron and Homer. I was going to read every page in every book on every shelf of that bookcase.

"Do you understand any of that?" Aunt Fanny asked sometime during the afternoon of day five. Books lay open around me, as if I were the center of a daisy and they were the beautiful petals.

"Of course I do," I said.

But I didn't. Not really.

"Grandmother found a doll in the attic for you," Aunt Fanny said. "Her name is Jeanne, and I think you'll like her. She's on your bed."

"Thank you," I said, not moving away from the books.

Even if I had tried to explain, Aunt Fanny would not understand. I had to keep reading. I had to keep turning the pages and trying to make sense of the stories, because Papa was coming for me—he'd promised he would—and if I finished those shelves full of books, if I could be good enough and read all of the thousands of words, we would have so many wonderful things to talk about on our way home.

There was a shaft that rose from the dust-stuffed sewing room up through the attic, and if I sat at the end of my bed and pressed my ear to the wall and listened with all of my might, I could hear some of the words that Aunt Fanny and Grandmother spoke while they darned.

"Not her fault. Poor dear. We'll just do what we can for her."

These people who acted like hugging was a crime, who could not bring themselves to kiss me goodnight—were they talking about me?

"She'll think I want to replace her mama. Maybe the best thing is to do nothing at all."

What were they saying? Did their words mean they cared, that maybe they loved me? And if that's what their words meant, well, then, did that mean I had to love them right back?

I didn't like dolls, but I kind of liked Jeanne. She had brown hair like Mama and pink rosebud lips. When I waggled her legs, she danced a bit, which almost was funny.

Even someone with a mission as important as mine had to take breaks once in a while, so when I paused my reading, Jeanne and I lolled on the bed that I'd shared briefly with Mama. On the day Mama left, Aunt Fanny had carefully swept away the shards of porcelain pitcher, then slowly stepped toe-to-heel and barefoot around the whole room before granting me leave to enter again. I didn't sleep in there anymore, though. My bed in the attic felt safer, but sometime I liked to lounge with Jeanne on the bed and think about Mama.

"Do you think she plays the piano or the banjo for the other mamas at Butler's?" I'd asked Aunt Fanny when she visited me during one of these lounging breaks.

"No," Aunt Fanny had said, gripping the doorframe. "But maybe she sings. Yes, Marjory, she probably sings to them while they all tend the garden or knit blankets or do any of the nice things they do all day."

I nodded. That sounded right.

Jeanne and I were resting one afternoon and thinking about what kinds of desserts Mama might've been getting at Butler's when I happened to glance out the high window and see something truly fantastic outside.

Papa! On the sidewalk in front of the house.

He held his hat in his hand and looked at the house the same way I had that first day, as if he knew it was watching. But did he know I was watching, too?

"Jeanne!" I shout-whispered. "It's Papa! See?"

Jeanne and I banged on the window with our flat palms, trying to get Papa's attention. Quickly—but not quickly enough—it became clear he couldn't hear me, so Jeanne and I flung the door open and flew down the stairs and ran smack into Aunt Fanny on the landing.

"Aunt Fanny," I said. "It's Papa. He's outside."

"Marjory, please. Your father's not here. Come upstairs and show me what you're reading now."

Jeanne and I tried to wriggle free of Aunt Fanny.

"I'll show you, Aunt Fanny. Look."

Aunt Fanny was surprisingly strong. She had to let go of me. I had to see Papa. I had to tell him about Lucie Manette, my most favorite character of all of the characters in all of those books that I'd read.

"Marjory," Aunt Fanny said, her voice sounding like Mama's violin strings when they're turned too tight. "Jeanne needs her nap. Let's put Jeanne down for a nap now."

Grandfather's footsteps thumped through the back of the house. The side door whined open, then closed, and Grandfather's shadow moved past the parlor windows.

"Aunt Fanny," I pleaded, looking her straight in the eyes. "He's come for me, just like I told you he would."

"Nonsense, Marjory. Your father is not outside."

We struggled without fighting, Jeanne and I trying to get around Aunt Fanny's blockade. I would not let her keep me from Papa, but I did not want to hurt her either. Her breath smelled like coffee. Bits of hair popped out of her bun like bug antennae. I wanted to stomp on Aunt Fanny's foot—I even brought my knee up in preparation—but I couldn't do it. I wasn't awful like Forrest.

She released me and Jeanne when the side door creaked and Grandfather once again thumped through the house. I moved without thinking, on impulse, fueled by a kind of lost lion cub need to find my father outside. The front door. The porch steps. No shoes because who could care about shoes at such a time? The shock of the late summer sun hurt my eyes, and I squinted, looked left, then right, searching and searching but seeing no one.

"Papa?" I yelled. "Jeanne, do you see Papa?"

A breeze swished the leaves on the apple trees, and the branches bent left ever so slightly, as if tipping me off. I looked in the direction they wanted. No one. But then I shifted my gaze to the other side of the street and saw a man in a hat turning the corner.

I dropped Jeanne and ran. Pudgy limbs pumping. Stringy hair whirling like trails of smoke from my head. But my legs were not as strong as my heart, and by the time I crossed the street and rounded the corner, the man in the hat wasn't there.

Papa was gone.

Grandmother waited for me on the porch when I returned. She held Jeanne in her lap and straightened the embroidered skirt that it only then occurred to me she had made.

"You're young," Grandmother drawled Frenchly as I dragged myself up the stairs. *You'rrrre young-uh.* She waved me closer.

I sat down at her feet and looked toward the end of the street. The apple tree branches were motionless. Fresh out of secrets, I guessed.

"I don't feel young," I said. Young children had parents to love them.

"You cannot understand yet what a man can do to a woman. What life with a man can do to a woman."

"You mean Mama?"

"Mama, yes."

I twisted my neck to look up at Grandmother. The creases near her eyes split and spread like lightning during a storm.

"But others, too," she said. "So many others."

Grandmother said nothing more, though I knew she had much more to say. I leaned closer. She rested her hand on top of my head, and I almost felt my skull crack, almost felt her gnarled fingers drop ideas into my mind. Ideas and hopes and wishes. The specifics were fuzzy. I was, after all, too young to understand, but I knew that what she had passed to me was important, that it had been gathered through generations and stowed for use in a future she would not see but would feel through me, somehow.

"Will Mama come back?" I asked.

"Yes."

"Will she be okay?"

"I don't know," she answered.

I squeezed Jeanne, let my head use Grandmother's leg as a pillow. We stayed like that—thinking and smelling the roses when the breeze brought them our way—until Aunt Fanny called us for supper.

Life, it seemed, had a way of normalizing, even in chaos. I learned the routines of my Taunton family and began waiting each morning for the click of Grandfather's hoe against the stones in the corn patch, began avoiding Aunt Fanny's temper when the tip of her nose flared pink and then red. After breakfast, when Grandfather left for the foundry or to meet clients in Boston at Faneuil Hall, the tension in the house shifted, changed shape, became something I always felt on the verge of grasping but never quite did.

"Why aren't you married?" I asked Aunt Fanny one day as she helped me dress for school.

"I'm too busy to have a husband, Marjory."

"Doing what?"

"Taking care of your grandparents."

"But can't they take care of themselves?"

Aunt Fanny sighed and pulled my dress tighter so the buttons could catch in the back.

"They are older, Marjory," she said through gritted teeth. Those buttons must have been really stubborn. "And the youngest daughter stays home to help. That's how it is."

I started to say something, but Aunt Fanny kept talking. "Besides, I have my bookkeeping for the foundry and the bicycle club and lots of good things to do."

"Bicycle club?"

Aunt Fanny's face brightened as if she'd stepped into sunlight, and she told me all about the bicycle club of young ladies—the puttees she wore on her feet, the longest distance she'd ever traveled by bike (seventeen miles).

"You should join me sometime, Marjory."

I couldn't help it. An image of Mama perched on my handlebars popped into my head.

"I don't have a bicycle, Aunt Fanny."

On a Sunday afternoon several weeks later, Aunt Fanny called me outside. I put on my coat, because it had suddenly turned to coat weather, and went out the front door. On the sidewalk, about where Papa had stood, was a shiny red bicycle, too small to belong to Aunt Fanny. Grandfather held it up by its seat.

"Is that for me?" I asked.

"Why, it certainly is, Marjory," Grandfather answered.

I couldn't control my arms any longer. I was so happy, I just had to give hugs. I started with Grandfather, then hugged Aunt Fanny and Grandmother so hard they both gasped for breath.

"Well, then," Grandmother said, flustered and smiling.

Aunt Fanny and I rode our bicycles after school when the weather was nice. Though I had a long walk to and from Barnam Street Elementary and was often quite tired when I got to the house, I never refused when Aunt Fanny asked me to ride. The trip we liked best was to the countryside just west of town, where the nut trees were generous and we could gather basketsful to bake into pies.

I raced home from school one day in October, eager to ask Aunt Fanny if we could go for a ride. The leaves were beginning to drift from the trees, and I wanted to hear them crunch under our wheels, wanted to see them whirl like mini tornadoes in the wake of our tires. Plus, on days when I went cycling with Aunt Fanny, Grandmother let me skip piano practice or a French lesson. An afternoon couldn't get any better than that.

"Aunt Fanny?" I called before I was fully through the front door. I hung my school bag in the front closet and listened for grumbling sounds from the kitchen, which would mean Aunt Fanny was elbow deep in gizzards and couldn't go for a ride.

Silence. Maybe, then, she would agree to go.

"Aunt Fanny?" I called again.

"In here, Marjory."

Aunt Fanny balanced at the edge of the blue chesterfield in the parlor, wearing the same pretty dress with the flowers she'd worn the day we arrived. Grandmother sat next to her. Neither of them seemed to know what to do with their eyes.

"Your mother is home," Grandfather said.

I jumped at the sound of his voice—I hadn't even known he was in the room—and turned to where Grandfather sat by the window. Mama lay near him on the settee.

"Mama!"

I hurried to her and kneeled so that our heads were close together. Her skin seemed more yellow than I remembered, but probably that was the light. When she exhaled, her breath came through her mouth, and it was thick with a sour smell that made me think of our old two-holer in Providence. I'd have to pick her some mint from the garden.

"Hi, Mama," I said again.

"Hello," Mama said. The word sounded less like an answer than a murmur in an otherwise soundless dream.

I looked to Grandfather for direction. He wiped his big hand over the back of his neck a few times before he spoke. "Marjory has a bicycle now, Lillian," he reported. "Red. Fanny taught her to ride, and she picked it up quickly. She's the only girl I know of on the street with her own bicycle."

"How nice," Mama dream-said. She watched the nearly bare trees out the window.

I moved my head closer to hers, hoping the nearness would force her to look at me.

"So much has happened, Mama," I said. "My teacher is Miss Florence Francis, and she doesn't care if I read ahead in the book while she's teaching. And not only can I ride the red bicycle, but I can ride very fast. Sometimes I pass Aunt Fanny, and she has to pedal hard to keep up. And, also, now I sleep in a bed in the attic, but if you wanted it very much, I could move back to our room. I wouldn't mind. Aunt Fanny swept up the shards of porcelain, and it's one hundred per-cent safe to walk around in bare feet."

I was aware of prattling on and sounding like Betsey Fairweather, the chatterbox I sat next to in school, but what else could I do? Nothing I said turned Mama's head, so I had to keep talking, keep hoping that something, eventually, would be interesting enough to catch her attention.

"And I love using the indoor toilet," I said, desperate. "I use it every day, usually after breakfast, and I even figured out that it flushes faster if you yank the chain down and to the right."

The fine hairs on her cheek touched mine when I got really close. Maybe my deepest, most secret thought would get her to look at me.

"Mama," I whispered. "Papa came for us once, but he had to leave quickly and hasn't come back." I paused to get the secret words right. "Mama, I think he went out west again to make money for us. And I'm afraid he got lost out there, Mama, because Miss Florence Francis says the west is so big, it could hold fifty thousand Rhode Islands."

Mama's lovely head finally turned. Even the whites of her eyes were a bit yellow. The effort it took to lift her hand to my hair seemed monumental, but she did it, even stroked the loose strands a few times.

"How nice," she repeated, then let her hand flop to the couch.

I turned to Grandfather. His eyes watched his knees. I spun toward Aunt Fanny and Grandmother, still side by side. My legs tried to move, but I could not go to them for the comfort I needed. They'd give what they had, but it would not be enough.

"You did this to her!" I yelled at them all. "You sent her away without me. I could have been there. They wouldn't have made her like this if I'd been there!"

I felt the stares of everyone but Mama as I ran from the room.

She was there and not there. Present yet incomplete. She'd broken to bits like the porcelain pitcher, and Aunt Fanny and my grandparents had swept her away, sent her off to be glued back together by people who could only guess what the original was supposed to look like.

"She still loves me," I assured Jeanne sometimes. "Even though her head is hurting a lot, her heart still works perfectly well. Because, you see, Jeanne, she's Mama. And she can't ever be anything else."

Some nights, Mama came like a ghost to my bed in the attic and curled her small body around me. We held hands under the covers and fine-tuned our breath till it matched.

In, out, in, out, I measured. If our breathing stayed synchronized for two minutes more, maybe Mama would get better.

I burrowed deeper into her curve, wishing the night to go on forever, and setting more magical little-girl goals: *Don't scratch at the itch on your nose,* I told myself. *If you don't scratch at it, Papa will come back and help you make Mama better.*

Always, at some point in the growing pink of near-morning, we turned inside out, and I cradled Mama. I topped her head with my chin and squeezed her tight. Somehow, without even trying, I'd become the mother and she the helpless, lost child.

WEST OF MIAMI, 1920

His voice slides through the swamp-night, searching the sawgrass for the person I may or may not still be. He's close now. The force of my name on his breath hurts my ears, but out here in the swamp, darkness and distance play dirty tricks, and he does not realize how close he is, how easily he could touch me if he just stretched his arm.

Like the mosquitoes, he is coming to take.

I don't know if I have anything left to give him.

Myriad unseen creatures await my response, eager, as he is, to portend my fate. Alligators steep in the murk with crocodilian malaise. Panthers, elusive and coy, stalk overgrown hammocks, the tree islands where those sleek cats make their homes. And somewhere in the unending black heat, curlews nest in their rookeries, dreaming of sweet morning krill.

Beastly, this waiting is, paralytic in its expanse.

He calls for me again. My name sounds regurgitated, sour and foul, as if he is vomiting not just my name but all of me, every last animal cell, into the sluice. I feel it, the heave and the thrust of my exit. I feel myself projected from the prison of his soul into the unseen wetland, where I sputter and swirl in the inimitable eternity of this place the natives call Pa-hay-okee. The thick water gets in my nose, in my mouth—thousands of years of strange brackish balm spreading over my tongue, down my throat. I am no longer in him. Now, this land is in me. It has entered me in a way no man ever could; it needs me more desperately than any person

I've ever known. And for the first time, I understand that I need the land, too.

My muscles awaken. The shock and the beauty of my revelation send me into the wild, running through high, saber-toothed reeds with only the faintest fear of the creatures I might disturb.

His feet hesitate in the marsh. Confusion, calibration, communicated through halting steps in the blackness. Then, with a splash and a grunt, the night cracks apart, and I hear him give chase.

I run. I run as fast as I can, as fast as I ever have, legs sloshing through mud, saw grass gnawing the fresh mosquito-made mounds of my flesh. I run as if the rest of my life depends on my escape because, in so many uncountable ways, it does.

TAUNTON, 1907

I came home from high school in Taunton every day for the noon meal, conjugating Latin verbs and reciting lines of the Aeneid as I strode down Harrison Street. Useless as anything other than an intellectual affect, Latin comforted me. Its declensions gave order to an unorganized world, imposed rigid boundaries where there were none. Some people had Jesus. I communed with Virgil.

The house, at midday, was like a traveling circus at the end of the season—I never knew what I was going to get. Aunt Fanny could be pawing the floor with her dainty feet, steam billowing from her nose like a penned bull as she polished the molding. Or she could be dodging the *Good Housekeeping Everyday Cookbook* that Mama liked throwing at her or using a couch cushion like Jimmy Collins to bat the cookbook away. As for Mama, if she wasn't hurling recipes at Aunt Fanny, she might be sewing or sleeping on the porch when the weather was nice. Sometimes she peeled potatoes. But she never sang anymore. The music, like so much of Mama, had disintegrated while she was at Butler's.

My grandparents, meanwhile, spent their time aging. Though not imminent, death was clearly their next big life event.

"Can we play checkers?" Mama asked when I arrived home one winter noon. She sat in the parlor with her hands folded on her lap and a full cup of tea steaming on the table beside her.

"Oh, Mama," I said as I unwound my scarf. "You know I only have time to eat dinner. Then I have to get back to school. I have a geometry exam today. Yuck!"

Aunt Fanny walked past with a stack of Grandfather's folded work shirts. "Please, Marjory. You did very well when we worked on geometry last week."

"That was last week," I called as I walked over to Mama.

She perched on the edge of the couch, hands still folded, and would not look at me when I knelt beside her. Blue winter light refracted in the tear slipping over her face.

"I really want to play checkers with you," she almost whined. She bit her lip in the sore place that her teeth liked to grab when she was sad.

"Oh, Mama."

She didn't flinch when I used my still-cold fingers to smooth hair from her face.

"I have to eat now and go back to school," I soothed. "Remember?"

"What about when you come home later? Can we play then?"

I nodded fast so she'd know I meant it. "Yes, as soon as I come home again later. You can be the red ones, okay?"

"Promise?"

"I promise."

I patted her knee and kissed the top of her brown head as I stood.

"I'm going to eat my lunch now, Mama."

"Marjory?"

"Yes?"

Mama looked at me now and brightened.

"Christmas is coming soon."

I breathed enormously, filling my chest with the kaleidoscope sorrows that fractured the room.

"You're right, Mama. Christmas is coming quite soon."

I left her in the parlor and went to the kitchen, where Aunt Fanny had put a serving for me on the stove. I didn't bother noticing what the food was. I just ate. Fork to plate to mouth and back, again and again until it seemed the very act of my eating was some sort of engine powering the snow that had begun falling outside.

When I'd eaten my food and washed my plate, I struggled into my coat at the front door and said a silent missive of thanks to Euclid and Mr. Fitz, the math teacher, and to Grandfather, who'd helped build a public high school in Taunton and required girls to go. If I hadn't had this reason to get out of my grandparents' house every day, I might've gone crazy, too.

"Bye, Mama," I called, once I was bundled again.

"Please don't forget," Mama answered. "Checkers. Remember, I'm red."

I nodded, even though she couldn't see me, and opened the door.

I lived under a wet, woolen blanket of obligation, beneath which my heart heaved and roiled, tormented by the stifling force of my love for Mama and her preciously simple demands.

"I'm going to the library now, Mama."

"The one near the fountain?"

"Yes, Mama. That one."

"Would you make a wish for me?"

"Of course, Mama, I can do that."

"I wish for snow."

"It's May, Mama."

"But, Marjory, I really, really want snow."

I made our wishes at the end of my visits, after I'd stood among the shelves and shelves of vast worldly secrets, peeking from beneath the corner of my heavy blanket, rapt and electrified and daring to wonder about college, a place I'd never be able go.

"Not just because of Mama," I insisted to the rows of waiting books. "Also tuition."

The fountain next to the public library squirted water from the scum-slick mouths of stone fishes. A collection of pennies massed like fish excrement at the bottom of the shallow pool, and a cherub with an actual chip on his shoulder presided over it all. I used one penny for both my wish and Mama's. Perhaps this thrifty approach is why my wish, always the same, never came true.

"Please let me be good enough," I whispered. "And let it snow soon for Mama."

I wasn't sure what *good enough* meant and didn't try hard to figure it out. But my chest ached with wanting it. I just knew there was more I could do—always, always, more I could do—to make Mama feel better. More I could do to be worthy, maybe, of drawing Papa back home. We could be a normal family again, maybe, if I tried hard enough.

The stone fishes gaped at me.

"Goodbye, then," I told them, then let the woolen corner of my burden fall once again and made my way back to Harrison Street.

"Let's go sailing," Grandfather said that May afternoon, when I'd returned from the library, weighted with books.

"Now?" I loved sailing with Grandfather, and he loved sailing with me. Of all the people in our household, I was the only one willing to get in his boat.

"Don't you have to get back to the foundry, Daniel?" Grandmother hollered from upstairs.

"Not today," Grandfather hollered back, winking at me.

We all crowded onto the trolley, then walked to the run-down boathouse at Field's Point, Grandfather's favorite spot to launch. I settled Mama on a bench in the boathouse with a hot tea and binoculars.

"There, you can watch the shorebirds now, Mama."

Aunt Fanny and Grandmother settled beside her. Aunt Fanny's lip curled just a bit and she blinked rather quickly, as if trying to decide whether she was pleased or put out by this unexpected excursion.

I helped Grandfather drag the boat to the water and climbed in when he nodded. The vessel was a homemade affair, hardly seaworthy, forged years ago from a wooden rowboat, with just a spit and a sheet and a tiller to move it. I loved its simplicity, the thrill of my doubts.

The wind pulled us from shore, further from Mama. At first I sat stiffly, but slowly, the waves worked me loose.

"Keep your hands off the gunwhale."

These were the only words spoken during our voyage. Grandfather was happiest when not under pressure to talk.

I kept my hands off the gunwhale and looked beyond the sides of the boat. The chop in the bay was hypnotic; the depth of the water so profound that I could only stare at its surface and guess at the darkness below. When the wind whipped the sheet out there on the bay, it also blew off my woolen blanket, flapped it about in the sky while I floated in a marvelous stupor.

"Headed in now," Grandfather said after too little time.

"Already?"

"Sun's considering setting."

As the boat neared the shore, the blanket found me again, draped itself over my back and shoulders. I pulled it close, like a good girl.

At least I'd had an hour of unburdened silence sweetened by salty sea air.

Mama was never far from my mind, but one February night when I was sixteen, I worried that she was too close.

I woke to find myself barefoot, flannel nightgown hanging from hunched shoulders, standing at the door of Mama's room. Snow fell outside. I was not near a window, but I could feel the crystalline flakes massing in drifts, inching up the trunks of the bare apple trees. Snow and more snow. Piling higher and higher, and then the walls of the sturdy old house falling away so that I was sinking, sinking, into the whiteness, unable to claw my way out, the unbearably cold crunch filling my nose and my mouth, down to my lungs, until the world up and died and there was no air, no oxygen, no life, anywhere.

Grandmother saved me. Her bony hand grabbed hold of mine and she pulled me from my snowy nightmare. Neither of us mentioned the long shard of glass I held in one hand.

"I suppose you'll be thinking about college soon," Grandmother said as we sat together in the sewing room, nursing our colds. Aunt Fanny had pulled chairs near the big steam radiator for us, and Grandmother and I both swiped at our noses with linen handkerchiefs while soiled cloths dried on the coils of the heater.

I looked over at Grandmother. She'd aged so much since Mama and I had arrived years ago. Grooves splintered over the skin on her face. Her hair, always pulled tightly back in a bun, was now entirely white. Heat still burned in her cloudy eyes, though, and it was this heat that made her words about college neither a question nor an attempt at manipulation but, instead, an obvious statement of fact.

"I should have gone," Grandmother continued. "Education." She honked into her hankie. "Synonym for liberation, you know."

Under my blanket, I shivered. That incessant tension between ambition and obligation pulled at me a little bit harder. I rubbed the flat, bony part of my chest, where it hurt most.

"But Mama," I said.

Grandmother looked straight into my eyes.

"Your mother wants you to go."

That was unlikely. Or, if it were true and Mama did want me to go to college, then she wanted me to go to the Framingham Normal School, where I could commute on the trolley each day and still be home to play checkers each night.

I would not go to Framingham Normal, though. If I were going to bother with college, there was only one place I wanted to go.

"But money, Grandmother. Really. Wellesley is so expensive. And the foundry. It's been—"

"It's been struggling for years because your grandfather doesn't know his ass from his elbow when it comes to running a business."

Not once in my entire life had I heard Grandmother curse or, even more improbable, criticize her husband. Thankfully, the handkerchief hid my gaping mouth well.

"He just kept making stoves," Grandmother went on. "And I told him, I said Daniel, you need to diversify and make something else. You need to invest in a bigger furnace. You need more than one lathe, more than one blower. But no. What did I know? And so he has struggled."

Grandmother sighed, twisted her handkerchief into an angry knot.

"I suppose I should be grateful, though. He didn't lose everything. He wasn't an utter failure." She looked at me hard. Apparently, Mama and I weren't the only ones who still thought about Papa.

"In any case, Marjory, the foundry is not your problem, and this house is nowhere for you to spend any more of your time. You will go to Wellesley, if Wellesley will have you, which I have no doubt she will. Now, get up from that chair and drag yourself to the writing room. In the desk, in the second drawer on the right, inside a sewing box, under a layer of pincushions, you will find a small book. Bring it here, please."

I returned to the sewing room with the book, its leather-bound covers held closed with twine tied in a neat bow. The book wasn't big, but its shape pressed on my palms, weighty, as if its contents were made of cast iron.

"Open it."

I settled myself again in the chair and tucked the blanket around me. Carefully, slowly, as if the book might disappear if I pulled too hard, I unraveled the bow and lifted the cover.

A bankbook. Pages and pages of entries listing deposits, some in Grandmother's tight scrawl, some in Aunt Fanny's flowery script. The first entry was dated April 7, 1899—my ninth birthday—in the amount of $1.17.

I looked at Grandmother, confused.

"Fanny does those bookkeeping jobs, you know," Grandmother said. "And those math lessons from time to time."

"And you?" I asked.

Grandmother smiled. She looked almost coy.

"On occasion, my housekeeping budget was open to interpretation."

It was, perhaps, the greatest act of sedition in her long life.

"I don't understand," I said. "This is for me?"

"Yes, Marjory. For you. For Wellesley."

The radiator hummed, louder now, thunderous, a steam-driven marching band heralding the rest of my life. I sniffled and snorted. Tears of disbelief and sinus congestion and gratitude streamed over my cheeks. I reached for Grandmother's hand, and I squeezed a million thank-yous into her palm.

"What will you study?" Grandmother asked.

"Everything!" I said, the word slipping through a smile I couldn't stop. "Anything! All of the knowledge in the world is there, Grandmother. I could study the Holy Roman Empire or evolution or philosophy. Or physics, though I'm not too sure about my math. But, probably, Grandmother, if you really want to know, I think I would like to study

English composition. Maybe become a writer. The department at Wellesley is one of the best."

My exuberance simmered in the radiator's chunky heat.

"A writer?" Grandmother laughed, incredulity lengthening her to her full height in the chair. "You'll die in a garret, Marjory. That's what happens to writers, they die in garrets. You don't want that."

We smiled at each other, imagining the possible paths of my future, a future she had just given me, wondering if any of those paths would indeed lead to a lonely death in a garret.

Then I remembered.

"But wait. What about Mama?" I said.

Grandmother let go of my hand.

"What about her, Marjory?"

"She'll die with me gone, Grandmother. She'll simply die."

Grandmother lifted her chin, stared at me over the plane of her nose.

"And so will you if you stay," she said.

Grandmother closed her eyes and succumbed to an episode of clumpy chest coughs. The decision, as far as she was concerned, had been made.

I closed my eyes too and considered the gift I'd just been given. Tuition money—yes, of course, a gift so generous I felt certain I'd never be given anything of the same order again. But the gift was more than the numbers in the bankbook. Grandmother, in her no-nonsense way, had given me something I didn't know I could have. She'd given me permission. Permission to leave. With her words and resolve, she'd reached over to my chair and yanked off that wet, woolen blanket. She'd said, without saying it, "Give it here, Marjory. Fanny and I will care for this blanket now."

"How far is it again?"

"An hour and a half, Mama."

"So far? How will you get there?"

"The train, Mama. I'll take the train into Boston, then change at South Station. The next train takes me right into Wellesley."

"That's so far, Marjory. How will I see you?"

"I'll come back, Mama. I'll take the trains back."

"Tomorrow?"

"No. Not tomorrow, Mama. In a few months. For Thanksgiving. And Christmas."

"I love Christmas."

"I know, Mama."

"Marjory? Can I ask one more question?"

"Of course."

"Do they have stars there? At Wellesley?"

"Yes, Mama. The stars are everywhere."

"Well, when you get there, will you look for the north one?"

I nodded. I could not get out the word yes.

Aunt Fanny took me to Wellesley. She sat beside me on the train, erect, not talking, her face puckered and tight but also a little bit dreamy. It was her eyes. She looked out the window, gazing at something that wasn't there, gazing, perhaps, at a past she hadn't lived.

"Will you take a math class?"

These were the first words she'd spoken since we pulled out of South Station.

"Not unless I have to," I laughed.

Aunt Fanny's mouth tightened. She pitched her gaze further afield.

If only I could explain things to her. Or even to myself. I just knew I couldn't take a math class because whatever I did at Wellesley, I had to be good at it. College was my chance. My chance to be good enough, finally, to make everything better.

"Aunt Fanny?"

She turned to me, lips squinting.

"Will you tell him where I am? If he comes looking?"

"Tell who where you are, Marjory?"

We watched each other, eyes steady despite the shuddering train.

"My father," I said.

"Your father," Aunt Fanny repeated. She broke off our stare and turned again to the window, where the brick buildings of Wellesley could just barely be seen.

The window in my little attic room at 7 Cottage Street in Wellesley looked over a garden filled with late-season bee balm and long-blooming asters. From the small desk I'd placed in front of it, I could see the tops of the fiery oaks that edged the flower garden, as well as the window of the attic room at 9 Cottage Street, but I could not, no matter how far I craned my neck, see the North Star.

"I'm sorry, Mama, but I can't see the North Star from my bedroom window," I wrote on the first postcard home. "One night, soon, though, I'll walk down the street and find a better place to look for it. I know it's there. It always is."

I stamped the card and went downstairs to ask the owner of the house where I might find the nearest post box. Classes had not started yet. In fact, none of the other girls who were to live at 7 Cottage Street with me had even arrived. So, from the moment Aunt Fanny had left two days before, I'd spent a gloriously indulgent forty-eight hours reading Matthews's *English Composition* as if it were a three-penny thriller and arranging and rearranging the clothes I'd hung in my wardrobe.

"Mrs. Fletcher?" I called when I reached the bottom of the stairs.

Someone was in the front reception room, but it wasn't Mrs. Fletcher.

A fog of glamour enshrouded the person standing before me. She stood tall, matching luggage lined up neatly around her. Peeking from beneath her skirts were high-heeled boots, the premium quality of which even I could discern from across the room. She surveyed her surroundings carefully, but without judgment, and when her gaze turned to me, she looked at me the same way.

Clearly, this person did not come from a town like Taunton. Most likely, she did not come from Boston either. I knew of only one place where someone with such an aura could reside.

"Carolyn Percy," she said, extending a hand. "New York City."

"Marjory Stoneman," I said, catching myself as I tripped on the edge of the rug as I approached. "Taunton."

Carolyn raised a thin, questioning eyebrow.

"Never mind," I said.

Carolyn wore some sort of gray fur around her neck with a matching gray hat. Squirrel? Fox? I couldn't tell, but the fur looked soft and I gripped my postcard with both hands so as not to pet it. From the side of her hat flared a red poinsettia, boisterous and bright, a detail so sophisticated I considered its addition to her attire to be the very first thing I learned at college.

"What will you study?" Carolyn asked. The poinsettia caught the sunlight and flashed as she moved.

I stuttered, though I obviously knew the answer to her question.

"Um, I'll study, ah, English composition."

"Fabulous!" Carolyn approved. "I'm partial to math,

but I'll tell you a secret." Here she leaned in. Carolyn Percy smelled like fresh linen. "I have a photographic memory. I read a page and—click!—I never have to study again because the information is stored in my head and I can find it whenever need be. Makes history—and literature, too—a little too easy. Math is quite interesting, though."

I instantly liked Carolyn Percy. She emanated joy and approachable refinement. She was plump, like me, but completely uninhibited by that fact. She'd brought a bit of the big city with her to sleepy rural New England, and for that gift alone I was smitten.

"A postcard?" Carolyn asked, big eyes looking at my hand. "If you post it by three this afternoon, it will go out tonight."

"Really?"

Maybe Mama would get it tomorrow.

"Oh, yes," Carolyn assured me. "Go! Go! If you hurry, you'll make it. The post office is on Grove Street. You can't miss it. Go!"

Carolyn shooed me toward the front door, and in that moment, I understood we would be friends.

"And now, an example," Miss Ferry announced on the second day of English 12. "An illustrative example of exactly how a letter should *not* be written. Apparently not all of you understood when I explained that flourish is inappropriate in a letter. Letter writing must be plain, though that does not mean inelegant."

I glanced at each of the other nine women seated at the large table, wondering whose work the instructor had singled out as an example of blatant inferiority. It was impossible to guess. I was not yet familiar with anyone's work, hadn't even heard most of these women speak. So I gambled. I bet it would be the girl to my left, the one with blond curls and pearl earrings.

Miss Ferry adjusted her glasses and held the substandard letter at arm's length before her.

"Miss Stoneman?" she called, looking up. "Would you please stand here and read your letter aloud to the class?"

Me?

Beneath the table, I clutched a fistful of my skirt. I was angry, terrified. My neck flushed. I rose and walked to the front of the room, where I used every ounce of control in my possession not to scream at my professor. Because—really!— of all the possible forms of composition, letter writing was the one that should be entirely free of restraint.

Ten people watched me, nine of them clearly relieved not to be me.

I cleared my throat. Carolyn was going to hoot when she heard about this.

"'Dearest so-and-so,'" I began, in the interest of privacy. "'The campus of Wellesley is full of unbearable beauty. I wake to the call of the whippoorwill each morning and look out the window at a garden that somehow, inexplicably, remains mostly in bloom.'"

Why, I wondered as my brain detached from my voice, did words sound so foolish when spoken aloud?

"'After classes each noon, I pause at the lake and allow what I find there to awe me in such a way that I feel I've collided with the Divine. Oak leaves blaze, stoked by unseen bellows of wind. Those brilliant scraps of scarlet tremble at the edges of their branches. They mirror themselves on the face of the water, igniting the lake. Above it all, the sky stretches cloudless and blue, and I imagine sometimes how it stretches the whole way to you. Wishing you love, Marjory.'"

I was afraid to look up. I held the paper in my hands and continued to watch it, hoping the ink marks could somehow relieve me of my fate. Miss Ferry inhaled, preparing to speak. But my nine classmates erupted in applause before Miss Ferry began. I raised my eyes. My gaze met Miss Ferry's, and I couldn't tell which one of us was more surprised.

The applause carried on. And it wasn't polite, this applause. It was loud. It was furious—the kind of applause that leaves the clapper's hands stinging, the kind that still thunders in your ears after it stops. I smiled, absorbing the riotous praise. That was the day I turned into a writer.

Most Saturday nights, Carolyn and the four other girls who lived at 7 Cottage Street came to my room in their night-clothes. The owner of the house hadn't extended electricity up to the attic, so we huddled in my small living space under the glow of two oil lamps.

Usually, we talked about sex.

Well, we tried to talk about sex. We talked around sex. We speculated and postulated about sex, but none of us had the faintest idea what it was.

"There are babies involved," Louise said.

"No there aren't," Carolyn answered. "Babies are the result. They're not involved."

Louise pouted in the soft light.

"Fine," she conceded, "but sex has something to do with babies."

I generally hesitated to speak in these conversations. If my housemates knew nothing of sex, I knew even less. But sometimes, I just couldn't help myself.

"I think," I began, pulling my knees to my chest and talking mostly to them, "the man does something to your navel."

"Your navel," Marian repeated. She was the only one of us who'd ever smoked a cigarette, and she was practically engaged to her high school sweetheart, so it was entirely possible she had some insight into the subject. "That sounds right."

"Yes," Carolyn affirmed, "the navel sounds right."

We basked in our innocence on those late Saturday nights, making guesswork of womanhood yet trusting in life to enlighten us eventually. We had so much to learn. Wellesley had so much to teach us. Like me, my friends savored the lack of maleness on campus. We thrived in the absence of boys' inevitable domination and looked to our brilliant female instructors and deans for inspiration. Ours was a world run by women, for the benefit of women, with men and their strange needs kept outside the gates.

But, still, we were curious. So very curious.

I read at Wellesley. Voraciously. And I wrote. Extravagantly. Ecstatically. And I thought thoughts I hadn't known I was capable of thinking.

"I don't believe Schopenhauer represented a true rejection of post-Kantian idealism," I proclaimed to Carolyn once while we studied.

My friend glanced up from her calculus work.

"Why on earth not?" she asked.

And then I explained, aware of the rush in my words, the hop in my tone. When I finished, I almost was breathless.

Carolyn reached across the table and squeezed my hand in hers.

"Isn't it splendid?" she asked. "How all we have to do here at Wellesley is eat and sleep and fill our heads with utterly useless knowledge while our parents take care of everything else?"

I looked down at the table. The wood whorled and rippled, like water in a fountain after a penny had just been thrown in.

Carolyn gasped when I looked up again. My eyes were wet, though no tears had fallen.

"Sometimes they don't," I said.

Carolyn squeezed my hand again. She was kind enough not to ask more.

I went home for Thanksgiving. The train seemed to take me not just over land but through time as well, conveying me to the far side of recent history, a place simultaneously simpler and more complicated than my new life.

The ceiling in the Taunton house felt lower. The floors, I was certain, dipped slightly toward the home's center. I hung my hat on a hook in the hall, but there was no room for my coat in the closet—the hangers were full of dark overcoats I'd never seen.

How to explain how I felt during that first visit home? *Angry* is too easy, though anger was there the moment I stepped through the door. I'd managed to sustain through the train ride a bit of the enchantment Wellesley had sprinkled on me, a little of the magic that came with knowing I now belonged at a place of intellectual exploration, a place full of thinkers who would shape the new century. These were all rather elitist, my private thoughts, but they excited me, inspired me. They enchanted me, really. But when the door closed behind me on Harrison Street, the enchantment—like sweat from my arms when the summer sea breeze blows—physically evaporated. This sudden loss was infuriating.

I was mature enough not to show it, however. I swallowed the anger, felt it slide like coffee sludge into my gut, where I could ignore it, at least for a while.

Even more than anger over the disappearance of my Wellesley fairy dust, though, was a nagging sense of fear. I didn't know how Mama was doing. I had no information. Though I'd written her a postcard every day since I left Taunton, she hadn't written back, not even once, and the only bits of news I'd gotten about her were quick mentions in Aunt Fanny's occasional letter: "your mother persists" or "Lillian has knitted another blanket." For all I knew from these pitifully inadequate statements, Mama persisted in slashing the parlor curtains to pieces with a carving knife every Tuesday or hurled an endless stream of invective at Grandmother while basket-stitching a pink baby blanket for the neighbor's new grandchild.

I'd chosen to assume the best while I was at school, though. Mama was fine! She sipped tea in the parlor each afternoon. She went to church with Grandmother on Sundays. She missed me, but not dangerously so. If I'd assumed anything less, I couldn't have stayed at Wellesley, I wouldn't have made it through the end of October. But now, my assumptions would be put to the test, and I was scared.

I'd figured, for reasons I hadn't entirely thought through, that everyone would be sitting in the parlor, looking out the window, anticipating me. I went there first.

A black curtain fully covered the parlor entry. The curtain seemed, with its thickness and width, meant to keep others out, yet I did not hesitate before pulling its frayed edge and peering beyond it.

A bed, unmade. An old table from the sewing room with a large jar and a leather strop upon it. On the floor, an open valise, crumpled clothing piled inside.

"Hello?" I called, pulling the curtain closed.

Aunt Fanny's voice answered from the kitchen, but I could not understand what she said.

I hurried down the hall, walking through stripes of fading sunlight, and, as always, found Aunt Fanny, with her hand plunged deep into the carcass of the Thanksgiving turkey. Strands of her hair fell from their bun, and I wanted to move them for her, push them away from her eyes, wedge them behind her ears, but her shoulders were drawn to her neck and her breathing was deep and stormy. If she'd been a horse, I would have backed slowly away.

Behind her, a man. Someone I'd never seen, with a wish-bone-shaped moustache and threadbare brown pants. He wasn't close to Aunt Fanny, exactly, but he was nearer than a man should have been, and the purpose of his nearness was not obvious. He held nothing, did not try to help Aunt Fanny with cleaning the meat. He just stood there and watched, hungry.

"Marjory!" Aunt Fanny said, pulling out gizzards.

"Aunt Fanny?"

She looked at me over her shoulder. I swept my eyes toward the loitering man.

"Marjory, this is Gerald. The renter."

I looked at Gerald, then back to Aunt Fanny, my questions asked clearly in my expression.

"Gerald," Aunt Fanny repeated, as if I hadn't caught the man's name. "He rents the front room." She blew on her hair through twisted lips, grunted, yanked out the heart of the turkey. "Gerald helps pay your tuition."

Gerald nodded at me, thick moustache bobbing over his chest, but quickly returned to watching Aunt Fanny.

"Does Grandfather know?"

Aunt Fanny plopped the turkey down on the table and turned fully to me.

"Of course he knows, Marjory. What do you think?"

"I mean," I started. "I mean, does he approve? Of having a renter? Of . . . of having . . . Gerald?"

Forgetting about the slime and guts, or perhaps simply not caring, Aunt Fanny put one fist on her hip and answered me in the sassy tone of a child.

"If he doesn't approve, he can figure out how to get more money out of the foundry. Until then, or until you graduate, Marjory, we have a renter. And his name is Gerald." She looked quickly at Gerald. I thought I saw her upper lip curl.

Had I ever, in the whole of my life, felt so awful? I didn't think so. When we'd left Papa, the awfulness had been mixed with confusion and hope, but this, right here, in Aunt Fanny's kitchen during my first visit home from college, this was pure wretchedness. Sickness churned with the stashed anger in my gut, cleaving, forcing me over in pain.

Aunt Fanny gathered the gizzards in her hands and marched to the back door, pink juice dripping in a trail behind her. Gerald scurried to hold the door open for her, as she seemed to know that he would.

"Don't worry," Aunt Fanny called over her shoulder. "You get used to it." Then she left, Gerald trailing behind, the slamming back door an exclamation point after her words.

I stood in the empty kitchen and clutched my stomach. What had I done by going to college? What else would these good people have to sacrifice for me?

And yet, I felt guilt but not remorse. I thought of my sweet attic room on Cottage Street and of Carolyn and of literature and of that pleasant, fleeting sensation when my mind hiccupped with brilliance. I tipped forward and tasted the black tang of bile at the back of my throat.

I wanted to see my mother.

Still holding myself at the waist, I struggled upstairs, guessing she was in the sewing room since the house no longer had a parlor to sit in. Her voice, soft and familiar, reached me before I got to the room. I paused in the hall and listened.

"It's been so long, hasn't it?" Mama was saying. "Twelve years already? Thirteen?" Her voice dropped to a murmur and for a moment I couldn't hear. I leaned closer to the doorway. "They said you went to Florida," Mama continued. "Did you really? I read that oranges grow there, Frank. Have you seen them? Have you seen oranges growing? And does the air smell fresh like orange blossoms?"

Had I not just discovered Gerald living in our parlor, had I not been doubled over from a toxic mix of unexpected emotions, I might have been more careful with my reaction to Mama's words. But my arrival had turned inside out what I knew of life in Taunton, and as I stood in the hall listening to Mama's chatter, it seemed entirely possible that Papa was in fact in the sewing room with her. It seemed eminently possible that I had stumbled upon the reunion I'd only recently stopped wishing for.

I stepped into the room without introduction, my six-year-old self bursting from the sickness and anger inside and welling with sunshine to fill my whole body. Gone was the partially educated Wellesley woman. For the few seconds it took me to digest the situation in the sewing room, I was pure little girl.

"Papa?"

Mama was alone in the room. Needlepoint spread over her lap, flirty smile playing games on her lips. She allowed herself a moment to recognize me, to shift from one world to the other, then she dropped the needlepoint and hurried to where I stood in the doorway.

Mama hugged my waist, buried her head in the sling of my neck, and squeezed hard.

"Sweet Marjory," she whispered.

I hugged her back, smoothed her hair with the palm of my hand.

"Hi, Mama."

She pulled away slightly and looked into my eyes.

"Do you ever hear from him, from your father?" she asked.

I shook my head.

"That's too bad," Mama said with a squeeze. "He visits me sometimes. Next visit, I'll tell him you say hello." She nodded, confirming the solidity of this idea. Then, "Oh! Do you want to play checkers?"

The sharp pain in my abdomen forced me into a chair. I sat, smiled at Mama.

"Sure, Mama. Checkers. Let's play. I'll be black."

"Goody!" she clapped her hands. "That means I'm red."

"Where's Grandmother?" I asked.

"She's napping. She does that now. I'll get the game."

Mama scurried to the hall cupboard, persisting. Everything in Taunton, it seemed, was persisting. Sickened and saddened and guilt-smacked, I couldn't wait to get back to Wellesley.

After first year, Carolyn and I lived together in Fisk, a building on the outskirts of campus where some of our living expenses were offset by chores. I doubted whether Carolyn needed Fisk the same way I did, but either way, her decision to live there made me admire her even more. Because if she did need the financial assistance, then I was amazed by her ability to affect a demeanor of wealth. If, on the other hand, she did not need the money, then I admired her willingness to work anyway for her room and board, in order to live close to me.

I wiped dishes, spinning a rag over the smooth porcelain until I saw the shape of my face floating in the curved expanse. Carolyn, with the big broom she liked best, funneled dirt and dust from the hall into the waiting jaws of an industrial-size dustpan. Most nights, she sang as she did this. Loud and off-key, Carolyn sounded nothing like Mama's long-ago song voice, but there was something about her enthusiasm, about her joy in the freedom of melody-making, that reminded me of those lost days in the Providence duplex.

"Keep going!" I'd call from my polishing place at the table.

"But there isn't any dust left! I got it all!"

"I mean with the singing!"

And she would continue, happily, her train wreck of a voice filling us both with delight.

Carolyn was the first person I told when my story—*Lost Balls*, a wistful little piece about the pleasure of taking a walk when golf balls go astray—was accepted for publication in the Wellesley literary magazine.

"Marjory!" she squealed. "This means you're a writer! A real live actual writer!"

Is that what publication meant? I was—it was true—beginning to think of myself as a writer, as someone who sought clarity and truth through words. My stories were, in some ways, a rejection of the philosophy taught by Miss Calkins, who told us with ferocious authority about neo-idealism—the notion that the idea is the only reality. But if that were right, I reasoned, if an abstract thought itself constituted reality, then my story wouldn't need to be published. It wouldn't need to be written at all. Or printed and presented for others to read. But my story was all of those things. The ideas that had informed *Lost Balls* were harnessed by words and embossed on paper and *that*, I wanted to shout at Miss Calkins, was *my* reality.

There were times, though, at the edges of sleep, when I desperately wished to believe the postulations of Miss Calkins' neo-idealism. Mama, smiling, playing the piano; the parlor a parlor with no Gerald in sight; Aunt Fanny a mathematician at MIT—the possibility that these ideas were reality was awfully consoling. Those were the moments when I let go of my stubborn monist views and conceded that maybe, just maybe, Miss Calkins and her neo-idealists were right (or, at the very least, useful).

Going home during breaks became easier. The initial enchantment I'd felt that first semester at Wellesley had solidified into more permanent magic, magic that would not blow away in the slightest wind. It was mine, this magic. I held it within me. Thirty-two Geralds could rent rooms in the house on Harrison Street, and still the thrill of my education would not disappear. I knew this now, and it comforted me.

Mama seemed more beautiful each time I came home. Her madness hadn't aged her. It had, instead, somehow deepened her loveliness, as if making up for the many other aspects of her it had taken away. Her dark hair, without a strand of gray in it, whorled around her head in a gossamer cloud, and the skin on her face was as smooth and fair as a child's. She remained dainty and thin, with the disproportionately long fingers of the violin player she'd been long ago. I loved to look at her when I was home, just sit and stare at her beauty and imagine the conversations we might have been having.

"Marjory?" she asked as I tucked her into bed one night during a Christmas visit. Outside, the strand of bells Grandfather had hung jingled merrily in the wind.

"Yes, Mama?"

"I'm scared."

"There's nothing to be scared of, Mama. I'm right here."

Her small body shifted under the pile of blankets. She squirmed and sat up.

"But there's something in me. Something that shouldn't be there. I don't like it."

Her pale face shined in the shadows. I clutched the side of the bed, bracing myself for this new twist in her madness and what it would bring.

"What's in you, Mama? What is it?"

"Can you light the lamp?"

The room soon filled with gentle gold light, the sort that reminds you of just how dark the world is beyond the window, even with the jingle bells ringing.

"Look."

Mama started squirming again, this time to free her left arm from her nightdress.

"Look at what, Mama?" I leaned closer.

"Right here. Please see it."

I did see it. A lump the size of a lemon swelling from the placid curve of her breast.

"Does it hurt?"

She bit her bottom lip and shook her head.

I touched the lump with one finger. It was hard, unyielding. I didn't know what it was, didn't know what to say. All I wanted was for her not to worry, not to cry.

"It's a swollen gland, Mama. We'll put a warm cloth on it tomorrow, and it will go away."

She worked her arm back into her nightdress and snuggled under the covers again.

"Promise?"

"Yes, Mama. You don't have to worry. There's nothing bad inside you."

"You're a good girl, Marjory. You've always been such a good girl."

"Thank you, Mama." I turned out the light. "Get some sleep now. Christmas is coming, remember?"

"I love Christmas."

"I know you do, Mama."

I kissed my mother's forehead and slipped out the door to my room. Did I believe what I'd told her? Yes, because I had no idea what else that lump could be.

After the holiday, I returned to Wellesley for the spring semester of my junior year. Mama and the lump were far from my mind. I was focused instead on the Suffrage Club, which Grandmother, when I'd told her about it at Christmas, had approved of by smiling impishly and whispering, "*That's* why I saved the money for you, Marjory. *That's* why! Go back to school and get me a vote!" Every few weeks an envelope arrived for me at Fisk, with one question written on the folded paper inside:

"Can I vote yet?"

Grandmother didn't even sign the letter, if that missive could be called a letter, yet her essence was all over it, from the scratchy writing to the crooked stamp to the stale smell of the paper that had likely been sitting in her desk drawer for a decade. I brought her letters with me to Suffrage Club meetings, for inspiration. D. Q. Applegate, the boisterous chair of the group who never revealed her first name, cheered when she saw the envelopes and shouted, "Let's get Florence the vote!" as a sort of rallying cry to open the session. I thought more about Grandmother at that time than I did about Mama.

Until March.

We endured, at Wellesley, an unfortunate series of lectures on the subject of sex hygiene. Nothing about these lectures addressed the real questions we had, questions about the mysteries between men and women that Carolyn and I had discussed with our housemates on Cottage Street years before. Instead, broad-shouldered nurses offered clinical recommendations on how best to minimize the discomforts of monthly bleeding or dampen the effects of the headaches to which our sex was, apparently, so prone.

"A doctor this time?" I asked Carolyn as I settled into a seat beside her that March. The lecture hall slowly filled with young ladies who, uncharacteristically for Wellesley women, watched the floor as they walked and squeezed their books close to their chests. Nobody liked the sex hygiene lectures.

"From Boston," Carolyn answered. "Big shot."

I arranged my coat around the back of my chair and waited, sighing, wondering what might be offered for dinner that night.

"Ladies," the doctor began when we were all seated. He was handsome, and not entirely old, which ignited an extra spark of self-conscious twittering among the audience members. "I'm going to inform you today about several maladies specific to the female person." The doctor's voice swelled to the edges of the large room, a feat not many speakers accomplished.

I glanced at Carolyn. She pressed her fingertips to her lips as if staunching a yawn.

Excessive monthly bleeding. Nervous fatigue. *I'm sorry, dear doctor*, I thought as I shifted in my chair, *but I'm bored out of my mind.*

Almost as if he had heard my silent complaint, the doctor paused, adjusted his tie. When he spoke again, he spoke even louder.

"Now, we will turn to a condition of the utmost serious-ness, the condition of malignant cancer of the breast tissue."

The word *breast* startled me to attention. Christmas bells. The size of a lemon. Firm to the touch.

"The first symptom is often a painless lump in the breast that grows bigger. This mass is the cancer. If it is not excised, it will spread to other parts of the body until the functional-ity of one or more bodily systems is compromised and death is the inevitable result."

Christmas bells jingle-jangled between my ears, loudly, so loudly, an entire herd of horse-drawn sleighs dashing over the snowy fields of my brain.

"What did he say?" I whispered to Carolyn.

She glanced at me without turning her head. We were, under no circumstances, allowed to chatter during sex hygiene lectures.

Bells ringing even louder, clanging now, the horses col-liding and the sleighs flipping sideways and the bells banging as they crunched under hooves.

"Carolyn," I whispered again. "What did he say?"

She spoke from the side of her mouth, still looking ahead.

"Cancer. Breast cancer. A lump that spreads."

Hard to the touch. Big as a lemon. Jing-a-ling-a-ling.

I groped the seat arm, searching for Carolyn's hand. Then I turned to her, wild-eyed, panicked, the force of the doctor's words pushing my chest into the seatback.

"What's wrong, Marjory?" she whispered, finally looking at me, risking the wrath of professors who ringed the large room.

"I have to go," I said.

I shoved one arm through a sleeve and let the rest of my coat drag behind like a misplaced tail as I scrambled up the aisle to the exit. The good doctor paused but graciously did not comment on my hasty escape. Miss Pendleton, the president of the college, watched me from beneath her corona of white hair. She let me pass, but her stare made it clear there would be questions later. When I reached the main door, I exploded into a disheveled run.

I posted the letter home within an hour, walked straight to the station, and bought a train ticket to Taunton for the day after next. A day would give me enough time to talk to my professors, to ask friends to mail me their lecture notes. My studies, my studies, my studies. What would become of my marks this semester? I told myself over and over, until I nearly believed it, that I didn't care about marks, then wrote a quick letter of explanation to Miss Pendleton.

Mama had breast cancer. I did not fault myself for not knowing this, for telling her to put a warm cloth on her swollen gland until it shrunk, for sweeping away her worries because I could not bear to see them. My ignorance could be forgiven—I was a student of English Composition, not medicine. No, the depth of my guilt ranged far deeper than a misdiagnosis. I was to blame for the illness itself. The very existence of the malignant mass currently gorging on her left breast was my fault. I'd known going to Wellesley would kill her. I just hadn't known how.

"Want to play with me?"

Mama sat on the hospital bed, deflated, sunken. Her shoulders rolled forward in their sockets. Her belly looked scooped and hollowed. Though her question was a relief—she wanted to play, even here, even now—she asked it without cadence, without any contours in tone, and I found it hard to believe she'd be able to play anything, even checkers.

"What if I braid your hair instead?"

Mama nodded. A small window near the ceiling let in the twitters and chirps of early spring.

I settled behind her and combed my fingers through her black locks. I was not good at braiding hair, mine or anyone else's, but I wove the strands slowly, gently, with great determination.

"It looks pretty," I said as I tied the end with a scrap of cloth from my pocket.

"It's bad, what's in me, Marjory. It's really bad."

She spoke of the breast cancer, but I thought of the madness. If only the doctors could remove both during the operation. If only they could cut away all of the darkness inside her.

"I know, Mama."

"I told Frank. I told him about how those doctors are going to cut me open with a knife and take out the badness and then sew me up again. He said they better be careful, those doctors. He said he'll come to the hospital and watch them and make sure they cut me up right."

"Oh, Mama. I'll be here. I'll make sure they do it right."

"Frank, though. He's always looked out for me. He can make sure."

Later, when Mama was sleeping, I found Aunt Fanny and Grandmother in the hall. Grandfather still waited downstairs in the men's area.

Aunt Fanny paced. Her face was pinched tighter than normal, and she clutched her little silk change purse as if she were hanging off the side of a cliff and it was a fast-fraying rope. She had paid the advance for Mama's operation. There couldn't have been much in that purse.

"Is she sleeping?" Grandmother asked.

I nodded.

"Poor thing."

We were quiet. The hall had a greenish tinge, as if the building itself were ill. I felt dirty, vulnerable here.

"Has anyone sent word to my father?"

Aunt Fanny stopped pacing. Grandmother gaped at me from beneath wrinkled lids.

"That's not an actual question, is it, Marjory?" Aunt Fanny spoke the words, but Grandmother may as well have said them with her eyes.

"Mama wants him here. I think we should tell him."

My relatives sputtered, looked to each other in disbelief, wondering, I'm sure, how I'd managed to get stupider at Wellesley instead of smarter.

"He's worthless—"

"He wouldn't come—"

"We don't even know where he is—"

"Florida, I heard. And with a woman. Without even being divorced. That's the kind of man he is—"

"Despicable—"

"The last thing we need is Frank Stoneman here—"

And on and on, a verbal whipping of my absent father, an assault so brutal I didn't know how to defend him. *Not true, not true, not true,* was all I could think to say. In the end, finally, when Aunt Fanny and Grandmother were breathless and spent, I pleaded only for Mama.

"But I think she would really like it if he at least knew."

They huffed their *oh wells* and marched past me to Mama's room, where Aunt Fanny asserted with little compassion that everyone who cared about her was already there.

Night in a hospital amplifies sound, makes shouts out of noises that are usually purrs. Tender footsteps become drumbeats. Unbidden sobs turn to howls. And the resistance of a heavy door wails like a poorly played violin. I heard all of these noises as I lay in the bed the nurses made up for me in the room next to Mama's—Mama walking closer, Mama crying harder, Mama opening my door and climbing into my bed.

I lifted the sheets like an invitation. Her small, shaking body curved against mine the way it used to, years ago, when we first moved to Harrison Street. Mama shifted. The bedsprings shrieked, loud enough, I was sure, to wake other patients. She shifted again, then again, metal scraping on metal, until she found a place for her breast that did not push on the lump.

Inside those loud hours, we struggled through sleep, waiting for—but not wanting—morning to come. I authored a dream that took place in the Providence duplex, before illness and madness, when Mama was still lively and lovely and full of moxie and grace. It soothed me, the sunny contours of the dream, and turned Mama's thick breathing into Brahms's lullaby.

Aunt Fanny and Grandmother and I nibbled jam sandwiches and waited. Every now and then, from somewhere in the cold hospital labyrinth, a woman screamed from pain or exhaustion or the triumph of finally having birthed forth a baby, but we could tell these screams did not come from Mama. Too soon, or too shallow a moan. Hours passed with the same warped lethargy they'd possessed in the night, and when I looked down, I wasn't sure if the sandwich I held was the same one I'd had since the morning or if the nurse had brought me a new one.

Grandmother and Aunt Fanny sat side-by-side, sunlight highlighting the etched skin, the heavy eyes, of them both. Aunt Fanny had not spoken to me since I'd asked about contacting Papa. Most likely, she was distraught over having spent her life savings to send a dunce such as myself off to college. What a moron her niece had turned out to be! What a waste of good money! With Grandmother, though, I seemed to have been forgiven. She squeezed my hand when I got lost in the waiting room fog and gave me calm, steady stares as surges of panic roared through me. With these gestures, she assured me that she understood what it felt like to worry like a mother for Mama.

Without warning, an animal cry split the silence. Now we had no doubt this was Mama, clawing her way from the ether. The cry came again, then again, let loose in bursts so rapid they merged into one long, anguished howl.

"She's saying your name," Aunt Fanny observed.

I strained to listen. She was right. Woven deep in the threads of Mama's baying were the liquids and glides of my name. *Marrrrjorrry*. A guttural plea. She was calling me. She needed my help to get back to this world.

I stood, preparing. My skirts fell in creased angles around me. The sandwich dropped to the floor, and I accidentally stepped on it as I looked for my bag. During my search, the waiting room door opened, and when I turned, the doctor was there—the youngish one who'd given the lecture at Wellesley.

"Is the daughter here?" he asked, loud even in the small room.

I kicked the jam sandwich from my heel and stepped forward.

"I'm here."

"Lillian can see you now."

I followed the doctor down the hall. He walked quickly, without talking, and gave no indication at all that he recognized me. My footsteps trailed his like weak afterthoughts. We turned. Turned again. As I scampered after him, it occurred to me that I owed this man a great debt, the greatest of debts, because without his appearance in that lecture hall three weeks ago, I would still be at school—studying, writing, working for the vote—without any awareness of the cancer eating away at my mother. I'd be ignorant. Still giddily, girlishly lost in the magical world of Wellesley, where the sole purpose of each day was to indulge my capacious curiosity. Instead, thanks to this fast-stepping doctor, I was here. In the glaring, green halls of the women's hospital. Going to see my mother, who would need me now with a ferocity that had surely doubled in strength.

I hated them. I hated them both, my mother and the good-looking doctor. And I hated myself for that hatred.

"Here we are," the doctor announced, as if I didn't hear, from the other side of a closed door, the syllables of my name pulled through the violated corridors of Mama's chest.

I waited for him to say more—instructions, or perhaps a prognosis—but the doctor simply opened the door and stepped aside so I could enter. The door wheezed to a close. The doctor was gone.

Mama lay under a blanket from the waist down. Above, she was bandaged, propped up on pillows. A nurse stood at her side, mopping her brow with a damp cloth and doing nothing to staunch the moans issuing from Mama's insides.

"Is she okay?" I asked the nurse, a question so unanswerable as to be almost ridiculous.

"No sign of a fever."

I took that to mean that Mama, in that precise moment, was not in immediate peril.

Mama looked woozy but awake. Half in this world and half out, which, I thought with a smirk, was how she usually looked. When she focused her eyes on me, she stopped moaning, and the sudden silence made the echo of my name sound even more wretched. Mama reached up with her good arm, the one not near the targeted breast. I stepped toward her, believing she was reaching for me, but instead she snatched the damp cloth from the hands of the nurse and threw it in my direction. "You'll do it better," Mama said.

I apologized to the nurse with a look. Her shrug suggested she'd seen it all.

I took my place next to Mama and dipped the soft cloth into the water bowl. She closed her eyes, and I pressed the cloth to her brow.

What came over me as I stood there, tending my etherglazed mother? Was it truly hatred—not of her, exactly, but of what she and her several illnesses required of me? Or was it more of an anger born out of fear? Fear of what my life would become if she needed my constant care. Even worse—fear of what my life would become if she weren't in it, if she didn't survive, if she left me all alone, with no hand to hold in the vast, starry night? That last thought was unbearable. I'd lost most of her when the madness set in, but to lose her completely, to lose her forever—that was not possible.

Irate and inflamed, I dabbed at Mama's clammy forehead. The unknown had backed me into a near-feral state.

"He wouldn't come," I said, my voice flat, heartless. These were the most malicious words I'd ever spoken. "Papa, I mean. I sent him a telegram, and he answered that he wouldn't come."

Mama's big eyes flipped open. She searched the room with terrified urgency, eyeballs darting, head swiveling. Only when she progressed to twisting her whole body to look behind the bed did the pain arrest her. Immediately, I regretted what I'd said yet could not stop myself from saying more.

"He said his new wife wouldn't like it, if he came to

see you, and if you'd wanted him here, you shouldn't have walked out on him that summer."

The pleasure of the cruelty made my legs tremble. It was as if years of unassigned blame had finally found an outlet, and the outlet felt good. Blame Mama. Blame her now, when she was weakest, when her fragility threatened to completely ruin my life. She'd taken me away from Papa, and although she could visit him whenever she wanted in the nonsensical chambers of her mind, I was without him. Always.

"I don't understand," Mama whispered. "He told me he'd be here."

"Well, he's not," I said, but the vitriol was waning. Mama held the ends of the sheet in tightly clenched fists and glanced around the room, not looking for Papa this time but for the demons she sensed approaching. When she spoke again, her voice was timid, exposed.

"Marjory?"

"Yes?"

"Will you ask the nurse if I can have an ice pop? She said before that I could, if I was good. I've been good, haven't I, Marjory?"

I sighed.

"Of course you have, Mama."

I leaned down and kissed her damp forehead. She was good. I was horrid. I would deserve whatever punishment the fates delivered.

"Marjory?"

"Yes, Mama?"

"Will you ask if they have cherry? Cherry's my favorite."

"I'll ask, Mama. You rest."

Mama closed her eyes, pulled the sheet even tighter. Dust motes danced like ballerinas in the stream of afternoon sun, and I understood that, even after the operation, all kinds of blackness still ate away at her insides.

I paused outside Mama's room, wondering which way the nurse might have gone. The hall was empty, quiet, allowing me to hear the doctor's quick steps before he turned the corner. When his image finally caught up with his footfalls, he walked toward me but without intention, distracted, it seemed, by the need to get to another room, another patient, another raging illness awaiting assault. When he was near, though, he slowed his pace slightly.

"Go back to school," he said in a hushed voice. I did not think him capable of such moderation in volume, and this surprised me almost as much as his words. "She might survive this, but she probably won't, and nothing you can do will change the outcome. So go back to Wellesley. Do you understand me? Finish your education."

My heart kept pace with his footsteps as he walked away. Had I just been granted permission? Absolution? An invitation to ignore the fact that my mother was free-falling to her death?

"Marjory?" I heard from beyond the closed door. "Is there cherry?"

"I'll check for you, Mama," I answered, then rushed away.

From my room next to Carolyn's in College Hall senior year, I could see Lake Waban with such clarity I felt I lived on a ship on its waters. Serene and placid some days, wild and frenzied on others, the lake felt like a friend, a gracious, dependable, yet ultimately unpredictable friend whose beauty refreshed and intrigued me.

"It's freezing in here," Carolyn commented that winter, whenever she stopped by before breakfast. "What are you, a polar bear?"

"I leave the window cracked open at night."

Carolyn would *hmmph* in that loving, exasperated way that she had, and I would not try to explain the comfort I found in the wind's stinging freshness. Like secrets whispered from Waban itself, the frigid airstreams indulged me, brought me out of myself and connected me to the glittering greatness beyond the brick walls of College Hall.

In the bitter freeze of that winter, Waban's water hibernated under a sheet of blue ice, its edges so covered in snow it was impossible to tell where the land ended and the lake began. This solidity, this petrification of my visible world, gave an illusion of permanency that I extended to all of the other parts of my life: to Wellesley, to Carolyn, to Mama—surely they would forever be as they were now, connected to me, nothing would change. I would not change. No tears or decisions or farewells would ever be made. The perfection, the stability, of this moment in time would be unending, unalterable.

Then, one morning in March, I woke to the sound of a guttural moan. The first faint, pink streaks of sun came with the strange sound through the opened window, and for a moment I forgot where I was. Was Mama making that noise? Did she need me? The contours of my room in College Hall slowly came into focus. My brain churned into motion. I was still at Wellesley. The moan came from outside. With my robe pulled tightly around me, I padded to the window and witnessed the sun lift slowly above the lake, heard that rough, inexplicable cry once again. The surface of the lake shifted. Its ice cracked apart and the newly-formed floes strained to move.

I pulled the window shut, turned my back to the lake. I couldn't stand to hear Waban crying as it emerged from its freeze. The world was melting. Spring was coming, as I surely should have realized it would, and time, no matter how hard I tried, would not be restrained.

A spot behind my right ear began thumping, a terrible sound, like soldiers marching to battle. I pressed on the spot with two fingers, but this only made the thump louder, longer.

Taking my fear and this drumbeat with me, I climbed back into bed and slept through my literature class for the first time since coming to Wellesley.

"You missed last Tuesday's class," Miss Sullivan noted as I slunk into my seat.

"Yes, ma'am."

"You've not graduated yet, Miss Stoneman. Please find the time to attend your classes."

"Yes, ma'am."

When I thought she'd surely have turned away to attend to other business, I looked up from my lap toward Miss Sullivan, a young instructor who seemed to play at being stern. She still watched me. Her dark eyes filled the portholes of her glasses, and before she turned away, she smiled slightly, softly. I'd been forgiven, which only made the transgression seem worse.

Though Carolyn had her life after college mapped out and planned, she understood my inability to imagine a post-Wellesley world.

"You could teach," she suggested. "Like me."

"Absolutely not. I'd be a terrible teacher. You, you can do it. You have patience and you can explain things clearly. But me? I'd be incomprehensible. The students would hate me."

What I could not say to Carolyn was that teaching, to me, felt like failure. To have studied so much and worked so hard—for what? So someone else could take hold of my wisdom and put it to use? So someone else could find greatness with the knowledge I had? Unlike Carolyn, I had no high-minded righteousness about the importance of the teaching profession, and—even more—I believed that to be conscripted into the job would support the popular notion that there were only a few limited kinds of work that women could do.

The problem was, I didn't know what else would suit me. I did not want to roam far from Taunton. According to letters from Aunt Fanny and my grandparents, Mama was well. She was stable, and I wanted to be able to see her quite often. But if I stayed close to home, what work could I possibly do? Teach in a small country school, maybe, if I were lucky.

"You could write," Carolyn suggested. "You're good at it. Look how much people liked *Lost Balls.*"

"That's not a job," I answered, meaning not a reliable job. Not a job that pays money. Not a job Aunt Fanny and Grandmother would consider a worthy return on the investment they'd made in me. It was not a job that would make me *good enough.* And so I continued, with increasing anxiety, to watch the world beyond my window defrost and change.

Carolyn knocked on my door before sunrise one morning.

"Dress warmly," she instructed. "And hurry."

I followed her down to the lake, where only glossy lily pads of ice remained on the surface.

"What are we doing?" I asked.

"Just watch."

Carolyn, Carolyn Percy of New York City, Carolyn Percy with the matching luggage and custom-made shoes, looked a bit out of place on the shores of Lake Waban in her gray rabbit furs before dawn. I hadn't known her to care much for nature, to be taken by its surprises and variances as I often was, so whatever we were doing that morning, she had planned it for me.

"Look, look!" she finally said and shoved a set of binoculars in my face.

I held the double glass to my eyes. A cluster of small birds moved across the orange sky. They were brilliant, even from a distance, with yellow patches glowing above tail feathers splayed like a winning hand of playing cards. When the flock passed from view, I turned to Carolyn.

"What was that?"

"Migratory myrtle warblers. They move. They leave one place and go to another. And it's okay. It's beautiful. They're very happy, didn't you see?"

I smiled at my friend, at the effort she was making for me.

"And you just happened to know about them?" I asked.

"Of course not!" she laughed. "But there's a girl in my chemistry class who's in the bird study group—did you know there even was such a thing?—and she told me. I thought you should know." She looked at me crookedly. "It can be done."

I left my room early every morning for a week after that, went and huddled alone in a blanket at the edge of the lake. The spots of ice thinned and then disappeared, subsumed into the warming, waking water. The slightest buds emerged on bare, outstretched branches. I waited there for the warblers, for a new flock to spirit across the sky in a mess of yellow and gray, eager to learn from them. Graduation was coming. Like those small birds, I wanted to know what to do when the seasons changed.

WEST OF MIAMI, 1920

The sound of my breath is enormous. Each viscous huff hangs in the air, suspended, forming a hood that amplifies the following breath. I try to run faster. The swampland resists. It's meant for gliding and skulking, not pounding. Not fury.

The night knows the difference between anger and fury. One is fleeting, an acute response to an acute injustice. The other is relentless, insatiable. The other forms over a lifetime and heats your insides until your heart becomes a thumping purple mass of rage trapped in your chest.

"Marjory!"

Closer now. So close.

What does he want from me? He wants everything. He's desperate. Without me, he will fail, he will die. He wants to whittle away at me until I sustain him, until I save him. Until I become his canoe.

I cry out with exertion. His footfalls come faster.

The darkness of this wilderness has layers. Ahead, a blacker mass is pasted against the everywhere blackness. It must be a hammock, a tree island. I will go there. I will catch my breath among the bromeliads, then turn and breathe my fury upon him.

"Marjory!"

The world tilts as I fall. Thick, wet earth shifts to the sky. Stars are slick underfoot. For a moment, nothing makes sense. I can't see. I barely can hear. Mud seeps from my ears as if my brain is melting and trickling away. And then:

"So, there you are."

I am caught.

He hovers above me, shrouded in the thick, buzzing night. Our breathing slows. And then, because there still exists a gentleman somewhere inside him, he crouches, offers an arm to help me rise from the sludge.

"You can't run away," he says. "I love you too much."

I pull my body from the wet earth with a slurp and answer, "I love me, too."

He shifts. The movement is sudden, hostile. On his breath, I smell the panic that accompanies his frequent bouts of confusion.

"What does that mean, Marjory? What the hell does it mean?"

I swallow, afraid of the answer, afraid of his response to the answer.

"It means," I say, "that I don't think I can love both of us."

His glare is hot on my skin, even through the dark. There is no question anymore about what I want, about what I must do. The same is true, however, for him.

"I think you can," he says.

His hand seizes my wrist, and the night falls even further.

NEWARK, 1913

I knew nothing of Newark, New Jersey, and knew no one who lived there, so in a way, the city was perfect for me during those twisted first years after college. I could retreat after work to my rented room in Mrs. McMahon's apartment house for young women, where the walls were so thick I wrote letters to Carolyn without being disturbed; I cried into my pillow without fear of being heard.

Mama was gone. She'd died in my arms two months after graduation, the cancer having overtaken her spine, her organs. Her shriveled, once-beautiful body surrendered while I'd held her, and as she'd left me, she sang. She sang sweet, tender songs with meaningless words, gentle music that I thought she'd forgotten how to make. But she hadn't forgotten. The music had stayed inside all these years, trapped by her madness but not extinguished. The songs escaped through her chapped lips, dancing into this world as my final gift, as a glimpse of the glory she'd find in her forever world. I listened, and I wondered at the cruelty of her many sufferings.

In the weeks after her death, what overcame me was not more guilt—it was too late for that—but a sense of disorientation, of failure, so complete that I felt, night and day, that I was floating through outer space, billions of miles from those stars that had once seemed so close to earth.

"Come live with me in St. Louis," Carolyn had written when news of Mama's death reached her at the boarding school where she taught. My groundlessness at that time was so profound that I could not figure out how to get to St. Louis, how long it would take. I did not answer Carolyn's letter for weeks.

"You have to do something," Grandmother had insisted as I'd mourned and moped around the old house in Taunton. "Or Fanny's going to start giving you chores, and you'll never get out."

Grandmother had aged since Mama's death. The cancer, I think, had seemed to my grandmother like a more legitimate illness than the sickness in Mama's head, and she'd dealt kindly with Mama as she'd declined. They'd become friends again; she'd cared for her daughter with real tenderness, pressing balm to her lips when they dried out, clipping her toenails as carefully as she'd surely clipped them when Mama was a baby. The loss, then, slammed the old woman into the wall, and when she'd stood after the impact, it became clear how much of Grandmother's strength Mama had taken with her into the grave.

"Go," Grandmother said, practically shoving me out the door.

But go where? With Mama gone, the burden I'd felt since we'd left Papa had lifted, but I didn't feel free. Mama called to me, needy and sweet, in my dreams, in my waking thoughts. I found myself incapable of making decisions because I could not think through the pleas of her ghost-voice.

Carolyn must have contacted some Wellesley friends, because D. Q. Applegate showed up at my grandparents' house and informed me I was enrolled in a training course in Boston.

"Training for what?" I asked as I watched her pack my suitcase.

"Training for salesgirls. At department stores."

This sounded like a terrible idea. Worse than being a schoolteacher. Worse than almost any professional job I could imagine. But I did not have the composure to argue with D. Q., and I allowed myself to be ferried along.

"You need a college degree to do that?" Aunt Fanny huffed as I hugged her goodbye in the kitchen. She floated in a cloud of white baking flour.

"Oh, yes," D. Q. assured her. "It's very prestigious."

"Be smart," Grandfather offered as farewell.

"Just go," Grandmother interrupted.

"Florence?" D. Q. said brazenly to Grandmother before the front door swung closed. "I'm still working to get you that vote."

Grandmother smiled at D. Q. in a way that made me wonder if she didn't wish D.Q. were her granddaughter instead.

"The two of you'd better hurry, then, dear," Grandmother said.

After completing the training course, I got a job at Nugent's department store in St. Louis.

"You'll live with me," Carolyn insisted. "The school gave me an apartment. It's not big, but there's a nice view of downtown, and I can hang up a curtain and make you a bedroom. You'll love it. I promise. Oh, and I'll sing while we clean. Just like old times."

In St. Louis, despair called to me constantly—beckoning from the toneless taps of the cash register, from the grinding of the streetcar brakes, from the everywhere flatness of Midwestern vowels and land. I didn't succumb. Not so much because I resisted but because Carolyn held me so tight.

Carolyn picked out clothes for me using my Nugent's discount ("Powder blue is your color, Marjory! I'm telling you, it really is!"). She put food on my plate and, since she didn't put much, I slowly lost weight. I also did away with my glasses because my wandering eye had corrected itself, and the glasses were no longer needed. From the outside, I looked the best I'd ever looked, but this attractiveness—if it could be called that—merely patched over the chaotic aimlessness I still felt inside.

Sometimes, I walked the streets of St. Louis at night, searching the sky for constellations I knew. Nothing. I could identify nothing up there. I thought more during these walks about Papa than I did about Mama, probably because thinking about him hurt a little bit less. He hadn't come back. He was never going to come back. I no longer believed, as I had as a child, that the west was so big he'd gotten lost. Whether he'd gotten richer or poorer out there—whether he'd even gone west at all—the one thing I knew was that he wasn't lost. He could have found his way to me if he'd wanted to.

I guess I hadn't been good enough, not even at Wellesley. Mama was dead. Papa was really gone. And I worked in the ladies' section at Nugents.

"I need to tell you something," Carolyn said after nearly a year living together.

"Yes?"

"I'm leaving. I'm going back to New York, to my family. I'm sorry, but I don't want to live here anymore."

"I don't either."

"You don't?"

"There's nothing here for me but you."

"So you're not mad?"

"Of course not."

Being mad would have required more verve than I currently had.

"Will you come with me to New York?" Carolyn asked.

"New York?"

I didn't feel able to handle living in New York—the streets crowded with urbanites dressed as smartly as Carolyn, the mile-high buildings and endless opportunities.

"I can't," I said.

Carolyn squeezed my hand, nodded gently.

"I've looked into it," she said. "Bamberger's in Newark has an opening for an educational director, and that would put you close enough to New York to see me sometimes."

We left St. Louis within a week of each other.

I lived in Newark—among its buildings and shops, beneath its street lamps and flowerboxes—but, like St. Louis, I did not see it. I had no sense of the city's personality, its peculiarities. I had no idea if the place was charming or gritty, sprawled or condensed. My rented room in Mrs. McMahon's house was a block and a half from Bamberger's, and I commuted between these locations in a vacuous head-fog, surviving, barely, on the outskirts of life. Women passed on the street with small children. I did not smile at them. Salesgirls at the store chattered about their engagements, their holidays, their favorite music. I nodded politely but did not ask questions. I existed in a self-imposed vacuum, a void, and the only things I allowed into that emptiness with me were books.

My rented room sat directly across the street from the library. I don't think I knew this when I took the room, but it's possible my eyes had noticed the small building without telling my brain and this sighting had influenced my decision. I spent whatever free time I had in that library, cocooned among the bound pages, comforted, as I'd been as a child, by the reliability of all of those words on all of those pages. Occasionally, I'd look up from a book and imagine Aunt Fanny at the library's main entrance, exclaiming that I couldn't possibly understand all of what I was reading.

One Sunday, with the library closed and work a whole day away, I decided to empty a box that had made the move to and from St. Louis with me. It was labeled, in Aunt Fanny's print, "Marjory's things," and that is exactly what I found inside. The blue quilt from my attic bed. Jeanne, the floppy doll Grandmother had made. Essays and examinations from high school. Then, at the very bottom, as if it had been the first thing packed into the box, I found a dark leather-bound book with a gold-embossed title. *Alice in Wonderland.* My father's copy. During all those years in Taunton, I had not read the book I'd taken with me when we left Papa. I hadn't even opened it. I'd feared its power. I'd feared that turning its pages would have been a treasonous act of betrayal. But now, Mama was gone. Did I still owe her such strict allegiance? I lifted the book from the box, tilted it under the light to see if the glare would reveal Papa's thumbprints. None showed themselves, but that didn't mean they weren't there. I sat cross-legged on my bed. Carefully, I opened the book. Then I consumed it as if it were sacred text.

Soon after the Sunday I'd discovered the book, Mrs. Henry approached me at work. She was a tall woman, with a dominating presence and a cultivated, precise sort of friendliness. Her title, officially, was "Store Social Director," but she seemed to be more of a mother hen, keeping an eye on her working-girl chicks.

"Marjory?" she interrupted as I went over basic arithmetic with the nineteen-year-old working the cash.

"Yes, Mrs. Henry?"

"You're pale."

I looked at the woman.

"Yes, ma'am," I said.

"Of course, pale is fine—it's lovely, really—but I mean to say there's no heat in your cheeks. No rosy glow."

"Mrs. Henry," I said, "I'm not sure I've ever had a rosy glow. I don't think I'm capable of it."

"Nonsense," Mrs. Henry answered. "You simply need something to do. You'll come with me to a party. This Saturday afternoon at the home of my friend Paula Laddie. Be ready at noon."

"But I work this Saturday, Mrs. Henry."

The older woman lifted her chin, considering. She looked at me, looked at the girl I was teaching, looked back to me.

"Charlotte, isn't it?" Mrs. Henry asked my student.

"Yes, ma'am," Charlotte answered.

"Tell me, Charlotte, have you learned a lot yet?"

"Oh, yes, ma'am." Charlotte nodded for emphasis. "Marjory has taught me so much."

"Fabulous," Mrs. Henry declared. "You'll be working from eleven to three this Saturday, Charlotte."

I survived the Saturday afternoon of teacakes and small talk and did my best not to look sullen, but the hours at Paula Laddie's house were, for me, an exercise in social endurance, an exhausting attempt at engagement with the world that I would have rather not made. My books were more interesting, my little room better vented.

Paula Laddie, though kind, seemed rather desperate to impress, and by the end of the party, I knew the cost of her tea set, the thread count of her linens, the name of her hair stylist. She was, perhaps unsurprisingly, unmarried, and for this reason Mrs. Henry assumed we should be friends.

"You two should lunch together," Mrs. Henry suggested as she filled her plate with petit fours. "Paula works at the bank, not far from Bamberger's. Three blocks at most."

"I often shop during lunch," I stammered. "Or rest."

Paula Laddie, in fairness, seemed equally uneager to lunch with me.

"I hardly get more than fifteen minutes for lunch," Paula chirped. "Scarcely even time to freshen up."

I left the party without further obligation to the hostess. The next week, I began rouging my cheek before work, with the hope that Mrs. Henry would find me sufficiently heated and leave me alone.

Yet that was not the end of Paula Laddie. Somehow, we found ourselves in the same line at the grocer or walking through the same door at the post office. Perhaps we'd been crossing paths all along and not noticed until after the party, but, in the weeks after I met her, it seemed that Paula Laddie was everywhere. Fortunately, neither of us ever stopped to make conversation.

"Hello, Marjory."

"Oh! Hello, Paula."

And then we'd move on, forcing ourselves in opposite directions, even if we'd needed to go the same way.

Our mutual unwillingness to engage was a relief, and I began to expect nothing more than a quick greeting or nod when we met. So I was confused when, one cool summer day, we ran into each other on the street during lunch and she stopped to talk.

"Marjory! Marjory Stoneman. It's so good to see you."

I stumbled in my low heels. It was as if Paula Laddie's effusive welcome was physically lying across the sidewalk.

"Hi, Paula," I answered.

It was only then, after I'd regained my balance and greeted her, that I understood the reason for her sudden chumminess: Paula Laddie was with a man, and though he looked old enough to be her father, from the way that she grinned, I could tell that was not who he was.

"Please meet Mr. Douglas," Paula said. She was proud, as if Mr. Douglas were part of her fine linen set.

"Kenneth," the man said. "Kenneth Douglas."

Kenneth Douglas wore wire-rimmed glasses that gave him the air of a professor. His suit—which I could confidently evaluate, having worked in department stores for more than a year now—was of average quality and several seasons outdated.

"Mr. Douglas writes for the *Evening News*," Paula boasted.

"Congratulations," I said, with more annoyance than I intended to let on. "I'd really better be going. It was nice see you both."

I had no interest in talking to Paula Laddie and even less interest in talking to the man she was with. I wanted to get to the library. At most, I had fifteen minutes before I'd be expected again at the store.

"A pleasure," Kenneth Douglas assured me, as Paula hung her arm around his.

I smiled and hurried away, trying my best not to break into a run.

I continued to run into Paula Laddie but never again saw her with the old man. She greeted me even more tersely now, worried, perhaps, that I would ask about her absent companion. And then, sometime that October, my Paula Laddie sightings abruptly stopped. She completely disappeared.

"Oh, Paula's gone and moved to Philadelphia," Mrs. Henry explained with a little grin. "More, ah, *opportunities* there."

The exit of Paula Laddie from my life seemed to create space for the entrance of someone else, and I began to see the man with whom she'd been walking that day on corners, at park benches, even once at the stationer, where I bought nice paper for my letters to Carolyn. These encounters were insignificant—they tasted as nuanced as water, lasted as long as a blink—but because of them, our eventual meeting in the library seemed less a serendipitous alignment of stars than an unavoidable collision.

"Howd'yado?" the now-familiar figure asked in his soupy croon.

I had three books in my stack and resented his silent appraisal of them.

"Fine, thank you," I answered, then turned to leave.

The near-empty library stretched between me and the door. Books hid on shelves in the shadows of the autumn afternoon. The walls themselves seemed hushed by the heft of the treasures they held. I hugged my books close to my chest. The only way I ever could bear leaving a library was by taking part of it with me.

"It's Miss Stoneman, isn't it? Miss Marjory Stoneman?"

I stopped. The significance of this follow-up attempt at conversation was not lost on me, even at the exact moment it happened. No man—anywhere, ever—had made an effort to keep me engaged, to pursue me as I tried to leave.

"Yes," I said, turning. "And you are Mr. . . . ?" I thought I remembered but wasn't sure.

"Douglas," he filled in. "Kenneth Douglas."

His elongated head bobbed atop a thin walking-stick body. He was not handsome, but there was all about him an air of forced refinement, a calm civility that fell just short of actual elegance.

"You work with Mrs. Henry at Bamburgers, don't you?"

"I do."

Kenneth Douglas nodded a few times, as if I'd said something worth mulling over.

"Think it might be all right if I come by there next week?" he asked. "To see you, I mean?"

Because this sort of request also had never happened before, I agreed.

He showed up on a Thursday, milling about in the ladies' winter wear section until I was free. During my break, we walked through the streets of an increasingly cold, overcast Newark. The trees, by this time, were almost entirely bare, except for the occasional leaf near a maple-top that persisted like a stubborn cowlick. Pedestrians wore scarves and overcoats that were perhaps too heavy for the weather but which signaled a preparedness reminiscent of the habits of New

Englanders. With resigned anticipation, the city seemed to be waiting for the first snow to fall.

"Are you cold?" he asked more than once.

"I'm fine."

When I shivered, it was from the feel of his gloved hand on my elbow, not from the weather.

Our courtship was hurried, fierce, an experience so utterly foreign to me that I reveled in the adventure of it, if not in any actual affection. Thirty years my senior—yes, thirty—and guarded with even the most mundane personal information (Were his parents alive? Had he gone to college?), Kenneth Douglas was not, objectively, an ideal match for me. But I'd never been the kind of girl to cling to fairy tales. I'd never awaited a frog, much less a prince, and so he did not fall short of any dearly held expectations.

In her letters, Carolyn supported the courtship. She mistook my curiosity about Kenneth for actual happiness, and I did not dissuade her. Clearly, I had recovered from the turmoil that had plagued me since graduation, since Mama's death, if I could maintain a relationship with such a mysterious man.

Kenneth proposed on a cold winter night in the vestibule of my apartment house. The mahogany paneled walls glistened with lemon oil—Mrs. McMahon must have rubbed them that afternoon—and the small space choked with the smell. I stood near the stairs, one foot raised, one hand clutching the banister, headed to my room after our evening at the local theater.

"Think you might marry me, Marjory?" Kenneth asked my back. "Think you might like to be my wife?"

I was supposed to feel something just then, in the aftermath of this momentous request, wasn't I? Wasn't my heart supposed to pound—from either excitement or fear, it did not matter which, so long as some sort of heart-pounding ensued—and weren't my palms supposed to sweat and all manner of involuntary physical responses sweep over the length of my virginal body? Instead, I stood still. Unmoving. One foot on the vestibule floor. The other perched on the first step. Frozen in my ascent.

It was carpeted, that step. Dark green faded to brown in the center, edged with peeling gold trim. My brain urged, then begged, my body to react. Even a twitch would have sufficed. Nothing.

The only thing I seemed capable of doing was observing that step, worn down to bland in the middle. How many shoes had rubbed away those green fibers? How many young, unmarried women had stepped in that spot, headed up to rooms of their own, only to trod upon it again in the other direction, leaving for a conjoined life with a man in a home?

Behind me, Kenneth shifted. Small bits of ice, dragged in on his soles, crunched expectantly.

Had Mrs. McMahon raised children whose small, eager feet first eroded the carpet? I imagined she'd had a gaggle of them, seven or eight in rapid succession, wearing her down like the rug.

Kenneth coughed. I had the decency to look over my shoulder at him when I finally spoke.

"Okay," I said.

Then I used the leg that had been poised on the step for so long to heave myself forward, feeling suddenly and overwhelmingly tired.

"What is it, Marjory?" Kenneth asked gently from behind. "What's wrong?"

"It's nothing," I answered. "Goodnight."

I pulled myself up the stairs and left my fiancé staring dumbfounded at the space where I'd been.

Marriage without love wasn't bad. Like tea without sugar or sleep with no dreams. In those first days after our wedding, I learned the mechanics of kissing, an activity that was, to my mind, both arbitrary and thrilling. *Why lips?* I thought as Kenneth pressed his mouth against mine. *Why are those two strips of flesh so important?* I had an erudite theory— because the mouth is a portal, a bridge between body and soul, between outside and in—but the longer the activity in question went on, the less I was able to theorize. A buzz would begin in my gut and slowly spread lower, smothering all rational thought and leaving me disturbingly mindless. These sensations were fun. Delightful and simple in a way most other things in my life had never been.

Our wedding was a quiet, nearly covert affair in the Newark courthouse. I told no one except Carolyn because the only other person I wanted to tell was my mother, dead almost a year. I shared the news with Mama during the last moments of dawn on the day of the ceremony.

"I'm getting married today," I whispered to the ceiling, imagining I was a child and she was there with me on the bed. "His name is Kenneth. I don't love him, Mama, and don't expect that I ever will."

"Even if you did love him now, Marjory," Mama answered, *"it doesn't mean you always would."* She was more sensible in death than she'd been in life.

Kenneth and I took the train out to Belmont for our honeymoon. The winter sky in western New York seemed to sit on the roof of our compartment, so weighted was it with ice and snow and unfallen grief. I read—*Alice in Wonderland*, because both Alice and I had fallen down a strange rabbit hole. Kenneth draped an arm over my shoulders and read my book, too. More than the kissing, more than anything we were about to do in our room at the Belmont Hotel, his reading along with me felt like an intrusion, a breach of the boundaries of my being.

"Did you not bring a book?" I asked sweetly.

Oblivious to any possible reason for my asking, Kenneth answered, "I did, darling. But it's at the bottom of my valise."

And so we read. Pained, I waited at the end of each odd-numbered page for a nod signaling that I could turn to the next. This went on for a full chapter and a half until I could take it no longer and placed the book on his lap.

"Go ahead," I offered. "These metaphors are exhausting. I'll just close my eyes for a while."

"Of course," Kenneth said, thinking he understood. He lifted the book, and I tipped my head to the seatback.

Sex. An even more curious endeavor than kissing. I knew nothing about it, not even lies, and when it happened to me in the honeymoon suite at the Hotel Belmont, I had the ridiculous urge to take notes, so I could one day compare with my friends who'd broached the subject with me in my attic room that first year at Wellesley.

"This is unfamiliar to you, I assume?" Kenneth asked as he assiduously unfolded the bedcovers until the sheets were exposed.

I nodded. His tone was didactic, instructive. Clearly, sex was not unfamiliar to him.

"Well," he continued, "it's probably easiest if we disrobe first. Get that out of the way."

1. Disrobe first, I would have written in my sex notebook.

Kenneth attended to the heavy, lined curtains, pulling at them until the panels overlapped. Then he turned on a few lights, turned off a few others, rearranged logs on the fire the bellboy had set in the hearth, creating, with these calibrations, the darkly primitive feel of a cave just after sunset.

2. Adjust lighting.

Kenneth turned from the fire and came close to me. The smell of burned wood and ash hung on him like cologne.

"We're married now, Marjory," he said, touching my arm. "It's okay to undress."

I was not scared as I unbuttoned my blouse and tugged at my stockings. Carolyn had given me a set of pink silken undergarments, of which I felt quite proud, and I was eager for Kenneth to see them.

3. Flaunt new undergarments.

"Those are nice," Kenneth acknowledged, touching a pink shoulder strap, and for that small kindness I was grateful.

Kenneth hung our discarded clothes in the armoire, then invited me, with dramatic a sweep of one arm, to lay on the bed.

His body, like his clothes, was handsome but worn, graying and wrinkled in places, though not wholly unattractive. He lay down. The nearness of so much uncovered skin was startling, then quickly thrilling, and I wondered with growing impatience what would happen next.

4. Keep waiting.

What I wanted was to get a good look at his penis. Would it be rude to ask? I'd never seen one before, though I'd often discussed with my Wellesley friends its mysterious structure and function.

"Kenneth?"

Surely, he belonged to me, in body and mind, as much as I now belonged to him. Surely I was entitled to ask for a peek.

"Mmm?" he responded, rolling to his side to face me.

5. Ask embarrassing questions.

I glanced down. His anatomy was hidden in the shadows of the sheets.

"Do you think I could—"

Kenneth's hand interrupted my question. As effectively as if he'd clamped it over my mouth, his hand stopped my breath, pushed my words into oblivion. A man's fingers had never been there before. Those particular nerve endings had never before sparked to life.

6. Gasp.

7. Shift self-consciously.

8. Banish any outward displays of revulsion.

9. Tell yourself it's okay that he stopped just as you were beginning to get interested.

10. Refrain from saying "giddy-up" as your husband climbs on.

11. Gasp again.

12. Perhaps gasp a third time.

13. Understand—almost!—what all the fuss is about.

I possessed, at the conclusion of our honeymoon, a great sense of accomplishment, having lain with Kenneth at least once, and occasionally twice, during each of the five days we spent in Belmont. I'd been eager to be near him, to feel him, to sweat sex out of my system like a fever until its power diminished and it no longer held the allure of the unknown.

Indifference to sex—yet another way in which I was truly becoming a wife.

We returned to Newark in the late afternoon and headed first to my apartment house to gather the last of my things. From the end of the block, the street looked the same as it had when we'd left, but the air smelled different, full of unnamed misfortune. Kenneth noticed it, too. We squinted and sniffed, trying, like hound dogs, to understand.

"Something's happened," he said needlessly.

We walked like a married couple now, same pace, me a half-step behind, with an arm looped under his elbow. This was how we approached my apartment house, or rather, what was left of my apartment house.

Much of the shell of the building still stood, though its wood was charred and fragile-looking, as if a strong wind might bring what remained to the ground. The inside was hollow, blackened, rotted.

"Good thing you were away," Kenneth observed.

I stood with Kenneth Douglas in the chill winter air, staring at the gutted remains of my burned-down boarding house. As a reader, a once-upon-a-time writer, the symbolism of the moment was not lost on me: Marjory Stoneman had gone up in flames; I was Mrs. Kenneth Douglas now.

After the fire, domesticity descended like a heavy snowfall. We found our own apartment, a quaint two-room plus bath and kitchenette that smelled like wet dog but got beautiful morning light. I made blue throw pillows for the sofa we'd bought on credit. I carefully arranged my cooking utensils on a sideboard next to this sofa and solemnly vowed to learn to use an iron.

At Bamburger's, on my first day at work after the honeymoon, Mrs. Henry looked me over critically, as if assessing through my clothes the extent to which the marriage had been consummated.

"Nice trip?" she asked when her eyes had settled again on mine.

"Very," I answered, with just enough of a smirk to stop her inquiry.

A week later I gave Mrs. Henry notice that I'd be leaving the job. Kenneth didn't think matrons should work. Lost in the fog of all my recent life changes, I'd agreed.

"Are you sure?" Mrs. Henry asked when I told her.

No.

"Yes," I answered.

The job had not been fun, or even mildly interesting, but it had been mine, and I missed its place in my life almost immediately.

"What do you think I should do?" I asked Kenneth over dinner one night. I had cooked liver and potatoes, an uninspiring meal that left me hovering indifferently over my plate. Kenneth ate quickly, though without any apparent satisfaction. "Did your mother work? Do you have sisters who work?"

Kenneth watched me through the screen of steam still rising from our plates.

"No sisters," he said flatly. "Mother took in laundry sometimes."

I waited for more, but nothing came.

"Maybe I'll read to the blind," I offered. "I've heard of married ladies who do that."

This pivot away from discussion of his family seemed to please him, and Kenneth answered in his usual tone.

"That would be suitable, Marjory."

So I found an organization, and twice a week, I sat in the library and read to a person who could not read alone. This work, I had hoped, would be fulfilling, or at least modestly satisfying, or at the *very* least, somewhat distracting, but I found I couldn't stand the sound of my voice after two or three pages. I sounded nasal, whiny, the least suitable person for reading aloud. And when my listener failed to grasp obvious symbolism or appreciate an especially beautiful metaphor, an unscratchable itch began to torment my insides, and it didn't stop until hours later, when I'd had a quiet moment to contemplate the writing myself.

But the very worst part was when Mr. Culligan fell asleep, as he was prone to doing, before I'd finished reading the first chapter of a book. Angry, I'd let my voice fall lower and lower, reading, finally, in barely a whisper and waiting for him to say something. He never did. I'd make a sour face at him, knowing that even if he woke he wouldn't see me, then angrily pen a letter to Carolyn while Mr. Culligan snored softly beside me.

There was one woman, though, Amy Lovelane, with whom I truly enjoyed my time. She had soft apricot-colored hair and was not much older than me. Married, with five children—a burden she carried more gracefully that I, with full vision, ever could have done—the weekly hour with me was her singular indulgence. I chose her books carefully, eager to give her a story that her mind could drift back to during the week when she needed a break from her duties. She liked mysteries and British writers. To make the very most of our time together, I invited her to read in my apartment instead of the library, so we could sit in armchairs warmed by the sun and sip tea and eat biscuits.

"You have a lovely home, Marjory," Amy said, as she did every week, when she arrived one Friday in April with her walking stick and thumb-sucking baby. "So sunny."

Was it wrong to be relieved that she could not see the dust motes piling up in the corners or the crusty layer that still coated the breakfast dishes? I enjoyed the fact that her milky eyes could not evaluate my housekeeping skills, though I was aware that, at some point, her fully functioning nose might give me away.

Amy and I settled in the armchairs. The baby fell asleep at her breast. I'd chosen a Sherlock Holmes story, her absolute favorite, and we were just getting to the good part when a succession of hard, urgent raps at the door interrupted.

The baby startled awake, as if she too felt her gut drop, felt the earth roll to the edge of a previously unknown celestial cliff.

Police officers, one tall and one taller, stood in the hall. With their somber expressions and inelegant mustaches, they looked as if they'd stepped directly from the pages of our Sherlock Holmes story and into my front entryway.

"Mrs. Douglas?" the taller one asked.

I nodded. In doing so, I gave permission for a conversation of laughable typicality to take place.

"We have a warrant for your husband's arrest."

"Is he at home, or do you know his whereabouts?"

"If he's fled town, he is considered a fugitive of the law."

The apartment turned sideways, and I looked back to make sure Amy was still holding tight to the baby so she wouldn't fall. I put one hand on the doorframe, squeezed my eyes shut. The only things stopping me from tipping over were the scripted hilarity of the officers' statements and the fact that, at bottom, I was not entirely surprised by their arrival.

"A fugitive?" I asked.

"Of the law, yes ma'am," the tall one confirmed.

"I don't know where he is," I told them, "if he's not at work."

The officers said something else, used their deep voices to thank me, remind me, assure me, implore me. I was not sure if I heard their words or words from the books I'd spent my life reading. Did I even exist, or was I a character in Amy's favored English detective stories?

"I'd better go," Amy said not long after the officers' footsteps had stopped echoing on the stairs. She collected herself and her baby and quickly was gone. *Of course*, I thought. Of course she went home. We were not friends. She had her children to think of.

The hours that followed were nerve-wracking, yes, but they also were thrilling in way that was utterly new to me in real-life, non-fictionalized form. My husband was a fugitive! The police were searching for him! I did not know what crime he was accused of committing; the officers had not said, but the charge, essentially, did not matter because I— his wife, Mrs. Kenneth Douglas, Mrs. Marjory Stoneman

Douglas—had absolutely no idea what actions my husband was or was not capable of taking. I did not, in truth, know him well enough to say. Murderer? Maybe. Bank robber? Probably. Vagrant or thief? Without a doubt. I became jittery, restless. When I could not contain myself in the apartment one moment longer, I headed outside. The night was cool and starless. I wished I'd worn a coat. Along the riverbank, the air swirled, marbled with the stink of industrial waste and April renewal. I thought of Kenneth and found him newly appealing.

"My husband's a criminal," I wanted to whisper to strangers, the way I would have wanted to if he'd gotten a raise or a promotion or a prestigious award. I felt as if his fugitive status gave me an imprimatur of fascination and intrigue. "My husband? Yes, he's on the lam. Oh, that's how we are."

I wandered the streets of Newark until the chill I'd absorbed had so thoroughly permeated me that I felt bodiless, massless, more of a cloud than a physical person. At home, the apartment was dark and cold. It failed to warm me, so I pulled blankets from Kenneth's steamer trunk and piled them on the couch, anticipating the relief of their weight. A cup of tea would help, too. My afternoon cup of tea still sat on the table next to Amy's half-empty cup. I took them both to the kitchen but stopped before I got to the sink.

The sugar canister lay open on its side, tiny grains spreading like sweet lava over the counter. I peered inside. The pouch we kept in the canister was gone. Kenneth, it seemed, had returned while I was out and taken our savings.

It turned out that Kenneth was not a skilled fugitive, and he was caught a day and a half after he'd fled. I immediately went to see him in the Newark jail, an excursion for which I dressed up, wore my best hat, slipped my hands into a pair of scarlet kid gloves I'd never before had occasion to wear. My heels *tap-tapped* like secret code in the corridor of the police station.

"I'm here to see my husband," I announced to the officer at the desk. I leaned forward, lowered my voice. "Kenneth Douglas. The fugitive."

The officer looked at me, shook his head slightly. It was a gesture I did not know how to interpret.

"This way, ma'am."

I *tap-tapped* deeper into the jail. The officer leading me belched, excused himself half-heartedly. I pulled off my gloves and shoved them into my purse.

"Here you are, ma'am."

The officer dragged a stool close to the bars of a cell. I sat.

"Ten minutes," he said as he walked away.

No one offered to take my coat or my hat or purse, so I piled these belongings on my lap and peered over them into the cell.

Kenneth stood in the shadows. He leaned against the far wall, one ankle crossed over the other. If he'd had a hat, he would have had it pulled low over his eyes. If he'd had a cigarette, he would have blown smoke in rings. He was doing the very best impression of a criminal I'd ever seen.

"Hi, doll," he said.

This was the first time Kenneth had called me "doll." Apparently, he too was enjoying this game.

"What are you in for?" I asked.

He stepped close to the bars.

"I bounced a check."

I wrinkled my nose, tipped my head to the side.

"Really? That's it?"

Kenneth shrugged.

"Yeah. It was no big deal. Trivial. Misunderstanding at my friend's store."

I stared at my husband. He looked thin enough to slip between the cell bars.

"A bounced check? But that's so . . ."

I stopped myself from finishing the sentence because what adjective could I possibly have used? Unexciting? Disappointing? Unattractive? I did not want to offend him. Or let on that, until this very moment, I'd been taking great prurient pleasure in the whole situation.

"Did you bring bail?" Kenneth asked.

"Bail?"

"Money. To get me out, Marjory. Did you bring any?"

"I know what bail is," I answered. "The only money we had was in the sugar jar."

"I used that."

"For what?"

"Train ticket."

"To go where?"

Kenneth sighed.

"I went to Taunton. First, I went to the apartment, and you weren't there, so I figured you'd heard about stuff and run off to Taunton."

I closed my eyes, breathed deeply so I would not scream at him to leave my family out of it when escaping the law.

"Then I guess we don't have bail," I said.

Kenneth nodded, watching me, then stepped to the shadows again.

"But I could ask around," I offered. "See if we can borrow. I'm sure there's someone . . ."

"Naw," Kenneth said from across the cell. "It's not so bad here."

I waited for Kenneth to say more but heard only the sound of water dripping somewhere down the hall. I stood.

"See you tomorrow," I said, then shuffled away, heels complaining as I dragged them slowly over the floor.

The glamour of the predicament faded quickly after that first visit to jail. *The Evening News* promptly fired Kenneth, and our furniture, most of which we'd purchased on consignment, was repossessed in less than a month. I gave up the apartment and took a drafty room in a ramshackle boarding house at the edge of the city.

"You absolutely cannot live like this," Carolyn proclaimed when she visited.

"It's just until he gets out."

"And when is that?"

"Six months. He got six months at Caldwell."

Disgusted, Carolyn shook her head.

"It will be fine," I told her. "You'll see."

In place of the excitement I'd felt during those first hours of Kenneth's ordeal, there settled inside me an unquestioning and familiar sense of resignation, obligation. The feeling was comfortable, if not exactly welcome, for it returned me to the state of loving servitude that had defined most of my childhood. All of the pieces were in place once again; the roles were all defined. With relief, I returned to the self I knew best and became Kenneth's provider, his comforter. I brought him cookies in prison each week and read to him from the newspaper. I begged Mrs. Henry for my job back at Bamburger's and began saving for the life we'd restart when he got out. My fidelity, my commitment to Kenneth and to our marriage, was never in question, at least not for me. I was too good at carrying the weight of another's fraught life to give up so easily.

No one else, however, saw it this way.

"You need to leave him, Marjory," Carolyn wrote. The ink was thick, dark. She'd pressed so hard with the pen she'd practically engraved the paper. Sometimes, those few words were the extent of her whole letter.

"This is not a life, Marjory," Grandmother argued when I visited Taunton. "Working so hard and living in a rat hole. Spending your days off in a prison. And for what?"

"That is not a man," Grandfather added.

Aunt Fanny, for her part, said nothing but did not try very hard to hide her contempt. She did not like Kenneth, did not approve of him any more than my grandparents did, but her disdain was edged with something more, something sharper.

"He couldn't find someone his own age?" she asked, working a rag over the dining room windows. The skin of her neck had begun to drape from her chin to her chest, and purple puddles had pooled under her eyes. Without a doubt, Aunt Fanny had aged out of marriage. I felt sorry for her then. Sorrier, perhaps, than she felt for me.

In the summer, the visits to Caldwell felt like excursions. I packed a picnic lunch, which I ate in the field while staring at the outer walls of the prison, musing over how hard it must have been to quarry and tool so many massive red stones. A tower stood in the middle of the façade, flanked on both sides by low-roofed expanses. Under different circumstances, perhaps, without the razor-wire, Caldwell could've been an Italian renaissance palace, a honeymoon hotel like the Belmont.

Where in that maze of stone and iron did Kenneth sleep? Where did he work? I longed for him, not in any sort of passionate way but with a neediness I found both unstoppable and frightening. I felt blurry. Rubbed away at the edges. I wanted my husband to define me, to give shape and purpose to my self and my days. The disorientation I'd felt in the months after my mother's death had returned with multiplied force. I needed Kenneth to need me so I could know who I was.

"I have a job," he informed me through the slats of his cage one afternoon.

"You do?"

"Secretary. For the Warden."

Was this good news? I couldn't tell. I shifted on my little stool and tried to figure out what to say.

"It's a lot of responsibility. And he likes me. I'm smarter than most of the guys you'll find here."

So it was good news, then.

"That's wonderful, Kenneth. You're . . . you're really getting ahead." What else could I say?

Kenneth reached a hand through the bars, touched my cheek with one dirty finger.

"Not getting ahead, Marjory. Just getting by. It's not so bad, actually—getting by without getting ahead. Kind of relaxing. I'm sleeping well here. Better than I've slept in years."

That made one of us. I often lay awake most of the night listening to the scurrying in the walls, to the raised, angry voices beyond. One night, I woke to the sound of a clap, like a door slamming shut. I found out the next morning that there'd been a fight in the street below my window—drunkards, the neighbors said, arguing over owed money. The sound that I'd heard was a man's skull hitting the side of the building. The dark marks on the sidewalk were his blood, baked by the overnight heat into the concrete.

"I should be going," I said, rising from my stool.

We tried to kiss through the bars when the guard wasn't looking, but instead of his lips, I tasted mostly metal.

"Can you bring shortbread next time?" Kenneth whispered, glancing at the tin of molasses cookies I'd brought.

The bridge of my nose pulsed as if it had its own heartbeat.

"Sure," I answered. "Of course."

I strode out of Caldwell with as much dignity as I could muster. Surely, the women I passed on my way to the door—the ones with dirty-faced kids on their hips and eyes sunk deep in their sockets—surely they were worse off than me.

My husband was getting out in a few months. My husband worked for the warden. I, meanwhile, I had a room and a job and a college degree.

Lucky me.

As fall hardened to winter and Kenneth's date of release inched closer, I found myself noticing ads for three- and four-room apartments in neighborhoods near the city center. I began collecting recipes for meals I thought might please him and picking out furniture we could buy on consignment again once he had a job. Prison, I believed, had been an unfortunate newlywed hardship, and I was ready to get back to the business of marriage.

"When does he get out again?" Carolyn asked during yet another visit.

"January," I said.

"Great!" Carolyn clasped her hands together. "That gives us three months. I'm moving to Newark this weekend."

"Excuse me?"

Carolyn batted her big eyes at me.

"I'm moving to Newark," she explained. "Just until Kenneth gets out. You need some company. Now, you can live with me in the apartment I've rented near Bamburger's, or you can stay in this dump and I'll visit you every day."

"I'll stay here," I said, though I was tempted by the nice light and good smells her place would certainly have.

"Fine, that's fine, Marjory. But I'm going to be here, I swear to you, I'm going to be here every day. Even weekends. Especially weekends! We're going to go to the library on the weekends. And to the museum and to the shops. Do you promise?"

I looked at my friend. Such calculated innocence.

"I go to Caldwell on the weekends," I reminded her.

"Yes, well, you've done enough of that. I'm here now! We're going to have fun."

Carolyn tried, she really did, and I was grateful for her efforts when I was not busy resenting them.

"A party, Marjory. I got us invited to a party! The daughter of the cousin of the mayor is throwing it. Let's go to the stores and find you a dress."

"I'm going to Caldwell."

"Not today. Come on, Marjory. We'll go to Bamburger's and use your discount. I'll get a dress, too. I could use a new one."

"I'm going to Caldwell."

"Forget Caldwell."

"My husband is there."

"Forget your husband. Let's go."

And so it went every weekend, Carolyn trying her very hardest to keep me from Kenneth, and me fighting equally hard to get to him for no reason other than that it was my obligation.

"This is ridiculous," Carolyn lamented as I pushed past her one Saturday. "I mean, what is the worst that will happen if you don't go to prison today? *You're* not the criminal. You don't have to spend all your time there."

"*He'll die!*" I wanted to scream at my friend. *That's what happens when I don't do what I'm supposed to, isn't it, Mama?*

"He'll worry," I answered instead.

"So?" Carolyn yelled at my departing back. "Let him worry! Let him not eat cookies one week!"

But I went to Caldwell. I always went to Caldwell.

Both 1914 and Kenneth's prison term were nearing an end. Once again, I quit my job at Bamburger's ("I'm not giving it to you again," Mrs. Henry had warned) and packed up my rented room. Carolyn had gone back to New York. She loved me still—I could tell by how closely she held me when we hugged goodbye—but I also understood that she'd had enough of my pigheadedness and felt entitled to return to her life. My plan, therefore, was to spend Christmas, and the weeks following it, in Taunton. When Kenneth got out in January, I would return to Newark and not visit my family again for a while. I'd be too busy restarting our home. Kenneth wouldn't want to go and, worse, would not be welcome.

My grandparents' house felt entombed. The slow-stepping, desiccated figures within it moved like ghosts through the rooms, and I walked among them, trapped. Not trapped in the condescending way I'd felt trapped when I came home from Wellesley that first year, but actually trapped in the sacrificial role I'd acquired during my childhood in the Harrison house. It was as if the house itself could ensnare a girl, hold her captive forever. Aunt Fanny's hunched back and chapped hands were my proof. Grandmother's useless, motionless longing for the vote—as if suffrage would bring her, at this late day in her life, emancipation—was confirmation. I saw these truths but, unlike during my Wellesley days, I was too tired, too resigned, to rebel. Returning to Kenneth, to the confines of a marriage that was at least better than the confines of these faded walls, was the most I could do.

One afternoon, Grandfather brought a cup of tea to me in the parlor. The room had been returned to its original state, the renters not needed for tuition after my graduation, and we sat opposite each other in threadbare armchairs.

He'd always been kind, my grandfather. Gentle and fair. But I'd never felt able to get close to him, perhaps because he'd seemed to me more of an island than a man, content in his stolid isolation. Or, more likely, I'd seen him as a poor substitute for my father and loved him as much as I could, which was not nearly enough.

"Marjory," he said. My name sounded forced. Clearly, this conversation was going to take more effort than his interactions usually did. "Marjory, that man is going to get out of prison soon, and you should not return to him. It's that simple."

Grandfather worked his lips over his teeth in the aftermath of his verbal exertion.

"Grandfather, that man is my husband." I was not angry or worked up, the way I would have been if Aunt Fanny had approached me.

"Yes, of course he is. I know that, even without being at your wedding or hearing about it before it happened and whatnot. And being married should be taken seriously. Of course it should. But he's no good, Marjory. You should walk away." He paused, then lit up as if struck by a flash of inspiration. "Your mother, Marjory. Look at her. She stayed married. She left a bad situation but stayed on as married. It can be done."

"She didn't leave a bad situation," I said, struggling now for equanimity. "She left a *good* situation. She left because she was crazy." I felt on the verge of a tantrum.

Grandfather smacked his lips frantically now. He had edged past his conversational limits in terms of both duration and dexterity.

Aunt Fanny, who'd been listening from the hall, flew around the corner to Grandfather's rescue.

"And you're as crazy as your mother if you go back to that man!" she yelled. Her pinched, inflamed face resembled Grandmother's more than ever. "We did not put you through college so you could marry a felon. We did not share our house with strangers for years so that you could live with a criminal, Marjory. A criminal!"

"It was just a bad check," I tried.

"Please, Marjory." Aunt Fanny's spittle sailed through the air. "People don't get six months in prison for a bad check. You don't even know what he did. You. Don't. Know. You realize this, right? You realize you have no idea what *crime* your husband committed?"

"I do," I muttered, but I didn't.

At some point, Grandmother scuttled into the room and joined the chorus of well-meaning, furious voices.

I should have, perhaps, given more weight to their pleas. They loved me. They always had. But as I sat there with my cooled tea, their cries felt like ropes winding around my ankles, holding me here, among their dilapidation, their stagnation. I thought of Papa, another man they'd wanted to keep me from. How wrong they'd been, had always been, about him.

"I'm going back to Newark when he gets out."

Their voices quieted. My resolution sucked the oxygen out of their fiery appeal, and we watched each other with disappointment and pain.

Grandmother's thin frame trembled.

"You're ruining yourself," she said.

"Maybe, Grandmother, I'm already ruined."

I did not get a job during those weeks in Taunton because I was not planning to stay. Instead, I tried to be helpful without over-committing, to contribute without becoming essential. I did simple things, like check the post or shovel the snow, of which there was not very much in the early part of that winter. My family eyed me warily. They were still angry, and I was not working hard enough to earn their appreciation.

No matter. Kenneth would write soon and tell me the date of his release.

His letter arrived on a Thursday in the middle of January. I opened it in front of the house, under a bare apple tree, shaking with relief.

He'd been released early. He'd borrowed money and was in New York already, looking for work. I should join him as soon as I read this. Our new address was on the other side of the page, with directions. He would send money. If I didn't come, he'd come to Taunton and get me.

The letter, with its urgency and its vaguely threatening tone, ignited a bit of the dark drama I'd felt when Kenneth was first arrested. My husband—my older, swarthy, mysterious husband—had been released from prison. I was now married to an ex-con, a man who'd seen things, done things. Together, we'd navigate the mayhem of that place I'd been too timid to take on alone: New York City.

I shook the January chill from my shoulders and entered the house through the back door. Aunt Fanny stood at the counter, shaping biscuits.

"Post is here," I announced, placing an envelope from Grandfather's foundry on the small table.

Aunt Fanny did not turn around. Watching the back of her head, I slid Kenneth's letter into my handbag and snapped it shut.

"Can I help you?" I offered.

"No." She did not look up.

"I'll be upstairs, then. If you need me."

Her resentment followed me down the hall, up the stairs. I dipped into Mama's old bedroom and watched Aunt Fanny's resentment move past, searching for me.

Mama's room. I had not gone in there since she'd died, but I felt I could go in now. It was time.

Dust and death had thickened the air, laced with a faint, lingering hint of lavender soap, or at least the memory of it. I took a deep breath and tasted Mama, all of her—the soap and the sicknesses and the sweetness of the songs that she'd been able to sing again only when dying. The bed did not shift when I sat on its edge. It did not bulge when I lay down, as if Mama were there, weighting the mattress, holding the cushions motionless.

Outside the window, snow began falling. Was it falling in New York right now, too? Had Kenneth found a warm apartment for us? I could not wait for the answers. I wanted to leave Taunton soon. Tomorrow. Now. I just needed to rouse myself from my mother's deathbed and gather my things.

"So he's out?!"

Aunt Fanny's shrieked question entered the room before she did. I sat up, looked around in time to see her careen through the doorway, hair wild, with Kenneth's letter held like a head in the hand of the executioner.

"You went through my bag?" I said.

Aunt Fanny ignored the question.

"You're not going to him, Marjory. You can't go. You absolutely must listen to reason."

My aunt stomped her foot, shook the letter in front of my face. Her weary eyes raged.

"He served six months," she yelled. "You'll serve a lifetime."

Any anger I felt about her rummaging through my bag dissolved, replaced instead by a pity so deep I did not think my heart could contain it.

"I'd serve a lifetime here, too," I said. "Wouldn't I, Aunt Fanny?"

Aunt Fanny—who once, long ago, before the bitterness set in, might have been lovelier even than Mama—let tears run over the arid skin of her cheeks, let the tears course like rivers in the gullies of her neck. For a moment, I hoped, as I had long ago, that she would come to me, hug me, let us console each other in our great sadness, but she pushed back her shoulders instead. She gave no acknowledgment of her tears, did not even wipe or dab them away.

"The trolley leaves in an hour," she said.

I knew I had won but felt no sense of victory.

"I'll get my things."

My departure from the old house on Harrison Street felt different this time than it had felt all the times I'd left before. A sense of finality was there in each hug, a premonition of closure, as if my returning to Kenneth signaled a true and lasting end to my grandparents' and aunt's obligation to me. Aunt Fanny continued to cry while pretending not to. Melancholy—in all its phlegmatic turpitude—seeped through the walls, dripped from the ceiling, coating us all in despair.

"Goodbye, Marjory," was all Grandmother said. Unlike every other time I'd left home, she did not wish me luck or send me off with a mission. This time, it was simply goodbye.

The trolley took me to Boston, where I barely caught the next train to New York. The trip took too long, delayed on both legs by the now fast-falling snow, and I tried, without success, to peel away the despondence into which I'd fallen during the Taunton farewell. As the train chortled south, I pictured Kenneth, wondered if he'd kept the mustache he'd grown while in prison. I imagined the apartment we'd live in, the city streets we'd explore.

But these thoughts didn't stir me. I couldn't break free of the gloom. I pulled a book from my bag and I read, though my eyes merely circled the page, aimless, and my mind could not commit to the words. Disgusted, I snapped the book shut with such force the woman next to me woke, grumbled, and sneered at my apology.

There will be so many new things to discover, I assured myself. *Important things—essential, existential things.* Then I spent the remainder of the trip trying to determine what on earth those things of such significance might be.

When I arrived, finally, at the hotel on the west side that Kenneth had described in his letter, I was exhausted from the effort of rousing myself. Instead of emboldening me, the attempt had left me weak, susceptible, certain of nothing except my own unique ineptitude. I collapsed in my husband's arms with the expectation that it was his responsibility to lift me.

Kenneth had become stronger in prison. Whereas before, his arms had been wiry, almost bony, they had now the contours of cultivated muscles. His chest too had perhaps become wider and thicker, though this was less obvious than the arms, and I couldn't be sure.

Between us, silence. And not an eager, expectant silence during which we each grasped for the right and perfect thing to say. This was a vacuum.

"Here," he said after one or three or five minutes.

His eyes turned toward the bed, and I understood that "here" was a directive, an order.

If sex during our honeymoon had been an adventure, the exploration of a land undiscovered, sex after Kenneth's release from prison was a trip across town to give the mob boss an overdue payment—obligatory and shameful but not without its own kind of thrill. I performed amid an uncomfortable and dark sense of duty. *Lift my hips now. Grab here. Allow him to do that (wait, what was that?).* Every thrust, every grunt, every mild yanking of hair had a rough edge to it, a suggestion that this was not something good people did. Afterward, lying alone in the wet sheets, I did not wonder for more than a moment about why Kenneth had not been more tender, more gentle, after his long-awaited release. Perhaps this lack of questioning was an exercise in self-preservation. Or perhaps I just didn't care.

But even if I didn't care, I believed that I should, and I raised myself from the man-dampened bedsheets. Near the door, Kenneth was already threading an arm through a coat sleeve.

"Shall we go for a walk?" I asked.

Our hotel was near Central Park, and I imagined that a stroll over the snow-covered paths, clinging to one another for warmth, would be a nice thing for us.

"Going looking for work," he responded.

Kenneth opened the door, paused, came back to me. He pushed his lips against the top of my head in an approximation of a kiss, then resumed leaving.

"Bye," I said just before the door closed.

Going looking for work became a refrain Kenneth crooned often—in the mornings, with the detritus of breakfast still scattered over the little table, or, as happened that first time, after a daytime bout of faintly menacing sex. At first, I wished him luck. I inquired about his endeavors when he returned. His answers ranged from vague ("Saw a few people") to cryptic ("Won't know until the boss hears from his southern supplier") to baldly aggressive ("How's your own damn job search going, Marjory? Or do you not work anymore?"). I absorbed each of them with a tepid smile and a concentrated refusal to consider how we'd continue paying for our room, our food, with the passing of each jobless day.

"I'll ask in the stores," I offered with about as much enthusiasm as I put into our physical coupling.

"Good."

What about Newark and Kenneth's disapproval of my job at Bamburger's? Apparently, prison had changed Kenneth's views on what work was and was not appropriate for a married woman.

But I did not go to the stores. I did not do much beyond brushing my teeth in the mornings. Some days I brushed my hair, though mostly I didn't. Other days I made a meal of boiled eggs and cabbage, which Kenneth and I ate from the pot because the dishes were still dirty from the last time we used them. Occasionally, I thought of contacting dear Carolyn, then I looked at myself, at my husband, at the untended home we'd not so much created as let happen, and I knew I could not see Carolyn now.

Joseph Conrad was my only real companion. I found him on the shelves of the branch library near our hotel and read him with a near-feverish focus. To forget the city around me, to forget the life I wasn't living and the man I wasn't loving—that's what Conrad did for me that winter.

I was well into *Lord Jim* one afternoon, reading by the weak, waning sunlight that made it through our one window, when Kenneth arrived home with a box. Foolishly, like an idiot child, I believed he had brought me a gift.

"What is it?" I asked, wide-eyed and expectant.

The box was fairly large and seemed to make use of, if not actually strain, Kenneth's new muscles.

"Could you do something?" he asked, extending his neck like a rooster toward the cluttered table.

I jumped up and began transferring items from the table-top to the dresser.

"Oh, for the love of God," Kenneth muttered, presumably over the care and time I was taking. He then performed the admittedly impressive feat of holding the box, balancing on one leg, and using the other leg to sweep the remaining things from the tabletop to the floor.

"There!"

The box clanged when he set it down.

I chewed at the side of my thumb and watched as he pulled open the flaps. His long body bent forward, and Kenneth extracted from the box a black typewriter.

"Kenneth!" I gasped.

How long had it been since I'd written? Since I'd tried to write? Three years at least. I hadn't attempted a story since Wellesley.

"This is a really good idea," I complimented him. Maybe writing a story was exactly what I needed just then.

"I thought so," he said. "Rented it from a shop a few blocks away. Man there said I could keep it till March."

With that, Kenneth pulled the dining chair from under the table and arranged himself in front of the typewriter. He licked his thumb, smoothed it over his moustache.

"What?" he accused me, staring down my dumbfounded gaze.

"Nothing," I whispered.

"Well, could you leave me alone? I'm writing a story so we can pay the bills around here."

I hurried into my coat and left the hotel. The world outside the apartment was as gray as within. Tears blurred my vision. Sidewalk and sky, steel and soot-stained snow melded together to forge a cityscape as bleak as my heart. I was useless. I could not identify one single thing I was good for. I did not cook. I did not clean. I did not work. I did not write. I did not present myself well. I had no friends. I had no family. I did sordid things with my husband in bed (though, arguably, those things were useful to him, but they unraveled me further). This self-flagellation felt good, the way very hot bath water sometimes made me shiver. I continued to wallow in my worthlessness as I crossed Central Park.

Winter was alive in the park. Snow balanced on tree branches as if it had been dared to do so by the children below, and wind raced over walking paths with the vigor of a businessman late for a meeting. On a sledding hill, tightly wrapped kids succumbed to gravity atop garbage-can lids. I walked in the midst of this frost-fringed excitement. I walked straight through the gales and the beauty and the snow-muffled squeals of delight, and I felt nothing. Nothing. I had only a detached awareness of deadness inside, of gangrenous rotting whose rejection of life was complete, save for the myriad maggots it spawned.

I pulled my coat tighter, dipped my head like a penitent to the wind. Let me decay. Let my heart fester and my soul

decompose. I had no desire, no reason, to fight the putrefaction inside. Snowflakes rose from the ground, hauled by
furious currents of air into an upside down blizzard. Voices
shouted from holes in the tree trunks, calling names, my
name, bad names, Mama's name, mean names, calling Jim
and Ahab and Carolyn and Alice and Vronsky and Fanny
and Defarge and Marlow and Marlow and Marlow, until I
felt nothing, knew nothing, saw nothing, heard nothing, only
the names of these people, real and not, swirling around me
with the same mysterious nothingness as the snow.

I was breathing hard when I reached the far edge of the
park. Sweat trickled under my stockings, tracing paths to the
places Kenneth had claimed. The sense of deadness remained,
but the confusion of moments before darted like exposed rats
into the bustle and traffic on Fifth Avenue.

Was I mad? Was I mad like my mother?

I grabbed the back of a bench to steady myself, displac-
ing a strip of snow that rested on the wood slat. On the busy
street, a bell jangled. Someone selling something. No, that
would not do. I needed more than warm peanuts. I needed a
place that would arrest my thoughts, grab hold of my brain.
It was okay if my soul slowly died, I didn't care, but I would
not—*would not*—give up custody of my mind.

The Met. Rising from the avenue like a great pyramid in
the desert, the Metropolitan Museum beckoned, urged me to
save myself by getting lost in its halls. Fearing the near-madness
of the park, I hurried up the steps to the museum, entered,
and gasped at its grandeur. I wandered the hushed rooms until
closing, returned before noon the next day. The Met gave me
nothing as great as salvation, but it allowed my mind to cling
to this world while my body and soul entertained death.

"Where were you?" Kenneth asked when I came back
one evening. The hotel room was thick with unmoving air,
and pages were crumpled like snowballs around him.

"Looking for work," I answered.

"And?"

"And nothing."

He grimaced. I shrugged. We stepped toward the bed.

I returned to the room another evening, about a week later, after hours of staring at an oversized oil by Bastien-Lepage. *Joan of Arc in the Garden,* painted in 1879. My head pounded with the colors and textures of the artwork, with the beauty of the saints calling Joan forth and the deference with which she listened to their pleas. It was with no small amount of disorientation that I walked the hotel hall toward our door that night.

Kenneth was at our threshold. Inside or out, coming or going—I couldn't tell. But he held in his hands the box with the typewriter, plus a bag on each shoulder, and he seemed to be surveying the hall.

"Come on," he hissed when I got close.

"What?"

"Rent's due. We have to leave."

"Oh, Kenneth, we can't do that."

My husband's eyes bulged with exasperation.

"Wait. Were you leaving without me?" I asked. "Leaving me with the bill?"

His eyeballs bulged wider, frog-like.

"Of course not, Marjory. I was waiting for you. Looking for when you came down the hall."

I did not believe him but lacked the will to interrogate further.

Kenneth and I became vagrants. We stumbled over the streets of the city in search of cheap rooms, staying long enough in one place to get a few nights of sleep, then leaving well before anyone would come looking for money. Sometimes we shared rooms with strangers—bums with gruff voices and unfocused eyes. On those nights, I clung to Kenneth for safety, acknowledging the existence of a spectrum of dangers that different men posed. But it wasn't only the men who were shiftless. Once, in an abandoned apartment in a tenement on the Lower East Side, a woman with nits in her hair put her arms around me in the dark, then, when I screamed, she ran off with the only suitcase of clothes I had left. After that, I hugged my last small bag of treasured possessions, my *Alice* book and a photo of Mama, while I slept.

This kind of life sallowed my skin, emptied my eyes. I let Kenneth tow me around. I let him leave me for days at a time in dirty rooms further and further from our first midtown hotel. The Met now seemed like a dream, like a fairyland I'd conjured in a long-ago time. Sometimes, huddled near a soot-caked window with a stolen library book in my hands, I tried to picture the Joan of Arc painting, remember its oiled nuance. Deep tangled greens of the garden. Joan roused by the gossamer saints. The days when I could recall the details were brighter, better, than the days I could not.

We settled, sort of, in a room in a suburb of the city. Kenneth had sold a story to *McClure's*, and though the money they paid him was not nearly enough to sustain us, it allowed us to pause for a moment and try to reset.

"See, babe," he said when he came home from the butcher with the first piece of meat we'd eaten in months. "Your husband takes care of you."

I nodded. There was some truth in his words. He'd managed not only to create but also to sell a short story. I hadn't done more than wander the Met. Kenneth was now the writer. The provider. The leader. The doer. And me? I went along, like a supplicant or a dog.

"Can you sign this, babe?" he asked, sending boozy breath down my neck. It was morning. I was drinking weak tea and trying to calculate at what time in the night he'd returned.

"What is it?"

The paper had numbers printed on it, as well as the name of bank in Florida, of all places.

"It's just a thing." He waved a long arm. "For a possible job."

I did not have a job, possible or otherwise. I signed the paper.

Every few days, Kenneth presented another paper for me to sign. Each time, the name of the same Florida bank was printed in the corner. Each time, I signed, believing—in some vague, undefined way—that my very survival depended on him.

"Pack up," he directed one afternoon.

"Where are we going?" I did not like the place we'd been staying, but its semi-permanence had been a comfort.

"You're going to Newark. You're going to stay with a man I know, a retired minister. He and his wife will have you until I get back."

I looked at Kenneth as if he were speaking a language I did not understand.

"Where are you going?"

He waved a long arm again.

"Looking for work. Won't be long."

The minister and his wife seemed as pleased about the arrangement as I was. They set up a cot for me in the back of the kitchen, where I roasted through the hot summer nights. Because I'd managed to retain a thin thread of decency through my time in New York, I offered to help the minister's wife with her chores.

"No, no, dear," she dismissed me. "I've been doing this work alone for so long, I've developed a system. And we certainly don't want to mess with the system." Then she scuttled quickly away before I could insist.

I wandered the house, adrift without Kenneth. At least when he was at Caldwell, I'd been able to visit. Here, I just waited, watching the orioles outside the window, muttering songs Mama might have sung years ago. Kenneth phoned the house often but irregularly, and I couldn't count on knowing when I'd speak with him again.

The minister and his wife prayed as often as they did other essential things, like eating or going to the bathroom. There was a space at the front of the house—a large closet that would have fit a cot nicely—with a table, two chairs, and two Bibles. At least three times a day, the minister and his wife would convene in that room and praise God, His works, and His glory.

Sometimes they sang hymns. When they did, I knelt in the hall, enjoying the sound of glad voices conjoined in harmony.

"Lord," the minister intoned once, following a hymn. "We ask of you one further blessing. We ask that you watch over young Marjory, for she knows not who she is nor who she may become. Please allow her into your flock, and please allow her to be on her own path again soon."

They wanted me gone. Though the minister's words were generous, they were also self-serving. The prayer may have been a rallying cry for my reformation, but these kind, older people needed some space. They did not need me loitering among them day after day, despondent and worn, a moving mass of lifelessness haunting their halls.

So I forced myself out on a walk every morning. Newark remained unknowable to me, its streets and shops anonymous and bland. Had I visited this neighborhood when I lived here? I had no idea. Nothing looked familiar, but that didn't mean I hadn't seen it before.

There was, on the corner, a flower shop full of glorious blooms—petals of yellow and pink and marble-swirled violet. Most days, I stopped and admired the stems, displayed on the sidewalk like lollipops in a penny candy shop.

"How much for a lily?" I asked the shopkeeper.

"They're sold as a bunch," she replied.

I fished around in my skirt pocket, which also served as my savings account.

"Seven cents for a stem," I offered.

The woman considered the offer and finally relented. I chose a flower from the middle of the bucket, rubbed its fuzzed pinkness for a moment before turning to go. I would present the lily to the minister's wife. I was not an orphan, a hobo. I had manners. I could be courteous when I pulled myself from the gloom long enough to remember how.

I walked the lily to the minister's house. The day felt different, as if the hours themselves held some sort of secret. It must have been the strangeness of my bringing someone a gift.

By the time I stepped through the front door of the house, I'd worked myself into a state, certain that the unusual feeling I had was due to the extravagance of spending seven cents on a flower or the audacity of assuming the minister's wife preferred lilies. The self-critical loop in my head affirmed my worst beliefs—I was a dunce. I'd spent the little money I had on a worthless, probably unwanted, flower while my husband was off scrounging for a job to support us. *"Nice work, Marjory,"* I heard Kenneth's voice say. *"Real helpful."*

"And here she is now," the minister said when I closed the front door behind me. I could not see him, but his voice seemed to come from the parlor.

The minister sat in a seldom-used chair, a cup of tea in his hand and a man in the chair opposite him. When he saw me, the minister set the cup on a little table and stood. The other man rose as well.

He was tall, this stranger, with thick glasses backlit by bright-as-sun eyes.

"Marjory," the minister said with a great gust of gladness. "I'd like you to meet your uncle, Dr. Edward Stoneman."

There is a particular sort of relief that comes when you find something you hadn't known you were looking for, like a forgotten best book, like *Alice in Wonderland* packed at the bottom of a box of personal items. This kind of relief makes you tingle with both the comfort of the faded familiar and the possibility of renewed joy. Struck by that lovely sensation, I squeezed my eyes shut, let the minister's grandfather clock tick a full twenty times, then greeted my uncle.

"Hello, Uncle Ned."

Uncle Ned smiled.

"So glad to see you, Marjory," he said, as if it had been only a few weeks since we'd visited instead of decades since he came to Mama's concerts in the Providence duplex.

I thought perhaps I should hug him, or at least shake his hand, but I still held the lily and the choreography of it all seemed too hard.

"Let's get settled, shall we?" the minister's wife said, coming to my rescue. I handed her the lily with less fanfare than I had planned.

"This was a kind gesture, Marjory," she said, taking the flower. With a smile, she arranged me and my uncle on nearby chairs.

"We'll let you two talk," the minister allowed, as he and his wife left us with freshly warmed tea and as much privacy as the doorless room could provide.

Perhaps because he was a doctor, Uncle Ned seemed to see the fragility of my well-being. The flutter I'd felt at our introduction had quieted, smothered by the tireless malaise that engulfed me. I smiled at him. I truly was pleased to see him, but my capacity for pleasure was limited, and the best I could do right about then was not yawn.

"I'd like to get to know you, Marjory," Uncle Ned started. "And your husband, too. I would like to acquaint myself with you both."

The situation didn't make sense. Questions gurgled just below my consciousness. Questions I knew—by the way he looked at me over the top of his glasses, the way he dipped his head to cede me the floor—that Uncle Ned anticipated I'd ask. But to probe deeper into my thoughts seemed exhausting. To inquire would take all of the strength that I had. It was enough, I decided, to release myself into his presence and answer his questions without forming my own.

"Can you make arrangements with him?" Uncle Ned asked. "With your husband, I mean? I'd like to meet him as soon as I can."

Without any embarrassment, I answered, "I don't know where he is. We'll have to wait for him to phone."

Uncle Ned and I fell into silence, waiting.

Kenneth phoned two days later. Since he was in Hoboken, meeting with some business associates, it would be easy for him to pass through Newark, and he agreed to come the next day. The three of us met in a park near the minister's house. The day was cloudy but warm, and we sat in an awkward row on a bench near the pond.

Kenneth had shaved and put on his charm. He had one long arm draped casually behind me and addressed Uncle Ned with the familiarity of a peer. These two men weren't, I realized looking from one to the other, very far off in age.

"I'm in the business of this and that," Kenneth explained with something that sounded like pride. "Started out in newspaper, local work here in Newark, but that's not always reliable. I do magazine work from time to time. You know, whatever pays the bills, as they say. Got to keep the little lady fed." Kenneth gave my shoulder a squeeze.

"Of course, of course," Uncle Ned answered. "Newspaper's not an easy profession. At least, that's what I hear from my brother."

This was the first mention Uncle Ned had made of my father, and with the jolt the reference sent down my neck, I hardly noticed Kenneth stiffen beside me.

"Here's what I'd like to propose," Uncle Ned continued. "I don't know much about Marjory other than how loudly she cried as a baby. So let's make the most of this reunion. Marjory, why don't you come and stay with me in my house in Springfield? We'll get reacquainted while Kenneth pursues his, ah, his job prospects. And, Kenneth, you can join us a week or so later. When you're ready."

Instinctively, I looked toward my husband for a response.

"That's awfully kind of you, Dr. Stoneman," Kenneth said. "And Marjory does seem to have become a bit of a burden on the minister and his wife." Kenneth flexed his lips, fishlike, while he considered what to say next. "But I'll be settled again quickly," he went on. "Probably for the best if we just leave things alone."

Uncle Ned sat up taller on the bench and took on a tone he likely reserved for difficult patients.

"Now, Ken—may I call you Ken?—I'm just going to have to insist that Marjory come with me. You're welcome, too, just as soon as you can get there. All right now?"

Kenneth shifted on his skinny seat bones, tightened his hand so that it firmly cupped the curve of my shoulder.

"Well now, Dr. Ned—I'm just going to call you Dr. Ned, since we're so friendly—I've got to be honest. I'm just not so sure about all of this rearranging. Marjory and I can get along fine."

Uncle Ned frowned and nodded with the practiced sympathy of a physician.

"I have no doubt that you can," Uncle Ned said. "But I'd really like to take this time to get to know my niece. She seems awfully special. You understand that, don't you?"

Kenneth relented. "Fine then. But I assure you, we won't be with you long. I've got my plans nearly settled."

Kenneth left Newark that afternoon. He seemed jumpy, nervous, his long limbs unable to quiet themselves as we said goodbye.

"Remember," he whispered, with a hard hand on the back of my head and a kiss pushed on my brow. "Remember who you're married to. Remember who's on your side."

His warning didn't make sense. Nothing, since Uncle Ned's arrival, made any sense.

Uncle Ned's house felt familiar, though I'd never been there before. The trees in the yard looked like the ones I'd lived under in Taunton; the walls breathed the same mix of cedar and mold. I felt the need, as soon as I walked through the front door, to let loose a sob, and I quite rudely asked to be shown to my room.

The bed upon which I collapsed was soft and forgiving, and tears effortlessly gave way to sleep. How long it had been since I'd rested unburdened. How sweet to feel the very, very distant reach of my faraway father.

Over the next few days, Uncle Ned and his family cradled me in a compelling kind of convalescence. I drank bone broth soup and ate lemon biscuits. I curled on the porch swing for hours, undisturbed, reading Balzac not with desperation but with real enjoyment. The best treat, though, was my cousin Lloyd, a floppy-haired, slant-smiled young man who played the piano as if inspired by angels. Nothing in the world mattered to him more than music, and for four hours each day, he filled Uncle Ned's house with the sound of Schoenberg, movement after movement, again and again, not so much practicing the pieces as discovering them, reveling in them, savoring their tonal mystique.

It was nice, being surrounded so completely by music. I'd forgotten how comforting music played with compassion could be.

Uncle Ned allowed me these dream days. Sometimes he offered a wink or a smile nearly as lopsided as Lloyd's, but that was all. There were no grand declarations. No firm ultimatums.

"Uncle Ned?" I asked one afternoon. We were picking late-summer zucchini from the side garden, Lloyd's music drifting from the windows above.

"Yes, Marjory?"

"Where is my father?"

Uncle Ned did not seem surprised by the question.

"He's in Miami, Marjory. He's gone there and started a daily newspaper."

Uncle Ned waited for me to ask more, and when I didn't, he turned again to the zucchini.

Miami. Newspaper. This was more information about my father than I'd had in twenty years. I rolled those two facts around in my mind as if they were sucking candies that I wanted to make last all day. Newspaper. Miami.

In the semi-dream state that was life at Uncle Ned's house, I'd nearly forgotten that Kenneth was going to join us. His shadow at the screen door the next day startled me, nearly made me recoil.

"Lloyd," I shouted, interrupting my cousin's piano playing. "Can you take a break?"

The piano quieted. I hoped Lloyd wasn't upset. It just didn't seem right for that music and Kenneth to be in the same house.

My husband moved with a mix of swagger and shame. He smelled foul, though his suit was neatly pressed.

"How are you?" he asked.

I nodded, a non-answer. I thought I'd been well, but now I wasn't so sure.

"Everything okay here?"

Kenneth turned and did not see me nod. He walked to the table, sniffed, lifted the corner of the tea towel that covered our fresh-baked zucchini bread.

"Aren't you going to offer me some?" he asked.

"It's not my house," I stammered. "Not my bread."

"Did you bake it?"

"I helped."

"Then it's your bread. The polite thing would be to offer me some."

I looked at my husband. I looked through the familiar assumptions until I saw the pores, shallow and wide, at the tip of his nose and the deep dip of his right eyebrow. Where would we go when we left Uncle Ned's house? How would we live?

"I think it's for later," I said.

Kenneth pulled at his ear, fidgety, ready to protest. If Uncle Ned hadn't walked in just then, he might have even found a knife and cut himself a slice of the bread.

"Kenneth!" Uncle Ned greeted him, stepping far into the room for a handshake. "So glad you've come. Let me reschedule some patients, and we'll spend the afternoon getting acquainted."

There was, in Uncle Ned's voice, a hint of transgression, as if he were already more acquainted with Kenneth than anyone knew.

I parked myself on the front porch with a glass of cold tea and waited. The absence of Lloyd's music left the air heavy and fraught, and I found myself humming a strained approximation of the notes in an attempt to fill the strange silence.

After a few hours, the two men emerged from Uncle Ned's office. Lloyd joined us, and we ate zucchini bread on the porch. We talked of the weather, the war, the merciless aphids central Massachusetts had suffered that summer. Kenneth sat with his arm around me, and it nearly felt pleasant. When the last crumbs of the bread had been pushed onto fingertips and eaten, Kenneth and Uncle Ned returned to the office.

I looked at Lloyd, hopeful.

"You want me to play?" he asked.

"Yes. Please."

Lloyd shrugged and gave me his lopsided smile.

"Okay," he agreed. "Since the lady insists."

Schoenberg soon floated out the front window, softly at first and then with a force that shook me more fully awake. I gripped the arms of the porch rocking chair. For the first time since Uncle Ned had appeared in the minister's house, it occurred to me that his sudden desire to know me, to know Kenneth, was more than familial graciousness. He had a reason, a purpose. I breathed deeply, music filling my lungs. Something was happening in Uncle Ned's office. Something significant.

I shook my head like a wet dog, felt the shadow of an approaching decision. I was not equipped these days for decisions. I'd been drifting through life for so long now—riding Kenneth's misguided wind, mistaking mere existence for life—that the prospect of a choice terrified me, made me rock the chair faster, harder, feigning escape.

"He's a threshold case, Marjory."

Uncle Ned leaned against his desk, long legs crossed at the ankles. Through the orbs of his glasses, he looked at me kindly but without condescension. We were alone in his office.

"A threshold case? What does that mean?"

"It means that he drinks alcohol. Too much. More than you realize, and this drinking puts him over the threshold. It makes him unable to keep a job or tell right from wrong."

I heard Uncle Ned's words but had trouble applying them to my husband. I could barely recall seeing Kenneth have one drink of alcohol, much less enough to push him past this so-called threshold.

"Drinking," Uncle Ned continued, "makes Kenneth capable of troublesome things. Illegal things, like forging names on your father's bank drafts."

I closed my eyes, saw the papers on the table before me. The ink mark of a Florida bank. A bank I'd never heard of, in a place I'd never been. How strange it had seemed at the time. How strange it still seemed.

"The bank told your father about the forged drafts. He became worried about you, and we tracked you down. It wasn't easy, believe me. Anyway, once we found you, your father asked me to see if you needed help."

Though Lloyd had stopped playing the piano, a feeling like music swelled in my chest, expanding, rising, until it reached a crescendo behind my wide eyes and leaked forth as a single, unbidden tear.

"Papa was worried about me?"

"Yes," Uncle Ned confirmed. "And after talking with Kenneth, I'm now worried too. He's not a bad man, Marjory. I really believe that is true. But because of the drinking, he is doing some dangerous things, some illegal things, and he will get caught. If you continue living with him, I have no doubt that you will be implicated, eventually, as an accessory."

In the quiet that followed his words, Uncle Ned looked at me, his gaze steady and expectant, as if he believed I were capable of rationally evaluating this information.

"So what should I do?"

A breeze stirred the curtain at Uncle Ned's open window. We both watched the cloth swell and swirl, then forced ourselves to once again look at each other.

"You should leave Kenneth. Go down to Florida and live with your father. You've been apart for too long."

On the other side of the office wall, Lloyd began playing again, the music a proxy for words I couldn't form.

"He talked this over with his new wife, Marjory. They want you there, your father and the new Mrs. Stoneman."

"They do?"

Uncle Ned nodded.

My heart beat with Lloyd's use of the minor keys. I could not go on with Kenneth, with the hunger and fraud, with the profound deadness that our marriage had wrought. There was no music in our life together. No sunshine or joy.

"I think I should go to my father."

Uncle Ned smiled just enough to let me know he was proud.

"I'll call Kenneth in," he said.

My marriage ended in the late afternoon, in a small room swirling with music and wet summer air. Uncle Ned spoke of divorce, of how long it would take and what it would mean, while Kenneth shrugged with real or put-on indifference. Any tenderness I felt toward him blew off with the breeze. I would not need it where I was going, would no longer need to summon it to get through the dark night.

We walked to the trolley together, not touching, not talking. He boarded. I waved. The trolley pulled away with a jingle, and just like that, I was no longer somebody's wife.

WEST OF MIAMI, 1920

To the night creatures, our struggle must look like a dance. We sway, spin, leap, skin slicked with sweat, fingers entwined, hot breath whorling in the inches between us. So similar, the motions of loving and of loathing. Pull and grasp. Push and claw. Movement building on movement until we cannot define our own edges or remember a time that was not this moment.

Abruptly, a pause, but I remain upright. He fills his fist with my hair and holds tight, offering up my neck to the moonlight. I feel him stare at this vulnerable, vital piece of my body. Behind my back, his other arm holds me, keeps me suspended above the sludge, the end of a tango. We breathe together, hard and ragged. A drop of sweat, or perhaps a tear, falls from his chin to the moonlit plane of my neck, where it lingers before rolling into the darkness below. I wonder what it would be like now to kiss him.

Then, with an unspoken agreement, we are in motion again. A knee to his gut. A flat-handed shove to his chest. I fall. He staggers. We are not touching but are still connected— every lunge balanced by recoil, every protest balanced by insistence. The perfection of our coordination gives me an instant of sadness, of jagged doubt.

"Please, Marjory," he begs, pouncing on my infinitesimal hesitation. "I need you."

"I know."

But I don't want to be needed. Sustaining the soul of another means starving my own, and my soul is hungry. It's been hungry for such a long time.

"It will be good," he promises. "You'll see."

"No," I say. "No."

As he hurtles toward me, I slink sideways and escape, again, into the rank thickness of the Florida night.

MIAMI, 1915

The train cut a path through Florida's thicket of slash pines. The trees were skinny, scrubby, with branches raised to the sky as if jubilant that their spindly trunks still held them upright. I hadn't slept much since St. Augustine and watched as dawn woke the pines under the gaze of a still-high full moon—a sight far better than anything I could have dreamed had I slept. Day kept on breaking. The train kept chortling south. It was a journey both monotonous and momentous.

Like rain water, Florida seeped through the steel walls of the Pullman. The air was denser, more brackish, than it had been in Georgia; the heat seemed almost sly. More than the air and the heat, though, was the wildness that pushed its way in from outside, insistent and undeniable, intensifying with each mile gone. I thought of Joseph Conrad. Perhaps Florida thickened forever. Perhaps Miami, the Magic City, was simply a ploy by the swamp to lure people in deeper.

"Miami," the conductor sang out as he passed my compartment. "Miami in forty-five minutes!"

I rose from my seat, disbelieving that a city would in fact rise from this dank wilderness, but I began to get dressed. Just in case.

Twenty-five years old, older even than the city to which I'd escaped, and sweating through the blue serge dress Uncle Ned had bought me in Boston the week before—that was how I stepped from the train and into the candy-coated shine of Miami sun.

So the city was real. Heat mocked my twilled woolen sleeves. It was a ridiculous dress to wear this far south, but it had been cool in New England when I bought it and, anyway, I liked the hot chill that ran down my arms, the unceremonious sense of defrosting.

I looked at the rail station clock. At least an hour until my father was to meet me. My father, Frank Stoneman: Pioneer. Failed entrepreneur. And now, according to Uncle Ned, editor of the second daily paper in a third-rate frontier town. Twenty years had passed since Mama dragged me and two suitcases away from Papa and the Providence duplex. I'd long ago forgotten the shape of his face and the arc of his smile, but I could still hear his voice—thick and animated and full of baritone love—as he read those stories to me by the upstairs firelight.

Though I was desperate to hear that voice again now, I was glad for the extra hour alone. It was all too much, too fast. I needed time to indulge in the unabashed blare of this sun a bit longer.

I left the little lemon-drop depot and turned east. The streets were bare lonely stretches with wooden box buildings and absolutely nothing growing out of the ground. Some of the boxes were boarding houses, named—longingly? ironically?—after faraway states. *The Minnesota. The Indiana.* Others were single homes, distinguishable from the boarding houses only by the absence of name-states. I thought of my grandparents' house in Taunton, with its towering elms and wrap-around porch, so different from this strange, perspiring place.

Further east, the houses, and then the streets, dwindled away, as when I'd drawn pictures for Mama as a child and become distracted by a bird and run off. Everything simply ended, unfinished. Except for the sky, which tumbled on and on, a blue wilderness just a little too far to touch. I walked with my eyes swimming in the sky's brilliance, so lost in its cloudless expanse that I crossed the beach and nearly fell right into the bay.

Oceans, as I'd known them until then, were messy, monochromatic affairs whose waters were too cold or too choppy to immerse yourself in. They were for sailing upon. Maybe gazing upon, if you felt maudlin. You would not, however, want to get any closer than that.

But this water! It sparkled like a Byzantine jewel. It beckoned and winked, and a sweet breeze blew from its edge like little kisses. I walked closer, then closer still, and when I stepped into the bay, I actually saw my shoes straight through the clear ripples. I laughed at myself, at my wet shoes, at the sound of myself laughing at the edge of the earth, but I stayed where I was, letting the warm water welcome me to my new home.

Maybe I really could recover down here. Salted water clung to my stockings. When was the last time I stepped off solid ground like this and stood in the pulsing waves of my own volition? When? Not during the years of caring for Mama. Certainly not while married to Kenneth.

The ocean approached and retreated, almost licking my wounds. Maybe Miami would be the place where I picked up the pieces of my shattered life and reassembled them, turned them into something beguiling, something that—with a little bit of good luck—might be worth living.

I was not surprised that my wet shoes gave me blisters on the way back to the depot, only that the blisters came on so fast. Big, swollen pustules above each of my heels before I'd even reached *The Missouri*. I considered removing the shoes and walking the rest of the way in my stockings, but what kind of impression would that make on my father? So on I tottered instead, now truly eager to see him.

The depot was empty, its shade a blindness after the glare of the sun. My train still sat on the track, so I boarded again to wait for Papa in the comfort of the leather seat. *Ah, sweet relief*, I thought as I slid my heels out of the shoes. But as I bent to examine the blisters, I caught, with my not-quite adjusted eyesight, a pulsating image at the end of the car. Mama. Not a ghost—I knew better than that—more like memory incarnate, her presence conjured by the force of my guilt. She said nothing. She was a wavering wisp of the beauty she'd been, weak but for the weight of her gaze, which sent her sense of betrayal across vacant worlds. I squeezed my eyes shut. Pushed her away. And though she no longer hovered there near me, sad-eyed and hungry, I felt smothered by something that must have been shame.

She'd left him.

I was going back.

My loyalty to my mother had been fierce, unyielding, even after her death, but I'd always been skeptical of the blame Grandmother and Aunt Fanny had cast on Papa, and so I did not consider it wholly disloyal to go to him now, to let him help me when I most needed help.

"Don't you agree, Mama?" I whispered to the gauzy vision at the other side of the car. "You wanted his help, too. Remember the hospital?"

Before she could answer, the car trembled under the measured thud of a confident gait. The disturbance shook the image of Mama away, sugar dissolving in water. I stood, turned. And there he was.

Papa was nearly as tall as the train compartment, nearly as wide as the aisle. He held himself stiffly and looked at me with wise, kindly eyes that were, I noted, the same indescribable hazel as mine. I'd forgotten we had this in common.

Papa took off his hat, used it to wipe away his surprise as the brim passed over his face. I had not grown up to be as lovely in appearance as my mother had been.

"Hello, sweetheart."

The voice was the same. Absolutely, wonderfully the same.

"Hello, Papa."

I pushed myself against him in an unstoppable hug. He chuckled, wrapped his long arms around me. We stood there, embracing each other and all the lost years and unknowns, all the scraps of shared memories that had survived most of my lifetime and a good chunk of his. We stood there until the porter at the back of the car cleared his throat.

"Ready, then?" Papa finally asked, pulling away.

I nodded. There was no fussing. No awkwardness. He just pushed a swatch of gray hair from his forehead and lifted my suitcase.

We walked to his automobile, which he'd parked at the back of the depot. If Papa noticed my wet shoes and limp, he didn't comment.

The auto rolled over barren streets I hadn't yet seen, past more box buildings and featureless earth. The pained image of Mama that had come to me on the train receded. Once again, she slept in the core of my heart, where I could love her graciously, without obligation. I glanced at my father, at his steady jaw and dignified nose. They must have made quite a couple.

"We're right over here," Papa said, turning the car. "Just over the bridge."

More treeless land. Stumps like chicken pox spotting the ground. And everywhere, the fruit of the destruction—small wooden houses forming a subdivision my father called Riverside.

"You should know," Papa said as he drove. "I want you to know that I waited two years after your mother's death to marry Lilla."

I nodded, unsure how to respond.

"How did you know?" I asked. "That she was dead?"

Papa took a hand off the steering wheel and pushed the flop of gray hair from his face.

"Your grandmother wrote and told me."

"Grandmother Stoneman? How did she know?"

"No, your Grandmother Florence. Your mother's mother."

I swallowed this information. It was too big for my throat and I struggled to push it down. Grandmother had done that for Mama, had contacted Papa, a man she despised. It had been her last act of motherly love.

We were quiet. Should I ask if it had been him I'd seen on the sidewalk outside the Taunton house so many years ago? Should I ask if he'd come to get me like he'd promised he would? My lips parted, but before the words could come out of my mouth, before his answer could never be unsaid, I clamped them shut. It was enough that Papa had come to get me, through Uncle Ned, when I'd needed to be rescued the most.

Papa drove further, then slowed the car, let it roll to a stop in front of one of the small, wooden houses. He turned to me.

"Marjory," he said, and I had to smile and the sound of my name in his voice. "What is it that you do?"

The question did not feel like a challenge or a test. It felt like a search for an answer he truly wanted to know.

"Well."

I thought of my jobs at Nugent's and Bamberger's, of the mindless repetition that came with teaching new girls to use the cash. I thought of wandering the streets of New York, aimless and drifting, doing nothing and barely existing.

"Well," I repeated.

My eyes closed, and what I saw under my lids was that moment, that unforeseen and electrifying moment during my first week at Wellesley, when I read my assignment aloud to the class and applause exploded the instant I'd finished. When the applause quieted, I'd been asked to reread certain lines and been questioned about my inspiration. The praise had given me more than my classmates' approval. It had given me a secret sense of self, of purpose, that I hadn't before put forth as fact.

"Well, what I do is. Well, Papa. What I do is, I write."

Did this sound like a confession? If it did, Papa granted me absolution.

He nodded once. He opened the car door. In the sun, his gray hair turned silver.

"You write," he said before he got out. "That, my dear, will work out quite well."

The windows on either end of Papa's unremarkable little house let in both bugs and a breeze. It was a worthwhile trade-off, the breeze being as essential as the cool glass of water his wife Lilla gave me.

"You're really here!" Lilla exclaimed more than once. I found it hard to believe she'd been so eager to see me, but a smile like that didn't lie.

The three of us sat in the living room, surrounded by shelves of books organized alphabetically by author. Dickens. Hawthorne. Shakespeare. The same books that had populated our sitting room in Providence when I was so small. I remembered them. Not just the names and the stories but the actual books—gold letters embossed on smooth leather, pages like papyrus under my fingertips. The smell of old glue and dust. It comforted me to imagine my father reading these books over the years, even without me tucked at his side.

Papa let Lilla carry the conversation that night, which she did with warmth and gusto.

"I've lived in Florida my whole life," Lilla said. "But never this far south. Not until now." She threw her head back and laughed, anticipating her own next words. "You'll see, Marjory. It's unreal down here. Like the wild west, only hotter. And with more gators."

How soon would I get to see one of those?

"And the politics!" Here Lilla hooted and slapped her knee. "The politics, Marjory. Wait'll you get a load of what happens here. Did you know your father was elected Circuit Judge, but Governor Napoleon hates him and his ideas so much he wouldn't certify the results? True story! See what I mean about this place?"

"Really, Papa? He wouldn't let you sit on the bench?"

"I got to be a magistrate of the police court for a little while instead."

"That's ridiculous!"

"Welcome to Florida, Marjory!" Lilla crowed. Then she stood, smoothed her dress over her rounded frame. "I'll be getting to bed. Give you two some peace." Lilla went to the side of Papa's chair, leaned over and smacked the top of his head with a kiss. "'Night, now," she said, and before she left the room, she touched her fingers to her mouth and blew me a kiss. "'Night to you, too, Marjory. It's good that you've come."

When Lilla was gone, Papa looked at me through the dim light. He watched me for so long, saying nothing, that I wondered if he'd somehow fallen asleep with his eyes open.

"You're not upset with me, Marjory? For the past twenty years?"

The lamp warmed his face, and the world beyond the square windows was full of night. I could have been six years old again in that moment.

"I was upset with myself, Papa."

"Why?"

"For . . ." I looked at a long ceiling crack, counted the tributary cracks that emanated from it. "For not being good enough to make you come back."

Papa stood, pulling his long body from the chair. He walked to a cupboard and shifted items around until he found a box.

"These are for you, Marjory."

He lifted the lid of the box and handed me a fat stack of envelopes, tied around the middle with a frayed length of twine. I leaned closer to the light, tried to read the ghost ink.

To Marjory Stoneman. 10 Harrison Street. Postmarked each year on my birthday, with *Return To Sender* stamped on top.

"Return to sender?" I whispered because I'd lost most of my breath.

"I didn't think I was wanted."

I wanted you, Papa, I tried to say with my eyes because my mouth was not brave enough yet to speak the words. *Maybe they didn't, but I wanted you so very much.*

In my room later that night, I lifted my favorite framed picture of Mama from the bottom of my unpacked suitcase.

"Here we are," I said to her image. It was an old photograph, taken in the early years of her madness, when there was still so much of her untouched inside. She'd looked straight at the camera. Her eyes were ebullient but her smile restrained, as if she'd known darkness was coming.

I placed the picture on my bureau. Though Lilla evoked no sour feelings in me—in fact, I quite liked her—I hoped she would see Mama's photograph soon. The picture, I believed, would set boundaries that I couldn't speak. Mama's presence on the bureau would remind the rest of us in the house of exactly how we all fit together.

I lay down for the first time in my new bed, listening to the croaks and calls of unfamiliar night sounds and thinking about Lilla's claim that Miami was as wild as the west. That Papa had come here, to the very bottom of Florida, made a good deal of sense. He'd failed so many times in his ventures out west, but he still had a pioneer's spirit—it had simply taken him a while to figure out that his frontier lay not beyond the grand mountain ranges but in a desolate swamp to the south.

What would have happened if Papa had thought of going south with Mama instead of out west? Would the humidity have driven her as mad as the prairie winds did? Would Papa's success in Florida have saved her from a return to Providence and Grandmother Stoneman's incessant rebukes?

Impossible questions. Unknowable answers.

I crept out of bed, rummaged through my unpacked valise in the dark. There it was. With the book in my hands, I tiptoed to the main room, ran my fingers over the spines until I found a just enough space. The book slid over the wood as if drawn by a magnet, as if it knew it would fit.

Alice in Wonderland. Back on Papa's bookshelf, where it belonged. Where it had always belonged.

I walked back to the room, and I slept, rocked by the phantom sensation of the train's movement. At some point in the thick night, I rolled over, stirred slightly, and understood that Papa's land of rebirth was now also mine.

No one knew what to do with me those first few days in Papa's house—not Papa, not Lilla, not even me. Did I need time to rest? I didn't feel tired. Did I need time to mourn the end of my marriage? I didn't feel sad. I went for long walks every morning, seeking the bay, and returned around noon with pink, fiery skin.

"Northerners," Lilla muttered kindly as she showed me how to snap the arm off an aloe plant and rub its cool goo on my burn.

I read but was restless. In the afternoons, I took my journal outside and sat in the scant shade of a Caribbean pine, but the words wouldn't come. Not because I couldn't find them. The opposite, actually. So much had happened since Wellesley, and so much time had passed since I'd written anything down, that the words had massed inside me, creating a blockage. I wanted to feel the pen moving over the paper, feel the soft scratch of the ink staining the paper, even if the words stayed stuck inside. So I drew pages and pages of concentric circles, a journal full of ripples soundlessly stretching to the white paper's edge.

By the end of my first week in Miami, I'd filled twenty-three pages with circles. Page twenty-four looked up at me on a breezy, blue afternoon. The page was defiant, just daring me to deface its creamy blankness with my loop-de-loops. I stared back at it while the words that wanted to be written lined up like school children in my head.

Not yet, I said to the restless words, to the expectant page twenty-four. Then the shadow of a butterfly drifted over the paper's expanse, showing me how beautiful the page would look filled in with life.

Okay, okay. Fine. I relented and let loose the line-up of words, the ones that needed to be written before anything else:

Dear Carolyn—
I'm sorry for disappearing. I was ashamed of my life with Kenneth and didn't want you to see any part of it. I'm in Miami, Florida, now (with my father!). I hope you are doing well. I hope you will respond to

*this letter, and though I would be heartbroken if you
didn't, I would understand.*

Love,

M

I pulled the paper from the journal and rushed to the
front the house. Lilla squatted on the porch, sanding a bench.

"Lilla, is there a post office in this city?"

Her eyes laughed at me over the half-moons of her glasses.

"Of course there's a post office, Marjory. We're not *that*
uncivilized. It's on First Avenue. In the new government
building."

"Can I get there on the trolley?"

"You can. But if you wait, I'm sure your father can post
something for you tomorrow. Why rush?"

"No, it's very important. Do you have an envelope?"

"In the desk drawer."

The government building rose three tall stories above street
level, far higher and grander than any other building around. I
hurried up the sun-stained stairs and through one of the many
arched porticos, clutching my letter to Carolyn. Inside, my
eyes were slow to adjust to the shadowed lobby, and I stood
dumbly for a moment as I waited for my vision to return.

"It helps if you turn your head to the side and breathe
deeply."

I tried to force my eyes to focus on the woman who suddenly stood beside me.

"Stop trying to see me," she said, "and turn your head
to the side. That's it. Now a deep breath."

I did as she instructed.

"There," she said. "Look at me now. Isn't that better?"

I nodded as the woman came into focus. Her face was as
dignified and authoritative as her voice.

"You're from up north." It wasn't a question.

"Yes, ma'am," I said.

"Not *ma'am*. Mary Elizabeth. You may call me Mary Elizabeth. And you are?"

"Marjory Stoneman."

Mary Elizabeth nodded once.

"Very well. Marjory." Mary Elizabeth picked up a briefcase I hadn't noticed she'd set by her feet. "Just remember what I said. Head to the side and deep breaths. At least five of them. Six would be better. Seven if you're an over-achiever. You'll see. You need a big bag of tricks when you live in Miami."

"Thank you, ma'am—ah—Mary Elizabeth."

Our conversation over, Mary Elizabeth strode to the exit. A man in a suit hurried across the lobby to open the door for her, but she swatted him away with the briefcase.

"You know who that was, don't-chya?" the sweaty post teller asked when I finally made my way to the window. He leaned forward on one elbow, ready to tell me a secret.

"It was Mary Elizabeth," I said, stating the obvious.

"Right-o. Mary Elizabeth Baird Bryan."

"Baird Bryan?"

"Wife of William Jennings Bryan? The Secretary of State?"

Oh.

"They live here?" I asked.

"Sometimes. You know how it is with rich folks. Can't live in one place all of the time."

Sure. I knew how it was with rich folks.

"Ah, I'd like to mail this," I said, remembering Carolyn's letter. I pushed the envelope across the small counter and watched the teller place a two-cent stamp with a picture of the Panama Canal in the corner. Maybe Carolyn would respond quickly. Maybe she'd forgive me, and then I could write back and tell her that the wife of the Secretary of State had taught me how to deal with sun blindness in this swampy little town on the underbelly of the country, and she'd hoot with laughter.

I'd been in his house nearly two weeks when Papa approached with an offer.

"The *Herald* needs a new society editor," he said as I squeezed aloe onto my flambéed cheeks. "Would you like the job, Marjory? I think it will be good for your skin."

"Do you think I can do it?" I asked.

Papa smiled.

"I have absolutely no idea, Marjory. But I'd like to find out."

The job kept me out of the sun. I sat at Lilla's long Jefferson dining table and made telephone calls to the most prominent of the city's five thousand residents. A typical phone call unraveled like this:

> Hello! This is Marjory Stoneman from the society page of the *Herald*. I'm calling because . . . yes, I said Marjory. . . . No, she's not here any longer. . . . No, no, she's fine, but her mother is ill. . . . She went to Georgia to care for her. . . . Stoneman, yes, he's my father . . .

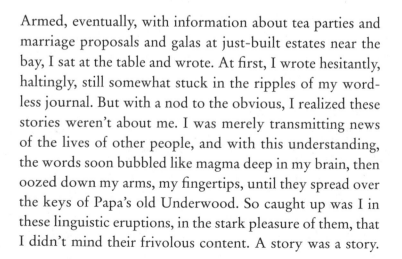

Armed, eventually, with information about tea parties and marriage proposals and galas at just-built estates near the bay, I sat at the table and wrote. At first, I wrote hesitantly, haltingly, still somewhat stuck in the ripples of my wordless journal. But with a nod to the obvious, I realized these stories weren't about me. I was merely transmitting news of the lives of other people, and with this understanding, the words soon bubbled like magma deep in my brain, then oozed down my arms, my fingertips, until they spread over the keys of Papa's old Underwood. So caught up was I in these linguistic eruptions, in the stark pleasure of them, that I didn't mind their frivolous content. A story was a story.

Words were words. And the ones I formed into newspaper columns were read by a city eager to legitimize itself through even the most mundane social conventions.

"There you go," Papa said each day when he handed me a copy of the society page. "Well done."

I liked seeing my name on the delicate newsprint. Thick letters. Dark ink. Undeniable proof that I really was here.

And yet.

The job quickly grew boring. There simply wasn't enough of a society scene in the tiny town of Miami to keep me busy all day.

Lilla noticed my agitation a few weeks into the job. She sat down at the Jefferson table and put her hand over mine.

"Marjory," she said with a conspiratorial grin, "I have an idea."

Lilla was the sort of woman you loved instantly. I understood why Father had fallen for her, how hard it must have been to wait to marry her. Lilla's blue eyes twinkled even in the dim center of the house. Her belly laugh could be heard from outside. And she was eager to hug and whisper and otherwise act like she'd known me forever. I'd made a half-hearted attempt to dislike her—it had seemed the least I could do for Mama—but I'd given the effort up quickly. It would have been easier to fly to the moon.

"What is it?" I asked, leaning close.

"Tell your father you want to do more."

"But, Lilla," I whispered, as if Papa were in the next room, "there *isn't* more. There's not enough of a society here to fill more pages. Unless you count pirates. I'm pretty sure I saw an actual pirate at the bay the other day, Lilla. Big, poofy beard down to his chest. Wild eyes. Maybe he has some society news. "

Lilla screwed her mouth to the side. "Will you stop, please? Listen, there are only two reporters at that paper,

Marjory, and the *Herald* is never going to catch the *Metropolis* if its best writer keeps reporting on tea parties."

This was the first I'd heard of a rival paper.

I watched Lilla watch me.

"Tell him," she insisted when I didn't respond. "Tell him you can do more."

The *Herald* operated out of a two-story corner building on Avenue D. From the street, it gave off the tricky allure of a cabaret or gambling hall—mysterious and anonymous, not open to good little girls.

"I guess I'll go in, then," I said to myself.

The lobby was small and dank with the smell of old rain. A steady *chunk-chunk* sound came from somewhere unseen, and I assumed—correctly, it turned out—that this was the pulse of the printing press.

"Hello?" I called, for other than the press, the room was still.

A head popped up from behind a desk.

"Hello," the head said, then the body to which the head was attached rose as well. "Joe Cotten here. How can I help?"

Joe Cotten was so handsome that he had absolutely no effect on me. I stepped close to the desk.

"I'm looking for Frank Stoneman," I said. "I'm his daughter, Marjory."

Joe's face busted into a smile.

"Miss Stoneman!" he exclaimed. "It's a real pleasure to meet you. We've gotten a great response to your pieces. Follow me. I'll take you to Frank. It's a bit of an adventure to get there."

I followed Joe Cotten around the circulation and classifieds desks and past a bank of windows.

"Is that the printing press?"

A hulking, churlish machine swallowed and burped in a separate part of the room, spitting out stacks of newsprint faster than I could count. The machine had so many pieces and parts and cogs and ribbons, it made so many unnatural noises and repetitive movements, that I could not fathom how one would begin to fix it if it broke down.

"We call it Goliath," Joe Cotton said.

"Well, that's a good name."

"The *Metropolis* is making a big to-do about their new machine," Joe went on. "Did you hear about it? They say it's the most modern press in South Florida. Prints 20,000 complete papers in an hour." Joe shrugged, unimpressed. "I say, *la-dee-da*, what's the point of printing so many papers if there's nothing worth reading written on them? Am I right?"

Joe winked, and the tour continued. He led me up a staircase so steep it may as well have been a ladder.

"Okay, then," Joe said, stepping onto the second floor. "This is the city room. Exciting place, certain times of the day. Frank's office is straight back. Just keep going. You'll find it."

I thanked Joe Cotten and started across the city room. Even empty, the room had energy, and I could feel the beat of the big press through the floor.

"Hi, Papa."

He sat at a large, oblong table, pencil tucked in the gray tufts near one ear. He smiled when he saw me, almost surprised, as if he had forgotten that I lived with him now.

I walked to the window and looked down at the corner where I'd recently stood.

"The plumbing shop," I observed. "You have a nice view."

"Don't I, though?"

I sat on a chair near Papa and leaned toward him. What I meant to say next is not what came out of my mouth.

"Do you remember *Hiawatha*?" I asked, startling us both.

Papa pressed his lips together, turned them down into the kind of frown that means your heart is cracking a little.

"I do," he said. "How you cried, Marjory."

Papa and I watched each other for a long moment. It was a relief to us both to know that what little past we shared was remembered.

"What I meant to say," I started again, "is that I'd like to write more than just the society pages. I'd be a good reporter. I can write for the city pages."

Papa pushed his hair from his forehead. He watched me carefully, then answered so promptly that I wondered if Lilla hadn't already mentioned my request.

"There are rules, Marjory."

"Okay."

"Everything you write must be entirely accurate. Facts are supreme. Without facts, we have no paper."

I nodded.

"I will treat you no differently than the other reporters."

I nodded again.

"I will pay you the same as the other reporters."

I kept nodding as he spoke. No sense pausing between edicts.

"You will continue writing the society pages and put as much effort into them as into anything else."

"I understand," I said when it was clear he was done.

"Fine then. Good. Now get to work."

I worked in the city room with Judge Hill and Garrett Benson, who, to their everlasting credit, did not care in the slightest that I was a woman. These kinds of dynamics felt different in Miami than they had up north. Maybe it was because the city was so new, still in its infancy, a time when gender was of no consequence because there were so many other more fundamental things to figure out first. Or maybe it was because of the heat. A city unlike any other in the country, Miami simply cared less about convention, about propriety. With our clothes sweated tight to our skin, we were all swamp-soaked outlaws, irreverently dismissive of rules so rigidly followed up north. Or maybe I just wrote so well they didn't care about anything else.

We were a morning paper, which meant late nights and late starts. Most days, I didn't get to the office till noon and didn't leave until close to midnight. I loved those late-night walks home, when I could pretend I was alone on the Earth. Moonlight fell on the streets like mystical, vanishing snow, and the air was ripe with the smell of night-blooming jasmine. Sometimes I let the memory of Mama walk with me, and I grasped my own hands tightly together because I couldn't hold hers.

Papa appeared at my desk in the city room late one afternoon, as I bent like an ostrich over a draft of the next day's society news. Like Papa, I'd taken to tucking a pencil behind one ear, though sometimes I lost track of things and stashed two pencils back there—a testament, I suppose, to the sprawling canopy of my ears. I trimmed words from a story about the nearly constructed Vizcaya, the sprawling estate on the bay.

"Marjory."

Papa's voice was heavy with restrained urgency.

"Yes?"

"I've got something big for you to cover. You and Judge."

I pushed my pencil behind my ear and, finding the position occupied twice over, put it behind the other ear instead.

Judge rose from his desk and joined us at mine. He'd brought his notepad.

"Fisher is coming," Papa explained as Judge scribbled.

"Fisher?" I asked.

Papa nodded.

"Indianapolis businessman. Built the Speedway there. He's got a reputation for being as brilliant as he is restless and obnoxious, and the only reason we care about him is that he's nearly done constructing a road from Chicago to Miami Beach. He's calling it the Dixie Highway."

"Miami Beach?" I asked, more confused now. "Where is that?"

"Nowhere," Papa answered. "He's inventing it. Making it out of a sandbar."

"You're telling me he built a road to a destination that doesn't exist?"

"Yes, Marjory. That's right. Judge can elaborate later. For now, just listen. Fisher is coming with his motorcade—it's a publicity stunt for the highway. They're on the last stretch of the trip, and they're not expecting press until they get to Miami. I want you two to surprise him. Wait for him further north. I don't care where as long as it's somewhere he won't suspect."

Judge nodded, looked at me with a smile.

"Hounding Carl Fisher is a favorite pastime of your father's," Judge said.

"Why?" I asked.

"Because it's fun," Papa said.

"Because," Judge clarified, "Carl Fisher thinks Miami is his alone to invent, and a man like that needs careful watching."

Pencils fell from my ears as I nodded. Papa smiled.

"I'll drive," Judge said. "Be ready at sunrise."

I stood with Judge Hill in the narrow shadow of a Caribbean Pine. We'd been waiting for more than two hours at the side of the road, a word I use loosely because up near New Smyrna, where we'd decided to wait, the highway was nothing more than a washboard arrangement of old battered logs. We'd already eaten the biscuits Mrs. Hill had packed and drank most of the cold tea I'd brought along, so now there was nothing to do but listen for the grumble of automobile engines through the saw-edged petioles of the palmetto palms.

"Soon," Judge said. I couldn't tell if this was a prediction or a wish.

Judge Hill was older than me and a far more experienced reporter, but I could sense, even in him, a restless excitement, a feeling that the arrival of the first motorcar would bust a hole in an invisible wall and all the wonders of the world would come rushing through.

"Everything's going to change," I said.

Judge nodded. "I suppose that's the point."

Judge had explained on the way up that this was Carl Fisher's road, leading to the beach that Carl Fisher had built by pumping land up from the bottom of Biscayne Bay or by taking topsoil from the swamp west of the city and piling it all on a barrier island off the coast of Miami. And now Carl Fisher had organized the first motorcade ever to drive the length of the state of Florida. The *Herald* had covered the trip diligently but not without critique. The paper had put tough-talking articles about it right next to reports of the war, and while I was waiting to witness the passing of this parade, I was also—though I did not know it just then—waiting for the arrival of something far greater than anything Carl Fisher could build.

"You hear it?" Judge said.

And all at once I did, a buzz like a bold swarm of bees, accompanied soon enough by the rattle and thwack of metal chassis clattering over the logs. Then whoops, hollers, the deep tones of men caught unguarded when they saw me and Judge.

The lead cars of the motorcade lurched through the pines. Men leaned from the windows, waved their arms through the thick air or slapped at the roofs. One fellow even balanced on the running board of the third car, a shiny black Runabout whose top was pushed back like a breathless accordion. Though his shoulders slumped, he was tall, with a burning bush of wiry red hair that drew my eyes to him. He wore suspenders over his shirtsleeves. No jacket. No hat. And he shook hands like a politician with whatever tree branches came within reach.

"See him?" Judge asked. "In the Packard. He just tipped his hat."

"Who?" I was still looking at the man on the running board.

"Fisher, Marjory! Who else?"

I glanced up at Judge, then at the rest of the procession. The Packard was of course the first car, and sure enough, there sat Carl Fisher, as handsome as Judge had said, though in an untouchable and seemly way. If he was surprised to see us lurking in the pine trees, he didn't let on.

"How do you feel, Mr. Fisher?" Judge called out.

"Like a million bucks!" Fisher answered.

"Can I quote you on that, sir?"

"I don't say anything that you can't print, Mr. Hill."

The cars rattled on, taking the man on the running board with them, and I realized with some mortification that I hadn't yet asked the questions I'd prepared, that I could not even recall the questions I'd prepared, that even if I *could* recall one of the questions I'd prepared, my mouth would not be able to produce the sounds needed to form the words of this barely remembered first question. Some reporter I was turning out to be.

"For heaven's sake," I muttered, then—heels be damned— trotted over the root-ridged, hot ground.

I never would have caught the Packard if Fisher had finished this stretch of his highway. Thankfully, though, he'd focused his efforts to the north and the south, leaving this sad middle ground pocked and splintered. The autos struggled and sputtered. Some had to restart. All this dysfunction gave me time to catch up, catch my breath, flip through my note pad until I found scratches that resembled a question.

"Mr. Fisher," I started and forced all thoughts of the man on the running board from my mind.

"Ah, Miss Stoneman," he interrupted, his car slowing to a crawl. "Tell me, please, how is your father?"

I glanced back at Judge. He was still under the pine.

"He's well, thank you," I said, flustered again.

"Good to hear, good to hear. I wouldn't want all of his coverage of me wearing him down."

I took a deep breath and refocused.

"So, Mr. Fisher, the *Herald* would like to know if you plan on paying the state for the topsoil you removed from the Everglades because—"

"—I tell you, Miss Stoneman, it's a wonder your father has time to print anything else in that little paper of his, seeing as how he's so concerned with my private dealings in that God-forsaken swamp. I'll tell you what." He leaned further out of the car, grinned in a way that might have made other girls swoon. "You just take that little pencil there and write this down. Are you ready? There now. Write down that Carl Fisher's Dixie Highway is complete and Miami Beach is open for business!"

Fisher concluded with a resolute tap of his knuckles on the side of the car. The whole procession heaved forward as I stood seething in the wake of the Packard.

He was stealing the land—changing it, moving it, using it—but unlike a common thief, he felt no need to hide.

I stamped my foot on the ground and glared after the departing Packard. Blood pulsed on my temple, giving rhythm to my outrage. Then, as if to compensate for the cutting down I'd just endured, something lifted me, something inexplicable and unexpected grabbed me around the middle and quite literally raised me up. With a quiet slurp, my feet rose from where my heels had punched holes in the soil, and I felt myself floating, for the quickest of moments, alongside the clattering convoy. I landed. But I was still moving. And the mysterious something still held me at my hips.

"Andy Walker. *Miami Metropolis.*"

It was the tall, fiery man in suspenders. He'd grabbed me as the Runabout thunked past, and now we both surfed on its long running board.

"Marjory Stoneman. *Miami Herald.*" I would have offered my hand but I groped instead for a part of the vehicle to hold on to.

Andy Walker's smile became lopsided as it grew wider.

"Don't let that rich gas get to you," he said, jerking his thumb toward the Packard.

I shrugged one shoulder and looked him straight in the eye.

"It would take a lot more than Carl Fisher to get to me," I boasted.

The Runabout dipped into a ditch. I gripped the doorframe.

"I won't let you fall off," Andy Walker promised. He held out his arm, making a railing of sorts next to me.

I rattled along with the motorcade until a curve in the road, about a quarter mile from where I'd left Judge.

"This is my stop," I said as Fisher's front car started into the bend.

"It's been a pleasure testing the strength of my knees with you, Miss Stoneman," Andy said as, with almost comical timing, the Runabout dipped in and out of a rut.

"Likewise, Mr. Walker."

With a flourish that brought me pleasantly close, Andy lifted me past him and placed me back on the ground. He tipped an imaginary hat. He waved. Then his car disappeared into the curve and the motorcade continued on to Miami, where, I was certain, nothing would ever be the same.

I began to spend my mornings at the edge of the Bay, finding, each day, something magnificent I hadn't noticed before: a giant school of mullet jumping through eyelets of sunlight, sewing invisible threads through the undulating fabric of the water's surface; a flock of great ibis turning cartwheels in the sky, their long white wings made iridescent by the new sun. More than once, I arrived late to work, having been so captivated by the gradual change of the water from blue to green that I lost track of time and had to hustle, breathless and sweating, over to Avenue D. The spectacles of nature down here were astounding. Miami took things that I thought I knew—birds, fish, beetles—and transformed them, turned them inside out and dipped them in vast vats of colors until they were nearly unrecognizable. Sometimes, I brushed my bare feet over the wet turtle grass and thought about Andy Walker. Sometimes, I wondered what else besides the wildlife might be different here, too.

The main room in Papa's house had the air of a library, with its wide dining table and floor-to-ceiling shelves of great books. This was especially true at night, when the house was hushed and the standing lamp cast a teepee of soft light over the armchair. I threw myself into Papa's collection of Dickens. Some nights, he'd join me, pulling a dining chair close enough to share the cone of my light, and we'd pass the dark hours in contented silence.

"This reminds me of Clapp," I said once, putting a finger between pages to hold my place. "The library at Wellesley. It's new. Built while I was there."

Papa's gentle face hardened. He did not look up from his book, but I could tell his eyes had skidded to a stop mid-sentence. I did not know why.

"Except there were more lamps in Clapp. And more women." I said this lightly, making a joke.

"That's enough about that, Marjory."

"About what, Papa? Libraries? Or lamps? Or women?"

I thought I was being very funny, but Father's eyebrows drew so close they almost merged.

"About your grand education."

Ah, so there it was. Cerebral yet uneducated, my father did not want to hear about college because if he did, he would have to resent me.

"I'm sorry, Papa." And I was. I understood well that past pain did not always recede with time.

Even without a college diploma, Papa easily melded with the intellectuals of the young city, of whom there were startlingly few. Lawyers, scientists, a couple of poets— these were the friends Papa collected like beautiful shells, preferring their company to that of the feverish developers who ogled every wild space still untouched. At least once a month, Father and Lilla hosted a dinner for their brainy friends, turning the dark little box of a house into a humid, backwater sort of Parisian salon.

Lilla insisted the electric lights made me look jaundiced and, despite my protests, placed lanterns on every flat surface before one of these parties. The little house then teetered between firelight and shadow, giving it a heady, intimate pulse. Though she was not a great cook, Lilla managed to fill the table with soft breads and baked fruits and meats seasoned generously enough to compensate for being much overdone. I once tried to help in the kitchen. Five minutes hadn't gone by before she asked if I could kindly crank the Victrola instead.

It was 1915, and Dade County was officially dry, but the law did not seem to reach as far as Papa's Jefferson table. Rum, smuggled on schooners from the Bahamas, could be found on the shelf behind Chaucer. Syrupy wine from heaven-knows-where hid behind Tolstoy. Papa himself did not drink but felt strongly that guests in his home should do as they pleased. And they did. The contraband loosened the tongues of his learned friends, and conversation swirled in that room like a tropical storm.

At the table one night, along with two gray-haired jurists, sat David Fairchild, a middle-aged botanist with a dark, brooding look, his stylish wife Marian, and a youngish couple, Pete Robineau and his fiancée, the wide-eyed Frances Cowe. Papa had spoken of Pete before, seemed to admire the bookish young lawyer, but I couldn't help thinking that the couple's appearance was an attempt by Papa and Lilla to find me some friends.

"Marjory," Pete said, and I could hear in his voice a hint of the Frenchness that was his birthright, bits of his native tongue that a childhood in America had not erased. "You write fiction now, no?"

My cheeks flamed. I looked down at smiled at my potatoes.

"Ah," said Papa from the other end of the table. "So, you read the society pages, do you, Pete?"

"Indeed. Francis here was disappointed not to have attended Mrs. J. Augustus Snuanpuh's tea dance."

Francis winked at me and added, "I *am* good friends with Mrs. De Yellowplush, after all."

I looked up from my potatoes long enough to peek at Father. At least he could finally joke about the ordeal. When he'd discovered an article about the invented tea party in his newspaper, he'd been so livid I'd thought the blood vessel at his right temple was going to burst. He was laughing now. But still. The laughter was stiff.

"It had been," I offered by way of explanation, "a very slow week in Miami society news."

Papa harrumphed. The night carried on. Talk turned to the war, and when we could no longer bear Pete's descriptions of the front, the wiry botanist spoke of his past travels to Indonesia and the Philippines and of the orchids he'd studied deep in the Everglades the previous month. This was the first I'd heard of such beauty in that dank, mosquito-plagued place, and I swooned a little at the thought of those delicate flowers hidden like pearls in the swamp.

"Of course," the botanist went on through a swig of his rum, "the dredging will kill them all. It will slaughter them just like those boys at the front."

Firelight flickered over the botanist's face. In the space between light and dark, I imagined a battalion of irreplaceable orchids, crushed like the young men at Gallipoli by machinations of conquest.

"I should like to see it sometime, Mr. Fairchild," I said. "The Everglades, I mean. And the orchids. Before it's all gone."

"And I should like to take you sometime, Miss Stoneman. I have taken reporters before."

"My friend!" Pete Robineau piped up. "My friend told me he joined you on a trip to Immokalee once. Mr. Andy Walker. Do you recall?"

"Yes, of course," Fairchild confirmed, "Mr. Walker. Though perhaps we best not speak of *Metropolis* agents here in the home of the *Herald*'s Stonemans." His eyes cut toward Papa.

"Nonsense," Papa insisted. "The *Metropolis* has fine reporters. Pour yourself some more of that rum and let's talk all night."

And with that, the little wood house came alive, swelling at its joists with talk of rare orchids and saw grasses and a certain reporter whose name intermingled with those of Fairchild's fine flowers. At Francis's urging, I poured myself a glass of rum and hung on for dear life as my heart pounded hard in my chest and I reeled at the many beautiful things surviving in this outlandish, unpredictable land I now called my home.

Later that night. Darkness. Moonlight barely a trickle through the glass in my room. The rum—it had come loose in my brain, and my thoughts churned unchecked in its caramel current. The hope and excitement of hours ago lingered still, but they were mixed now with memories and madness, with shards of childhood nights when I wandered wraithlike though my grandparents' house in my flannel nightgown, searching for the pieces of Mama that she had misplaced.

What was I doing here in Miami, among the botanists and beasts, the grizzled newspapermen and the insufferable heat? The night was, after all, just as dark this far south, and sometimes as long.

"Mail for you," Joe Cotton announced one day, dropping two envelopes on my city room desk. The top envelope was thick, pulpy, with an elaborate and interlocking V and S embossed at the top.

"Anyone know what this is?" I asked, holding the rectangle up.

"'V. S.?'" Garrett said. "That's the Bryan's new estate, ain't it, Judge? Villa Serena?'

"Yessir," Judge nodded. "Like a kid or a dog, an estate's got to have its own name."

Garrett was right. Inside the envelope, I found an invitation from Mrs. Mary Elizabeth Baird Bryan. She'd read my columns, the printed words said. She remembered meeting me in the government building that sunny day. She'd like me to join her for tea.

"Glad it's you and not me," Garrett said after I'd read the card aloud.

"What does that mean?"

Garrett turned back to the work on his desk.

"You'll see," he said without looking up.

Judge tipped his chin toward my other envelope.

"Where's the other one from?" he asked. "The White House?"

I took in the second envelope's handwriting, its postmark, its return address. Without answering Judge, I unsealed the flap and rushed my eyes over Carolyn's words. She was teaching in New York, living in the city, but, really, she just wanted to know about me. The questions that followed were the same as she was: direct and earnest and bubbling over with compassion. Did I like Miami? Was my father as I'd remembered him? Did I still think of Kenneth? When would I visit? She'd love to have me.

"Better than the White House," I answered Judge and slid the letter into my bag for safekeeping.

Villa Serena edged Biscayne Bay. Disarmingly symmetrical, with almost reflective white walls and two pointed red roofs, the house seemed to play tricks on my eyes. It was hard to gauge its height, its depth. Its halves were nearly too identical to make a believable whole. I puzzled over this for several minutes before a housemaid opened the front door and I had no choice but to approach.

I adored Mary Elizabeth before she opened her mouth, before I again heard her inimitable voice or was made privy to her uncompromising ideas. She was a stout lady with the most intelligent, ambitious eyes I'd seen on a woman since my days at Wellesley. She seemed out of place in the large, airy loggia, as if even a room on the edge of the wide, wild ocean could not contain her.

"I'm so happy you came, Marjory," she beamed and gestured to a chair near her. The housemaid poured two cups of tea.

"I'm happy to be here," I answered.

"I trust you've been turning your head to the side and breathing deeply as needed?"

"Oh, yes," I said, though I suspect she could tell that I hadn't.

A china bowl brimming with radishes sat on the table between us. I eyed them, unsure if decorum dictated that I should or should not take one.

"Oh, don't worry about those," Mary Elizabeth said, noting my confusion. "My husband. He loves radishes. He could eat nothing but radishes all day and be very happy. We have bowls of them placed strategically all over the house."

My hostess sipped her tea, then hurried right to the point, brushing aside the chatter of deep breathing and radishes.

"Are you aware, Marjory, that some states have come to realize a woman might have opinions separate from those of her husband? That the women's suffrage amendment has passed in some states?"

"Oh, yes," I assured her. "I'm quite aware. I worked with the suffrage club when I was at Wellesley."

Mary Elizabeth smiled, leaned more casually against the arm of her chair.

"Honestly," she confided, "the idea that a woman must be of one mind with her husband. Pure rubbish. You will understand the absurdity of this, Marjory, when you marry one day."

Something came over me. The woman was so honest, so free with her thoughts, that I did not hesitate to reply with the truth.

"Actually, Mary Elizabeth, I'm married right now. But my husband is an alcoholic felon with whom I no longer share a bed, much less a vote."

My words dropped to the stone floor of Villa Serena and rolled away like a loose marble. Perhaps I'd gone too far. For the longest time, Mary Elizabeth's face didn't move.

Maybe I should get up and show myself to the door, instead of enduring the shame of her having to ask me to leave. But then her lips twisted. Her cheeks pressed up into her eyes, and she threw her head back and guffawed.

"You, Marjory," Mary Elizabeth said while catching her breath, "you are exactly what the state of Florida needs." We had long a discussion about the likelihood of Florida's women getting the vote and how best to move the process along. Could I write articles about it in the *Herald*? Of course I could. We spoke also of women who could argue our case most effectively. Mrs. Stranahan, for sure, and perhaps Mrs. Broward as well. Listening to Mary Elizabeth, it was easy to forget that she was a statesman's wife and not the statesman herself. She seemed to know what I was going to say before I said it, seemed to have crafted a response before it was needed. She was kind without being too friendly. Interested in me without being intimate. I knew, sitting across from this woman, that Secretary Bryan never could have prevailed at his post without her.

"Perhaps *we* should travel to Tallahassee this spring and make our case to the legislature," she suggested with a twist of a smile that questioned whether I had the gumption to join her. Maybe I didn't.

But maybe, just maybe, I did.

An undefined ache began in my gut as I sat on Mary Elizabeth Baird Bryan's blue brocade chair, an ache for a wide, open space that allowed me to believe I could make the impossible happen. Yes, I was still tied to a man who had so nearly destroyed me, but why should he also possess my vote, my voice? Why not free myself from Kenneth at the ballot box while I waited and waited for the State of Florida to free me from him in all other ways?

"Mary Elizabeth," I said, leaning forward with elbows on knees, "I think we should go."

Mary Elizabeth let loose a gentler version of her previous guffaw, a noise full of chortles and indelicate snorts.

"I don't drink alcohol, Marjory," she said when she settled, "but, we need a toast." Mary Elizabeth raised her teacup. "To the vote!" she exclaimed.

"To the vote!" I echoed, raising my own, and then we set about plotting our trip.

The second time I saw Andy Walker was months later, at the end of December, while covering the party celebrating Villa Vizcaya, the Italian Renaissance estate on the Bay, next to Villa Serena. I was not expecting to see Andy there and suffered through the first hours of the party in the usual way.

I wore the same dress—pale blue linen embroidered with daisies and occasional French knots—that I wore to all the society parties. If people noticed this about me, they never said, never even slipped a furtive, critical glance in my direction. And why should they? They were not there to watch me. I was there to watch them. Like an ornithologist, little notebook in hand, I kept to the fringes and observed the society ladies and pioneer-baron gents in their rainbowed plumage, recording their movements and their conversations as they strutted through whatever polished rookery they happened to be in that night. I was tactful, of course, with the information I chose to print. If I published half of what I observed at the parties in the next day's *Herald*, I would not be invited again, and then my job . . . Well, an ornithologist can't work if she has scared away all the birds.

Tonight, though. Tonight was not like anything I'd seen before on the society beat. There was almost too much to keep track of, too much to note, as the guests grew drunk on salted night air and Mr. Deering's contraband Chianti. A hundred people or more milled about the interior courtyard.

Some had arrived in the usual way—by automobile or carriage—but many had giddily floated in from the bay on gold-edged gondolas (provided, of course, by Mr. Deering, who, I was beginning to think, really had gone too far with the whole Italian renaissance trope). Instead of the customary subtropical finery, the guests tonight had dressed in the drab and shapeless frocks of eighteenth century Umbrian peasantry, another indulgence, I supposed, to Mr. Deering's apparent fetishism for all things Italianate.

High above the bustling courtyard hung a square of star-pocked black sky. I ached for a taste of that sky. I wanted nothing more than to surface from the depths of this ridiculous scene and lose myself in the galaxy's splendor. But I had a job to do now, and stargazing would not get it done. I forced my eyes lower. They slipped down the coral-stone columns, slid over humped archways, swung from the fronds of the potted palmettos until they settled once again on the swarm of faux peasants. In the corner, by the lute players, stood Mr. Chalfin.

Paul Chalfin exuded an air of possession over Vizcaya that exceeded even that of James Deering, its owner. His high, rounded forehead glistened like the marble floors he'd commissioned, his suit was made of material as fine as those of the curtains he'd ordered. He had not, I noted wryly, donned peasant garb for the evening.

"Mr. Chalfin?" I asked, approaching the man. He was shorter than I expected, and I stopped an awkward distance away, in an effort to mitigate our height differential. "Marjory Stoneman, of the *Herald*."

"A pleasure," Paul Chalfin said, peering around me. I suspected this statement was not entirely true.

No sooner had these words been exchanged than Pete Robineau appeared at my side, winking at me when Chalfin looked down. I introduced the two men.

"A pleasure," Paul Chalfin said, looking directly at Pete. This time he seemed to mean it.

Pete dipped his head.

"Congratulations on Villa Vizcaya's completion," Pete said.

"Ah," Chalfin cooed before Pete finished speaking. "A Frenchman! I studied for three years at the École des Beaux Arts."

"One of the finest schools in the world," Pete noted, making the little man grin.

I was glad Pete had joined us. I took notes as he questioned Chalfin about Vizcaya, looked to him when I got lost in Chalfin's rococo descriptions of the estate's grandeur. Having been born in Versailles, Pete had, I assumed, an innate comprehension of these sorts of things.

"You must come by again," Chalfin told us, looking only at Pete. "The gardens will be complete in just a few months."

With that, Chalfin excused himself into the throng of peasants and left me and Pete standing alone. I turned to my friend, enjoying the continental solicitude he somehow still possessed.

"I don't think he'd like Francis very much," I observed.

Pete laughed, put his arm over my shoulders and agreed.

"So here we are in Renaissance Italy," he said. "I expect any minute we will find Leonardo DaVinci playing the lute."

"I'm surprised Chalfin didn't have the David shipped over and installed in the courtyard."

"Perhaps it will be unveiled later," Pete said. "In the meantime, let us go see Francis. She's talking with a friend. Come, we will join them."

Pete maneuvered through the crowd, listing to the left as he always did since returning from the war.

"Francis is there," he said, pointing, "at the end of the loggia, you see? Talking with our friend from the *Metropolis*."

I saw Andy before he saw me. He was fresher, more combed and pressed, than he'd been that day on the running board, but he stood with the same playful readiness I remembered. He was nearly a head taller than anyone else in the room and shined like a torch in a darkened chamber.

"Francis, darling," Pete said, touching his fiancée's elbow, "you remember Marjory?"

Francis turned to me, beaming, and touched her porcelain cheek to my sweaty one.

"Of course! How are you, Marjory?" Then, without waiting for an answer, Francis spun me toward Andy.

"Miss Marjory Stoneman," Francis proclaimed, "I'd like to introduce you to Mr. Andy Walker. He's the reporter we told you about. The one who went into the swampland with Dr. Fairchild."

As Andy watched me, I could almost feel his hands at my waist, feel the earth falling away as it had on the road near New Smyrna. He reached forward, took my hand in his.

"It's nice to see you again, Miss Stoneman."

The breeze blew off the bay, waggling his tufts of red hair. I smiled. I told him I was happy to make his acquaintance again.

"And did you arrive via gondola?" Andy asked, grinning crookedly.

"Why, is there any other way to arrive, Mr. Walker?" I scoffed.

I was not a woman accustomed to the attention of men. Heck, I'd married the first man who'd remembered my name. That beauty was not going to get me anywhere in this world was not breaking news, and I'd long ago dismissed the quotidian concerns of corsets and curlers and thrice-daily devotions at the dressing table. But here in Miami, it was beginning to occur to me that strongly held convictions and a sharp wit were nearly as attractive, at least with the right man, as a slender waist and long legs.

"Well," Andy said, "I happen to be a gondolier when

I'm not swashbuckling among orchids and alligators, and I insist you come for a ride, Miss Stoneman. Pete, Francis, you must come along, too."

Pete and Francis begged off.

"It's late."

"We leave for Chicago in the morning."

"Come on, old man," Andy urged, draping a long arm around Pete's shoulders.

"No, no," Pete insisted. "We'll leave the gondoling to you two."

"*Gondoling* isn't a word, darling," Francis teased.

"Au contraire, sweetheart," Pete said. "I just made it one."

Engulfed in their repartee, Francis and Pete disengaged, leaving me alone with Andy Walker and the prospect of a midnight gondola ride.

"Well, Miss Stoneman?" he asked. "If you are not also leaving for Chicago tomorrow, I expect you will join me?"

The small fleet of gondolas was moored near the house, in the lagoon formed by a massive stone barge built, like a sandbar, to temper the bay. The barge was effective. It calmed the lagoon water, which nipped the boat like a puppy; out beyond the stone barrier, the bay strained and howled.

Andy stood tall at the stern. Under the million-eyed gaze of the stars, I climbed into the boat and settled on the middle bench.

"Ready?"

I nodded and felt the earth become liquid beneath me.

Andy pushed on the pole, and the gondola drifted from shore. It was a small lagoon, barely bigger than a New England pond, and we were halfway to the barge by the time Andy had crooned three lines of what may or may not have been an authentic Venetian barcarole.

I looked up. Beyond Andy's long silhouette, Betelgeuse pulsed red, thumping in the night sky like a heart.

Andy followed my gaze to the sky. "Do you see Pleiades?" he asked in a lull in his song. "The star cluster there, over the moon."

Did I see Pleiades? As clearly as I saw my own hands on the typewriter each day. As clearly as I'd seen my own breath on a cold Providence morning.

"Sterope and Merope," I said. "And Electra and Maia and Taygeta and Celaeno and Alcyone. The seven sisters."

Andy whistled, appreciative.

"Don't forget their parents," he added.

"Pleione and Atlas."

We smiled in the darkness, impressed with ourselves.

"What about that one there?" Andy asked, pointing a long arm at the sky. "I bet you don't know that one."

"Which one?" I squinted at the infinitely rearrangeable stars.

"There. See how those three stars make the wing, and over there, those lines of stars make the rung?"

I leaned further back, nearly tipping.

"How do I not know what you're talking about?" I said, more to myself than to Andy. I looked harder, trying to draw connecting lines in the sky.

"Look." Andy used his arm to trace lines through the heavens. "See the beak there, and the feet there. And over there are two parallel lines."

"I don't—"

"I can't believe you don't know the constellation Little Chicken With Ladder, Marjory! Copernicus discovered it four hundred years ago."

I turned my eyes from the stars to Andy's face. His grin cracked into laughter. I smiled, too.

"Oh," I conceded. "Little Chicken With Ladder. Of course. You see, I only know it as part of the larger constellation Gondolier With A Strange Sense of Humor."

"A likely excuse."

It didn't take long to reach the barge. While Andy roped the gondola to a post, I climbed from my seat and onto the limestone platform. He turned toward my bench in the boat to offer assistance and, finding it empty, peered at the black water as if searching for a drowned body. "Hmm," he murmured like a fictitious detective. "There'd likely be bubbles."

"I'm over here," I said.

He looked up and, with mock relief, clapped his hand to his chest and exclaimed, "Oh, thank heavens!"

We stood facing the house. On the other side of the lagoon, the tall windows of Vizcaya blazed with lamplight, and the motley sounds of drunken enjoyment mingled with the calls of tropical night birds. From this distance, though, the house did not look as indomitable as Deering had surely intended it to look. It looked instead like a hiccup, a mistake, for beyond its curated grounds, the shoreline darkened and filled with thick-legged mangroves.

"And what do you think of Miami so far?" Andy asked.

What an unanswerable question. I closed my eyes, listened to the shuffling of the bay against our stone island.

"It's like nothing I've ever known," I said finally. "It's so beautiful, I'm almost afraid to trust that it's real."

"It is beautiful," Andy agreed, "but so is that Venetian urn Chalfin stuck in the foyer. And so are all the paintings he's got covering the walls."

"So if Miami is more than a pretty picture," I said, "then what is it, exactly?"

Andy's excitement burned in the moonlight. "It's *alive*, Marjory. It's a beautiful baby with a heartbeat, and it's going to grow up to be something amazing one day."

I tried not to laugh.

"That's why you're here, then?" I asked. "To raise Miami as if it were a child?"

"Yes. That's why I'm here. And that's why you're here. And your father and the *Herald* and the *Metropolis*. And Flagler and Fisher. It's why we're all here. There's no place else like Miami. Not in the whole country. Maybe even the world!"

Andy was breathless. His narrow chest heaved, and his eyes shined as if they were small suns.

"And what if Miami has other ideas?" I asked, thinking of the peckish alligator who had strolled past our back door last week and breakfasted on one of Lilla's young kittens.

"That's okay. That's the point," Andy said, still giddy. "We're all going to grow up together."

I swallowed hard and turned from the lagoon to the bay, where the water roiled endlessly, without restraint. I didn't know what to make of this conversation with Andy. It wasn't his words that befuddled me so much as their spirit. I was used to people who drained me, who left me tired and weak. My mother. My husband. Both of them always needing more than I had to give. But tonight, Andy had filled me instead. His ideas had been gifts, not expenses.

Andy stood beside me, watching the bay. He squeezed my hand quickly, one impulsive pulse, as if he just couldn't help himself.

"There's absolutely nowhere else in the world I'd rather be," he said. Did he mean in the city of Miami or on the stone barge with me?

I moved toward him—not even a step, barely more than an imperceptible shifting of weight so that the tips of the tiny hairs on our arms grazed one another, contact so slight, so dazzling, it was like being knocked over by the sea breeze.

"Me either," I said.

We stood together on the unmoving platform, a respite of solidity between the carousing waves of the bay and the brackish lagoon. I could have stayed there forever, sustained by his nearness, but I feared the magic would extinguish if dragged on too long.

"Get in, Mr. Walker," I eventually said, lifting the gondolier's pole. "I'm supposed to be taking notes about high society folks."

"Of course," Andy said. "I forgot that you're on the job tonight."

Andy sprang from the bench into the gondola, causing the small boat to teeter with comic imbalance. He rode the disturbance like a bow-legged rodeo clown, then settled onto the bench and let me haul us back to Vizcaya.

"You may be driving, Miss Marjory Stoneman," he said as I stepped aboard and pushed away from the barge, "but I'm still going to sing." And with that, Andy threw his head back and bellowed the rest of his barcarole to me and the myriad constellations.

Dearest C—

I could fill fifteen pages with descriptions of the colors and sounds and smells of Miami. I could then fill fifteen more with news of my father, and my work, and the fascinating people who have chosen to live in this mysterious place. But I have neither enough paper nor ink for all of that, and surely even you do not have enough patience. I'll try my best to stay to the point.

So much is happening here, so quickly. Every day feels like a week, every week like a month—though it's a marvelous bending of time.

My time here in Miami is filled mostly with work for the paper. Silly society news, of course, but also real pieces. Papa seems to trust me more now, and about half my articles are for the city room. He has made some noise about going out west with Lilla this summer. I'm not sure what that will mean for the paper, but Papa wouldn't just let the Herald get smothered by the Metropolis. He will have a plan, surely, as he always does.

Not to worry—my days are not all spent in the newsroom. There is a group of young people—writers, reporters, engineers, and scientists—with whom I pass my free time. We argue and laugh and, if someone has been out to the stills in the swamp, sometimes drink moonshine (it is hideous stuff—I never manage more than a swallow or two). On Saturday nights, we sprawl in the sawdust at the open-air theater, watching the silent movies and breathing the night-blooming jasmine. There is an energy among us, an inescapable sense that we are all on the verge of the rest of our lives, and that those lives are, in all ways that matter, tied to this city. In my best moments, I feel it too.

Love you from here to forever,
Marjory

My orbit and Andy's orbit began, slowly, to intersect. The gravitational force of Miami's young intellectual life drew us both in, and, like me, he was there most Saturday nights when we built campfires on the empty beach after the movies and talked nearly till dawn. Wrapped in a moonless March breeze, Frank Ashworth once told us about a Tequesta burial mound on the north point of the river, dug up and destroyed when Flagler built his hotel. There was no assumption among any of us that this exchange of a gravesite for the Royal Palm was entirely bad or entirely good. We talked instead about progress, about the moral labyrinths that growing a city could form. My mind swelled on these nights. The vehemence, the profundity, of our conversations was almost too much to ingest. For so long, I'd been mired in the black, tangled fates of others that I'd forgotten, or perhaps never known, the pleasures of philosophy, the simple joys of thinking beyond the confines of someone else's personal drama.

"What are you thinking about?" Andy asked the night we learned of the Tequesta mound. Flames flickered and snapped in the campfire, burning a hole in the dark sky.

I looked at his warm, open face. At the scrub-brush stubble on his chin—capable, maybe, of washing me clean.

"My speech for the legislature," I answered. "Demanding suffrage."

It's not that I didn't trust Andy with my real thoughts. It's not that I didn't want him to know. I wiggled my bare toes deeper into the sand, down to where the grains were packed hard and cool, and understood that I felt unburdened with him. Andy felt like the future. I didn't want to tarnish him with my past.

I shifted in my small rut in the sand, hitched my hands behind me for support. After a moment, Andy shifted, too. His arms also went back. We stared at the fire, almost afraid to look at each other, and—as I somehow knew that he would—Andy inched his hand closer until he could loop one of his fingers around one of mine.

"See up there?" I whispered, jutting my chin toward the sky. "The cluster of stars above the Big Dipper?"

"No."

"Look, it's almost as if there are spikes coming out of the cluster."

"Oh, yeah, okay. I see it now."

"That's Ananyas."

"Ananyas?"

"The Slayer of Regicidal Pineapples."

Andy was quiet. Then, after a moment, he started laughing so hard Frank Ashworth had to shush him.

After that night, we often sat near each other, often walked home together in the first drips of daybreak. The ghosts of the leveled live oaks listened as we tried to converse in Latin, bringing the dead language alive, teasing each other about our respective newspapers in a cumbersome tongue that knew nothing of the invention of the printing press. Our discussions sometimes became so absurd that we stumbled over our laughter. Grabbed one another for balance. Quickly let go.

"You know," Andy said as we shuffled inland, "It's all I can do to keep up with you." He gave a sheepish smile, the one that lifted half his mouth and squinched his big nose to the side. "The constellations. The Latin. In case you couldn't tell, I'm trying to impress you, Marjory Stoneman."

A small burrowing owl watched us from the side of the road, head cocked, eyes wide, as if he were as surprised as I was. Not wanting to scare the creature away, I waited until we were well past it to speak.

"*Eh bien*," I answered. "*Ça marche.*"

"Wait, that's French, right?"

I nodded.

"Great." Andy threw up his hands with exaggerated despair. "Now I need to learn French!"

His playfulness was as refreshing as iced lemonade. I hadn't known anyone, ever, so steeped in joy.

Above, the owl streaked past, gliding toward the pines on the other side of the road. *Who cooks for yooou?* it seemed to hoot. I tucked my arm around Andy's and rose onto tiptoes, getting a little closer to his faraway ear.

"I said that it's working," I whispered.

Andy smiled, injected a little hop into his step. For once, he seemed to have nothing to say.

Past the Suwanee—that tannin-stained river forever yoking southern Georgia and north Florida—the red hills of the region spread their dust like dandelion puffs on the breeze. I found the copper dirt in my hair, tasted it on the back of my tongue, tried to wipe it, unsuccessfully, from the hem of my best skirt. The dust seemed to blow right through the gaps in the caulking of the walls at Tallahasee's Leon Hotel, where I stayed with Mary Elizabeth, Mrs. Broward, and Mrs. Stranahan while we petitioned the Florida legislature for the vote.

"We'll present to a joint committee in the morning," Mary Elizabeth confirmed. "So you ladies get yourselves a good night's sleep."

I was too excited to sleep. The possibility of having a voice in the future of women's suffrage in the state was intoxicating. My words, affecting Florida's fate—it was almost too thrilling to bear.

Jittery and wide-eyed, I spent most of the night on the main staircase landing, sitting on a gold-tassled bench and listening to the raucous arguments among the political lobbyist who also seemed to have no need for sleep. Their verbal punches and counterpunches wafted upstairs from the lobby. Prohibition. Taxes. Infrastructure. During the many hours I listened, none of these vehement men spoke of the women's vote.

"Looks like you're just about finished eavesdropping."

I startled awake on the bench. Apparently, I had needed some sleep. A round-bellied man with white-tufted triangles growing on the sides of his face stood on the landing, squinting at me through his monocle.

"I wasn't eavesdropping."

"I say you were, but no matter. A lady such as yourself could not have made sense of the arguments anyhow."

I sat taller on the bench, wiped the vestiges of sleep from my eyes.

"With all due respect, sir, of course I understood those arguments. I understand politics very well. In fact, I'm presenting in front of a joint committee of the legislature in the morning."

The man's mid-section shook as he chuckled.

"And what are you presenting, young lady? Your best pot-pie recipe?"

"Actually, sir, I'm advocating for women's suffrage."

This time, the man's belly tried to wiggle loose from the vest containing it.

"With those wool-hat boys," he said when his laughter settled, "you'll have an easier time convincing them that your chicken pot pie is better than their mamas'." He bid me goodnight and shuffled toward the hall, shaking his wooly head and muttering "women's suffrage," as if I'd just told him the punch line to the funniest joke he'd ever heard.

By late morning, however, I'd come to be grateful for my midnight encounter with the old man and his jiggling belly. His rudeness had been but a dainty aperitif to the main course of disrespect served up by the Florida legislature.

All four of us wore our best hats. We sneezed the red dust from our noses before entering the hearing room, then walked in pairs through the mahogany doors. Being more senior, Mary Elizabeth and Mrs. Broward went first, followed closely by me and Mrs. Stranahan. Despite hardly sleeping, I felt fresh and jumpy, eager to make our case before these important decision-makers.

The room was enormous, with wood-paneled walls and a faraway ceiling, yet somehow the place still felt stuffy, confined, as if the air, so full of stale tobacco and backward ideas, gagged on itself. The bodies of men, presumably legislators, sat propped against two of the walls, a long table before them, creating a smorgasbord of mustaches, cravats, pocket watch chains, and glazed-over eyes. Until one of the men leaned forward and shot the brown contents of his mouth into the spittoon he shared with his colleague, I wasn't sure the bodies were alive.

"Thank you for allowing us the honor of addressing this chamber," Mary Elizabeth began.

No one stirred. No one granted her permission to continue, but no one stopped her either. I watched the chairman, identified as such by the brass nameplate near his spittoon, as Mary Elizabeth spoke. He cleaned his fingernails with the thumb of his other hand.

By the time it was my turn to speak about how suffrage would increase the pool of educated voters, two legislators were asleep, one was reading the newspaper, and three had fired up their pipes. So be it.

"As many women as men graduate from high school in Florida, and granting them the right to vote would nearly double the number of educated voters in our great state."

My voice filtered through the smoky room, bold and impassioned. The ends of my fingers tingled, my heartbeats per minute likely exceeded the heart rates of all the legislators combined. I believed in the right of women to vote. Not only that, I began to sense a belief in something even greater, broader—my right to advocate against all of the bad policies, whatever they might be, promoted by these uninspiring men.

When I finished my piece, the legislators did not react. In fact, at least two more had fallen asleep. They did not care what we said, did not even feign granting us half their attention.

"Ignorant, that's what they are," Mary Elizabeth fumed on the Pullman later that day. We sat together in the dining car, trying to skim red dust from the surface of our soup.

"Rude and infuriating," Mrs. Stranahan added.

The legislators had been all of those things and more. By traveling north, we'd gone deeper into the south, to a place steeped in overturned thinking, a place still governed by customs and rules that the more enlightened parts of the country rejected. But instead of being discouraged, I felt invigorated, alive. Miami was not Tallahassee. I was going home to a place bursting with new ideas, and I'd gotten to sample the thrill of advocating hard for something important.

"Galvanizing," I said.

My three companions looked at me over the puddles on their soupspoons.

"That's what those wretched men are," I explained. "Galvanizing."

Mary Elizabeth threw back her head and let loose a signature snort.

"That's what I like about you, Marjory Stoneman," she crowed. "Yes, that's what I like about you."

She winked at me across the table. I settled back in the seat. I couldn't wait to get home and scrub the last of the Tallahassee red dirt from my skin.

⁓

Papa and I sat in his office, recent copies of the *Metropolis* spread everywhere. The clock read 5:30, but the sun remained high in the sky. This was still a marvel to me, how the Miami sun stayed afloat so much of the day.

"Continues to be mostly a mouthpiece," Papa observed, dropping one *Metropolis* to the floor and lifting another. "A daily advertisement for Flagler and Fisher and the rest of them." Papa turned a few pages. "Not much about the war. Nothing about prohibition. Though I will say, this Walker fellow has some good bits about Governor Trammell."

The tips of my ears burned at the mention of Andy. I glanced at Papa. Was his comment intentional? I had no way of knowing. His head remained bent over the papers, gray locks shielding his face. I shifted. Very little about Papa was unintentional.

"They should write more about the war," I offered, shaking my head at the newsprint I held. "How myopic a paper is it? I mean, I know Florida is dangling here in the middle of the ocean like some sort of anchor dragged behind a big ship, but really. *War*. You'd think it would get covered."

Papa ignored me, continued skimming his section.

"Walker says here Trammell will consider a run for the Senate when he leaves office. I'll have Judge look into that." Papa unwedged a pencil from behind his ear and made a note to himself. "Oh," he said, noticing something next to the pad on his desk. "This came yesterday."

I took the thick paper from Papa's outstretched hand. It was a letter, addressed to him, from a lawyer in Orlando. My eyes pored over the cramped, uneven type.

"Seems you're still married," Papa said when I looked up.

"I don't understand."

"Kenneth hasn't agreed yet."

"But he has to."

Papa watched me, his eyes full of compassion but his lips pressed in a firm line.

"Doesn't he have to?" I asked.

"No," Papa said slowly, "He does not."

For some reason, I pictured Kenneth's hands—large, lined with meandering veins, nails short and square. I saw those hands holding a fork, upon whose tines sat a piece of my badly poached egg. The dry feel of that leathery yolk in my mouth came back to me now. The bitterness with which I'd prepared it. The sourness with which I'd seasoned it. Desperately lonely. Painfully bored. Not knowing if he'd come home, which was worse than when he was in prison and I did not have to listen for the scratch of his key in the door.

"Isn't there anything we can do?" I asked. "To move him along? He was trying to defraud you, Papa. Can't we threaten to press charges?"

Papa's compassion turned, I thought, into pity.

"I'll talk to the lawyer, Marjory. We'll see what can be done." He picked up a paper again, straightened it with a declarative snap. Andy's byline stared me in the face.

"Until then," Papa went on, "you must remember that you are married. You must conduct yourself accordingly." He peered at me over the top of the paper. "Because this may feel like the wild west, Marjory, and Miami may be completely unlike Taunton, Massachusetts, but there is still a right way and a wrong way of doing things."

I watched Papa, admiring—even in my agitated state— his ability to offer instruction without domination; advice without condescension.

"No one told you to wait so long to marry Lilla," I countered, though softly.

Papa nodded. He folded the *Metropolitan* until it would not fold any further. Then he leaned forward on his elbows and looked at me with eyes full of unspent fatherly love.

"No one had to tell me," he said.

I looked down. My hands had freckled in the incessant sun. Constellations, right there on my skin.

"Andy Walker is my friend, Papa," I said. "He is nothing more than my friend."

Papa leaned back in his chair, exhaling slowly. He closed his eyes. It must have been hard for him to be a father for the first time in so many years.

"Then keep it that way, Marjory."

On an April night at the edge of the bay, ghost-light from the full moon drizzled over our small strip of sand. The night was somehow *more* than most of our Saturday nights. More people. More moonshine. More Andy. Men with stringy beards and lost gazes milled among our usual crowd. They looked like pirates but called themselves Gladesmen. They'd come in for a few days from the swamp.

"They're outlaws, most of them," Andy whispered. I liked the feel of his breath on my ear. "Frank found them when he was out surveying last week."

What had drawn bookish Frank Ashworth and these raucous, rough men together? Frank wasn't even drinking the moonshine they'd brought in from their stills, though the Gladesmen seemed willing to share.

Myrtle appeared at my side, nearly floating. I'd sipped some of the moonshine from Andy's tin cup, and we'd all somehow disengaged from the pull of the earth. We were weightless. Groundless. The only thing keeping us on the sand was the gravity of each other.

"He needs them," Myrtle shared, speaking of Frank, her husband, and the Gladesmen. "They can take him to places out there that he'd never get to in a million years by himself."

I leaned into Andy, who was still close. The thought of exploring the depths of that sticky, beast-plagued wetland was thrilling in its impossibility. Though unseen unless you ventured west of the city, the Everglades loomed large over Miami—an open secret, a constant and mysterious presence that seemed at once utterly indomitable and fantastically frail. Frank often spoke of his journeys. Myrtle, who, like Andy, wrote for the *Metropolis*, frequently published columns describing what Frank had learned on his trips. The railroad encroached. The speculators dug canals. The Everglades was everywhere and nowhere at the same time.

Myrtle drifted away as easily as she'd appeared. Though no one played music, the night had a rhythm, a pulse that filled my head and my ears and created the illusion that everyone on the beach was nearly dancing.

"You went, right?" I asked Andy. He was close. I could feel the sweat through his shirt. We moved together, side to side, in time to the thumping non-music.

"Where?"

"The Everglades."

"Mmm hmm."

Shadows moved at the edge of my vision—Gladesmen and poets, surveyors and pirates, the myriad inhabitants of this chrysalis city—but all I saw fully was Andy.

"What is it like?"

"What? The Everglades?"

I nodded.

"It's hard to describe."

I stepped even closer to him.

"You're a journalist," I said. "I think you can do it."

"Well . . ." Andy squinted, thinking. But he did not finish his thought.

Andy touched his lips to mine, lightly, like a breeze, and we hung on like that, mouths hardly pressed together, suspended in an exultant and momentary eternity. Nothing in my life had prepared me for this. The voices of strangers and friends swirled around us, beyond us. Exhilaration. Terror. So much of each that one became the other and I capitulated to their fevered demand. I pushed into Andy, felt him push against me. The silent music beat louder.

Then we came apart, trembling, laughing.

"It's like that," Andy whispered.

Well, then. The Everglades was someplace I wanted to go.

"You're sure you're okay with this?" Papa asked, for what must have been the tenth time that morning.

"She's fine, Frank," Lilla answered for me.

"I'm fine, Papa."

Papa swung the last of Lilla's suitcases into the back of the car, looked at his watch.

"The train is at noon, Frank," Lilla said. "We have plenty of time."

"But the editorials," Papa clarified. "You're okay with the editorial page?"

I stepped closer to Papa and put a firm hand on his shoulder. This was not something people ordinarily did to Frank Stoneman.

"I will be fine. The editorial page will be fine. The *Herald* will be fine. Go and have fun."

It was summer, my first summer in Miami. Sometime weeks ago, late in May, humidity had joined the ever-present heat to form a paste that coated the city. Each day, the paste became stickier, denser, until at midday it was so thick I could hardly breathe. The sky sought relief the only way it knew how—by exploding. Rain fell in panes. Rivers formed in the streets that had gutters while lakes formed in the streets that did not. Water fell mightily until, suddenly, it didn't, and after a moment of absolute stillness, the paste began churning, forming again for the next day.

During one of these storms, Papa had told me about his upcoming trip.

"A month," he'd said. "California and Denver. Lilla and I, we want to see other unfinished towns."

The *Herald* was finally in a place where Papa felt he could leave it for a short time. Circulation and advertising had increased with Miami's population. And though we were a morning paper in an afternoon paper town, it seemed that at least some of the newcomers to the city liked to get their information at the start of the day.

"And, ah," Papa had gone on in a rush, needing to get the words out but almost afraid to do so, "you can do the editorial page while I'm away." He'd glanced at me. "So, that's that. Everything's all set."

Now that the day of his departure had arrived, Papa seemed less certain about things being set, as perhaps he should have been. I didn't know what I was doing. Despite my firm assurances, I was in no way prepared to manage the editorial page of the *Herald*. I had a plan, yes, but it was not a plan of which Papa would have approved.

After a roundabout of sweaty embraces, Lilla and Papa rattled away in the car, leaving me in charge of their home and their livelihood. I stepped onto the porch as rain started to fall, earlier than its usual afternoon appearance. The first warm drops came slowly and scattershot, like the exploratory notes of one of Mama's piano pieces, then they picked up the tempo and fell in a furious and prolonged crescendo. I lowered myself onto the wobbly three-legged stool and pulled it close to the porch railing for a front row viewing of the rain.

Water rushed toward the ground, screening my eyes so thoroughly that I thought perhaps I had closed them. The sound of the rainstorm persisted, manic and glorious, reminding me of a concerto by Rachmaninoff that Mama once played. I smiled. I took a deep breath and listened. The storm was beautiful in its madness, and though I dismissed the thought as preposterous, I couldn't help thinking that through it, Mama had come to keep me company while Papa and Lilla were gone.

The city room at the *Herald* hummed with conceit. With Papa away, Judge and Garrett and I were orphaned, yet like the best kind of Dickensian orphans, we were wily and self-assured. I kept hidden the terror I felt each time I submitted the editorial page for printing. I boasted to the men about what a good job we had done when we left the office late in the night, and they agreed.

My editorial columns were, to be very honest, low in accuracy but replete with grammatical correctness and sophisticated sentence structure. That was the first prong of my plan—to so stun, or perhaps confuse, *Herald* readers with my elegant prose that they forgot to concern themselves with my content. The tactic worked. For two days.

On the third day, Judge Hill dropped a copy of the *Metropolis* on my desk, folded so that the typeface of their editorial page screamed in my face.

"Hattie Carpenter has your number," Judge said.

Hattie Carpenter, the *Metropolis* editor, did indeed have my number. In a column whose obsessive quotation marks strangled the life from the words that they gripped, Hattie exposed the mistakes in my recent editorials. The Halcyon Hotel had opened in 1906, not 1905. The Fort Dallas Park houses sat on thirteen acres, not fifteen. The tone of her piece was one of sheer delight, peppered with an implicit invitation daring me to test her knowledge of local history.

"This woman," I said, trying to hide my panic, "uses far too many quotation marks to act so superior."

Judge shook his head. He spoke kindly but firmly.

"You're disgracing the paper, Marjory."

At that moment, a headache began at my left temple. Over the next several days, the headache advanced, curling like a snake around my left orbital socket and down the side of my nose. The pain was constant, relentless. Probably, excessive stress was the cause. But couldn't excessive stress cause so many more troubles in the head?

"Is this what it felt like, Mama?" I asked the dark night, while I lay curdled in my hot sheets. "When your troubles started?"

The night did not answer, but I felt Mama there, watching. Waiting. Enjoying the chance to wander around while Papa was gone, to search Lilla's spice rack, to rifle through her underwear drawer. Each pulse of my headache made Mama's footsteps louder, her wheezy songs louder. I began to fear the implications of the headache more than the pain that it brought.

"This is not going to happen," I whispered, resolving again, as I had in Central Park, not to go mad. Then I peeled the top sheet from my body like a strip of old sunburned skin and set upon the only headache remedy I could think of: implementing the second part of my ridiculous plan for running the *Herald*.

With a regrettable kind of exhilaration, I began raiding the wire services for good editorials. The Associated Press, Reuters, they all had very good writers. Not one to plagiarize, of course, I put the credits in small—very small—print at the bottom of the page.

"Hattie doesn't know what to do about you," Myrtle confided over lemonade one June afternoon. "She's furious about the wire pieces but thinks it would be tacky to point it out in a column."

With that, my headache began its slow dissolution. I might not have fooled Hattie Carpenter, but at least I shut her up.

"Anyway," Myrtle went on, swirling the ice in her glass, "on to more important matters." She smiled, her little nose wrinkling. "A few of us are renting a house on the beach this summer. Fisher finally finished filling it in. Do you want to join us? There's plenty of room."

I swallowed the last of my tart lemonade.

"How would I get to work?" I asked.

Myrtle smiled wider, pleased that I hadn't immediately said no.

"You can take a jitney over the Collins Bridge. Or there's a ferry. It looks like a washtub, but it really does float. Mostly. I think."

"That's reassuring."

I studied the bottom of my empty glass. Would Mama stay alone in Papa's house or follow me to the beach?

"Besides," Myrtle chirped on, "we'll all have to get to work. Me and Frank. The Keenes. Andy."

Andy?

I looked at Myrtle. She winked. She actually winked.

"Okay, fine," I said, cheeks hot. "I'll go."

Myrtle clapped like a girl at the circus and poured more lemonade. As our refilled glasses sweated and the promise of the summer grew larger, Myrtle prattled off details I was too flustered to hear.

Until Carl Fisher got to it, Miami Beach had been nothing more than a strip of palmetto scrub sitting off the eastern tip of the peninsula. The sandbar had peeped, just barely, above the waterline like a wary crocodile, guarding the mainland, perhaps, from marauders. On the bay side, the steamy strip had been full of leggy, tangle-rooted mangroves and the creatures that loved them: immortal snakes; iguanas with stony eyes and sticky tongues; mosquitoes in such abundance they darkened the sunset. It had been a place where only a dreamer could look and see treasure.

When we parked ourselves there in the summer of 1916, the beach was not yet the vacation paradise Fisher had promised his rich northern friends. The place was desolate and pale, its foundation literally exhumed from the sea floor and piled higher and higher upon the ancient sandbar until the strip looked something like land. Hundreds of tons of Everglades topsoil had been spread like birthday cake frosting over it all, and saplings—scrawny and wrong—had been poked into the cake as its unsteady candles.

"This is Fisher's paradise?" I asked, incredulous. It wasn't hard to imagine wealthy northerners rattling down the Dixie Highway for days, then crossing the bay on the two and a half wooden miles of Collin's Bridge, only to arrive here, in the vacant memory of a swamp.

"Not yet," Andy said. "But he'll do it. He's going to raise paradise right out of the sea."

Andy's bottomless optimism, his sugary belief in the future magnificence of Miami and its various appendages, created a pain in my chest that was, in its tone and ferocity, almost maternal. I pushed this sensation quickly away. Maternal was not the feeling I wanted when it came to Andy Walker.

"Isn't he almost bankrupt?" I asked.

"Fisher?" Andy shrugged. "He's always almost bankrupt, and then he isn't. That guy will never give up."

There was, in the breeze that blew over the beach that summer, a sense of upheaval, of nature redefined. It was as if we had moved into Carl Fisher's unfinished dream: streets laid out but not paved; houses marked but not built. The silent battle of prehistory and progress raged all around us, and I began to have a sense of whose side I was on.

"Maybe it would be a good thing if Fisher doesn't finish the beach," I mused one Sunday morning as the shadows of sea cows drifted through the still water. "He could leave it just like this. We could watch the jungle regrow and take over. It would be like looking back millions of years and seeing the Earth come into existence."

"It'll never happen," Andy stated. "I'm telling you,

Marjory, Fisher does not let things go. And besides, people all over the country want Miami Beach. They need it. They just don't know it yet."

He smiled. Something in that grin suggested there were other things that other people might want but not yet fully know. My cheeks flared, and I could not look at Andy. I watched the ground. A tiny crab scuttled into a hole in the sand.

Our house was less of a house than a hut, a shelter left by the workers who had cleared Fisher's swamp. One room. One table. One chair that nobody bothered to use. No lights, no doors, no glass in the windows. No matter. We stored our work clothes in the house and lived on the sand, running like children for no reason at all, getting drunk on the lovely scent of sea lavender that wafted over the ridge.

"Race you," Andy would say, boyish and earnest, and we'd crash into the surf and head out to sea.

We swam farther each time, pushing ourselves into deeper, colder water. If we got far enough, the beach succumbed to the horizon. The strip of sand and its saplings nearly disappeared.

"I didn't know I loved salt water," I told him one morning as we floated in liquid sunrise. "I used to go fishing with my grandfather sometimes, but it wasn't like this. There was no connection to the water. It was just something to sit on. A road."

We floated on our backs, splayed like starfish, the waves heaving us up, pulling us close, the ocean our endless dance floor. We held hands, watched stars evaporate in the growing daylight. I was, during these moments, acutely aware of Andy's skin—the heat of it, the nearness of it, the plentitude of it beyond the cover of his bathing clothes. So much of wanting him, of desiring him (which I now clearly did) appeared in the form of an unbearable urge to be close to his skin, to touch— perhaps breach—his most basic and final barrier.

When we kissed on the beach after a swim, I resented the granules of sand that clung to our bodies because they impeded absolute contact.

"You smell like seaweed," I said as we stood in the surf.

"Probably better than how I usually smell," Andy answered. His self-deprecation, in its obvious falsity, gave him an air of playfulness but also of complete confidence. Only someone sure of who he was could make fun of himself for being something he wasn't.

Andy and I would return to the hut separately, fooling no one but maintaining at least the pretense of decorum. Myrtle, believing herself a conspirator, looked away with a smirk.

Maybe I should have felt guilty. Probably, I felt guilty for not feeling guilty. I was, after all, knowingly defying my father's instructions about not carrying on with Andy Walker. But on this scrap of unreal beachfront, in this outpost of a city that was itself nothing more than an afterthought, I felt freer than I'd ever felt in my life. I felt unburdened. Awakened. Civility and its rules were a lifetime away.

"Kiss me," I'd instruct Andy while we boiled water for coffee over the morning campfire. And he would. Without hesitation. A most delightful sort of nausea would wash over me then, as if my body simply could not handle the ache that a kiss from Andy inspired.

At night, Judge Hill usually drove me to the beach after work. Each time the front wheels of his car rolled onto the first wooden slat of the Collin's bridge, we both held our breaths, as if we did not believe in the bridge, in its strength or ability to transport us over the water. In the dark, the bridge was a complete leap of faith. We trusted that the next slat, and then the next, would appear beneath the chassis, but we could not say for sure that it had until we were over it, and even then, it was not entirely clear that the bridge wasn't just a mirage, a magic trick conjured by Carl Fisher to bring people to his funny playland.

"How long are you going to be staying?" Judge asked one night as we drove through our suspended disbelief.

"I don't know," I said. "It was supposed to be a week, but we're just staying on. Nobody really wants to leave."

Judge nodded. It occurred to me, probably later than it should have, that Papa had asked Judge to keep an eye on me while he was away.

"Be careful, then," Judge offered when we'd survived the trip across the dark water and driven as close to the hut as we could. "It's damn near a wilderness out here."

I gathered my bags and turned back to Judge.

"Maybe that's why I like it."

Judge shook his head. He turned the Ford slowly and drove off at barely a crawl, as if he expected I might change my mind about staying and chase after the car.

The hut was empty. A lantern burned on the table, giving enough light to change by. I quickly took off my work clothes, hung them carelessly with the others, and groped through my pile of stuff until I found my bathing suit. Still wet, the suit was a struggle, but one I'd grown used to because it never dried. I never gave it a chance.

My friends had the fire going in its usual spot close to the water. I could hear them singing—cowboy songs the Keenes had learned when they traveled out west. The songs were of wide-open land, of mountains and deserts and the calls of coyotes. The words felt out of place here. South Florida needed songs of its own.

Beyond the circle of firelight, the ocean water glowed, phosphorescent and bright, as if stars had fallen right out of the sky and sunk in the shallows. The heady scent of seagrape rolled down from the ridge to the foam at the shoreline, promising sea turtles protection, promising me exultation. Something was different this night.

Not wanting to interrupt the sad song, I greeted my friends with only a smile. They smiled back through the lyrics and all shifted slightly, making room for me in the circle. There was, I noticed that night, no question of which way they inched. Everyone moved so that space opened near Andy. That we'd sit together was now a given.

His arm circled my shoulder. I burrowed into the space at his side.

"Keene's blotto," Andy whispered into my hair. "See him sweating?"

"We're all sweating," I whispered back. "It's July in Miami."

"Yeah, but just wait. When he stops singing, he's going to start retelling bad jokes about the Kaiser."

A few minutes later, I found myself laughing at Keene's jokes, not because they were funny but because they'd been so aptly predicted.

"It's blowing in, even here," Keene wheezed when he'd run out of punch-lines. "Even in our little wilderness. The war's blowing in. Smell it?" Keene sniffed hard at the air.

Helen, Keene's fiancée, patted his hand as a comfort and warning. Keene paid no attention.

"The Somme," he went on. "You people writing about that in your papers yet? We can't pretend it's not happening just because we're over here knee-deep in alligator shit."

"Nobody's pretending," Frank said through the firelight. "It's just not our war."

"Bull shit," Keene spat. "Chlorine gas, Frank. Chlorine gas makes it everyone's war, goddammit."

Helen pulled on Keene's arm. He shook her off like a fly.

"Wilson knows we can't stay out of this. You'll see. Sure as Satan's in hell, we'll be in this war soon enough. Because we already are. Or we should be. Do we have a national conscience or not? That's what I want to know. Chlorine gas, Frank. On boys. Boys young as Andy."

Little Helen tugged Keene to standing. He wobbled on the uneven sand and dragged a hand through his sweaty hair. "Good night," she said to us. An apology.

Half Keene's size, Helen kept the man upright as they stumbled together toward the house.

When they were gone, the four of us still at the campfire exhaled at once, sending the flames even higher. Our silence was desperate. Keene's truth had been too much for us tonight.

"We've got to keep him away from the bottle," Myrtle said. It wasn't clear from her voice if this was an attempt at levity. If so, it hadn't worked. The renewed silence was torture.

"I think I'm done for tonight," Andy finally announced, easing me away from his side and unfolding his limbs to standing. He was leaving. This felt somehow like a personal rejection, as if I had done something to ruin his night. Had I? I didn't think so. It was the talk of the war that had done it, that had flattened our spirits and sucked the mirth from the air. Damn your drunken diatribe, Frank Keene. Damn it. Just damn it.

"Marjory?"

I looked up. Andy's hand extended toward me. The hand was an offer, an invitation.

"You want me to come?"

Andy nodded.

Accepting his hand in front of Frank and Myrtle would be nothing less than a scandal.

I lifted my hand and placed it in Andy's. Our palms sparked, then pushed so tightly together the skin couldn't breathe. He urged me up from the sand. Without saying goodbye, we left Frank and Myrtle at the campfire and walked away from its light.

The shoreline was endless. We moved along the edge between water and land, our feet salted, our balance unsteadied by the dark and the gentle suck of receding waves. Our mood was serious, profound. Gone was the goofiness, the playful banter we usually used to hide our trembling chins and quivering knees.

We stopped walking and drew ourselves close. The smash of the waves became louder—ocean current and blood rushing around us, through us, primal and unstoppable. There were not enough ways to fit together, not enough hands or enough tongues to touch enough places. The phosphorescent sea rolled on and on, over our toes, our ankles, until we were standing together in liquid stardust. The talk of the war, of all those poisoned young men, gave urgency to the beauty around us.

Everything, it seemed, had come to this. My teenage years at the edge of the dance floor. The midnight conversations with my Wellesley girls. The honeymoon with Kenneth. All of it had been bits and pieces of love and lust, clues about the secrets between men and women and the desires that can drive them to blindness, but not until now had it all fused together. Not until this moment, with Andy's sweat on my neck and the taste of his eagerness sweet in my mouth, had I understood the torrential force created by liking and loving and wanting and aching for someone who was driven to breathlessness because he felt the same way about me.

"Here," I said, and we lowered ourselves to the ground.

Our weight, our movements, displaced the soft sand, and we lay in a rut custom-made by the earth—a grave of sorts, where we could bury everything that had ever happened before and rise into a life filled with all that would come after. The moment—its significance, its heft—was almost too pure to bear.

"I'm not twenty-five," Andy confessed in a rush, feeling it, too. "I just said I was because I wanted you to . . . I don't know . . . to see me as equal."

I kissed him hard, to show him I didn't care.

"I'm twenty-one," he said, testing. I kissed him again. His hands were under my bathing suit. His body pressed long against mine. I arched into him, drowning in happiness, and returned his honesty with some of my own.

"I'm still married," I said.

Time fell from its precipice and hit the ground with a thud. Stunned but not broken, the fallen micro-seconds tried to reorganize themselves, tried to find linearity again in their shaken plane of existence. Moonlight and shadow contoured the night clouds, which bloomed like summer hydrangeas, while time faltered and I waited for Andy to say he didn't care either.

He had to not care. Because clearly the two of us answered to deeper impulses. Clearly, we were unbounded by the rules and restrictions that controlled everyone else. Out here, on unsettled land, we existed outside of the regime of convention, outside even of time.

Didn't we?

Andy had stopped moving. He seemed to have stopped breathing. The hush of the waves had replaced the hurried sound of his breath in my ear.

"I mean," I said, lifting myself on my elbows, "I am getting divorced. But it takes a long time. Years, sometimes. He's got all the power. But it's going to happen. I'm not *really* married." I kissed Andy again. His lips were slack against mine.

"Marjory."

He spoke with deflated passion and something else, something deceptively sharp, like a bread knife.

"What?"

"I don't think this can happen right now."

Andy pulled back. He looked away, but not before I saw that that sharpness was pain.

Stung, perhaps even shamed, by the rejection, I nodded and struggled from the sand pit to standing. I kept my arms wrapped tightly around me so that Andy would not brush against me and feel the fire, the rage, coursing just under my skin. Never, not even during those hollow nights squatting in New York City tenements, had I ever despised Kenneth Douglas so much.

I walked back toward the dying fire. Andy followed a few steps behind—too much of a gentleman to let me walk back alone, and too much of a coward to come take my hand.

In the days that followed our collapse on the beach, I reconstructed events until I believed that *I'd* told Andy no, that *I'd* decided extramarital sex was not worth the mess, that *I'd* decided to heed Papa's instructions and not get too deeply involved with Andy Walker. Remolding the past turned out to be easy, if the revisions were wanted badly enough. Like the fat subtropical sun, though, these revisions disappeared at the end of the day, and my night-thoughts were full of heartbreak and shame.

I avoided being alone with Andy. Maybe I needed to leave the beach and retreat back to my father's house in Riverside, but I just couldn't go. Fisher's mutant finger of beach land had curled around my belt loop and would not let me go.

Now that Andy and I did not take our morning swim, I'd begun watching the turtles drift through the seagrass before breakfast. They floated with arrogant ease, so sure of their purpose, so sure of how to go about meeting their basic needs: instincts honed over millennia, impulses acted upon without judgment. I sighed. How was it that I'd come to envy a sea turtle?

"Marjory?"

That voice, so gentle and deep. I didn't turn around. Perhaps I'd been hoping for a conciliatory speech of sorts, and now that it was coming, I hated the idea of it, hated the pretense of it. I loathed the notion that I had to be soothed, but like a child, soothing was just what I needed.

"Don't bother," I said.

Please bother, I hoped.

The sand muted his steps, but I sensed him walk closer, felt the latent heat of him warm my space.

"Then I won't say it," he said.

Andy crouched on his heels before me. Sitting like that, he could not get his feet to lay flat on the ground, and he tottered a little, blown like a palm frond by the breeze.

"You're blocking my view," I whispered. "I can't see the turtles."

Andy moved his face toward mine, softly wrapped my cheeks in his palms. Our eyelashes came close to touching. I inhaled. He smelled of black coffee and the baked-on remains of old ocean water.

This kiss was as full of impatience as it had been a few nights before, but there was in it now too persistence and promise, an implicit pledge to wait out the realities that kept us apart.

"I'm sorry," I said. "I should have told you sooner."

Andy smiled. His face was still close and glowed with anticipation. It was the same giddy optimism he had when he talked about Miami. That was a very good sign.

"Our time will come," Andy promised. "You'll see."

I should kiss him again. I should kiss him again before he moves away. Shouldn't I?

But I did not have time to decide. Andy tipped on his toes, pressed his lips against mine and left them swimming there long enough for a teardrop of my relief to roll into the trench of our cheeks.

"I love you," he said.

I felt my life gathering speed, swirling wildly around a motionless center, where I sat with Andy Walker on the shore of delirium.

"I . . ." It was hard to say. "I love you, too."

The waves grabbed hold of our words, stole them out to sea to put in an oyster, where they could grow into a pearl. Andy eased sideways. We sat shoulder to shoulder and watched the new sun stretch its burning tentacles over the sea. With night finally finished, the turtles moved on, hitching a ride on the current and disappearing into the deep. I wasn't sure I agreed with him, about Miami or about us, but the most joyful thing about Andy Walker was not whether he was actually right but that he believed he could be.

"What makes you so sure?" I asked, watching the last of the turtles retreat. "That our time will come?"

"I just am."

"No," I said, needing more. "How can you assume everything will be better one day? We'll work out. Miami will grow. Fisher will finish this ridiculous beach." There was an edge to my voice that I hadn't intended.

The rising sun snagged in Andy's loose curls. Beneath them, he watched the waves foam.

"You haven't answered my question," I reminded him after a moment. "I still want to know *why*. Why do you have so much faith in in the future? What's the secret, Andy Walker?"

Andy's face softened in a way I hadn't seen it soften before—jocular edge fading, screen falling away from sad eyes.

"You don't really want to know," he said.

"Yes, I do."

"Once you know, you'll wish you didn't."

"We'll see about that."

"Okay," Andy relented. He squeezed his eyes shut, then squeezed them shut further. "It was July, in the afternoon. A week before I turned eight." Andy loosened his grip on his eyeballs, let the lids work themselves up. "The panhandle heat was so bad, I swear I thought I might sweat my skin right off my bones. My mother was feeling it, too.

She got so hot, she opened the front of her dress, kept swabbing hard at her neck with the edge of her apron. There were streaks of pink on her skin. She'd thrown up twice while rolling out dough for my birthday bread, bloody chunks of breakfast eggs and last night's potatoes. 'This heat,' she said each time, shaking her head, not complaining. Never complaining. She told me to put the dough on the front stoop to rise, and then she let herself down on our one cushioned chair. I put the pan on the stoop. I went over to her. She pulled me onto her lap.

"'Bake it for three-quarters of an hour, Andrew Walker. And make sure Mabel drinks some water before she eats any,' she said. 'She'll be wanting some when she's up from her nap.' Then my mother closed her eyes, put her nose in my hair, and breathed in really hard. She held me tight and breathed and breathed until the blood bubbled in her throat and she drowned in herself. She was twenty-nine."

So many dead mamas. So many mama-less kids. Did Andy sometimes talk to his dead mother, too?

I looked sideways at Andy. He was so handsome, even in grief. The reverberations of his words faded away and his cheerful veneer begin to reconstitute itself on his face.

"Progress could have saved her," he said, grabbing my hand in his and jimmying it like a saltshaker. "Don't you see, Marjory? Telephones. Automobiles. Medicine. X-rays—have you ever seen one of those? Just think about what an X-ray machine can do, looking inside the body like that. Think about what an X-ray could have seen inside my mother."

I wasn't sure an X-ray would have been able to see anything inside his mother, but to find hope in such tragedy was a gift, a gift that made him perhaps the most extraordinary person I'd ever known.

"Even Miami Beach," he carried on, rising to his knees. "Let Fisher build it. Let him make it magnificent. People will come. The city will grow. There'll be a university. A hospital. Forward, forward, forward, Marjory." Here he took a big breath, gathered strength. "A few years later, my father took Mabel and went back to Kentucky. He said the land made more sense there, said the heat in Kentucky just held you tight, didn't all the way choke you the way it did in north Florida. He thought the heat killed her. Nothing you could do about that! But I knew better. I went south when they left. The industrialists were going to set their sights on Florida soon. Flagler already had. Fisher was forming his vision. These were men who didn't just leave things to God."

Andy's words settled around us, his ideas rising in the heat like birthday bread.

"And you?" I finally asked.

"Me?" He grinned, excited, and jumped up to standing. "Why, I document it all in the *Metropolis*. I make sure everyone knows what great things are happening. I'm not one of those men. Never could be. Wouldn't want to be. But I sure as hell can tell the world what they're doing."

I was quiet, almost afraid to ask my next question.

"And me?"

Andy pulled me to my feet so I could join him at the edge of the world. His answer came immediately.

"We'll go forward together."

This time he turned both my hands to saltshakers. His eyes were eager, puppy-like.

"I don't know how to explain it," he went on. "I've never met a woman like you, Marjory. Even when you were just standing there on the side of the road, waiting for the motorcade, there was something about you. You looked impatient. Like you couldn't wait to get your claws into Fisher. You looked like someone who might have a chance at beating me in a debate."

"A chance?"

"Fair enough. You looked like someone who *could* beat me in a debate."

"So you plucked me off the side of the road like a delicate flower."

"You're a lot of things, Marjory Stoneman, but a delicate flower is not one of them."

"Stoneman Douglas."

"What?"

"My full name is Marjory Stoneman Douglas. I'm married. That's why we're having this discussion, remember?"

Andy laughed.

"Fine," he said. "I love you, Marjory Stoneman Douglas. Now please get divorced already."

I smiled.

"Okay," I said.

We were quiet for a long time. The tide pushed the waves closer to our bare toes.

"What about the war?" I asked, pushing, pushing, testing the strength of this reconciliation. "Doesn't war lead to progress? The Kaiser has airplanes, Andy! Motorcars in the sky! If that's not progress, I don't know what is. So does that make war a good thing?"

"I don't think you could say war is ever good, even if it leads to progress. The sooner the war ends, the sooner the world can recover and get back to moving forward the right way. Airplanes? They would have happened regardless."

For a moment, we were quiet.

"I wonder which will come first," I said, as if setting up a joke. "My divorce or the end of the war."

"I want them both. Tomorrow. Tonight. Right now."

I laughed.

"You're going to have to wait longer than that."

"That is extremely unfortunate," Andy said.

Our fingers found each other, wove themselves into a determined grip. I tipped my head to Andy's shoulder and sighed. How strange everything was in this mangled, marvelous pit of the world.

Ordinary life resumed. The six of us left the beach hut one morning with our arms full of sand-crusted clothes and the feeling, unarticulated and vague, that we were leaving a rare bit of magic behind. Helen had not entirely recovered from the embarrassment of Keene's drunken outburst, but even she, in her diminutive way, was reluctant to let go of the beach.

"Maybe we'll do this again next summer?" she asked as we stepped from the shadow of the hut's roof into the sun.

"Sure." "Yes." "That would be super."

We all hurried to commit to next summer, though even as the words spilled from our mouths, we tasted their blandness. Our weeks on the beach could not be replicated. There had been something both timeless and fleeting about them. In a year, Miami Beach would be different, built up. The six of us would be different. My chest seized with the trauma of change, and I knew we could never be here like this again.

But that did not mean I couldn't come back to the beach next year with Andy, perhaps as his wife, if the Florida state courts got down to business. We seemed to have committed to an engagement of sorts. There was no ring, no proposal, no announcement in the society pages of either newspaper (I would have liked to see Hattie Carpenter try to scoop me on that one), but there was an understanding that we renewed with each sweaty kiss, each captured glance across the crowd at an event we were covering for our papers. We were together.

Papa and Lilla returned full of stories about their adventures out west.

"Mustangs," Lilla marveled, breathless with memory. "Running around like big, hairy fire ants."

Sometimes I wished I could tell them about my own summer adventure—how far out I'd swum into the sea, how much in love I was for the first time in my life—but I knew the memories would be diluted with the telling, even if Papa didn't explode upon hearing them.

"The west is so grand, Marjory. So wide and untapped." He hugged me sideways with one arm and sighed. "But I'm glad to be back in this swamp. I really am. The west is for men too young to know better and too old to leave. Those of us in between, we just shouldn't stay."

I believed he meant what he said. It had been, as far as I knew, the first time he'd gone west just for fun, not chasing riches or false opportunity. It also had been the first time he'd returned east without a hangdog expression and a profound sense of failure. Maybe Lilla was the richness he'd always been seeking. Maybe with her, he'd finally stopped looking for more. I thought these thoughts quickly, in case Mama, who hadn't entirely vacated Papa's house yet, could still somehow hear them.

"Everything go all right with the paper?" he asked. "While we were away?"

"Of course, Papa."

Neither of us mentioned the wire service reports. If he knew, he spared me the humiliation of saying so.

"Did Judge fill you in on everything already?"

"Yes," Papa assured me. "He told me everything."

No talk of the beach house, of Judge driving me there after work. We smiled at each other, trusting yet unsure.

Sometimes I watched my father in his office at the *Herald*. He sat erect but contained, subdued. He never kicked his heels onto the desk, never stretched his arms wide and held his head with his palms. He had no poses of domination, of powerful repose. The *Herald* was, I came to understand, his consolation prize. Fated never to be a titan of industry or even a circuit court judge, he'd settled instead for newspaper editor, a position from which he could check and critique the men he'd tried to be.

I knew what the *Metropolis* meant to Andy. I was pretty sure I knew what the *Herald* meant to Papa. But what did the newspaper mean to me? The answer was elusive, and, distracted by love and the waning years of my youth, I didn't try too hard to figure it out.

I hadn't intended to conflate my divorce with the end of the war when I'd asked Andy which would come first. Though pointed, and not entirely kind, the question had been mostly a joke. But in the weeks and months after that conversation, the overwhelming uncertainty of both ordeals became twisted together, our lives carrying on under their shadow—a shadow made longer, wider, broader by its muta-tion. Alone, the darkness of this huge shadow became truly insufferable. Together, though, Andy and I could suffer along, each buoying the other while we awaited the sun.

Or so I believed.

"Another letter came from the lawyer in Orlando," I told him one night after a movie. We were drinking bottles of Ola-Gay as we walked. The moon was full and heavy in the sky, a paperweight keeping the world from flying off orbit.

"Let me guess." His jaw pulsed. It did that a lot lately. "The divorce is still pending. Information forthcoming when available."

"Essentially, yes."

Andy threw one arm in the air. This was the point in the conversation where we usually pulled each other through the disgust, the despair, with a joke or a squeeze.

I hooked my arm around his elbow.

"Where will we live?" I asked. This had become a favor-ite game. "When we're married. Riverside? Or maybe the grapefruit grove? Merrick is making noise about buying up the land around his father's church and developing it."

Andy stopped walking, turned to me.

"I can't stand it anymore, Marjory."

"I know."

"You don't. I'm not just talking about the divorce." Andy sweated along his hairline. The beads slipped down his face, crooked and slow. "It's the war, too. Keene was right. It's everyone's war. You can't tell me it's not."

"I'm not trying to tell you it's not."

"Then you know that it's my war, too. If it's everyone's war, then it's also mine. I'm a twenty-two-year-old man living on Earth in the year 1916. This is my war."

The moon seemed to extinguish its light. All I could see was the dizzying glow of peripatetic fireflies.

"What are you saying, Andy?"

"I can't keep waiting for Wilson or your husband to wake up and do what they're morally obliged to do. I signed on with the American Ambulance Service."

Fireflies sparked near his head, set aglow by the heat of his words. The world was exploding in microbursts.

"You did?"

Andy nodded.

"It's already done?"

He nodded again. "I'll be back when the war ends. You'll be divorced by then, and we'll get past this whole stupid mess."

Abruptly, and without intention, I remembered the toilet in my grandparents' house in Taunton. How proud my grandfather was of that toilet—first indoor flusher on the street!—as if it had been an automobile or telephone. When I pulled the toilet's delicate chain, water swirled inward, downward, sucked away to the unseen pit of putrefaction. The war was that toilet now, pulling young men from all over the world, pulling Andy, into its rotting stink.

"I've waited for someone before," I said, thinking of Kenneth's long months in Caldwell. "It's miserable."

Andy offered all kinds of commendable assurances—he was sorry, he'd be careful, he loved me so much he had to do this—but his voice was already far away, as if coming to me through the breathy whorls of a conch shell washed up on the shores of Brittany.

He left a week later. Standing on the corner of 12th Street and Avenue D, our bellies full of dinner neither of us had wanted to eat, we made an attempt at goodbye.

"I guess there's nothing to say," I said. On his feet were heavy brown boots he'd never worn before.

"My train leaves at midnight."

I glanced at Andy's face, but I couldn't bear the innocence, the sweet righteousness, and had to look quickly back to the boots.

"Hey, Marjory?"

"Yes?"

"You see those stars there?" he asked, pointing. I forced myself to look up. "If you go from that one to that one to that one, and then over there, it makes a gondola. I believe that constellation is called Lucky Night."

I had to look down again, quickly.

"I know it well," I said to his boots.

We stood a while longer in the purgatory known as farewell. Couples passed on the sidewalk around us. A stray dog trolled for scraps.

"I'm going to meet some friends now," Andy finally said. "For a late snack before the train goes. Do you want to come?"

I hated this invitation nearly as much as I hated the fact that he was going. Did I want to go be one in a crowd of admirers who would see him off to war as a herd?

I shook my head no. We shifted uncomfortably in the heavy night-heat, a confounding, impossible heat that only the dawn, with its promise of fresh sun, would relieve.

"Well, okay. Okay, then. Well." Andy stammered on, words turning to shreds of misshapen sentiment, big brown boot shifting, stamping out cigarettes that weren't there. "All right. Okay."

Andy wasn't the first man to tromp wide-eyed into a warzone. I wasn't the first woman to love a man so much that she hated him for choosing to go. I knew all of this. I knew my sorrow was far from unique or even uncommon. Women had seen their men off to war for as long as there had been women and men. The difference was that I had made him go. The divorce that wouldn't come. The interminable waiting. The powerlessness to make anything happen faster. He'd needed to do something. Anything. He'd chosen war.

"Be safe," I said, a useless admonition if ever there was one.

Andy nodded. His mouth stopped moving, and I warned myself to savor the kiss that was coming, to remember it as it was happening, to long for it before it was over. But Andy didn't kiss me. He held out his arm. We shook hands.

The train took Andy away. I heard it. A hollow hoot at midnight, a sound that curled over the darkened city like a lone tendril of breath, winding into my open window and flattening me against my sweat-dampened bed. The whistle faded, absorbed into the night. Was there ever a lonelier sound than the silence that followed a waning train blast?

I turned to the ocean. The mornings I liked best were the ones when the water's mood mirrored my own—angry and restless. Discontent. Frothing. Sometimes I swam. Mostly, I stood knee-deep in the surf, letting the retreating waves force me deeper into the sand while looking east. Warships steamed somewhere in this very ocean. Warplanes flew over the distant cousins of these very waves. Andy was there, on the other side of it all, perhaps sometimes glancing at the wild Atlantic and thinking of me.

Eighty-seven mornings passed before a letter arrived for me from France. Enough time for a litter of Florida panther to gestate. Enough time for a great blue heron to lay and hatch three clutches of eggs. In all that time, I had not heard from, or of, Andy Walker.

"He's been taking injured soldiers from the battlefield in the Ardennes."

Fairchild, the botanist, and a few other guests were over for dinner with Papa and Lilla. He asked again about the young newspaperman he'd taken into the swamp long ago, and I'd answered, eager to share my new news.

"Ah, so that's why I haven't seen his articles in the paper," Fairchild deduced. Then, a moment later, "He's a good man. Bright and funny. He'll be all right."

I looked at Papa. He was considering the piece of tomato on the end of his fork.

"Andy's become quite taken with the war," I told Fairchild. "He's enlisting in the Lafayette Esquadrille."

Fairchild's eyebrows rose.

"Aviation?" Fairchild asked. "Americans flying as French?"

"Yes." I braced for the now-familiar cramp in my chest that came whenever I thought of Andy flying in a sardine tin over the death fields of Europe.

"Lordy," Lilla whistled, shaking her head.

Papa raised his eyes from the tomato and looked at me.

"It's admirable, what Mr. Walker has done," Papa said. "War is never the best choice, but sometimes it's the only one."

I loved Papa so much at that moment that I had to come up with a cheeky retort or risk collapsing in tears right there at the Jefferson table.

"You keep talking like that, Papa," I said, "and someone's going to brand the *Herald* a jingoist paper."

"I'm pretty sure someone already has," Lilla said.

"So be it." Papa shrugged. "I'd rather the paper be jingoist than unprincipled."

"Plants are unprincipled, though they'll do what they can to survive. Fascinating, really, how human they are." Fairchild looked through his thick-rimmed glasses at me. "You really should come with me, Marjory, into the Everglades. I'm hunting the fabled vanilla orchid. You can help me look. I think you'll find it a welcome distraction."

"Go, Marjory," Frances, now Pete Robineau's wife, spoke up. "Believe me, you need a distraction." She lifted her mewling infant from her shoulder and settled the child on her lap, where they cooed at one another. The sightline between mother and baby seemed to glow as brightly as the candles on the Jefferson table.

"How long has Pete been in France?" Lilla asked.

"Six months," Francis answered. The rest of us at the table heaved a quiet, awful sigh. Vivian, the baby, was eleven weeks old.

I agreed to accompany Fairchild into the swamp, to enter the wilderness that raged beyond the edge of the city. Andy had done it. During what felt like a lifetime ago, Andy had ventured into the Everglades with the fervent, spectacled botanist.

I closed my eyes, ran the tip of one finger along the smooth grain of the table. Perhaps, out there among the elusive vanilla orchids, a scrap of Andy lingered where I might find it.

* * *

"It's not grass," Fairchild explained. He spoke softly, more to himself than to me. "People call it grass, but it's a sedge. Ancient and resilient. The bottoms are edible, but the tops will slice your hand right open."

Fairchild pushed his glasses up and his hat down. He existed, I'd begun to notice, in a constant state of rearranging.

With quick tug on each sleeve, followed by a deft and practiced yank, he pulled a long blade of sawgrass from its muddy moorings and offered me the tender end. I bit it, chewed, and was grateful for the oranges and nuts I'd packed in my sack.

We walked for hours across the wet prairie, water sloshing over the tops of our boots, creatures splashing out of our way before I could identify them. Sunlight burned through my hat, through my blouse. When I insisted we pause for a breath, I bent forward, palms pushing on thighs for support, not so much tired and worn as concerned about how much further we still had to go. I closed my eyes. When I opened them a breath later, I saw before me, in a single drop of water at the purple tip of a bladderwort petal, tiny rainbows refracting forever.

"Such little surprises," I marveled.

Fairchild smiled. "It's a whole universe of miniscule delights."

We sloshed on. The hammock Fairchild sought was in sight, rising from the sawgrass like a medieval castle. Over the swaying expanse of the wetland, the shadows of a few sparse cumulus clouds formed a steppingstone path, leading us to the entrance of the tree island.

The feeling that came over me as we stretched over the shadow stones and neared the hammock is not easily explained. It was neither a sudden passion for the Everglades nor an epiphany about its earthly uniqueness. It was, instead, something far less poetic. A hunch, perhaps, that this place would have significance for me, that its wild, anonymous expanse would somehow, inexplicably, turn personal.

"I think I miss Andy," I said. I'd meant only to think this, not say it. I reached for my sack. Maybe I needed some water.

Fairchild pulled his hat lower and spoke to me as we approached the shade of the tree island.

"When the children were small, Marian didn't travel with me on my expeditions. This made sense, of course. To haul them through far-flung malarial jungles would not have been wise. But I missed her terribly." Fairchild paused to unbutton and rebutton his cuffs. "During the day," he went on when his sleeves were secured, "I studied mangoes and lychees on overgrown tropical islands, and during the night, I dreamed feverish dreams of my dear wife." He stopped walking, leaned close to be sure I could hear. "So when Marian appeared, with a small child on each of her hips, standing on the raised platform of my basecamp hut in Siam, I clutched my head violently, believing I was suffering hallucinations." Fairchild grabbed at his hat, reenacting the scene. "When I realized it was actually her," he confessed, "it was the most magnificent moment of our whole marriage."

"That's lovely," I said, meaning it.

Fairchild hit himself on the head and let out an undignified grunt.

"Lovely, yea, but I intended, Marjory, for the story to be instructive. Prescriptive, even."

"How so, Dr. Fairchild?"

"Oh, Marjory," he sighed. He stooped to re-tuck each pant leg into the tops of his boots. "You need to hone your sense of romance. Go to Europe, my dear. Get yourself to France. You can operate a switchboard for the Army or join the Red Cross. There are any number of things women can do over there. Worst that happens, besides getting killed, is that you help out with the war effort. Best that happens, besides helping out with the war effort, is that you find Mr. Walker."

I stopped walking. The sound of the breeze through the sawgrass flooded my ears. That I could take action—that I could move beyond the sitting and waiting that had so bothered Andy—had not occurred to me before.

"You really think I can go overseas?" I asked.

But Fairchild had already entered the cool of the hammock. He was on his knees, peering beneath broad bromeliad leaves, searching, still searching for his elusive orchids. I approached, grateful for the break from the sun.

"Can I help?" I asked, forgetting about my previous question. I did not need Fairchild to give me the answer to that one.

"Take these." The botanist gave me a small pair of tweezers and showed me, with great enthusiasm, how to lift the leaves carefully.

We spent hours in the pillowy darkness of the tree island, the place like a secret among the flat, exposed wetlands of the rest of the Glades. Though we found two clamshell orchids and a longclaw, we did not come across a vanilla orchid.

"Next time," Fairchild assured himself, and I understood that both he and his wife Marian prized the risks and rewards of a nearly impossible search. "Let's be heading back."

As we adjusted our hats and boots for the return trek, I pictured myself walking below the mansard roofs of Paris. I pictured winsome gaslights along the Seine burning holes in the blue morning fog, and a man in an aviator's uniform leaning against one of those lamp posts, arms crossed. Waiting for me.

WEST OF MIAMI, 1920

Nature becomes my accomplice. The moon—the glowing heart of my old confidant, the timeless night sky—draws me toward it as it draws the tides, urging me closer with its invisible will. Tired legs churn. Lungs strain for air. As I move, sawgrass parts like a curtain, then, shielding and defiant, the knowing reeds sway closed behind me and deny knowledge of my recent passage. "Marjory who?" the ancient sedges would ask if confronted. "No one's been through here, Mister." Beneath my feet, liquid land congeals for the slightest of instants, hardening when my soles touch down, then melting again into that mysterious, primordial brew.

I am determined now. No longer desperate, I run with purpose, away from him and the ghosts of those like him. Away from heavy obligations disguised as love. Away from the expectations, the assumptions, that hurl my own needs into the gurgling, gaping pit of well-meaning avarice that has stalked me since Mama first fell apart on our porch that summer day. I will not be the birch tree. I will not become someone else's canoe. I will grow tall and grow deep, rising to challenges I choose to meet, pushing roots into soil that nourishes me.

I have no bitterness, though. These resolutions taste sweet.

Around me, the Everglades weep with relief. Someone understands, the enormous river of grass seems to shout. Someone knows how it feels to be hollowed, emptied, your essence seized in the service of others.

"Run faster," I tell myself. And I do. I run so fast, I nearly fly.

PARIS, 1918

Even though the war had been raging for years, Paris was an elegant hostess. The small, cobbled alleys and wide, rounded boulevards greeted me unapologetically, confident of their enduring appeal. Over these city streets hung a pungent perfume of warm bread and cat urine, faraway gunpowder and the tart smell of anxiety that must have been on the breaths of Parisians since the start of the war. I'd arrived at dawn. The light on the Seine was pinker, more velvety, than I'd imagined.

Nearly a year had passed since my trip into the Everglades with Fairchild. It was not as easy as one might have thought for a woman to insert herself into the war. I'd tried the Navy first, enlisting by accident when a woman I'd gone to interview for the *Herald*—the wife of the plumber who owned the plumbing shop across from the paper, a woman who was supposed to be the first in Florida to enlist—had not shown up. One minute I was swearing under my breath at the absent woman's lack of conviction; the next minute I was swearing aloud an oath of allegiance to the defense of my country. Suddenly, I was a yeoman first class, stationed at the headquarters of the naval reserve base on Biscayne Bay, issuing boat licenses and wondering how, exactly, this position was going to get me to France.

It wasn't.

I was a well-meaning but terrible yeoman and filled the gaps in my day with plots and plans. Papa had found a replacement for me at the *Herald*—one Miss Jefferson Bell, a woman from Ocala whose manner of speaking and general world view were so deeply southern there should have been an *e* at the end of her last name.

"Mahhhjory," she mewed when we met, "there is just so much I can *do* with this society page."

With my replacement secured at the paper, I was freed to use my spare time getting to Europe. I began with French lessons. Each evening, I'd leave the reserve base and walk up Flagler Street, past Seybold's Bakery and the variety store that displayed in the window a quill pen I quietly coveted. The trolley then chortled me along to Madame Faudel's small house, where we'd sit under a key lime tree and converse in my halting, sporadic French.

"*C'est bien,*" Madame would conclude as she picked her teeth with a long pinky nail.

On the way home, I'd often conjugate irregular verbs, *crois, crois, croit, croyons, croyez, croient,* remembering the company I'd kept in high school with Latin declensions. Other times, I'd compose an unwritten letter in French to my grandmother, who'd insisted I'd find the language useful one day. "*Tu avais raison, grand-mère,*" I'd write in my head. "*La langue est une clé qui ouvre les portes du monde.*" In my actual letters to Grandmother, I could not admit that I was now learning the language she'd so desperately tried to teach me. Perhaps this would be yet another thing for which she would struggle to forgive me.

With my French skills improving, I next needed to persuade Captain Johnston, the commandant, to discharge me from the Navy.

"I can't take shorthand," I explained when I finally had audience with him. He looked exactly like a commandant should look—tall and solid, authoritative, with a trim gray mustache and an ache for the sea in his eyes that I'd seen before in the eyes of my grandfather.

"And I type like a reporter, not a secretary. Oh, and I can't stop myself from correcting the grammar of my commanding officers when they dictate letters to me, and I've gotten the distinct impression that they do not appreciate this advice." I paused, then fumbled to mollify my tone, adding brightly, "Sir."

Captain Johnston's gaze slipped down his long nose until it settled on me.

"And what will you do with yourself if you're discharged, Yeoman Stoneman?"

I had not yet told anyone my plan, and the words sounded bold coming out of my mouth.

"I'll join the Red Cross, Sir. I hope to go overseas."

The commandant's gaze lingered a moment longer, then he nodded his head curtly and dismissed me.

My discharge came through three weeks later. The lieutenant commanders I'd worked for at the Biscayne Bay base—men who rarely smiled and never laughed—seemed even happier than I was to receive the news.

"I'm joining the American Red Cross," I told them. "Civilian Relief."

"Best of luck to you," they offered. Then, "And to the Red Cross."

I left Miami with an overstuffed suitcase and the blind belief that, amid the bountiful horrors of war, I would somehow have a beautiful reunion with Andy. It was July, nearly three years since I'd first arrived in Florida. Heat clung to my legs like a needy child until I promised the city I would return as soon as I could.

"I'm proud of you, Marjory," Papa said.

We stood awkwardly, each knowing the other was also remembering that summer day long ago, when I'd left with a suitcase the first time.

"Papa?" I asked, almost shyly.

"Yes?"

"Has there been any news about my divorce?"

Papa exhaled through his teeth, perhaps with a new understanding about my desire to go overseas.

"No, Marjory," he said. "Nothing yet."

I left, retracing my path to the northeast. I was to spend a short time in Manhattan with Carolyn before sailing to Europe.

"You're really here!" she exclaimed in the middle of Grand Central, hugging me close, dismissing with her embrace any question about the state of our friendship. The purple cloche on her head and department store hues on her face assured me she'd been fine during the years that I'd missed. "Where should we go first? I know a place with the most fabulous cannolis! Have you ever had one?"

Did we pick up the germs from the rattling door handle of the Italian pastry shop? From the coins we exchanged with the paperboy on the corner? Or perhaps from the darling baby, held aloft by his mother, who sneezed when Carolyn cooed in his face?

My two-day visit turned into a month-long convalescence, during which Carolyn and I kept each other from succumbing completely to the Spanish flu. Even with the windows flung open, the air in her apartment hung still and lifeless, stoking our feverish torpor. We sweated through layers of clothing, through sheets and cool towelettes, soaking the twill of her couch and the brocade of her chairs while we shivered, impossibly cold.

My mind detached from my body, thoughts drifting like a child's balloon through dream-sodden landscapes. I moaned—maybe out loud, maybe continuously—a miserable, monotonous keening that assured me I hadn't yet died. From the circuitous depths of my sickbed confusion, Kenneth appeared. Mud crusted his neck, his fingertips. His eyes were hollow, the skin around them pleated and thin. He sat himself down beside me on Carolyn's couch, stretched his legs like a flock of geese into a vee.

"You don't look so good," Kenneth noted.

I tried to tell him that he didn't look so good either, but I could not stop moaning long enough to form the words. Struggling, tongue sticky against the roof of my mouth, brow bubbling with sweat and frustration, I listened as Kenneth recounted his perpetual hardships.

"Haven't had a job since you left. Haven't sold a story in almost three years. Haven't had a warm bath in nearly as long."

Beneath it all, running like a current of self-pity and blame, was the unspoken accusation that his troubles were primarily, if not entirely, my fault.

"I could use a warm bath. Might make all the difference. Could cure me, Marjory. Turn me into myself again. You know how that can be."

I turned my face toward Kenneth, to attempt once more a verbal response, but he had gone. Carolyn sat in his place. Her fuzzy, matted hair hugged her head like a cheap version of her stylish cloche, and drops of blood dotted her lips where they had cracked. Despite all this, she looked clear-eyed, alert.

"I'm going to try a bath," she announced. "I think my fever has come down enough." Carolyn extended one long hand and placed it on my forehead. "Maybe tomorrow. I just bet you'll be ready for a bath tomorrow."

She leaned over and pressed her parched lips to my brow. The gesture was so small, yet so much. Hot tears slipped from my eyes.

"Tomorrow," she promised, then left me to descend again into my swirling delusions.

It was not the next day, but three days later that I cooled down enough for a warm bath. A week after that, I hugged my dear friend goodbye and caught a train to Quebec, where a convoy of Red Cross women were to set sail.

Our ship was enormous, painted in wild dazzle designs to deceive enemy submarines. We pitched across the Atlantic on this striped monstrosity, tossed about by the waves as if the ship were an annoyance the sea wanted to shake off. I walked the rocking decks at night, savoring the solitude, the plentiful sky, the salty wind. This ocean, which had for months separated me from Andy, now brought me to him. I was not at peace, though. Never before had I felt so hunted, so vulnerable. Out there, among the star-crested waves, a periscope might be watching, waiting for the right moment to strike a ship full of women bringing relief to the wounded. Why, I'd ask the night, was humanity so utterly stupid?

Once we docked in Avonmouth, the journey to Paris was nearly as long as the one across the Atlantic. London passed outside the window of the night train in a terrible hush, the whole of the city darkened by curtains and covers. This was a shame I was certain I'd never get over—to have been to London but not to have seen its chiseled façades; to have passed the clock tower of Westminster at midnight but not to have heard its bells toll. Perhaps humanity was even stupider than I'd first thought—it sought to destroy not only itself but also its expressions of brilliance.

Even gritty with war and its deprivations, Paris electrified me. Its grand history and uncertain future fused into a buzzing, dizzying present. Along the Rue de Rivoli, which felt not only like the center of Paris but the center of the entire world, whispers of music wafted sweetly from darkened doorways and half-open windows. A man with his pants knotted at the knees laughed as his dog mouthed a rope and pulled his wheeled chair down the street. In the shade of a stone portico, a couple kissed as if they were alone in the city, while a child stopped to watch a white butterfly dance around them. No one seemed not to notice the smell of the Seine, fishy and thick, or the heavy clouds that hung over the rooftops like artillery smoke. And no one knew what I knew about France: that Andy was here.

The Red Cross had set up its headquarters in the Hotel Regina. Intended for happier use, the hotel bore its necessary burden with grace, allowing its luxurious lobby to function as a command center of sorts. Desk legs dented the plush carpeting, and instead of fine paintings, detailed, frayed maps of Europe adorned the walls. The lobby was smoky, bustling. It reminded me of the city room at the *Herald*.

"You're new."

A woman stood before me, clipboard in hand, pencil tip poised above it. Her features were dulled by fatigue, the kind that you get used to and wear like a daily skin tonic.

"Yes," I confirmed. "Marjory Stoneman."

The woman scanned her list.

"Stoneman Douglas?"

I nodded. "Yes, Stoneman Douglas."

"Okay, then." She walked over to a desk and returned with a key. "Room 417. The stairs are to your left. Just keep going up."

The room was small, with a window carved out of the severely curved roof. From a tiny balcony, I had a view of a golden statue in a small garden.

"Jeanne d'Arc," I whispered, practicing my pronunciation of the French *r*. The shining, immortalized woman sat erect on her horse, arm raised, focused on something beyond the Rue de Rivoli. I followed her gaze over layers of blue Haussmann rooftops, to the watercolor horizon, and, somewhere, nearly in reach, to Andy Walker.

I set about making myself useful to the Red Cross. Civilian Relief, the department into which I'd been hired, worked mostly in the field, and it was difficult to find many civilians needing relief in the lobby of the Hotel Regina.

"Can you tell me who runs the Civilian Relief department?" I asked anyone who looked like they'd been there a while. "Kaufman. Pearl Kaufman," was always the answer, though no one could say where to find her.

The operation was not so much disorganized as it was overwhelmed, with years of trauma and destruction pressing on a staff that teetered at the brink of exhaustion. New people like myself arrived every day, dozens of us, but no one had the time to teach us what we needed to know in order to help. So I sharpened pencils and fetched coffee. A few times I traveled outside the city with a relief doctor, who tended to the dirty, bloodied, shocked refugees as if they were nobility in a bright examining room. On one of these trips, I held the hand of a woman as she delivered her third child. The mother was in such a profound state of trauma that she just stared dull-eyed at the roof of the medical tent and did not make a noise as her baby emerged into the big, ravaged world.

"What do I do?" the mother asked, startled, when the doctor gave her the newborn.

"The best that you can," the doctor replied.

Between these extremes of idleness at headquarters and crisis work in the field, I kept company with other Americans at a restaurant in Montmartre called the Queen of Hearts. Here, in the low light of the wood-paneled room, across tables dotted with candlewax that had dripped into polka-dot puddles, we cawed with Yankee abandon and identified attenuated pathways of connection between us. "My sister's fiancé is at Marne. Maybe he's seen your cousin," or, "I must have been at Vassar at the same time as your friend." On these uninhibited evenings, I found a woman who'd graduated from Wellesley the year before I got there and a man who'd read about Miami in the Cleveland newspaper and wanted to buy farming land there when he left France.

"Tomatoes, probably," he said, dreamy-eyed. "That would be good."

But I found no one who knew Andy Walker.

"He's an aviator," I said every few weeks, when the crowd turned over a bit. "From Miami, like me."

Heads shook, sorry they couldn't help. I got a different response only once, when a dark-haired young woman sitting alone in the corner listened carefully as I described Andy.

"A scar on his cheek?" she asked through red lips.

I shook my head, feeling suddenly clumsy, the way I had at high school dances.

"Not the last time I saw him," I said.

The woman looked at me, then looked at the ceiling, conjuring an image of the man she was considering.

"Are you his sister?" the red lips wanted to know.

I shook my head again. "No," I answered. "His fiancée."

She nodded, then returned to her drink. When she left, she slipped out quietly, without saying goodbye.

The restaurant was below street level, off an alley that probably wasn't drawn on a map. I felt safe here, burrowed below the sidewalk and surrounded by people like me, who still dreamt in English. We paid for our meals with food stamps, kept our napkins for the week on a rack in the back. The napkins were worn thin from years of laundering and had blue fleurs-de-lis stitched into the corners. With no money ever exchanged for the food and the quaint domesticity of the napkins, the Queen of Hearts felt a little like home in a city whose charm came in part from its strangeness.

Rain slicked the restaurant's front windows the night Pete Robineau appeared, smudging the alley beyond the glass panes into a fugue. I did not see him standing on the sidewalk and shaking cold drops from his umbrella or adjusting the tilt of his hat, but surely he must have done these things, because when Pete listed through the door of the Queen of Hearts, he looked as composed as he ever had.

I jumped from my seat and hugged my old friend, surprised and delighted by his arrival. My Red Cross colleagues shifted chairs, making space for Pete next to me.

"How did you find me?" I asked. In the low candlelight, the sadness in Pete's eyes could almost be mistaken for fatigue.

"I'm working with an intelligence agency, Marjory." He half-smiled. "I have my ways."

Pete took my hand in both of his. This gesture—so intimate, so tender—triggered a panic that caused my heartbeat to stutter.

"Andy?" I asked, certain now that Pete had found me in the restaurant to relay terrible news.

Pete squeezed my hand.

"Andy has been transferred into the American Air Corps." Pete laughed, adding, "Probably, the French couldn't stand him any longer and gave him back to the Yankees. I checked yesterday. He is stationed at a base in the countryside."

I exhaled, felt my heart try to steady itself inside my chest.

"I'll tell him you're here," Pete promised.

Buoyed by the first news of Andy I'd had in months, I looked at my friend and again saw the sadness that I had myopically assumed had something to do with me. I leaned toward Pete and smiled until he could not help smiling back.

"Baby Vivian is as beautiful as Frances," I said. "Her lips are the color of a papaya—honestly! I've never seen such lips before. And when she sleeps, her eyelashes flutter against her cheeks. I don't know how she doesn't wake herself up with those tickling lashes."

Pete watched the sinking candle, constructing a vision of tiny Vivian among the flames.

"What else?" he asked.

"They are completely in love," I answered. "Frances and

Vivian. They look at each other, and the rest of the world falls away. All they need now is you."

Pete nodded, thinking.

"Thank you, Marjory."

I pushed my bowl of rice and jam toward him.

"Have some," I offered.

Pete took a spoon and shared my dessert.

"This war needs to end," he lamented as he ate.

"Yes," I agreed. "So you can go home to your girls."

"And so France can have good food again. Only you Americans can tolerate a dessert like this."

Pete and I laughed without mirth. Jokes during wartime, I'd discovered, were never actually funny.

Too soon, Pete stood to leave. Favoring his strong side, he lifted his hat from the rack and placed it low on his head.

"I'll get word to Andy," he promised again. I watched through the streaked windowpane as Pete's umbrella burst open and his silhouette dissolved into the cold Paris rain.

A sense of impatience infused daily life. In back rooms and on boulevards, rumors that the war would soon end spread over the city, but Parisians—among whom I now counted myself—saw little evidence that these rumors were true.

I was also impatient at work, mired day after day in a sticky mixture of ennui and urgency. I hadn't yet been trained to do anything useful, though the demands on the Red Cross grew daily.

"Can I help?" I asked nearly everyone at headquarters. "Please?" If I was sent to the storehouse to count jugs of water, it was a good day. If I was not, I took a cup of tea on a small balcony, corralled by a barrier of wrought iron curls, and gazed at the gilded statue of Jeanne before returning to the lobby and trying again. The chipped porcelain teacups at the Hotel Regina were like most things in Paris in 1918, damaged and suffering yet impossibly fine.

Perhaps more than anything, though, I was impatient to see Andy. Pete had not returned to the Queen of Hearts—I didn't know if he had even been able to send word to Andy. Perhaps Andy had been transferred before he'd heard from Pete. Perhaps he'd been shot down and killed without ever knowing I'd come to Europe to find him. These scenarios unfolded beneath my closed lids as I lay in the bath at the Hotel Regina, steeping like tealeaves in a large porcelain tub of hot water.

I took too many baths. I combed my hair too often and applied too much rose water to my face. But waiting was an insufferable game, and these small acts of preening at least made me feel like it was a game I still played.

In late September, Paris shivered with the first hints of cold. I laughed at myself, digging a scarf from my steamer trunk as soon as the Gallic wind started to blow. I hadn't felt anything close to winter in over three years and began to wear the scarf everywhere.

I was, of course, wearing the scarf as I bustled toward the hotel lobby one morning, arms full of various papers that Pearl Kaufman had requested I bring from the newsstands along the river. Walking quickly, grateful for the task and hopeful that its prompt completion would lead to another, I did not wait for the woman inside the lobby door to exit before I pushed in. Instead, I squeezed past her self-importantly, both of us forcing ourselves and our belongings through the narrow opening.

Plotting my route to the director's desk, I suddenly felt my head hinge backward and the scarf tighten around my neck, execution-style. The newspapers fell to the carpeted floor. I squeezed my fingers between the scarf's wool and my skin and tried to relieve its hard grip.

With the scarf somewhat loosened, I pivoted and saw the woman, now outside the hotel, swatting with annoyance at the fringes of my scarf, which had curled themselves, snake-like, around the clasp of her shoulder bag.

I knocked on the glass of the door that separated us. The woman's eyes followed the trail of the scarf until her gaze settled on my neck, then my face.

"Marjory Stoneman?" she exclaimed, her words dulled by the glass wall between us. She opened the door in a rush and came back inside while I unraveled the scarf from my neck before her maneuvering could choke me again.

Miss Ferry stood before me in the lobby of the Hotel Regina. Despite a decade having passed since I'd been in her class, she looked the same as she had at Wellesley, smooth-skinned and severe, with her hair, now graying, knotted on top of her head.

"You're working for the Red Cross?" she asked.

"Technically, yes."

"Meaning?"

"Meaning I don't actually have much work to do."

Miss Ferry nodded.

"I understand," she said. "War is nothing if not ineffi-cient." She looked at me for a long moment, seeming to recall with each passing breath the disgrace and the triumph that had been my letter home during her class.

"Come with me," Miss Ferry instructed, as if I had never graduated and remained under her tutelage.

"But the newspapers," I said. "I have to get them to Mrs. Kaufman."

Miss Ferry surveyed the rolls of newsprint that lay at my feet.

"Of course," she relented. "Go ahead, then. I'll wait here and try to disentangle your scarf from my handbag."

The delivery of the papers did not result in more work, as I had hoped, and I soon found myself walking down the Rue de Rivoli with Miss Ferry, my salvaged scarf once again wrapped snugly under my chin.

"There's a café on the corner," she said. "The coffee's not bad."

I knew the café she meant, and the coffee was pretty good, considering the proprietor had lost his two sons in Verdun and his wife had nearly starved herself into extinction in the years since.

We settled at a small table in the back of the café. The steam from my coffee warmed the inside of my nose, and I breathed deeply, enjoying its warmth. Intimidated by Miss Ferry, even after a decade, I waited for her to speak first.

In a rush, as if she hadn't talked to a friend in a very long time, Miss Ferry explained that she'd been in Paris two years, doing publicity work for the Children's Bureau of the Red Cross.

"What does that mean?" I asked. "Publicity work?"

"Reports," she answered at the end of a deep swallow of coffee. "Dispatches sent back to the States describing our accomplishments, such as they are, in helping the children."

"That sounds important."

"It's not nothing," she conceded. "But I'm tired. Two years is a long time to be here. I want to go home. They say the war will end soon, but I'm not going to wait. I can't. Just look."

Miss Ferry hovered her hands over the small tabletop, as if she were going to show off a beautiful ring. At the ends of her splayed fingers, she'd ripped the nails to bloody scraps.

"I write dispatches about all the children we've fed, all the coats we've distributed, but it's not as if the country-side is full of good news. I've seen them, the children we couldn't help. There aren't enough hours in the day to write dispatches about them." Miss Ferry began to scrape at a fingernail with her thumb but then stopped, squeezed her hands into defiant fists.

"But it will be better for you," the professor insisted. "The war will end. It has to. Everyone thinks so. And then the pieces of good news will outnumber the bad. Hospitals, the children's hospitals, will be transferred to the French—those will be good ceremonies to cover and write home about. Yes, more good things. Fewer bad. The balance will certainly shift very soon."

I tilted my head, not certain I understood.

"Better for me?" I asked.

Miss Ferry blinked rapidly.

"Well, yes," she said. "Better for you, seeing as I won't be here anymore."

"You want me to be your replacement?"

"Marjory. I'm sorry—did I not mention that? Yes, if I'm to be sent home, I need a replacement. And I remember you as such a fine writer. You'll be perfect for the job."

I laughed through my nose.

"Miss Ferry, don't you remember my letter? You used it as an example of how *not* to write."

"Oh, Marjory," she said, searching her cup for missed drips of coffee. "Your writing was beautiful—why do you think the whole class applauded? You just broke the rules of epistolary etiquette, that's all."

Outside the café windows, rusted leaves fell like snowflakes. A small dog on a leash barked at the leaves as they floated around him. Miss Ferry was depleted, spent, but the city was not. Merely subdued, Paris still promised adventure and excitement and Andy. Most of all, Andy.

"Okay," I told Miss Ferry. "I'll do it."

She smiled, flexed her violated fingers, waggling them as if preparing to type.

"Good," she answered. "I'll let them know at headquarters."

With that business done, Miss Ferry and I shifted in our chairs, not sure what to say next. I asked her if she still taught at Wellesley. She asked where I'd been living before coming to France. Neither of us particularly cared about the other's responses, and we rose and gathered our belongings as soon as civility would allow.

"Miss Ferry?" I asked, surprising myself.

"Mmm?" She fiddled with her large bag.

"I came to France for a man," I confessed. "Not because I was so eager to help with the war effort."

The older woman pressed her lips hard together, as if she were considering confessing something herself, as if the lost, gray years of the war held her secrets, too.

"History will judge you by your deeds, Marjory, not by your motives. Just do whatever you can while you're here."

I nodded, swirled the length of my scarf around my neck. Miss Ferry and I had said everything we needed to say to each other.

As we left, I smiled at the empty-eyed café owner. He dragged his hand through the air in response, not quite forming a wave.

Autumn in Paris raced toward winter, as if trying to keep pace with the whole of Europe's race toward the end of its madness. Night fell faster each evening, relieving the exhausted day and slicking the city with a sweet coating of frost, like the layer of sugar spread over a fresh palmier. I loved the darkened, chilled streets of the city at night, the endless alleys and intersections where echoes of the panoply of human exclamation could just barely be heard—babies wailing, widows grieving, couples reuniting on the crumpled sheets of their beds. From the bridges over the Seine, the river below seemed to slow down, contemplating turning to ice, at least at the edges where the ducks liked to loll.

I meandered each evening to the Queen of Hearts in Montmartre, telling my Red Cross friends after work that I'd meet them there. Instead of walking directly, I twisted and turned through neighborhoods, observing, absorbing. If I came across a group of men in uniform and heard them speaking English with an American drawl, I paused, fidgeted with the toggle buttons on my coat, searched for the only face I truly wanted to see. There were whiskered cheeks swollen with false bravado, little-boy eyes swirling with man-made terrors, mischievous grins, pimpled brows. There were men more handsome than Andy, men with trim moustaches and right-angled jaws. I passed all of them by, searching and searching the shadowed crannies of Paris.

I tempered my disappointment each night with the camaraderie of my colleagues at our Montmartre haunt. I diluted my increasing worry about Andy with sips of illicit absinthe from glasses passed under the tables on nights when a telltale green ribbon was tied to the to the coat rack at the back of the room. The liquid was the same emerald color as the coded ribbon; it was a secret escape that allowed each of us to forget what we no longer wanted to know and catch a glimpse of what we wished to remember. With the anise flavor slathered over my throat, I thought of Andy, his laugh as warm as sunlight, his kiss as sweet as coconut milk.

Andy did not walk out of the night-fog of Montmartre and into our basement restaurant. He did not scrape the absinthe from my mouth with his tongue and lead me to a darkened portico around the corner. When he appeared, it was on a Tuesday morning, as I sat in a small closet office in the Hotel Regina, scratching a dispatch onto thick, blue-lined paper.

"Marjory."

I did not immediately turn in my chair. A moment so long in the making needed to be held in one's hands—the heat, the heft of it imprinted on one's palms so that decades on, when those hands are twisted and weak, the memory of that moment remains, having been burned years ago into the skin.

"Marjory."

I could not hold the moment much longer. The heat singed the cups of my hands; the flesh was beginning to char where the suspension of time was the hottest. I turned. And there, his head nearly touching the doorframe of my little office, was Andy Walker.

He wore his dress uniform effortlessly, gladly. Beneath the crisp fabric his shoulders were full, his back long. The leather cross straps over his chest did their best to contain him. In his hands, he turned his hat round and round—the only sign of nervousness that he showed.

"Hi," I said, standing, hoping my trembling knees could keep me upright.

"Hi."

We looked at each other, the expanse of my office feeling as wide as the Atlantic, as vast as the thirteen months we'd been apart.

"I got this," Andy said. With two fingers he lifted a medal from his breast. "It's the *Croix de Guerre*. And look, there are two palms."

I took this as an invitation to approach. In three steps, I stood before him, knees shaking harder.

Andy no longer smelled like the sea. He smelled earthy instead, like wild mushrooms and ash.

I raised one finger toward the medal, looked up at Andy for permission before touching the cross. He nodded. The handles of the swords were ridged and intricate, the fronds of the palm firm beneath my fingertip. Below the palms, the

medallion's ribbon was the same color green as the cloth tied
to the coat rack in the back of the Queen of Hearts. Perhaps
absinthe and the *Croix de Guerre* served the same purpose
in this greatest of wars.

"For acts of gallantry," I said, pulling my finger away
from the cross.

Andy smiled.

"Yes," he said, then added, "I couldn't wait to show you."

"It's beautiful."

We stood there, so close, needing to touch. I wrapped
my arms around his waist, settled my cheek on his chest. The
beautiful bronze cross pressed on my ear.

"I've missed you," I whispered to his shirt buttons.

"Me, too," he said into my hair.

The bureaucrats of the Red Cross bustled about in the
hall. Europe smoldered around us. But Andy and I stood,
reunited and safe, still holding on.

"Will you have dinner with me tonight?" he asked.

"Yes," I said. "Of course."

Then we parted again, but briefly, the promise of the
evening just hours away.

When I wrote stories in college at Wellesley and after—fiction,
that is, not the newspaper stories I'd written in recent years for
the *Herald*—the thrill of the work lay in the power of deter-
mining a story's fictitious reality. As the omnipotent author, I
could make the lost dog return home on the heroine's birthday
or have the young girl pull through her fever just before dawn.
I could make protagonists fall in love and antagonists fall off a
ledge. I simply had to want something, and it could be.

Somehow, over the last year or so, I'd lost sight of the
fact that, while this phenomenon was the essence of fiction,
real life didn't bend quite as deeply to my desires.

Andy waited as planned on the Pont Neuf. Still in his dress uniform, with the blue-black of dusk further bruising the city around him, Andy stood stiffly, nearly at attention. Did they not issue coats in the American Air Corps? Even with my woolen cape and hazardous scarf, I shivered in the evening chill.

"Hello, there," I greeted him when I was close, sending my words off in a puff of mouth steam. I felt more relaxed than I'd been in my office that afternoon, the jolt of his appearance having softened into a milder buzz.

Andy loosened his stance, placed his hands on my waist and lifted me into the air, much as he'd done the very first time we'd met on the terrible road through New Smyrna. He held me high, pulled me close, let me slide slowly down the length of him until my feet once again touched the bridge.

"I saw a nice place," Andy said, tipping his head toward the Left Bank.

"Wonderful," I agreed. "I don't often get over here. When I leave the hotel, it's usually to go to Montmartre."

I hooked my hand around his elbow and leaned into his arm as we walked. I felt giddy, silly, bursts of delight rising from my gut to my chest like bubbles in a flute of champagne. As the city undressed for nightfall, I told Andy of my stint in the Navy and my lessons under the key lime tree with Madame Faudel. I told him of having the flu in New York and going into the swampland with Dr. Fairchild.

"Oh, and of course I have to tell you about Miss Jefferson Bell." I drew out the description in my best impression of a Southern debutante. "The *finest*, the *best-connected*, well, simply, the most *buttery* society page editor Miami, Florida, has ever known."

Andy smiled. It felt like a favor.

"There it is," he said, jutting his chin toward a wide-windowed bistro across the street.

We settled at a table in the middle of the room, ordered mutton because that was all the chef could offer that night. The echo of my preposterous Southern accent pinged about in my head, and I attempted to smother it with the telling of my near-fatal encounter with Miss Ferry a few weeks before. "So now I write dispatches about the hospitals we're handing over to the French and the orphanages we've established," I concluded. "I'm not fighting on the front, obviously, but I think it's important."

The small candle on the table between us cast a dim glow on Andy's mouth, on his chin, but left the rest of his face and his red hair smoldering in ashen shadows.

"I've really, really missed you," he said after a moment. Though this could have been some sort of response to my tales, the words had the helium quality of a non sequitur.

Occupants of the other tables turned over. The waiter cleared our food. Our wine was replenished, then replenished again, and still Andy said almost nothing.

"We've been apart a long time, haven't we?" I asked.

Andy put his elbows on the table, clasped his hands below his chin. The bronze *croix de guerre* winked at me in the low candlelight.

"Sometimes it felt like forever," he agreed.

"Why did you get the cross and the palms?"

"For valor."

"I imagine valor and terror are two sides of one coin."

Andy looked at me for a very long time, perhaps playing out something in his head that he could not put into words.

"You imagine correctly," he eventually said.

I reached my hand across the table. He took it, hung on. Blood pulsed in the tips of his fingers.

We left the bistro, drunk on wine but sobered by life and braised mutton.

"Want to walk for a while?" Andy asked.

We continued along Rue Dauphine. The streets—the shops and cafes, the cabarets and libraries—pulsed with repressed energy. Paris was like a racehorse kept too long in the gate. The city was desperate to be let loose once again. "I'm sorry," I said. "For prattling on like that before. For forgetting that your time has been spent much differently than mine."

"Please, Marjory," Andy said. "Don't say you're sorry. I just wish I had funny stories to tell you."

"*Something* a tiny bit funny must have happened in the last year."

Andy's boots made each step sound momentous. With every thud, I wished harder that he would come up with a story so that my presumption about something funny happening to him during war would not sound so stupid.

"Actually," Andy began, a hint of his old goofy grin slipping out. "I went to a dance hall once, when I was on leave. Somewhere in the Quartier Pigalle, I think. I danced so hard—it was so much fun, especially compared to shooting at Germans—but I didn't realize that the seam on the seat of my trousers had split open during one of my fancier moves. Wide open, Marjory, and I danced like that the whole night, with my undershorts on display in the middle of Paris. When we were leaving, a French Airmen asked if that was how Americans always dressed for a party."

Andy laughed. I chuckled along. When I pictured him dancing, it was not his seam-splitting backside I saw but, rather, his front. His arms, to be exact. And not just his arms, but the woman who must have been dancing within them.

"I'm glad you had a break from the fighting," I said.

We walked until we were lost, the city unwinding in familiar ways along unfamiliar streets. Andy took my hand. He slid off my glove and stuffed it into his pocket before weaving his fingers among mine. He lifted our fused hands, kissed the dip between two of my knuckles, kissed it again for a beat longer. We negotiated darkened cobblestone streets and laughed when we passed the same rectory twice, each time from a different direction. I smiled at, and he looked away from, beggars in old army uniforms, their pain exploited by moonlight.

"I had an affair."

We kept walking, did not miss a stride.

"Her name is Nadège. She's a dancer."

So this was how Andy felt when he'd found out I was married. So this is the shock of learning the person you love had lain naked with another.

"Nadège," I repeated. "A dancer."

The trials of war lurked all around us. Mutton for dinner and homeless men with no eyes. Church bells with too many sorrows to toll. Fatherless children, husbandless wives. Add to these horrors Nadège the dancer.

"Do you still see her?"

"No." Thump, thump, thump of his boots. "It was a few months ago. You weren't here. I wasn't supposed to survive my next mission."

Nadège the dancer, possibly Andy's last earthly pleasure.

"Have you killed anyone?" I eyed the medal on his chest.

Andy stopped walking. He looked at me, unsure whether to answer.

"Yes."

"With a gun?" I prodded. Like a candle snuffer, the question extinguished the little spark in his eyes.

"With my hands."

"The same hands that touched Nadège the dancer?"

"Those are the only hands that I have, Marjory."

I looked at Andy. My sweet, beautiful Andy.

"It's war," I said carefully. "I'll forgive you for the one thing, if you forgive yourself for the other."

Was there ever a woman as magnanimous as I was right then?

Andy nodded once as an answer. If he were going to say more, he did not have a chance. A jumble of ragged clothing crashed onto the street from an alley. Two men, fighting. In the sickly gaslight, they stumbled and careened, seeming to hold on to each other as much for support as for battle. At the edge of their invisible ring, a three-legged dog barked, cheering, it seemed, for one man or the other.

"Should we help?" I asked Andy.

He watched the men tumble over a sewer drain and stumble into the gutter.

"No," he decided and turned away. The drunken, foul expletives of the men's struggle followed us down the street.

It was after midnight when we found ourselves again over the Seine, this time on the Pont des Arts, the bridge that led almost directly back to my room at the Hotel Regina. We hovered over the ancient water while, all around us, the city feigned resignation.

"I live right over there," I said without gesturing toward the hotel, without even looking at it, just boring my gaze into Andy's so that he'd understand.

He took a step closer. The woolen hem of my cape touched his shirt.

"With a roommate?" he asked.

I shook my head. He took my hand, and we crossed the bridge.

Jeanne d'Arc didn't pass judgment when I left Andy by her side. Instead she looked over his head, golden eyes seeking the return of the sun.

"Count to three hundred," I whispered, though no one except Jeanne was near. "It's room 407."

I ran up the stairs to my room, huffing by the time I reached the door. Had it been five minutes already? Maybe

Andy wouldn't come. Maybe he'd wander away to the dark corners of the Quartier Pigalle, in search of Nadège.

Inside the room, I pushed unwashed laundry under the bed, tossed a quick splash of rosewater onto my face. I lit one lamp, decided the light was too harsh and lit another instead. Hadn't that been one of the rules I'd unearthed with Kenneth—get the lighting just right? This second lamp was perfect. It burned enough to show dewy eyes but not enough to reveal any hesitation within them.

Through the stripe of space where the curtains didn't quite meet, I peeked out at Jeanne. She was alone in her valor. Andy was either on his way up or had disappeared into the night.

Ten minutes went by. I looked out the window, and again, Jeanne stood alone.

When twenty minutes had passed, I took off my clothes and shoved them under the bed with the rest of my worn garments. Then I turned off the light and slid under the covers.

I'd been rejected again, as I'd been that night on the beach. And yet I must not have completely believed this. After all, the door was still unlocked, and I'd not put on nightclothes.

I slept a half-sleep, brief and filled with thoughts of my choosing: the cool of the ocean first thing in the morning, the haunted call of a burrowing owl. When the door finally swung open and the glow from the hall spilled inside, I wasn't surprised or upset, just relieved that I would not have to torture myself once again with heartbreak and shame.

"You count very slowly," I said from the bed.

Andy closed the door, slid the lock into place.

"I thought you said to count to three thousand."

"You didn't think that."

"You're right," he agreed. "I didn't think that."

I lay on my side, close to the edge of the bed. Andy pulled off his boots and walked across the room, crouched with his face close to mine, as he'd done on the beach in Miami.

"Sometimes my head gets heavy, Marjory," he whispered. I could taste our third glass of wine in his words. "Like it's full of wet sand. And I have to go think for a while before it clears up." He put his hand on top of the covers, rested it on the crest of my hip. "Do you still want me here?"

I slipped my arm out of the covers and lifted his hand from my hip. Holding it gently, I guided his hand under the blanket and placed it back on my naked hip crest. For a long moment, we both stayed utterly still.

"Yes," I finally answered.

Andy's palm traveled over the ridgeline of my side, first down to my toes, then up again to my shoulder, urging the covers away as it moved. His hand made this journey three times, then, in one quiet motion, he nudged me onto my back and turned me sideways, pulling me toward him, right to the edge of the bed, by both hips.

I had not known this was something that could happen, that this was something people did. The room swelled with my breath, with my animal exclamations.

"I love you," I said in the midst of it all, and this would not be the last time I said it that night.

We lay wrapped up in exhaustion, limbs tangled within twisted blankets, breathing mismatched and deep. In the unmoving darkness, our hands sought each other. My fingers filled the gaps between his and bent over his knuckles. Our palms pressed together. We slept hanging on.

"Andy?"

From the gap in the curtain came the gray light of near-dawn. His boots were still by the door, and little snores washed like waves through the room. But I was alone in the bed. His side wasn't warm.

"Andy?"

The snoring stalled. I sensed movement below, under the mattress. I rolled to my stomach, hung my arm off the side of the bed. Andy's hand quickly found it.

"What are you doing down there?" I asked. My voice was tender, simple, a voice I hadn't used in so many years.

"Sometimes I like it down here," Andy said. "It feels safe."

I was quiet. My thumb rubbed his.

"It's safe up here, too," I promised. "Will you come up?"

"Okay. I will."

But Andy still hadn't moved when I fell back into sleep.

He was next to me when I woke, the only sign of his hiding a few pieces of my laundry that he'd dragged with him from under the bed. With the covers pulled to my chin, I rolled toward him.

"Morning," I said.

He slid his arm around me and kissed my forehead.

"Morning," he answered.

I thought of the just-finished night, so good and so strange.

"So what happens now?" I asked.

"Well," Andy said. "The war is ending. Before I was discharged, my commanding officer gave it less than a month."

"Discharged?" I pushed myself up on an elbow.

"I'm done, Marjory. I'm going home. To Miami."

I strangled the top of the blanket. This was good news, wasn't it? I should be very happy.

"You are?"

"Yes. And I want you to come back with me. It's all done. Everything's over. We can get married."

I wasn't divorced yet. Papa had written in his last letter that the decree was in process but still hadn't gone through. In the year 1918, for a woman who abandoned her husband, there was apparently no such thing as a speedy judicial proceeding.

"I can't leave Paris yet," I stammered. "There's still so much the Red Cross needs me to do."

Andy blinked hard.

"Really?"

"I'm sorry," I said, touching his face. "You did your job. I need to do mine."

As I spoke, holding Andy Walker's warm cheek in my hand, I saw the scraggy pines of our Miami. I felt the wet heat on the back of my neck and heard the surf tempering the call of the roseate spoonbill. I tasted the moonshine we'd drunk on a beach in the starlight.

"But I will come back as soon as I can. I promise."

"And you'll marry me then?"

I smiled.

"That's what I've wanted to do for two and a half years, Andy Walker."

I burrowed my head into his chest, and he wrapped his long arms around me. I waited for him to ask about the divorce, but the question never came. Maybe he assumed it had gone through by now. Or maybe, in the maelstrom of war, he'd simply forgotten. The sun rose, and the room slowly pinkened.

We were young. We believed the war would be over when the ink on the armistice dried. We believed Kenneth would be gone from my life when a robed man on a bench in Tallahassee wrote his name on my divorce decree. We believed—perhaps willfully, perhaps with intentional, essential blindness—that we could simply pick up where we'd left off.

"Then I guess I'll see you in Miami," Andy said as he eased me from his arms.

"Yes," I agreed. "I'll see you at home."

Memorizing his movements, I watched him get dressed. Pants first. Then shirt closing happily around his muscled chest. He stood for a while in front of the mirror, fastening and refastening the *Croix de Guerre*.

"Come back quickly," he said, and I nodded.

This feeling was so horribly familiar—grief mixed with goodbye, happiness promised and then delayed—but I refused to return to Miami with Andy unless I was divorced from Kenneth Douglas. When I saw Andy again, when we swam past the breakers together into the tropical deep, I wanted there to be nothing that could come between us again, nothing that could ever keep us apart.

On the morning of November 11, 1918, I stood on a second floor balcony of the Hotel Regina with a dozen of my Red Cross colleagues. The streets below and the skies above were completely, eerily silent, as if, in the night, Paris had finally fallen to the foot soldiers of death. The city, the entire continent, was soundless and breathless and still. I am certain we could have heard a child sneeze in Berlin.

The silence persisted, longer than it seemed possible for silence to persist in a city the size of Paris. In collective isolation, every person in Europe mulled over their losses, their dead, mourned the minutes and the months and the years of their lives stolen by war—*How much laughter did I miss out on? How many embraces, how many kisses, did I forego? What foods did I not taste and what music did I not hear and how many beautiful dreams were replaced with nightmares? What children were not born? And if the misery can be over by putting a few men in a room with a pen, then why did it have to happen at all?*

War, it seemed to me as I stood in the aching quiet, was most senseless at the moment it ended.

Gunshots erupted over the Seine. To a populace that had braced itself against the sounds of invasion for years, the synchronicity and coordination of the explosions were not immediately clear. An invisible panic coursed through the empty streets, shaking tree branches, dislodging stones. Cats shrieked in terror. A choking cloud of soot-dusted pigeons rose from the pavement in the Place de la Concorde and dispersed, birds settling themselves nervously on the sloped roofs of the first arrondissement. Having been in Paris only a few months, I understood the message by the fourth gunshot. It took the more seasoned Red Cross workers a bit longer, but by blast ten, we were all hugging and jumping, testing the cantilevered strength of the hotel balcony.

Gradually, with trepidation and disbelief, the people of Paris grasped the significance of the gunfire, and by blast twenty-five, the city had turned itself inside out. Apartments, shops, hotels, schools, churches—every building in the city emptied its inhabitants into the streets, forming rivers of jubilant, exuberant humanity. Relief was no longer an emotion. It had become a tangible thing, passed from one stranger to another on the hot breath of a delirious kiss.

Some men stood beneath our balcony, urging us to climb over the railing and let them help us down to the street. I went first. I swung my legs over the balcony's iron bars and groped with my feet until I found a shoulder to stand on. Hands held my legs to steady me. A voice told me to let go of the railing and let them catch me. When I reached the ground safely, the man whose shoulders I'd balanced upon kissed my cheek and shouted something in French that I did not understand. The Rue de Rivoli swelled with reveling survivors. I hung onto a lamppost, tried to wait for my Red Cross friends to descend, but the momentum of the masses could not be resisted. I let go of the post, allowing myself to be carried away.

It is possible that my feet did not touch the street once as I traveled the length of the Rue de Rivoli, pressed shoulder to shoulder with strangers I'd known forever. As the celebration raged on, laughter turned to tears, then back to laughter again, all of the complexities of human emotion exposed in the starkness of this November day. Beside me, a woman with thick lines on her face carried a small boy on her shoulders, her arms hooked over his thighs so he would not fall. As we careened together over the pavement, she kissed me hard on the side of my head and shouted into my ear.

"Now my boy will always know peace! Such a thing will never happen again!"

I took her boy's hand and pressed my lips to his pudgy fingers.

"May his hands never know the weight of a weapon!" I yelled back in blessing.

The Rue de Rivoli deposited its raucous contents into the estuary of the Place de la Concorde. Given space, the mob spread but did not settle, using the expanse instead as a dance floor. Standing to the side was not an option, and for the first time in my life, I wagged my hips with abandon, jimmied my hands in the air. I kicked my heels up behind me and let my shoulders bounce as fast as they could. People danced with me. Old men. Little girls. Soldiers whose wide-eyed astonishment at not being dead was their most defining characteristic. Somewhere in the center of this hopping mass, voices congealed into a voluptuous rendition of the Marseillaise. The song rippled out from this center, people joining when the melody reached them, further and further until the whole public square vibrated with grieving exuberance and the rousing, reassuring permanence of the Republic's great anthem.

Hours passed. At some point, people realized they had no idea when they'd last had a sip of water or a nibble of food or had last changed the baby's diaper. They realized their dead were still dead and always would be. Though the streets remained packed, the intensity of the celebration waned, and it was possible, finally, to sit and catch one's breath. I found a fountain at the edge of the plaza and climbed into it. The basin was dry and elevated and curved in just the right degree to be comfortable. This was a day with no rules—I was free to sit like a pigeon in a fountain in the middle of Paris if I wanted.

I closed my eyes, let the magnitude of the day's events percolate. Perhaps I slept. The sun was setting when I heard my name called.

"Marjory Stoneman, what on earth are you doing?"

Three colleagues stood below me. Their cheeks glowed with chill and excitement.

"You can't sleep on a day like this," they shouted. "Not even in a fountain. Come on!"

I climbed to the ground, awake now and giddy. Though I did not know these women well, I hooked my arms through theirs and held on. We wove through the lingering smatters of people to the edge of the plaza, turned onto the Champs Elysees. The great boulevard looked somehow wider and deeper than I'd ever seen it before, as if, after four endless years, the street itself were shifting and stretching beneath the new day.

"Let's go," I said, and still linked at the arms, we began running down the Champs Elysees, eagerly throwing ourselves into the purpled gloaming of a city finally, finally, at peace.

The momentum of daily life after the armistice propelled me from one dawn to the next, making it difficult to dwell too long on the ache that pulled me with almost magnetic irresistibility toward Miami—and Andy. As Parisians feverishly sought a return to normalcy, I also sought a return to my pre-war existence. I dreamt of the smell of night-blooming jasmine, wandered through memories of summer on the beach. I could be walking the narrow streets of Montmartre—stepping on ancient stones, peering through patisserie glass at billowy croissants—but be so lost in recollection that I almost believed I was on Flagler Street by the Bay.

It's not that I didn't love Paris. I did, even more than when I'd first arrived. With the war over, the city had pulled back its hood, ripped off its cloak, revealed its beautiful, authentic self again to the world. On corners and in cafes, in basement studios and lofty ateliers, musicians and painters and writers grappled with the meaninglessness of the war, using their gifts to express what most of us could hardly shape into a thought.

Restaurants began offering more choices on their chalkboard selections ("Mutton wasn't even on the list," I wrote in a letter to Andy). Children played in the parks and squealed with a carelessness that hadn't been heard a few months before. Amid the unshakable sadness and persistent reminders of loss, there was, in the varied arrondissements of this indefatigable city, spectacular renewal.

But Paris was a long way from home, and I'd begun to long for the merciless sun and renegade ethos of the Miami I'd left behind. I found it difficult to imagine with any degree of specificity what married life with Andy would look like, but it was enough to know I would wake in his arms every morning, count the stars with him every night. We'd have a small house hidden in a grove of live oaks, Spanish moss dripping onto the roof. And we'd host dinner parties in the space under the trees, debating the future of the city long into the night with the Robineaus and the Ashworths and the Keenes. Perhaps there would be children, hanging from my hips as if I were the live oak tree and they the Spanish moss. This was as far as my imagination took me, however. Any attempt at further detail (Who would cook? How would we get to work? Who would wash the diapers of those hanging moss babies?) caused my thoughts to condense into a hard little stone and fall right out of my ear before any sense could be made of them.

But I could not return to Miami just yet. The divorce—it was coming. "Soon," Papa had promised in his most recent letter, as if he understood I would not come back still married to Kenneth Douglas. That this marriage had outlasted the war to end all wars was nothing short of amazing.

I let Paris distract me. I let my work engulf me. My life, for now, was an adventure, and I could not be sad about that.

A letter arrived from Carolyn Percy, postmarked a month earlier. She was in France, in the canteen service, and was likely to be assigned to a location in Paris. I used my Red Cross connections and found her working in the Gare du Nord.

"It's you," Carolyn yelped when she finally looked up from ladling soup and saw me standing in the station's dull light. We hugged madly while her supervisor cleared her throat again and again.

"I've been in Paris two weeks," Carolyn gushed. "Bordeaux before that, and I can't even remember where I was first. But a whole two weeks in Paris, Marjory, and I haven't even had time to look for you." She adjusted her hat, leaned very close. "Tell me the truth, do I smell like fish?"

"Fish?" I took a big sniff. "A little, yes."

"Ugh! I knew it! Marjory, I'm telling you, I've probably served two thousand trays of canned salmon in the past five days. Trays and trays and trays of slimy canned salmon. I'm never going to get rid of this stench. I'm going to smell like a fishmonger for the rest of my life!"

"Do the soldiers eat it?" I asked.

"The salmon? Yes! They can't get enough. Canned peas and canned salmon, like it's some sort of delicacy."

"Then you smell scrumptious to them, Carolyn. And, besides, I'm sure there are far worse smells to be associated with in a war zone or a train station than salmon."

Carolyn laughed and hooked her arm around mine.

"As long as you can stand the smell, Marjory, I'll be just fine."

Carolyn stayed in Paris through Christmas and went home just after the New Year. With troop levels dwindling and transport less fraught, the canteen service began winding down. We said goodbye outside the Hotel Regina, in the shadow of the gold Jeanne d'Arc.

"I'll probably go through New York on my way home," I said.

"Ooh, good! Oh, Marjory, you must stop and see me. You will, won't you?"

I promised I would, and I meant it. I did not want Carolyn Percy estranged from my life ever again.

The directors at the Red Cross, perhaps somehow intuiting my need for prolonged distraction, shifted the scope of my assignments and sent me into the deepest corners of the smoldering continent to cover the transfer of Red Cross clinics to local authorities.

"Your *ordre de mission*," Mrs. Kaufman's assistant said, presenting me with a sort of unlimited train pass. "And your traveling uniform." With this, the assistant deposited a stack of bulky gray cloth in my arms and wished me the best.

The uniform fit badly—baggy where it should have been fitted, tight where I needed it to stretch, too long in the hem, too short in the sleeves, and just generally not much better than wearing an oversized sack. Carolyn would have been appalled to see me in this getup and would have flat out refused to wear it herself. The unsightly outfit turned out to be a blessing, however, as many of the ceremonies I covered included lengthy speeches, abundant food, and wine so magnificent that two glasses weren't nearly enough. My stomach bloated with delight at these parties. I had to remind myself to write notes for the dispatch before accepting the next glass of wine.

Beyond the small portal of my train windows, Europe persisted, its meadows dappled with the first colors of spring, its mountains glossy with early snowmelt. The land had seen war before. It recovered faster than those who lived upon it.

My mission took me to Italy, to the towns of Turin and Montecatino. To Florence and Venice and Rome. At times I felt like an ancient explorer, discovering the secret beauty of unvisited empires. Other times I felt more like an aristocrat, enriching myself through the language and culture of distant lands. I was, of course, neither of these things, a reality driven home by the fact that my wallet and all of my money was stolen somewhere outside of Pisa.

In Venice, I met up with other Red Cross workers who were also stationed in Paris but happened to be in Italy at the time. We greeted one another as if we'd been friends since birth. There is something necessarily comforting, I supposed as I embraced them all, about seeing a familiar face in a strange location.

"It's good to see you again, Marjory," a man said as we passed around hugs like cigarettes. His name, if I recalled from our nights at the Queen of Hearts, was Frederick.

Our group quickly got lost in the maze of the watery city, depended on gondoliers to return us to our hotel. As a grizzled man poled several of us over the murky canals, I thought of Andy in the bay near Vizcaya, braying his barcarole.

"Hard work," Frederick said of the gondolier's efforts. I tried not to fault him for puncturing my sweet reverie.

I wrote furiously during this time, sending dispatches to headquarters daily for submission to the AP wire service. How much of this work the AP accepted, I didn't know, but my job was to provide written record of the transference of the Red Cross's responsibilities, and this I did quite well. Writing felt good. Even if what I produced was the most rote sort of reporting, I wove words into thoughts that had import, and this was better than not writing at all.

Every few weeks, I returned to Paris, noting each time how the city had brightened, had put the war ever so slightly further behind it. I went shopping in stores whose windows had for so long been darkened and felt good about the centimes I was able to give the shopkeepers. In one clothing store, I held several dresses to my chest but kept returning my attention to a pair of blue trousers.

"Are those really for women?" I asked in French.

The shopkeeper smiled, her makeup bending with her mouth's changing shape.

"For bold women, yes."

I bought the pants. That night, I wore them when I took myself to dinner at a bistro not far from the Hotel Regina. I was not the first woman in Paris to wear trousers around town, but it was enough of an unusual sight to get me a few bewildered looks and a couple of nods of approval. I sat in my new pants at a table by the window, and when the waiter appeared at my side, I used my newly-acquired appreciation of wine to order a full-bodied red from Bordeaux. He smiled at my choice.

"And are you waiting for someone?" he asked.

I've been waiting for someone for two years.

"No," I answered instead. "Not tonight."

The waiter's eyebrows reached for his hairline, but he said nothing.

City life streamed past the window, everyone with somewhere to be, even if that place was exactly where they were at that moment. The waiter delivered my soup, a hearty *garbure* chunky with ham and cabbage, and I spooned it with great relish while watching the people walk by.

I was nearly done with my soup and thinking ahead to my upcoming *poulet* when the faces on the other side of the glass began smiling at me, waving with the excitement of an unexciting coincidence. I smiled and waved in return, and the small group of my colleagues continued on to wherever it was they were headed. After a few steps, one of them called out to the others from behind a cupped hand, then veered into the bistro.

"Mind if I join you?"

Frederick was already pulling out a chair.

The waiter appeared as if conjured by some sort of professional wait staff black magic and set a second place without asking me.

I looked at my new dining companion. His face was pale and puffed like a biscuit but full of sweetness, too, as if the dough had been sprinkled with sugar before it was baked. His dark hair was cropped close to his head. He smelled yeasty with too much cologne.

"What do you recommend?" Frederick asked, scanning the chalkboard menu.

I tried to describe the positive attributes of the *garbure* without allowing too much irritation to creep into my voice. I had been enjoying dining alone.

"Sounds delightful," Frederick decided. "I'll order a bowl."

By the time we ordered dessert, we'd shared the basic details of our pre-war existence, gotten to know each other well enough to consider ourselves friendly acquaintances. He came from Philadelphia. His family ran a newspaper. As he paid the check, Frederick skittered around the one piece of information he'd perhaps wanted first.

"At home, do you . . . you know, are you . . . I mean, there isn't someone . . ."

I considered informing Frederick that I was both married and engaged, but the shock of that statement seemed far too cruel. Instead, I said nothing, changed the subject by fussily smoothing my pants when I stood.

"Nice trousers," Frederick commented.

I smiled and held the door open for him as we stepped onto the street.

My next assignment took me to the Balkans, right into the tinderbox that had sparked the global wildfire. Until the train pulled into the station in Ragusa, I hadn't realized that I held many assumptions about the region—that its streets would be blackened with the collective shame of being the epicenter of so much destruction; that its people would be coarse and unfriendly and its weather relentlessly gray. Only when I registered my surprise at the sight of the twinkling Adriatic and cloudless blue sky, only when I ate a spoonful of sun-sweetened jam with the gentle tribeswomen of Elbasan, did I realize that I had expected to know what the place would be like.

Weeks passed. We traveled narrow mountain roads, sometimes in half-broken trucks, often on the backs of horses so small I thought I would crack them, checking on clinics in tiny, lost towns and delivering powdered milk to refugees living in caves. The twin enormities of the beauty and devastation of the Balkans left me lurching.

I wrote my last dispatch for the Red Cross at Dr. Rosemary Slaughter's clinic in the farthest-reaches of Serbia. Then I eagerly made my way by train to Athens and, after a moonlit visit to the Acropolis, boarded an old steamer bound for Marseille.

The steamer was full of wandering souls. Students going to study in France. An anxious governess returning to Paris for the first time since the outbreak of the war. Sailors unsure of their port.

"Tchin tchin!" the sailors hollered before draining their glasses.

The only thing we all had in common was our distaste for the rancid olive oil the cook used in every meal.

"I'd rather they used motor oil," the governess said. "It could not possibly be any worse."

Among the seasick displacement of all of these travelers, I experienced a fierce longing for home and deep gratitude for the parts of the world I had seen.

The longing turned out to be something of a premonition.

In Paris, the Red Cross had begun dismantling its headquarters in the Hotel Regina. My job when I returned to the city was storing files in boxes, arranging boxes in stacks, and labeling the stacks much as one would in a library. Frederick had somehow been assigned to work with me, and his company eased the tedium of the work.

We had just labeled our third box of the day when a secretary poked her head through the office door.

"Marjory?" she asked.

I looked up from the file on my lap.

"Yes?"

"A cable arrived for you."

I'd never received a cable before in my life.

Frederick watched me as I followed the secretary from the room. I looked back at him before turning the corner and shrugged.

The cable had come from my father. I read it quickly. It was, based on its content, so much more than a cable. In fact, it was as grand as a second armistice. Maybe there'd be celebratory gunshots again on the Seine.

Divorce final STOP Come home STOP Be my assistant editor STOP

"I'm going home," I couldn't help announcing to Frederick when I returned to the office, clutching the news.

He smiled, but his eyes filled with stark disappointment.

"I'm happy for you," Frederick lied.

"It's okay if you're not."

"Okay, I'm not. I wish I could spend more time with you. I'm sorry."

Frederick's recent attention had made me feel a bit lovely. His interest in me had been a counterbalance to my desire for Andy. But I no longer needed such staid equilibrium. I was going back to Miami.

WEST OF MIAMI, 1920

The tree island chews on the darkness, savoring its last taste of night. At the base of a great mahogany tree, a shadow fox circles her den. She guards it with careful eyes but won't go inside. Not yet. Instead she sits, lifts one dainty leg and begins licking and licking and licking her paw, as if washing up after a crime. Not far away, perhaps on a curled peel of red gumbo limbo bark, a click-beetle chirps, warding off day—or some other predation—with its irascible noise.

Still, dawn persists. It's relentless, this trenchant blue prelude to day. It seeps between the chaos of cleaving tree branches and slips over wide waxen leaves. It drip-drip-drips onto the hammock's brown velvet floor, where I lay, unnerved and exhausted. Daylight continues to rise like an overwhelmed river—first reaching the roots of a needy strangler fig, then passing the floating finger-leaves of the bromeliads, until, finally, morning floods the whole place and I am drowning in light.

"Marjory?"

I sit, instantly alert and wide-eyed. Did he follow me here? I'd been so sure that I'd lost him, that I'd made my escape.

"Mar-jor-yyyy?"

My name, turned into sing-song.

I creep on hands and knees to the edge of the hammock, push against the wide pillar of an oak trunk. Through the tangle of mad leaves and branches, I peer out. He is standing in the open wetland, fists on hips, hair muddied, face scratched. All that's between us is the tree island's ring of deep water, a moat formed by millennia of acidic dead plants burning the limestone away.

"You in there, Mar-jor-yyyy?"

His voice can't decide if it's playful or menacing, desperate or firm. Every word is a little of each. Every sentence a mix of his very worst parts.

"I'm here," I say.

I climb through the scrim of branches and stand at the edge of the trees, ready for reckoning. In the sky, the stars and their myriad constellations are fading away.

He steps closer, and closer again. But he does not cross the moat.

"Go up north," I yell at him.

"With you. I'll go north with you."

"No. Not with me. Go north alone. Take that job."

"But why won't you come?"

I look behind me, into the hammock. There are no birches in this sub-tropical cove, but trees can teach lessons, give warnings, wherever they grow. In the blue shadows, the strangler fig clenches a doomed cabbage palm, loving its host with its groping air roots, loving and loving its host into shapeless oblivion.

"You'll suffocate me," I tell him.

"I promise I won't."

"But you already have."

The rising sun gets caught in his hair. We watch each other now over the expanse of the moat, silently undoing the past.

"Go up north," I yell. "Please, go north! If you really love me, go north."

My plea hangs suspended over the moat as he watches me, silent and undecided.

MIAMI, 1920

Once again, I sat on the upholstered seat of a Pullman car, chortling south. If only the train moved as fast as my mind, because, in my head, I was already home, lying in the salty shade of a big banyan with Andy while the city, our city, bloomed all around us. The train car was full, or nearly so, with people dressed in their traveling best—flowering hats and perfectly knotted bowties, lightweight stoles and newly shined oxfords. The children did their best to crease their freshly pressed clothes while they visibly dreamed of sandcastles soon to be built.

"Forty-five!" the porter called as he strolled the length of the car. "Forty-five minutes 'til Miami."

The first time I'd taken the train to Miami, I hadn't believed a city would really emerge from the wild flatness beyond the car windows. The possibility had seemed comical, almost absurd. The land was too thin, the air too thick, for anything as great as a city to grow. This time, though, the heart of the thriving metropolis thumped loudly, a drumbeat that reverberated all the way up the coast and pulled people to it.

"We're staying at the Roney Plaza," the woman across the aisle shared with me. She leaned sideways, beaming with anticipation. "Do you know it? On Miami Beach?"

"Roney Plaza?" I answered. "I'm not familiar."

"Oh," she exclaimed. "It's your first visit, too!"

I considered not bothering to explain, just letting this woman idle in her presumptions, but this particular presumption felt too much like an insult to let pass.

"No, no. It's not my first visit," I said. "I live here, in Miami. I even write for a newspaper. But I was away for a while. In France. With the Red Cross during the war."

The woman balanced on her armrest, considering whether to ask more. She blinked quickly and seemed to decide that this discussion was not part of her holiday plans.

"Mmmm," she murmured and turned toward her window.

I *had* been away for a while. Though I'd been desperate to get back to Miami, my steamer from England had docked in New York (how nice this second passage had been, without the threat of German submarines lurking below, though a Red Cross nurse had said while we'd watched the gray horizon one day, "There are, of course, still all of those nasty mines"—a thought that had not previously occurred to me). In New York, I could not pass up Carolyn's invitation to visit.

"Marjory!" Carolyn whooped when I showed up at her apartment door.

The strength of her hug matched the volume of her exclamation, and we embraced while doing a bit of a jig on her landing.

"I am *so* happy to see you," she said as we danced.

Carolyn lived in Greenwich Village now, in a small apartment above an art gallery on Fourth Street, and she taught at Washington Irving High School. I'd passed bookshops and treasure shops on my way to her place, tea shops and shops so non-descript they were bound to have speakeasies buried within. The Village had become America's Left Bank, and I welcomed this soft swirling of cultures as I eased back home.

"Come in, come in," Carolyn urged, hauling my suitcase across the threshold. She'd regained her plumpness and glowed in the dim lamplight of her living room.

"Hmmm," I said when I'd entered. I lifted my nose in the air and sniffed hard, like a hound on the hunt. "Hmmm," I said again, circling, sniffing some more.

"What?" Carolyn asked, concerned.

"Nothing," I said.

"Come on, Marjory!" she followed my trail. "What is it?"

"Nothing," I repeated, still sniffing. "It just smells a little like canned salmon in here."

Carolyn looked at me from under her long lashes, then we both toppled over and laughed until our stomachs cramped.

I spent four days in Greenwich Village with Carolyn, eating spaghetti the first night at her favorite restaurant, a strange little place in Washington Square called Grace Godwin's Garret.

"How do you measure the worth of your work?" Grace asked in a throaty whisper as she heaped spaghetti onto our plates. This seemed to be the start of one of the proprietress's soul-chats Carolyn had warned me about.

"Whether I have fun while I'm doing it," Carolyn crowed, to which Grace responded with a wink and an amen.

"And you?" Grace Godwin asked me as spaghetti dripped from her serving fork like wax down the side of our table's one candle.

I thought for a moment.

"My work is worthwhile," I said carefully, "if the world is better off when I'm done."

"Well, well." Grace raised one eyebrow, as if appraising my answer. "You just eat up that spaghetti then, Miss, and when you're all done, you tell me if it made the world any better."

The spaghetti made me feel bloated and full, but the chocolate cake and coffee that followed were perfect, and I assured Grace as we left that I was far better off than when I'd arrived.

"Then I've not wasted my time," she drawled after us.

During the day, Carolyn and I admired the storefronts, browsing in places like Her Shop, a clothing store that carried trousers as stylish as the ones I'd bought in Paris.

"I have a pair like these," I told Carolyn, holding up beautiful tweed pants.

"Oh, you do not, Marjory!"

"I do indeed. Bought them in Paris. I'll wear them tomorrow."

"No, Marjory. Please don't!"

I walked all the next day in the midst of a gaze from Carolyn that was at once admiring and appalled.

"Don't you feel, I don't know, *mannish* in those?" she asked as we headed back to her apartment with a dinner of fresh bread and ham.

"Not at all," I assured her. "I feel marvelous."

Carolyn cocked her head, skeptical.

"Carolyn," I said. "You live in Greenwich Village. Have you looked around?" I pointed across the street to a window that displayed a full-length coat made entirely of feathers. "My trousers are about the least shocking thing around here."

Carolyn laughed and tugged me along.

"You should get a pair," I said.

"Me?" she asked. "Oh, never."

But I wasn't so sure.

We sat on her couch my last night in town, reminiscing about our giggle-laced conversations in the attic at 7 Cottage Street.

"I have something to tell you," Carolyn said, dipping her head.

"Yes?"

"I met someone."

"Someone who doesn't mind the smell of canned salmon?"

"Marjory!" Carolyn swatted at me, then told me all about Kelley Cole, the handsome opera singer with whom she'd been talking marriage. "I think he's the one, Marjory, I really do."

"Then we should celebrate!" I exclaimed.

"Of course we should," Carolyn agreed. She pranced to the cupboard and pulled out a bottle of champagne she'd snuck home from France.

"To Kelley Cole!" I toasted as the bubbles raced to the rims of our glasses.

Carolyn giggled and blushed, and we spent the rest of the night draining the bottle and talking about the husbands and children we both surely, surely would have.

The morning after my few days in New York with Carolyn, I loitered near the ticket booth in Grand Central Station, undecided. North or south? Which way should I go? Though my heart tugged me south, I bought a ticket to Boston and held the stub between clenched fingers as I stared out the frost-crusted train window.

The upstairs shutters of the house on Harrison Street were closed tightly, as if the once-watchful house were now sleeping or dead. Though it was not snowing right then, drifts had piled high on the porch stairs. The slope's icy top sparkled pink in the winter sunlight. I'd need a pick-axe to get to the front door.

As I stood on the sidewalk—waiting, deciding—the door swung open and Aunt Fanny's shadow appeared, wrapped in a shawl.

"Go around back!" she shouted before the door slammed. Maybe it was the wind.

The path along the side of the house had barely been cleared, and the bottom of my skirt hung wet and heavy by the time I shook off my coat in the kitchen. It was warm in the kitchen, with the familiar smell of a roasting chicken, but when I sat at the table and accepted a cup of tea from Aunt Fanny, I noticed an unfamiliar layer of dust coating the tops of the chair backs, the handle of the teaspoon, the rim of the saucer. I looked up at Aunt Fanny. Her dress was blackened with soot where she'd wiped her hands. Where was her apron? Standards at the house on Harrison Street seemed to have slipped.

"I guess you'll be needing a change of clothes then, won't you?" Aunt Fanny sighed, poking her eyes at the puddle forming beneath the hem of my skirt.

"I've got my suitcase, Aunt Fanny. I'll take care of it. I'll clean up the water, too. Please, sit and have tea with me."

Aunt Fanny hesitated, glanced at the pile of unpeeled potatoes.

"I'll peel them when we're done," I promised.

Aunt Fanny relented. She flopped into a chair, enjoyed her slouched posture for a moment, then compensated for so classless a move by sitting uncomfortably tall in her seat.

"Where are Grandmother and Grandfather?" I asked after a moment.

"Your grandfather is in the parlor," she said. "Probably snoozing. He doesn't do much these days, Marjory. You'll see. And your grandmother is down the street playing bridge at Minnie Maxwell's house. I'll go get her in about an hour."

"She needs help getting home?" I asked.

Aunt Fanny laughed.

"She'll tell you she doesn't. In fact, if I don't get over there well before the game is done, she'll just start walking home by herself. But she needs an arm to lean on. She really does. The ice is too much. She fell a few weeks ago. No broken bones or anything like that, but still, I found her squawking on a snow bank, ranting about how I need to get her better shoes. Now we walk slowly, so she doesn't fall, but of course we also have to walk fast because your grandfather can't stay alone for too long. Some days Minnie's grandson walks your grandmother home." Aunt Fanny paused here, longer than necessary to make her point. "Those days are better."

I tried to exhale discreetly, so it didn't come out as a huff. My long breath blew ripples across the brown pond in my teacup. I waited until the ripples settled before starting to speak.

"You look very pretty, Aunt Fanny," I said. And she did. Beneath the weary life story she wore on her face and her hands, beneath the permanently puckered twist of her mouth, Aunt Fanny glowed like a sun that had not yet burned out.

"Thank you, Marjory," she said, smiling.

Aunt Fanny held her teacup in both hands, sat without touching the ladder-back of her chair, and glanced more than once at the potatoes. She was, I realized, completely unable to relax.

"You know what?" I asked Aunt Fanny. Sure, I would peel the potatoes and wipe up my puddle, but I would also try to help her in a way that actually mattered.

"What, Marjory?"

"When I was in France, with the Red Cross, you know what helped me with my work more than anything?" I didn't wait for her to answer. "Wellesley, Aunt Fanny. My Wellesley education. The education *you* gave me. I was able to write dispatches that were effective and grammatical and concise. And I got promoted to an even more important job because of a Wellesley professor I met at the Red Cross headquarters."

Aunt Fanny nodded, following, believing.

"So, if you think about it," I went on, "having sent me to college, well, it really means that *you* helped the children displaced by the war!"

I'd gone too far. Aunt Fanny's eyes hardened. She set her teacup down with a clatter and rose to her feet. By trying to make her feel better, I'd mocked her. I'd made her feel worse.

"I'll go get your grandmother now," she announced. "As I said, your grandfather is in the parlor. He'll need cleaning up. He . . . ah . . . he leaks when he sleeps."

In the quiet that followed Aunt Fanny's departure, I could hear the old creaks of the unsettled house, the creaks of an unsettled childhood, of unfulfilled lifetimes, the creaks

of Mama's dead madness—beams aching, foundation shifting, the ever-straining noises of a great, heaving force held
always in place.

"Grandfather?"

A hacking sound came from the parlor. I strode down
the hall and peered through the doorway. A very old man
sat in a chair by the fireplace, suffering the indignities of
time. Stained quilts covered him to his neck, and a scaffold
of pillows secured him in his seat.

"Grandfather?" I asked again, approaching. I knelt by
the side of the chair and rummaged under a quilt until I
found his hand. The skin on his hand was crusted, flaky, as
if he were molting.

"Grandfather?"

It's possible he shifted under the covers, but I couldn't
be sure. His eyelids opened halfway. Beneath were creamy,
pink orbs.

"Maahree," he grunted.

"Yes," I said. "It's me, Marjory."

"Um whurreed."

"Pardon?"

"Um whurreed."

"You're worried? About what, Grandfather?"

He grunted again, but the effort to speak was too much.
His wrinkled lids dropped, and Grandfather fell again into
his day-sleep. I did not disturb him, did not peel off the quilts
and check for damp underclothes. Perhaps I was afraid I
would hurt him if I tried to handle his limbs, but most likely
I was too repulsed by his deterioration to try. Instead, I hurried to the kitchen and peeled potatoes mercilessly.

The mood lightened when Grandmother came home.
She was aged and unsteady and a little deaf in one ear, but
she also was cheerful, as if the preliminaries of death had
eased the trials of life.

"Back from the war, safe and sound!" she greeted me. Grandmother shuffled to where I stood with the potatoes and squeezed my arm. "I'm proud of you, Marjory. You did a good thing, going over there. As brave as the boys, you are."

"Not exactly," I said as Aunt Fanny, hair shiny with snow, slid between me and the work counter. Displaced, I watched as she dropped potatoes one by one into a pot. The spuds fell like bricks, splashing hot water over the rim. Aunt Fanny didn't flinch.

"I think Grandfather said he's worried about something," I said in a low voice, as if he might hear.

"What was that?" Grandmother cocked her left ear at me.

"I'm pretty sure Grandfather said he's worried about something," I repeated, speaking more or less into her ear.

"Oh, he is," Grandmother confirmed, nodding. "He's very worried about being buried alive."

"What?" I asked. "Buried alive?"

"He thinks," Aunt Fanny explained from her station at the work counter, "that we'll think he's dead when he's not and we'll bury him while he's still alive and he won't be able to tell us to stop."

This wasn't funny. Grandfather's fear was quite sad and, to him, very real. Nevertheless, for the first time—perhaps ever, but at the very least in two decades—Aunt Fanny and Grandmother and I laughed out loud together. We laughed so hard tears swam from our eyes and we had to steady ourselves against the countertops.

"Oh dear," Grandmother said, recovering. "We humans and our human concerns." She dabbed at her cheeks with the end of her sleeve.

The boys at the front. Suddenly, I was ashamed of our laughter. The boys in the trenches—I bet they'd never thought about being buried alive until it was happening.

"Do you tell him you won't let that happen?" I asked.

Aunt Fanny spun toward me.

"Of course we do, Marjory. What do you think?"

Grandmother still chuckled a little, drifting just beyond the reach of Aunt Fanny's sharp tone.

"I keep telling him I'll hold my mother's old hand mirror under his nose until I'm sure he's not breathing," Grandmother said.

My days in Taunton passed much as that evening did—moments of pleasant camaraderie mixed with lightning strikes of Aunt Fanny's invective. Her resentment seemed only to have grown over the years, and while I didn't think she really wanted me to stay on forever in the house on Harrison Street, I also knew she thought it unfair that I could leave.

"But where else would you go?" Grandmother asked as we sat with Grandfather in the parlor. Beyond the large window, a black-capped chickadee sat on an apple tree branch, its marbled eye looking at me. "Besides Boston, I mean. At this point, where else would you go?"

Did they not understand? Had I not made it clear in my letters?

"I'm going back to Miami," I said. "I'm going home."

Aunt Fanny and Grandmother swapped glances. One would have thought, over time, this exchange would have grown more discreet.

"You're going back to him, then."

For a moment, I thought Aunt Fanny meant Andy, and my mind struggled to recollect any mention I'd made of him. Then I realized. Of course.

"Yes, I'm going back to Papa," I said. "But I'm also going back to a job as assistant editor of a pretty big newspaper, and back to a collection of the most interesting friends—do you know one of them has studied flowers in Borneo? And I'm going back to a smell, Grandmother, a smell that I can hardly explain. It's sweeter and saltier and richer than any smell in New England even on the best summer day."

And I'm going back to a man who loves me like no one has ever loved me before. It's a love without expectation, without obligation. It's a love that's as free as the wide, wild ocean. That's how he loves me, Grandmother. Doesn't that sound worth running to?

"Yes, well, smells can be very compelling," Grandmother agreed. She looked toward Aunt Fanny, this time for help.

"You know what smells nice, Marjory?" Aunt Fanny asked, leaning forward, eager, nearly licking her lips. "Your grandfather after he's been in that chair for four hours. Really rich. Earthy. You'll like it. So why don't you run upstairs and get his change of clothes?"

From her seat, Grandmother fretted. This time, she could tell all was not well.

"Now, Fanny, please," Grandmother said. "It's Marjory's life." Grandmother then turned to me, the skin on her neck sagging under the weight of her words. "It's your father, Marjory. We just don't want to lose another good Trefethen woman to that man."

I looked from one set of sad eyes to the other. Outside, the chickadee twittered in the cold. I smiled before I spoke, to let them know I wasn't mad.

"You're wrong about Papa," I said. "You always have been. He's a good man. He didn't cause Mama's troubles. He just tripped on them while he was walking through life and kicked them all out in the open."

I paused. Grandfather wheezed in the silence. When no one spoke up, I continued.

"Maybe I never thanked you the way I should have. For sending me to Wellesley, I mean. It was the greatest gift you ever, ever could have given me. Even greater than the red bicycle." At that, a flash of a smile swept Aunt Fanny's jawline. "So I'm saying it now—thank you. And it wasn't a waste. I promise you, my future is in Miami. That's where I need to be."

My grandmother dipped her head. My aunt stared at me, but not venomously. They were appeased, if not convinced.

"I'll go get Grandfather's clothes," I said. Then I stood and climbed the scuffed stairs, almost expecting to see Mama curled on our bed, hugging her knees, like an old kidney bean left to out to dry.

The next morning, I packed my bag and left Taunton. It was time. I was not going to stay and ease Aunt Fanny's burdens forever, and the longer I lingered, the more pointed that refusal became. As I stood in the hall arranging my hat and gloves, Aunt Fanny approached, her robe as tightly cinched as her mouth, her hair already, at this early hour, dusted with flour.

She stepped closer and hugged me.

Aunt Fanny put both arms around me and squeezed, pushing against me, as if searching for my heartbeat beneath the layers of wool. She touched her cheek to mine and held it there for an uncomfortable moment. Then, with breath that was too close to my ear she whispered something that sounded, almost, quite possibly, like "I'm sorry."

Grandmother ushered Aunt Fanny aside. It was her turn. She held my gloved hands and looked at me with bright eyes.

"I may just get to vote before I drop dead, Marjory. It looks like it's coming."

I nodded. I didn't trust myself speak. Such a small gasp of freedom, her possible vote. Such an essential, yet insufficient, measure of a life's worth. I needed to get back to Miami, where life—my life, my life with Andy—would be so much more.

"Let me just say goodbye to Grandfather," I said, slipping my hands from Grandmother's grasp.

He sat in his chair in the parlor, slumped to one side but

awake. Bits of breakfast clung to his whiskers, and he gave off the sticky smell of someone who has had a long night.

"I'm leaving, Grandfather."

I walked toward him, arms outstretched. This would certainly be our final goodbye.

Grandfather must have used all of the energy he had left in his body to lift one arm from the quilts, to hold it in front of him with a flat palm like a police officer, ordering me with one gesture to stop. Not to come closer. Not to embrace him. Our goodbye, it seemed, had already happened.

"Okay," I said. I retreated, pushed from the room by his anger or grief or whatever else gurgled inside him and needed to keep me away.

"You'd better go," Aunt Fanny said.

I straightened my hat, lifted my suitcase.

"Yes," I agreed. "It's time."

The door to the house on Harrison Street shut behind me. The lock scraped into place, keeping everything in. Everything, that is, but me.

If Miami had been a baby the first time Andy and I spoke of it, the city was now, in the winter of 1920, a complicated adolescent. With its carefully planted palms and burgeoning tendency toward the art deco, Miami was, like a teenager, as ravishingly beautiful as it might ever be. It was still innocent, too—still unburdened by debt or disease, by destruction or mismanagement—though barely. South Florida was on the cusp of discovering hard adult truths, but at the moment of my return, it was, like any young person, blithely unaware of what life would bring next and ready to believe that whatever came would be good.

The streets simmered with talk of a land boom. The population had doubled in size. The city limits themselves were misleading because, beyond those invisible lines, the unincorporated parts of Dade County were changing as fast as the official metropolitan area. South Florida was even stranger and more exciting than the first time I'd arrived.

Papa looked well. He had more gray in his hair and more lines near his eyes, but he moved with the ease of a man who was settled, content.

"I am so glad you're home," he said as we drove east from the train station. "You can't live with us, though."

"I can't?"

This was news. I wanted to tell him that Andy and I would marry soon and get our own home. I just needed a month. Maybe two.

"I sold the house in Riverside. Lilla and I are in a small apartment downtown until the new house is built. I made a deal with Seybold, remember him?" I didn't. "Two lots in his new development—Spring Garden, he's calling it, up a ways from the canal. Two lots for the price of one."

"Why did he make *that* deal?" I asked.

Papa laughed at himself.

"Because I'm his very first buyer," he said.

Still a pioneer, Papa was settling the unexplored territory of the Spring Garden subdivision.

"Not to worry, though, sweetheart. Fairchild and his family are in the South Pacific somewhere, collecting lichen or some such thing, and they've said you're welcome to stay in their guest cottage."

"In Coconut Grove?"

"Indeed."

Papa drove me to the Fairchild estate. Like a nesting doll, Coconut Grove was a town within a town, separate and unique, yet enclosed by the city around it. The foliage surrounding the scattering of buildings in the Grove grew lush and thick, giving each home, even the mansions, the sensation of being hidden away in a jungle. It was the perfect place for Fairchild, the botanist, to live.

Papa and I passed a few hours opening windows, unpacking my things, and discussing my role at the *Herald*.

"Thirty dollars a week," he promised. "Just like Judge gets."

"That's generous," I said.

"You're good, Marjory. I consider it an investment. And you'll have your own column, too, to say what you think needs to be said."

"What if I think there's a lot that needs to be said?"

"That's why it's a daily paper, Marjory."

Papa sat in a rattan chair with a glass of water while I set up the last of my belongings. I felt him watching as I balanced the photo of Mama on a side table.

"She was something, wasn't she?" he asked.

Mama.

"She definitely was," I agreed.

"Voice like a songbird."

I nodded.

"I loved her, you know," Papa said softly.

"I know, Papa." I looked at him. "But I think I loved her more."

Ever thoughtful, Papa did the math, considered the varied equations.

"I loved her more than I loved the sunrise, Marjory. The instant I set eyes on her in that boarding house in Minnesota, I loved her more than I'd ever loved anything in my life. Still, though," he concluded. "I think you probably did love her more. In that way, at least, she was quite lucky."

Talking of Mama left us both woozy, in need of distance and air. I ran one finger under my collar. Papa rose from the chair and surveyed the room for his hat.

"Well, I'll be getting back to Lilla now," he said.

"I'll be at work tomorrow," I promised. After I surprised Andy, of course.

Papa found his hat and placed it on his head. He paused at the door and looked at me from under the brim.

"I'm glad you're back, Marjory. I really am."

I smiled.

"Me, too, Papa."

The guesthouse had a small verandah off the bedroom, and after Papa's car chugged down the drive, I wandered out there. The Fairchilds had angled a few chairs amiably toward one another other. Between the chairs, a table held a magnifying glass and a set of binoculars, for examining wonders both near and far. I lifted the binoculars to my eyes, let my vision adjust to the altered scope.

The glass brought the deep foliage to me, as if I had plunged head-first into a thicket. Broad leaves so green they almost looked black. A single blooming hibiscus whose scarlet center overflowed my two lenses and filled my whole visible world with deep red. I pivoted, to see what other treasures awaited. When I paused, I saw in great detail the ridged bark of a ficus, a flurry of leaves like unbrushed hair all around it.

Something moved in the leaves. The movement was slight, careful, perhaps not a movement at all but the breeze. I turned the dial on the field glasses and brought the bush more into focus. Nothing. Just the patchwork of leaves and their myriad shadows. I started to move on, turned my sights on something else, when the foliage shook once again and I heard the unmistakable snap of a twig.

I pointed the glasses at the ground, where a cat or a possum or a skunk might be found. Instead, through my little hand telescopes, I saw the lump of a boot, the outline of trousers. Slowly, I lowered the glasses, grabbed onto the back of one of the Fairchilds' chairs.

"Who's there?" The January cool carried my words through the shade.

Silence. Only the trees seemed to breathe.

"Who's there?" I called again.

A rustle of branches and more cracking of twigs. The sound of a hurried retreat, and then the twittering nothingness of a backyard again. I lifted the binoculars, scanned the lush grounds over and over and over until I could probably map out the arrangement of flowering bushes and hardwood trees.

I could find no one.

The night birds sang like they'd missed me. I lay in the over-sized bed, staring at the slats of the Fairchilds' ceiling and listening to layers of birdsong.

"If no one was there, Mama," I said to the darkness, "then I'm just plain crazy." I tugged the covers up to my chin. "But if someone *was* in there, then maybe I should be scared." The bed sighed as I shifted. "I don't know which one is worse."

Night slogged so far into itself that it could travel no deeper and began slogging out. I slept a little as the songbirds changed shifts and the air tinkled with the first ditties of dawn. As sleep took over, I made a decision. Someone had to have been there, lurking in the overgrown bushes. Someone simply *must* have been hiding just out of sight—because I feared nothing so much as fearing myself.

I took the trolley downtown the next morning, but I did not go straight to the *Herald*.

"I'll get off here," I called to the driver, ringing the bell. The trolley slowed to a stop and I nearly bounced down the stairs, buoyed by the hundreds of butterflies that fluttered around my insides.

The day was bright and swept clean by a wind that rushed off the water and brushed the smell of the ocean over the city streets. I'd worn my trousers and put on pink lipstick, neither of which attracted attention as I crossed the road with the wind. How I loved Miami.

The *Metropolis* headquarters sat on West Flagler Street, in a two-story brick building across from the new courthouse. I'd never been there before. Never even walked past the front door. If I had, my father might have charged me with treason.

"I'm looking for Andy Walker," I said when I'd walked inside and finished tilting my head to the side while breathing deeply six times. "The reporter."

It wasn't clear whom I was addressing. A woman in a pink sweater filed papers at a desk in the corner and a man in the back of the room stared at a map on the wall. Neither of them acknowledged me.

"Excuse me, Miss?" I said, targeting the lady.

She looked up but her fingers kept filing.

"I'm looking for Andy Walker."

"Ain't nobody here with that name." She sounded like she'd just arrived from Brooklyn. "Ain't that right, Bud?"

Bud turned from the map and pulled his glasses off, presumably to help him think better.

"Andy Walker. Sure. Of course. One of the best. He hasn't been here since he went off to the war. He didn't get killed, did he? I don't remember seeing his name on the lists." Bud shrugged and returned to his map.

I'd written to Andy. He'd written back. He definitely had not been killed before getting home.

"Well," I tried again. "Is Myrtle here? Myrtle Ashworth?"

"Myrtle," said the lady in pink. "Yeah, Myrtle's in the newsroom."

We looked at each other. She sighed, put the papers down on her desk.

"All right, all right," she said. "I'll go get her."

When she came into the front room, Myrtle pulled me into a deep embrace, held me with less exuberance but as much love as Carolyn had.

"You're finally back."

"Yes," I said. "And I am so thrilled about it. I'm staying at the Fairchild estate."

"I heard about that!" Myrtle said. "I ran into Lilla a few times, and she told me."

We beamed at each other a moment.

"I've really missed Miami," I confided.

"I bet Miami isn't all that you've missed." Myrtle winked. "And I bet you didn't come here just to see me."

I laughed and hugged her again.

"True," I conceded, "but seeing you is a wonderful treat."

Myrtle took my hand suddenly and pulled me through the front door to the sidewalk. Even outside, she kept her voice low.

"Don't you know Andy's not at the paper? Didn't he write and tell you?"

"We've written," I said. "But we didn't write about work."

Myrtle glanced her big eyes around, dialed her voice down to a whisper.

"He came to the newsroom when he got back to town. Dean gave him his job back, but then Andy was gone a week later. I don't know if he quit or was fired. There was a betting pool on it in the newsroom—the good money was on him having been fired—but we still don't know what happened."

The flutters in my gut turned to hard thumps.

"Where's he working now?" I asked.

Myrtle's eyes grew even bigger.

"That's the strangest part," she said. "I heard he's gotten into real estate."

"Real estate? Andy Walker?"

"Yes! Isn't that a hoot?"

"It's certainly odd."

Myrtle and I fell quiet. I wasn't sure what to do next. We watched a motorbus full of large-hatted people move past.

"What's that?" I asked.

"A prospect tour. It drives around and shows investors all of the places they can buy land."

The motorbus rolled west on Flagler, headed, I supposed for the swamp.

"Oh, Myrtle," I said. "I have to talk to him. But what do I do—show up at his house? Send him a letter? I've waited so long to see him."

Myrtle smiled at me.

"Just go to him," she said. "He's been waiting a long time to see you, too."

I'd never been to Andy's house, but it was near the canal and easy to find. I went there as soon as I left Myrtle on Flagler Street.

He sat on a tree stump near the front door, reading, of all things, yesterday's *Herald*. He wore baggy trousers and a sleeveless undershirt. His arms had lost some of the tone they'd earned in Europe.

"Hello," I said.

Andy raised his head. He hadn't heard me approach.

"Marjory!" He jumped from the stump and came trotting over, left the newspaper flitting about in the breeze. "This is first rate," he gushed. "I didn't know you were back yet."

"I just got back. Yesterday, in fact."

We stood awkwardly, unsure whether, or how, to touch.

"And you waited this long to see me?" Andy asked, possibly teasing.

"I wanted to surprise you," I said. "Like you surprised me in Paris. I wanted to sneak up on you while you were working. I just came from the *Metropolis*. Can you believe it—Hattie Carpenter actually let me walk in the door without calling the police. Probably, she didn't know I was there. But I saw Myrtle. And she told me you weren't there, so, I guess, here I am."

What was it about reuniting with Andy that made me prattle on like a dipsy doodle?

Andy stiffened a little, pushed back his shoulders.

"You shouldn't have gone there," he said.

"No," I agreed. "Perhaps not. But I didn't know." I stepped closer to him. "And I really wanted to see you."

Andy stayed too upright for a long moment, then softened and let his shoulders dip to their usual slouch. A shock of his red hair fell forward, too.

"I couldn't wait to see you either," he said and took my hands in his. The feel of his skin after so many months sent a tingle straight up my arms and into my chest, where it gave my pounding vital organs a jolt.

"Come have coffee with me," he suggested. He tugged just a little on my hands.

Andy and I sat outside, in the morning shadow of a big banyan tree, just as we had in my daydream. The coffee was strong. Andy sat close. I thought I might faint from the perfection of it all.

"Are we still engaged?" he asked after a few gentle sips. I watched him watch his coffee.

"Yes. I mean, I think we should be," I said.

Andy looked up at me. He smiled that old, funny smile. "Me, too," he said.

Andy set his coffee mug on the ground, watched me as I finished a swallow. Then he leaned forward and kissed me. It was a beautiful kiss, a kiss that tasted even better than freshly brewed coffee sipped under a banyan one warm winter morning not far from the bay.

I called my daily column "The Galley" and treated it as a public diary filled with my musings and thoughts. There was something ineffable swirling throughout the city—a spirit, an essence, a primordial identity that vaguely suggested a destiny—and I tried with the column to express these inexpressible things. Not a poet, I often wrote poetry at the head of the column. No other form of writing was intoxicating enough to catch what I attempted to throw at the citizens of 1920s Miami.

"Keep it up!" Mary Elizabeth wrote a few weeks after I started. "This city is lucky you're back."

"Well done," Judge praised as he read copy over my shoulder.

Andy, however, did not like to discuss my columns.

"Our city's growing up," I commented as we walked among the massive humps of imported landscaping on Miami Beach. Dozens of people crowded the sand, making love to the sun, cleaning off in the surf. This was the same treeless strip of land we had lived on that summer, not five years before. "Did you read 'The Galley' yesterday? I wrote about how we must be the most confident city in the nation."

"How can a city be confident?"

I turned to him, confused. "A city also can't be a baby, but you thought it was. We're personifying here."

Andy shrugged, dismissive. "I guess," he said.

Andy did not like to talk about his real estate business either.

"Do you sell land here by the bay, or out in the swamp?" I asked him.

He shrugged. The gesture was becoming habitual. "Most times, I don't sell it anywhere," he said.

We liked to swim in the Roman pools Fisher had built

and to dance at the outdoor tea dances at Roney Plaza. For a time, Andy had a car and drove us around, but one day the car was gone, and Andy changed the subject whenever I asked after it.

"Look," I said, pointing upward one cloudy night. We were catching our breath after more than an hour of fox-trotting.

"What?" he asked.

"Up there," I said. "That constellation."

Andy squinted at the starless sky.

"There's nothing there," he said.

"Yes, there is."

"Then what's it called?"

I laughed and tilted my head to his shoulder, snuggled into his arm.

"The ancient Greeks called it Andy's Automobile," I said.

My giggles kept going until it became clear Andy wasn't going to join in.

"Sorry," I apologized. "I thought it was funny."

"It wasn't," he corrected.

We didn't laugh much. We never discussed the growth of the region, never marveled at the hospitals and libraries and schools being built. "The Galley" became my companion in those conversations, and each day, I fell a little more in love with my column.

"You've gotten a big response to this one," Papa said one afternoon at the *Herald*. He dumped a pile of letters onto my desk.

"The Everglades piece?" I asked.

"Yes, ma'am," he confirmed.

I'd gotten to know Ernest Coe, an older landscape architect from Connecticut who wore frayed seersucker suits and believed adamantly that the swamps to the west should be turned into a national park.

"One cannot simply redirect the natural flow of water in the name of progress and prosperity!" he'd cried during our very first meeting. His passion for the place was infectious, and I began to write occasional columns about the merits of his ideas.

After I'd read through the responses Papa had poured on my desk—everything from "Riveting insight, Miss Stoneman," to "Women must leave these decisions to men"—I tried to ask Andy, the formerly fervent believer in progress, what he thought of the park.

"Do you love me?" he answered, leaving my question suspended in the cricket-thick air. We sat on the chairs of my guesthouse veranda. The sun had set minutes before, and Fairchild's yard bulged with the chirps of new night.

"Yes," I said. "Of course I do."

"Then we shouldn't wait any more. We should get married."

"Yes," I said again. "Yes, of course we should."

"You don't sound excited, Marjory."

I wasn't. But I didn't know why. I could not grasp the edges of my feelings, could not pull them close for inspection.

"I'm just tired," I lied. "The newsroom was a circus today. Judge and my father were at odds about something, and they wanted me to weigh in as a tie-breaker. It wasn't easy."

"Very important, you are."

Was he mocking me? In the darkness, I couldn't tell.

"I'm sorry," Andy said. "That wasn't nice. You deserve that job. You're good at it."

I was. I was very good at it.

We sat in silence as the night deepened. Only a trickle of moonlight came through the treetops, dripping onto the grass like spilled mercury. Around us, unseen insects droned madly, their symphony played exclusively as a crescendo. At some point in this dark riot, Andy searched for my hand.

"Here," I said, letting him find it.

I held onto his fingers, the ones I had, for years, ached to touch. Who did they belong to now, these fingers I held? I could hardly imagine the man next to me breaking into an Italian *barcarole* or getting worked up over the invention of the pop-up toaster. And yet, the old Andy was somewhere in there, beneath this man's flattened expression, inside his unlaughing eyes. I saw him sometimes. Once in the aftermath of a failed joke. Once in the fast-fading bliss that followed a kiss. But I couldn't predict how long he'd stay or when he'd show up again. I just had to hope that he would.

"I should get going," Andy said, not letting go of my hand.

Since I'd returned to Miami, Andy and I had danced. We'd kissed. We'd sometimes pressed too close together in inappropriate places, like Myrtle and Frank Ashworth's front porch. We had not, however, repeated that one night in Paris, the details of which still replayed in my head. Vividly.

"Or you could stay," I said.

For a moment, Andy said nothing.

"Or I could stay," he agreed.

We didn't move, but a charge now coursed through our connected hands, my body like the July sky during a storm. Beyond the veranda, blackened treetops rustled. A warbler trilled, dry and clear, a sound that fluttered above the din of the yard.

"Sometimes I think there's someone out there," I said.

The warbler trilled again.

"Is there?" he asked.

"I don't know."

The warbler trilled louder, an aria in the opera of night song.

"There might be," Andy said. "Enemies can be anywhere. I learned that in the war."

I didn't answer. I did not know what to say. A minute passed. Maybe more. Long enough for the warbler to perform an encore.

"That bird!" Andy suddenly shouted. He stood, chair scraping the floor. "That damn bird is making my head hurt."

"She'll stop soon. She does this every night."

"Let's go inside."

In the bedroom, I lit several lamps. We'd sat too long in the dark, been too alone with the night.

"This is better," I said, stepping toward Andy. Though I was no longer sure that I wanted to, I was determined to salvage the evening.

"Do you still want me to stay?" he asked. His eyes were wide and unsure. I thought of the little boy, sitting on the lap of his dead mother.

I nodded, wrapped my arms around Andy's waist.

"Of course I do," I said.

Andy slid his hands up the back of my neck, tangled his fingers in the hair at the nape. He kissed the top of my head, my brow, the tip of my ear.

"You smell like newsprint," he whispered.

"There's a good reason for that."

"Maybe it's just on your clothes."

"Let's find out."

My memory of our night in Paris clashed with what happened next. Andy moved stiffly, limbs jerking, his long body clamoring for something he could not seem to find. From his mouth came animal grunts, desperate and dire. I tried to calm him, soothe him, with soft words and lies. He grew more feral as I grew more worn.

"I'm okay," he said when it was over, as if he knew I was unsure.

I rubbed his arm.

"Of course you are," I said.

I untangled the sheets with my legs and settled my head against his heaving chest. We'd sleep now. He'd hold me. We'd lift into our dreams. But before I could settle, Andy rolled from beneath me and got off the bed.

"Where are you going?" I asked.

"I can't sleep up top."

Andy pulled on some clothes and turned off the lamps. Then he came back to the bed and stretched his long body on the floor by my slippers. I peered over the side of the mattress. He scooted from sight.

"You're okay there," I said—neither an assurance nor a question, just words.

I let my arm drop off the side of the bed, and from below, he held my hand, as we'd done in Paris. I was nearly asleep when he tugged.

"Hmmm?" I murmured.

Andy tugged again on my arm, harder, more insistent.

"What is it?"

He pulled again. I tried to roll away, to ignore him, but his fingers held tight and he tugged.

Too tired to resist, I slid over the side of the mattress and squeezed my body under the bed's wooden frame.

"I'm here," I said.

The congested space was soupy and thickened with dust, the mattress no more than an inch from my nose. Its nearness pressed on me, heavy, threatening collapse. I fought off the panic of this new confinement.

"I need you, Marjory," Andy whispered.

And there it was, in my Miami, from the mouth of the man who'd always made me feel free: the oppression of someone else's deep need.

"I'm here," I said again.

"The Galley" had given me minor celebrity status in certain parts of Miami. I was invited to parties, not as a society reporter but as a guest whose discourse provided a curious sort of entertainment.

"What do you think about dredging, Miss Stoneman?" men in linen suits asked. Unlike when some women spoke, they shut their mouths when I answered, seemed to listen to what I had to say.

"It's going to ruin the land."

"So what? It's a swamp. Dry it out. Carve it up. Sell it in tracts that can be turned into something useful."

"Such as?"

"Farmland. Housing. More farmland. Those northerners can't get enough tomatoes, I tell you."

It was hard to counter this dogged and singular view of utility. The prospectors who had flooded the region believed only dollars were useful, only profits made sense.

"If you dredge part, you ruin the whole thing. Everything depends on water flowing south from the lake. Dry out the middle and nothing survives. You, sir, might have a nose and mouth, but you can't breathe without lungs."

"So develop it all," my companion would inevitably say, a glint of gold in his eye.

I'd parry then with a sensible argument about groundwater and storm barriers and temperature regulation, but what I really wanted to do was ask if he'd ever seen, among the endless reeds of sawgrass, the glimmer of the sun off a carrion fly's wing, a glimmer that signaled to the hungry vultures above, or if he'd ever felt the sudden, sweet cool of condensation in the Everglades air during the thickest, hottest part of the summer. These questions wouldn't come out of my mouth, however. They seemed only to flow from my mind straight onto paper. I raced home after these parties and wrote—wrote my responses to these men, the responses I hadn't said in the moment. The responses that needed, somehow, to be said.

Occasionally, I brought Andy with me to these parties, hoping the fiery discussions of the city's possible future would ignite his old fervor. But he mostly stood mute at my elbow, staring at some faraway thought beyond the coiffed heads of the guests. A few people remembered him as a *Metropolis* reporter and sought his opinion on the topics at hand, especially state politics.

"What do you think, Mr. Walker, about Tallahassee borrowing at such high interest rates? Is that foresight or foolhardiness?"

"Do you think women voting now will doom the Dixiecrats next election?"

"Our one-eyed governor is something, isn't he, Mr. Walker? Trying to run the monks and the Negroes out of the state?"

Andy would shift closer to me as the questions unfurled. I could almost hear his heart pounding harder, his breath getting shorter. The ends of the questions would fall off a cliff, into a conversational canyon, where they echoed among us in interminable awkwardness. Three, four, five sets of eyes watched him, waiting for a response. Eventually, as if it took heroic effort, Andy would offer the small crowd his only insight: a one-shouldered shrug. Sometimes, after the momentous shrug, he deflected the questions to me.

"That's something Marjory would know about."

But if I gave my opinion after he'd lobbed the question at me, he'd later get angry, accuse me of showing him up.

"You just had to out-do me, Marjory. Make me look stupid," Andy would pout as we walked to the late night trolley stop. We had no time to gaze up at the sky during these walks—too much arguing needed to get done.

"You gave me the question, Andy. You handed it right over to me and wanted me to come up with an answer."

But logic was irrelevant to his injured ego, and the only way I could soothe him was by diminishing myself.

"Besides, I didn't really know what I was talking about," I falsely confessed. "I just repeated some stuff I heard Judge say a few days ago."

This sort of talk made him feel better, coaxed him back to a more relaxed state. Not always, but often enough, he'd then do something, say something, that made me forget, or at least ignore, his ridiculous behavior.

"For you," he said once, before we reached the trolley stop. He paused at the side of the road, where flowers grew in loud bursts, and plucked a long stem of night-blooming jasmine.

I held the gift with my thumb and first finger. The little white petals perched on their stems like tiny starfish, their romantic perfume billowing about in a sultry, warm cloud.

"Reminds me of when we started spending time together," Andy said. "Our walks home from the movies. Remember?"

I did. I remembered. And, as Grandmother said, smells can be very compelling.

The one topic I would not genuflect on, however, was the Everglades. The more Ernest Coe ranted at my desk at the *Herald* and the more I learned from Frank Ashworth and the Gladesmen he brought around, the more the place bewitched me. To think of it! A vast, primal land at the very doorstep of our booming city. Nature, in its rawest form, butting against the frenzied momentum of civilization. The swamp could not be underestimated, dismissed, irreverently tamed. When talking about the Everglades at parties, I never minimized it later with Andy.

"You were trying to make me look like a dullard," Andy complained as we left Villa Serena one evening. His red hair had grown long and shaggy. It fell in his eyes, shaded his brow. "With all that talk of oolite rock and rookery protection."

"I was discussing the Everglades, Andy. It had nothing whatsoever to do with you."

"It felt like it did."

"Well, it didn't."

We continued in silence, curving with the road away from the bay. My heart cracked a little with every step.

"I have an idea," I said, scooping his hand into mine.

Andy looked at me, his face full of hope, as if I were the doctor and he my gravely ill patient.

"Let's go out there together," I said. "To the Everglades. We'll borrow my father's car and drive out on the Trail as far as we can go. You've been there with Fairchild, and I've been there with Fairchild, but we haven't gone together. Please, Andy. Tell me you'll go."

My plan was nothing less than brilliant. I'd make the Everglades bewitch him again, too—turn the place into something we shared, something that would rekindle his passion, his zest, for our south Florida life. The Everglades would extract the old Andy Walker forever from this cadaver of the man and put an end to my tedious soul-tending.

Andy was quiet. I waited, dreading the shrug.

"First rate!" he finally said. "Let's do it."

"Really?"

"Really," he said.

Our smiles mirrored each other and our faces inflated, cheeks expanding with relief and excitement and maybe our old kind of love.

"Next week?" I asked.

"You pick the day."

"Let's go Saturday."

Andy draped his arm over my shoulders. I slipped my arm around his waist. We walked like that, braided together, almost a regular couple, until Cutler Road ended and the trolley stop came into view.

I almost didn't hear the knock on the door through the clatter of my typewriter. It was late afternoon. I'd come down with a cold and hadn't gone into the office, but there was a column begging to be finished by the next day.

The knock came again, louder.

On the guest cottage porch stood a mailman, his uniform darkened by half-moons of sweat.

"Mrs. Marjory Stoneman Douglas?"

"Yes, sir." I resented the full married name. I was divorced now. But it seemed unnecessary to express my displeasure to the mailman.

"Letter for you."

"Delivered right to the house?"

"It was sent special. Important, I guess."

As the mailman hurried back to the road, I studied the envelope he'd handed me. Postmark, Newark, New Jersey. No return address. A small stain on the back that might have been coffee.

I unsealed the flap and quickly scanned the contents, unwilling to dwell too long in their words. Kenneth had a friend in Chicago. He was considering going up there and looking for work. He hoped I was doing well and didn't harbor bad feelings toward him. He sent his very sincerest regards.

Kenneth's paper. Kenneth's ink. Droplets of Kenneth's saliva on the back of the stamp. My former husband knew where I lived. Pieces of him had entered my home.

I crumpled the paper, wrung the life out of it with my fist. Beyond the open door, the verdant grounds of the Fairchild estate dipped toward dusk. Branches shifted in the pre-evening breeze. Leaves shook with anticipation of night. I closed the door and retreated to my waiting typewriter. I didn't want to think about who was or wasn't out there.

Andy showed up at the guesthouse at noon the next Saturday. I had Papa's old Model 29—whose paint had blanched to gray in the sun and whose side lamps had been missing for years—parked by the road. Papa had assured me the car would hold up just fine, but he wasn't without concern. He'd wanted to know where, exactly, we were headed and how long we planned to stay.

"In case the skeeters pick up the Buick and carry it off to Cuba, I can come looking for you," he'd explained.

"The mosquitoes aren't that bad yet. It's only May."

"Just in case," Papa said with a wink. "And don't forget to take some notes about the Trail. We can run an article about it next week."

"Of course," I promised.

Andy looked awake, almost excited, when I opened the door to the guesthouse. His limbs jiggled with their old restlessness. His smile threatened to pop off his face.

"Hi there," I said.

"Top of the morning to you," Andy answered. He bent and, almost bashfully, placed a kiss on my cheek.

"I don't think it's morning anymore."

"Well, then, top of the afternoon to you."

I laughed and pulled the cottage door closed.

"Want to drive?" I asked.

"Your father's car?"

"It's the only one I've got."

Andy stretched and stood a bit taller, pleased with this manly assignment.

"Well, sure. If you think it's all right."

"Of course it's all right."

Summer had not yet begun. It was mid-May, the air outside warm but not yet as damp as it would be in June. The motion of the car cooled the breeze only slightly. I'd dressed for the swamp—heavy boots, light pants, long-sleeved shirt. A hat with the widest brim I could find. Enough protection, I hoped, to keep the sun and the insects at bay.

"I brought lunch," I told Andy as we drove. "Sandwiches. Oranges. Oh, and some little cakes Lilla made."

"Wait, she's not very good in the kitchen, is she?"

"No," I confirmed, laughing. "But these are pretty good. Ginger, I think."

Andy drove the Model 29 west, then south, away from the city, the metropolis fading gradually, like stars in the dawn. I was surprised to see how far inland the buildings had crept, how intrepid, or irreverent, the prospectors had become.

"What will happen to these houses when the rain comes?" I wondered out loud.

"I guess the owners will have boats instead," Andy replied.

Swollen cumulous clouds hung low in the sky. Pinelands gave way to marsh. Somewhere along the edge of these wetlands hid the end of the incomplete, perhaps never to be completed, Tamiami Trail.

"How far out is it finished?" Andy asked.

"The Trail? I don't know where exactly they stopped. The Dade County line, maybe."

The two-lane road was intended, eventually, to connect Tampa to Miami, with the east-west portion slicing right through the heart of the Everglades. Judge Hill liked to report on the construction, which was expensive and strenuous and perhaps structurally impossible.

"Do you think it will ever get done?"

For a moment, I couldn't answer Andy's question. I was too busy delighting in the fact that he'd asked it, that he was curious about something beyond today.

"Not without a big infusion of cash from somewhere."

We turned west onto the Trail later than we'd intended, the car having an unexpectedly low top speed.

"You still want to go?" Andy asked. Beyond his profile, the river of grass stretched forever.

He was still smiling, eager, and I felt this was it, my best chance to save him, to keep him awake and help him remember all that he was before the war poisoned him. To turn away now would be to give up. Denying him the inspiration of the land's beauty would be accepting defeat.

"Yes."

As the Trail's narrow paved lanes beckoned us deeper into the soggy sawgrass, I left all thoughts of the city back on dry ground. We followed the road, that great headless snake, headed not toward any particular destination but, simply, toward wherever the purveyors of progress had surrendered and ended construction of the audacious Trail.

"There's everything and nothing out here," Andy said, and again, I swooned at these glints of his rejuvenation.

We stopped to eat lunch in the late afternoon, sitting cross-legged in the middle of the road, hot pavement warming our legs as if we were reptiles. Above, a hawk circled, eyeing our corned beef.

"Lilla's cakes aren't so bad," I commented.

Andy lifted a cake, bit it, and chewed with great care.

"I can't call it first rate," he concluded. "But definitely a strong second rate."

"In any case," I said, "it's better than I could do."

"Aw, I bet you could learn."

After lunch, we kept driving, ever westward, passing motionless, open-mouthed gators drinking in the final hours of sun and twig-legged herons piercing the sky with their beaks. Everything moved slowly out here—the water's imperceptible journey south to Florida Bay, the wading birds' stillness as they digested their latest meal. This quiet land was a contradiction, perhaps a refutation, of the break-neck speed with which Miami was growing.

"Maybe the city's moving too fast," I said.

"Feels far away from here, whatever its size."

"But for how long? What happens when this road finally connects up to Tampa?"

The question lingered, unanswerable.

The road was there, and then it wasn't. It ended abruptly, without celebration. A single pick-axe lay on the crumbled edge of the pavement, like a bookmark holding the workers' place.

"I guess we're here," Andy said.

We got out of the car and stood together on the final, crumbling inches of the path, poised as if at the edge of the sea, surrounded almost entirely by the richness of untamed, unclaimed wide earth. Beyond it all, the sun's color deepened to orange, preparing to bid us farewell.

"It feels good, being out here."

Did I say this, or was it Andy? Either of us could have said it. Either of us would have meant it.

Andy put his arm around my shoulders, pressed his lips to the side of my head.

"I've been scared lately," I said, as the top of the world turned to purple.

"You have? Why?"

"I don't know. It's foolish."

"You can tell me."

I put my arm around Andy's waist, felt myself click into place at his side.

"Sometimes," I began, "and I know this sounds ridiculous, but sometimes I think there's someone in the foliage at the guesthouse. Hiding in the bushes and watching me."

Andy said nothing, giving me time to say more.

"And the thing of it is," I continued, "I'm not entirely sure if someone is there, and in some ways, I guess because of my mother, I'm more scared of the possibility that I'm imagining it than I am of someone actually being there."

We watched the last of the sun settle behind the sawgrass, felt the world slip toward night all around.

"Please don't worry," Andy said. "I don't want you to worry. It was me."

"What was you?"

"At the guest house. In the bushes. It's been me hiding back there."

My brow turned clammy, like a sudden and instantaneous onset of the flu. In the deep space behind my left eye, worry began to throb, prescient and black.

"I don't understand."

"I wanted to see you."

"You could have knocked at the door." I exhaled, my breath wobbling. "Andy, I thought I was losing my mind, seeing legs in the bushes. I stayed awake night after night, worrying that I was turning into my mother, and the whole time it was you out there. Watching."

I withdrew my arm from Andy's waist. He tightened his arm around my shoulders. As if to remind me exactly where we were having this conversation, the orchestra of swamp insects burst at once into dissonant song.

"Please," I said. "Let's talk about this on the drive back."

"But we just got here," he said. It was almost a whine.

"It's getting dark, though. It's going to be a difficult drive."

Andy stepped so that he stood squarely before me, each hand now capping one of my shoulders. In the last, dying breaths of daylight, his eyes bored into mine, hot as irons.

"Sometimes I just need to see you," he said. "To know I'm okay."

I tried to step back. His grip held me in place.

"And then I see you," he went on, "and then I'm okay, and it's really not such a big deal, right?"

"Let's drive back to the city and talk," I insisted.

"I don't want to go back," Andy said. "Not until you promise you'll marry me, Marjory. And soon. Then I won't have to hide in the bushes because you'll always be there."

"I can't promise that, Andy."

"But you already have! So many times, remember all of those times we talked about marriage? And I've got a job offer, Marjory. Up north. Pittsburgh. You can come north with me. We'll start everything over."

The throbbing in my head pulsed harder, slamming the side of my skull in rhythmic confusion. My chest tightened. Breathing was no longer easy.

"I don't want to leave Miami," I managed to say. "I don't want to leave the newspaper."

Andy threw his arms up in disgust or outrage or frustration. While his hands flailed in the air, I backed slowly away, felt my heel fall off paved ground and sink into the primordial muck.

"Your job won't matter as much when we're married," he countered. "Please, Marjory. I'll be okay if you're with me."

The weight of the thousands of needs of Mama and Kenneth and Andy pushed my feet deeper into the mud. I staggered further from the road to keep from collapsing. Someone I loved was hurting, in trouble. Wasn't I obligated, by some unnamed birthright, to come to the rescue?

"I just. I need a minute. To think. Okay? Just a minute."

I lurched deeper into the sawgrass, stumbling but not falling down. Like the moment after a flash of lightning, the darkness got darker, and then I heard it. Faintly at first, then louder, the buzz filling my ears and blocking all other sounds.

It was the feverish night-song of a swarm of famished mosquitoes.

WEST OF MIAMI, 1920

His eyes grope for me across the moat of the hammock. Everything about him, even his gaze, is needy and sore. The sun has nearly cleared the horizon. It sets his red hair aflame.

Please go north, I beg Andy in my head. *Go north and find someone else to ease your nightmares, someone who can give you all that she is. Go north and find someone who is good enough to help you because I am not that person. Not for you, and not for anyone else. Not anymore.*

You see, Andy, I'm not good enough. I'm better.

"Go. Please." This time out loud.

No response.

Maybe he's had a mental break, like Mama had on the porch years ago. Maybe he's unable to move or to speak or even to hear me.

"Go!"

Silence.

"We could have been happy," he says, finally, his words thick with defeat.

"We could have been, once."

"You won't forget, will you?"

"Forget what?"

"Me."

"Never."

Andy nods, accepting. His long shadow stretches over the moat. I touch the dark shape where his cheek would be.

I close my eyes as he moves away, and when I open them, great ripples of sawgrass lay between his shadow and me. He's walking toward the Indian village.

I am alone. And I'm free.

This dawn has broken the known world apart. I can see now that I will never again do what others expect me to do. I will not marry—I have no use for men after Andy—and I will not have the children I've never craved. Instead, I will give birth to books and to stories. I will fill my life with powerful thoughts and more powerful action. I will not be restrained by the shackles of guilt and obligation.

Around me, the Everglades awaken. These wetlands begin another day of misunderstood, primordial splendor. Do the wading birds know the dredgers are coming? Can the bobcats feel the Trail encroaching? This place, and these beautiful beasts, have made sacrifices. Perhaps that's why we understand each other so well.

All at once, in the east, where Miami bulges in from the coast, a great commotion erupts over the sawgrass. I gasp, steady myself against the hammock's oak tree, and watch an enormous circle of white ibis leap from the earth and soar brazenly through the sky. They drift in one effortless wheel, spinning without seeming to move, around and around with dizzying solicitude until, one by one, they settle again among the reeds of sawgrass.

I watch the sky where the birds were just floating. I can't turn away. The pink air is stamped with the imprint of so many hundreds of majestic beings, their sky wheel not so much a memory as a promise of perpetual grace. Into this space, a space that is both empty and not, a single white ibis suddenly rises and dances alone. She twirls slowly, as if the sky is full of water not air. Her long, narrow neck arches back, her orange feet reach for the sun. As she moves, the world fills with music.

"You're free now, too, Mama," I say.

Then I step from the shade of the hammock and turn toward the road. The rising sun reaches over the sawgrass, over the water that slides forever between the sky and the land, warming the creatures that burrow and glide and scurry throughout this beguiling place. A new day has indeed begun.

EPILOGUE: MIAMI, 1998

The stars are nearly gone now. Faded, rubbed away at their crepuscular edges by the blaze of hotel lights on South Beach. By my deteriorating retinas. By the call to sleep that overtakes me earlier and earlier each evening, when some of the best stars, my favorite stars, have yet to make their appearance. I wander instead beneath a constellation of memories that shines brightest in the afternoon sun.

I'm there now. In the sun. On a chair in front of the Coconut Grove cottage that I built, short story by short story, in 1926. Each payment from the *Saturday Evening Post* or *Black Mask* meant construction could continue—on and on, publication by publication, until my home was finished, finally, just before the great unnamed hurricane whose winds were so strong the weathermen could not measure them. The little house survived that storm, and every one since.

So have I.

Has there been madness? Small bouts of it, yes. Nights here and there when I stumbled through jasmine-thick air, wearing only bedclothes and calling my dead. These were just moments, though. Nothing that lured me too far into the deep. Nothing the morning bay breeze skimming my skin couldn't fix. My life has been long, full of meaning and joy, and these bouts are like bad meals I've mostly forgotten.

I've won awards. I've had buildings dedicated to me and streets named in my honor. I've met a queen and a president (neither of whom, by the way, was as regal or poised as my

own mother and father). But these accolades were inciden-
tal. Completely beside the point. I would have fought for
the rights of the exploited even if no one had ever asked me
my name.

One thing I have noticed, over my many decades of
fighting, is that no matter which direction I'm facing, I list
slightly west, toward the vast Everglades. It's been the enduring affair of my life, my relationship with that inimitable land.
We helped each other become independent, gave one another
a shot at survival. The place became a national park the same
year my book about it was released. Some described that
book as an ecological history, others as an environmental-
ist's call to arms. Me, I call it exactly what it was: a love story.

I'm 108 years old now. The Everglades is nearly five
thousand. This place that I love will outlive me. The question
is, by how long?

I try not to be maudlin, really I do, but I wonder sometimes what dying will feel like, when death inevitably comes.
Maybe it will be a lightening, a lift, a weightless escape from
the grip of the earth, like being plucked from the side of the
road near New Smyrna and placed on the running board of
an old Runabout thunking headlong into forever.

My friends will scatter my ashes, when the time comes.
I want to be sprinkled during a summer storm in the wide,
grassy prairies of the northernmost Glades. I want the imperceptible tilt of the land and the unrelenting mid-August rain
to carry me south, carry me west, over the ancient, brittle
oolitic limestone, through the uncharted sloughs panting
with imperceptible life. The water—primordial and polluted;
essential and exploited; a lifeblood that is also bloodstained—
will carry me on, carry me further along this river of grass,
past tender outcroppings of pinelands and into the tangled,
teeming root-webs of the coastal mangroves. I will mingle
there with the sea, in a dance of salt water and fresh. Perhaps

I will linger, wait for a roseate spoonbill to splay her delicate feathers and float with me into the restless, eternal currents of the Florida Bay.

The Everglades is my home. It's where I'll live on when I'm no longer lucky enough to be alive on this beautiful earth.

ACKNOWLEDGMENTS

This book is the realization of a lifelong dream, and I could not have created it without the help, guidance, and inspiration of many special people.

First, endless thanks to my agent, Anna Geller, and to Shannon Green and Brooke Warner at She Writes Press. I've learned that writing the book is just the beginning of the journey, and I'm so grateful to have had your expertise as the adventure continued.

I'd also like to acknowledge Ellen Alvin, Ken Westlake, Marianne Kjos, and John Kendall. These are the Miami-Dade public school teachers who introduced me to my own creativity, to writing and literature, and to the myriad worlds I could imagine into existence. I'd also like to thank Professor Terry Osborne, whose freshman seminar at Dartmouth showed me the importance of place in creative writing—the ability of the setting to itself become a character in a story.

Deep, deep gratitude goes to the brilliant women in my life who read and commented on the many iterations of Marjory's story and who supported me as I wrote it: Danielle Loevy, Nicole Phelan, Eliza Fournier, Erica Zolner, Katherine Dorsey, Katie Wise, Heike Bryant, Liz White, Angela McCurdy, and Allison Holzer. Also to Margaret Clayton, whose ability to see bravery in me has made me stronger in so many ways.

Author Laura Munson deserves an enormous, Montana-size thank-you. When I first attended Laura's Haven Writing

Retreat, this book was just an idea and a few dozen pages long. With Laura's insight, perspective, and encouragement—and the help of my Haven II friends, Jule Kucera, Jennifer Johnson, Sasha Woods, and Lydia Pugh (WORDS!)—those pages turned into a finished novel that Laura believed in long before I did.

There are not enough words in the universe to thank my mother, Sheila McMullen, who gave me a "Girls Can Do Anything" poster when I was six and then spent the next couple decades making sure I had all of opportunities she'd never had.

Finally, heartfelt, bottomless thank-yous to Lee—who has given me unwavering support and has endured the drama, frustration, and sacrifice that being married to a writer requires—and to Taryn, Emily, and Tessa, whom I've tried to make proud. I love you.

ABOUT THE AUTHOR

Lori McMullen grew up in unincorporated Dade County, outside of Miami, and now lives with her family in Chicago. She is a graduate of Dartmouth College and Harvard Law School, and her short fiction has appeared in the *Tampa Review* and *Slush Pile* magazine. *Among the Beautiful Beasts* is her first novel.

Author photo © Lisa Geraghty

SELECTED TITLES FROM SHE WRITES PRESS

She Writes Press is an independent publishing
company founded to serve women writers everywhere.
Visit us at www.shewritespress.com.

The California Wife by Kristen Harnisch. $17.95, 978-1-63152-087-7. The sequel to *The Vintner's Daughter*, this is a rich, romantic tale of wine, love, new beginnings, and a family's determination to fight for what really matters.

The Silver Shoes by Jill G. Hall. $16.95, 978-1-63152-353-3. Distracted by a cross-country romance, San Francisco artist Anne McFarland worries that she has veered from her creative path. Almost ninety years earlier, Clair Deveraux, a sheltered 1929 New York debutante, becomes entangled in the burlesque world in an effort to save her family and herself after the stock market crash. Ultimately, these two very different women living in very different eras attain true fulfillment—with some help from the same pair of silver shoes.

Estelle by Linda Stewart Henley. $16.95, 978-1-63152-791-3. From 1872 to '73, renowned artist Edgar Degas called New Orleans home. Here, the narratives of two women—Estelle, his Creole cousin and sister-in-law, and Anne Gautier, who in 1970 finds a journal written by a relative who knew Degas—intersect . . . and a painting Degas made of Estelle spells trouble.

Portrait of a Woman in White by Susan Winkler. $16.95, 978-1-938314-83-4. When the Nazis steal a Matisse portrait from the eccentric, art-loving Rosenswigs, the Parisian family is thrust into the tumult of war and separation, their fates intertwined with that of their beloved portrait.

Don't Put the Boats Away by Ames Sheldon. $16.95, 978-1-63152-602-2. In the aftermath of World War II, the members of the Sutton family are reeling from the death of their "golden boy," Eddie. Over the next twenty-five years, they all struggle with loss, grief, and mourning—and pay high prices, including divorce and alcoholism.